Capturing Wishes

A WHISPERING PINES CHRISTMAS NOVEL

BY KIMBERLY DIEDE

CELIA'S GIFTS SERIES

WHISPERING PINES CHRISTMAS NOVEL

FIRST SUMMERS NOVELLA

Capturing Wishes

A WHISPERING PINES CHRISTMAS NOVEL

By Kimberly Diede

Celia's Gifts

Ebook ISBN: 978-0-9992996-7-8
Print ISBN: 978-0-9992996-8-5

To Alecia, may the magic of Christmas always live in your heart

"Star light, star bright,
First star I see tonight,
I wish I may, I wish I might,
Have this wish I wish tonight."
—Anonymous

CHAPTER 1

Gift of Anticipation

"*D*id you hear that?"

Nathan glanced toward his cousin in the gloom. He'd been too busy focusing his attention elsewhere in the room to notice much else. "Hear what?"

Robbie was staring intently through the window into the darkness. A log in the fireplace hissed and popped, sending out a shower of sparks. "That noise, it . . ."

"All *I* hear is a bunch of forty-somethings making a racket downstairs," Robbie's sister, Julie, said as she balanced a plate of Halloween treats on her lap, careful not to spill on her costume. "And that stupid 'Monster Mash' song playing for, like, the *tenth time*. It's late. I'm surprised so many of them are still up." She took another bite out of one of her aunt's famous caramel apples.

"That's weird," Robbie said, still staring into the dark. "I thought I heard tapping on the window . . ."

Nathan grinned. "Of *course* you heard something, cuz. It wouldn't be a legit Halloween party without a little tapping on a second-floor window in an old lodge at an even *older* resort. Remember the stories they always tell around the campfire out here about Albert and Arthur, the little ghost boys who roam around Whispering Pines? Maybe it's *them*, levitating outside the window. Or the vampire kid from *Salem's Lot*."

Nathan suspected his younger cousin had probably never read the classic tale by Stephen King. Maybe he'd watched the movie. *Nights like this would make the perfect setting for any ghost story,* he thought. *Maybe something by Shirley Jackson, or Edgar Allan Poe.*

Before Robbie could do anything more than flip Nathan off for making fun of him, the window panes flanking the fireplace rattled hard. Rivulets of moisture reflected off the glass in the firelight.

Kaylee, a girl they'd all just met that night, smiled at the cousins' banter but said nothing. She was a few years younger than the rest of them, the daughter of the man Nathan's mother was dating. He'd brought her along to the Halloween party, something Nathan's mom had been nervous about. But as far as he could tell, Kaylee was fitting in just fine.

Nathan pushed up out of a deep-seated chair and walked across the scarred hardwood to the window. "Dang, looks like we have our first sleet storm of the season, folks," he said. "I can't see the lake, it's too dark, but I can hear the waves crashing out there."

"Good thing we weren't planning on going back to school tonight, Grace," Julie said to the pretty girl sitting next to her—the subject of Nathan's focus when Robbie had heard phantoms outside. Julie shivered in the chill air, set her plate to the side, and pulled an afghan off the back of the sofa. She covered her own bare legs then handed a corner of the throw to Grace. "And knowing Aunt Val, she has plenty of food for everybody. We won't go hungry."

Julie's comment pulled Nathan's attention back to Grace as she accepted the edge of the throw from his cousin and tucked it around her knees. Grace and Julie shared an apartment at college. While Nathan's and Julie's moms were sisters, the roommates' dads had been brothers. It was complicated, but Nathan was glad he wasn't technically related to Grace.

"Let me see if I can't warm it up in here," he offered, flicking his eyes toward the old copper boiler full of firewood.

"Nathan," Grace, the girl he couldn't seem to get out of his head, finally addressed him directly. "Julie mentioned you were moving . . . ?"

Guess she does *know I'm alive,* Nathan thought.

As he crossed from the streaming window to the fireplace and picked up a poker, he tried to keep his response casual. "Yeah, I started dumping my stuff over at my new place earlier today. I have to be out of my old apartment by the first. I should be able to finish moving everything else tomorrow." He used the poker to rearrange what remained of the smoldering wood in the fireplace and then added another big log from the dented metal container. "That should warm it up in here. *And* chase away any ghosts."

Grace grinned in Robbie's direction, then turned back to Nathan. "Are you going to have the same roommates?"

"Nope," he replied with a shake of his head, brushing his hands against the legs of his jeans. "Some dude is subletting my room at the old apartment. I have a pretty sweet deal lined up with this old guy my mom knows. He owns Book Journeys, a bookstore in this cool old building, and he needs some help running the place. He hired me and is letting me live in the apartment above the store. Rent's pretty cheap, but I'll be working quite a bit. I start on Monday."

Nathan sunk back into his chair, glad the fire was again chasing the chill from the air and the shadows from the corners of the room.

"I thought you worked at Barnes & Noble. Won't that be a conflict of interest?" Grace asked.

"Nah. I wasn't getting enough hours over there, so I quit to do this instead. I'm sure I would have gotten plenty of hours between now and Christmas, but I was worried I'd get cut once we got past the holidays. I need to work."

Talk about money sent Nathan's mind back to the last time he'd visited his dad. His poor excuse of a father had chewed through all their money—including his and his sister's college funds. Luckily, Nathan was a senior, but his sister Lauren was just getting started. He'd graduate in the spring. He had considered going on to get a master's degree, but his dad's sins put those plans on the back burner. At least for now.

"Are you going to be the manager or something?" Robbie asked.

"It's just me working there plus the old couple that owns it, Frank and Virginia. I guess that makes me *assistant* manager, salesperson, and grunt, all rolled into one. They don't want to work as much as they used to."

He could see Grace watching him closely, her head tilted as if in concentration, while he explained his new living arrangements and job. She twirled a strand of her snow-white hair between her index finger and thumb. Her thoughtful gaze sent the butterflies in his stomach fluttering. He'd told no one about the crush he'd had on her for the past year, and he hoped it didn't show on his face now. He'd been wanting to ask her out but couldn't seem to get up the nerve.

She chimed in again. "Since you aren't quite done with school yet, you'll probably have plenty of time to study. I can't imagine a small, independent bookstore would be very busy."

Nathan shrugged; he'd had a similar thought, but her comment grated on him. He was surprised to realize he already felt a sense of responsibility when it came to the Fisks' store. "I filled in for them once when Virginia needed some medical tests. She'd been having some trouble with her heart. It was busy that weekend because Frank had scheduled an author reading and book signing. He didn't want to cancel on the guy, so he asked me to help out. It was fun. The store is in this vintage building, lots of character. Not sure why I like it so much, but Frank and I hit it off, and when we started joking around about me coming to work there, we both decided maybe it wasn't such a bad idea. Now I need to figure out a way to bring in more business for them."

And since she threw me off when it only took her a second to pinpoint my biggest concern with my new job, I'm blabbing, he thought with embarrassment. Maybe some day he'd master the art of talking to women. Now they just flustered him.

"They can afford to pay someone, huh?" Grace asked.

Nathan wasn't sure why she was peppering him with so many questions. Normally he wouldn't mind the attention from her—he'd have *loved* it, in fact—but a part of him felt almost defensive of Frank and Virginia.

"Jeez, Grace, lighten up," Julie chimed in with a laugh. "You sound like you did back when Mom was trying to get her retreats up and running out here at the resort."

Grace shrugged. "Sorry. I guess I do tend to be a little *too* realistic sometimes."

"Or pessimistic?" Julie shot back with a pointed look.

Grace grinned, her cheeks flushing. "Didn't mean to drill you, Nathan. It's just that I hear all this theory at school, and we work on business cases, but the real world is so much more interesting."

Nathan relaxed back into the comfortable recliner angled toward the fireplace, content with the idea that Grace found him—or at least his new working arrangement—interesting. "Well, to be honest, Frank did consider closing up the store so they could retire. But his wife loves it and doesn't want him to shut the bookstore down. So one of the conditions of Frank and Virginia hiring me was that I find ways to drum up business and eventually bring in more than the cost of having me work there."

"That might be tough," Grace said, setting her cup of punch down and leaning toward Nathan, elbows on top of her blanketed knees. She was wearing a flapper dress in emerald green. Nathan couldn't help but notice how the rows upon rows of fringe on Grace's dress matched the green flecks in her big blue eyes.

Her dress was similar to Julie's purple one. The girls had come to the party in costumes—as directed. The boys had ignored the suggestion, showing up in jeans and sweatshirts.

"I'm pretty good at coming up with ideas for drumming up business. Just ask Julie here," Grace added. "Give me a call if you need some help."

Don't get excited . . . it's not like she's asking you out on a date, Nathan warned himself. Her words had his heart beating a little faster, and he worried someone might notice the flush creeping up his face. Despite being a senior in college, he hadn't dated much. One disastrous prom experience and a handful of dates with another girl as a college freshman made up his short list of dating events. *Pathetic. Dear old Dad would laugh in my face if he knew. He* never *had that problem.*

"Yeah, sounds good," he said, smiling at her. "I'll just get your number from Julie if things don't pick up and I'm fresh out of things to try."

Grace pulled her phone out. "Here, what's your number? I'll send you mine, so you have it."

After that, the conversation around the room moved on to other topics. Nathan was more than happy to forfeit the spotlight. Would he be able to get up the nerve to take Grace up on her offer? Asking for her help with the store would be the perfect excuse to talk to her again.

***

Nathan slept on the floor of Robbie's room. The pillow and throw blanket his cousin had tossed him a few hours earlier did little to soften the hard ground.

The creak of a door, followed by wet kisses on his face, brought him fully awake. He sat up, rubbing the cocker spaniel behind her ears. He yawned. A glance at his phone revealed it was a few minutes before seven. The rest of the house was quiet. "Hey, Molly, how'd you know I needed to get up early?"

"Shut up, man," Robbie groaned from the bed above.

Nathan pushed to his feet. He threw the pillow at his cousin, but Robbie just scooped it up and shoved it under his head, flipping over to his side and showing no signs of getting up.

"Come on, girl, I'll take you out," Nathan said to the dog as she pranced next to him. She trotted out of the room at his offer, leading him to the stairs.

No one else seemed to be up yet on this side of the duplex, but now he could hear voices through the wall separating his aunt and uncle's half from his mom's half of the duplex they shared at Whispering Pines. He could also hear babbling, which meant his baby sister was already up.

He stepped out onto the back patio to let Molly do her business—and slipped on a patch of ice. It took plenty of fancy footwork but, somehow, he managed to stay upright. There came tapping on the window to his left, which meant, unfortunately, that someone had witnessed his less-than-graceful stunt. He resisted the urge to look over his shoulder. Instead, he kept an eye on Molly as her nose led her in large, looping circles, leaving tracks in the wet grass. Trees rimming the yard bore evidence of last night's storm, their ice-encrusted branches dripping in the early-morning sunshine.

"Thank God that storm blew through. It would suck to move the rest of my stuff out of the apartment and over to the bookstore in the rain," Nathan said aloud, although Molly was too busy exploring to pay him any attention. "Come on, girl."

The spaniel glanced up but immediately resumed her sniffing. Nathan slapped his leg, bringing Molly trotting in his direction. He petted her golden head as she loped past him. He let the dog back in on Robbie's side and then knocked on his mom's back door.

Seth, his mom's boyfriend, opened the door, nodding and stepping back to let Nathan in.

"Thanks for giving up your bed." Seth grinned. "Little slick out there?"

Nathan returned his nod with a grimace, relieved he hadn't wiped out in front of witnesses. "Little bit. But it's melting fast." He made his way over to his youngest sister in her highchair. "Hey, squirt, you up already? Keeping Mom on her toes, I bet."

Harper babbled in reply; she was clearly happy to see her big brother, but at just nine months old, she didn't have many words to express it.

Seth turned to Jess. "I'm going to run up and shower quick if you don't mind."

"Go ahead," she said. "You want to get in there before Lauren or Kaylee get up, or you'll be waiting a while."

Nathan watched Seth squeeze his mom's hand as he walked by, heading for the stairs. He was still trying to get used to the thought of his mom dating. Seth was a good guy, but still. He turned back to his baby sister—another person he was getting used to. He loved having his baby sister around, but sometimes the sight of her brought up too many bad memories.

He supposed he'd done all right in the parent lottery. His mom was pretty great—especially with all the things she'd taken on this past year. On the other hand, Will, his dad, was worthless. The man had everything going for him, but he threw it all away. Nathan suspected it was because, deep down, his father was a narcissist, caring only about himself.

The man's mistakes had landed him in prison, a fact Nathan was still grappling to come to terms with in the months since he was incarcerated. But even when Nathan was growing up his dad wasn't around much. As a surgeon, he worked long hours. When he wasn't working, the man was usually golfing or attending conferences. When he *was* around, he'd continuously nagged on Nathan. For Will, it was all about status and reputation. Nathan thought back to when he was younger and his dad had bought their new house, forcing them to move away from their old neighborhood and best friends to a new development filled with big houses, snotty kids, and treeless concrete. Nathan knew his mom hadn't wanted to move, either. But his dad insisted they'd *earned* the right to upgrade. Nathan never saw it that way.

Harper banged on the tray of her highchair, pulling Nathan's attention back to his mom's small kitchen with its dated appliances and scarred countertops. The room felt more like home than the fancy kitchen at their last house ever had when he'd lived there. Nathan ruffled Harper's pale, baby-fine strands, then poured himself a cup of coffee and started rummaging around in the cupboard for food, all the while aware that Jess was looking at him as if expecting him to say something.

"What?" he asked, not sure what he'd missed. He dropped two pieces of bread into the toaster.

"I asked what you thought about your uncle bringing a date to the party last night," Jess repeated.

Nathan shrugged. He *had* been surprised to see Ethan, his mom's only brother, show up at the party with an attractive, obviously *younger* woman, the night before. Not that Nathan ever gave much thought to his uncle's love life. "His date seemed nice enough, and cute, but I guess it was kind of weird. I do wonder if Lizzy knows he's dating. I don't think she'd like her dad going out. I bet she's not ready for that yet."

Nathan knew from the look on his mother's face that she'd taken his comment personally, so he quickly backtracked. "Before you go getting all mad, I swear to you, Mom, I didn't mean that as a dig. You know I think Seth is cool. I'll admit, it was a little tough when you two started dating, but I've known for years that you and Dad weren't happy. This mess with Ethan's marriage blowing up was a big surprise."

"I suspect you're right," Jess agreed with a sigh. "I think Lizzy's struggling with the divorce. Do you ever talk to her?"

"It's been a while," Nathan admitted. "Maybe it's easier for her to stay away, to stay busy, and not think about it. You know, with how her mom walked out on all of them."

Maybe Lizzy's avoidance tactic isn't such a bad idea, Nathan thought.

But he knew better than to say this out loud. Running away from the pain *would* be easier—it was hard when family dynamics changed so drastically; but his own mother had too much on her plate for him to stay away. *He* couldn't abandon her, too.

"I'll call her sometime," he assured Jess, then switched gears. "I need to finish moving out of my old apartment and into my new place. If I don't want to sleep on another floor tonight, I better at least get my mattress hauled up there. And then I need to start coming up with a game plan for the holidays at the bookstore. We need to make the most of these two months coming up."

Nathan knew his mother was painfully aware of the lack of business at the bookstore in recent months. Jess had a small ownership interest in the store, passed on to her from Nathan's great-aunt, Celia—it was how they'd met the Fisks in the first place. Nathan knew Jess loved the old store and wanted this new plan to work. If he couldn't help turn things around, Nathan doubted the doors would still be open next Halloween. He was already feeling the pressure to make a difference. He didn't want to disappoint his mom.

"So, do you have any brilliant ideas yet?" she asked.

He spread peanut butter on his hot toast and took a seat at the table. "A few . . . but I need to work on them more before I start talking details."

Jess poured a glass of orange juice, pulled up a chair, and sat next to Nathan. She set the juice glass in front of him. "Honey, are you sure you aren't taking on too much? After all, this is your last year at college. Are you going to be able to juggle everything, plus the long drive between the bookstore and school?"

Nathan took a bite of his toast, gathering his thoughts before responding to his worried mother. He needed her to have confidence in his ability to turn things around. He didn't need them *both* to have doubts.

"I'll be fine, Mom. Don't worry about me. I learned how to juggle from an old pro."

"Hey, watch who you're calling 'old,' kid," Jess said, trying to sound stern but failing. "Just be sure to call if you get in too deep, okay?"

Nathan thought about receiving Grace's number the previous night. He smiled. "Okay, Mom."

"Oh, and Nathan, see if you can't squeeze in a haircut today, too," Jess suggested as she stood and ruffled his dark hair.

Nathan ducked out of her reach. "Stop! Come on, Mom, I'm not twelve. I can take care of myself."

He caught the look she gave him as she turned back toward Harper—as if he had yet to convince her of that fact.

CHAPTER 2

Gift of Buried Secrets

*N*athan collapsed back onto his bare mattress, tired from hauling what little furniture he owned down three flights of stairs at his old place and then back up another, narrower set at the bookstore. He was lucky the new apartment was partially furnished. Two roommates had helped him with the heavy lifting, but they'd gone home midafternoon. All was quiet.

He'd get the bed frame set up later. For now, the mattress worked just fine on the floor. His sheets were here somewhere.

I only need ten minutes, Nathan told himself, allowing his eyes to drift shut.

***

His eyes popped open. Ten minutes had turned into a fully-fledged nap.

Beams from the setting sun shot through the window, highlighting dust motes as they danced in the air of the tiny apartment. *His* tiny apartment. He'd never had a place all to himself before, and after nearly four years with roommates, he was looking forward to his own space. But before he could enjoy it, there was unpacking to do.

Then he remembered his homework. He checked the time.

"Oh *man*, I've got an online test due in an hour . . . and I *still* have to get more crap out of my car," Nathan moaned to the empty apartment. It would take some getting used to, this living alone. He turned up his music to cut the silence.

Forty minutes later, he submitted his test with fingers crossed, hoping his answer to the essay question would earn him back a few points. The immediate results for the multiple-choice portion of the test were less than stellar. But he'd had too much on his mind to focus.

Snapping his laptop shut, he stowed it in his backpack and propped it against a red leather couch, scooping his keys off the counter. The burst of color from the small couch seemed oddly out of place in the tight quarters, and Nathan could tell just by looking that his long frame wouldn't fit comfortably on it.

He jogged back down the stairs and out to his car to grab what would hopefully be the last load for the day. Minutes later, he'd lugged a plastic tub of kitchen items, piled high with clothes on top, back across the gloom of the deserted bookstore and up the stairs. He could barely see over the tall load, and he had to keep shifting the tub as he climbed to keep his clothes from sliding off. The squeaky board told him he'd reached the top of the stairs. He headed for his mattress in the corner—and plowed right into an old desk he'd forgotten was there. His clothes fell in a heap on the floor.

Cringing, he set the tub down and bent to check the wooden antique for damage. It was the *one* thing Frank specifically warned him to be careful with, saying it was special to Virginia. He'd promised he'd take good care of it.

Great way to start, klutz.

He found a tiny dent in the upper corner of the wood where he'd rammed the tub into it, but he'd gotten lucky. The plastic hadn't scratched the surface. There didn't seem to be any noticeable damage.

Close call.

As he bent down to scoop up his clothes from the floor, he noticed the bottom desk drawer had popped open. He was about to shove it closed with his foot but thought better of it. Not wanting to chance damaging it, he leaned down and tried to close the drawer by hand. Something jammed and the drawer wouldn't close.

What the . . . ?

He shimmied it and tried again. Still stuck. Getting down on his hands and knees, he laid his head on the linoleum to peer underneath the vintage desk. It looked like a bottom piece had broken loose. One end was hanging down to the floor.

Crap. Maybe he hadn't gotten so lucky after all.

Hoping he'd be able to fix the piece and *not* irritate his new boss and landlord, he eased the drawer out all the way. Something thudded to the floor. Thinking it was part of the desk bottom, he examined the drawer he now held in his hands. It was heavy; full of what looked like old letters and papers.

This surprised him. He'd assumed the desk would be empty.

The drawer itself seemed to be intact, but the bottom looked odd. Setting it aside, he glanced back at the desk for the fallen piece.

There, lying on the yellowed linoleum underneath the frame, was a thick sheath of paper, now slightly fanned out.

He crouched down and piled the papers back into a neater stack. Underneath where the paper had fallen was a flat piece of wood, its dimensions similar to that of the drawer.

"Looks like I've found myself a secret compartment," Nathan said, even though there was no one to hear his announcement. "Nothing like a little mystery to wrap up a Sunday night—and two days before Halloween! Next there'll be scratching in the walls and a blood-curdling scream."

Having always been an avid reader, Nathan liked nothing more than a gruesome horror story. His vivid imagination could conjure up all kinds of scary scenarios that might play out in a historic building like this. Kind of like the scratching on the window at the old lodge the night before.

Who knows what secrets these walls hold?

He took a minute to pop the real bottom back onto the old drawer, admiring the craftsmanship that had created the hidden compartment. Reassembled, the drawer looked fine, and it slid shut easily when he tried again.

He did think it was strange that the desk was full of stuff.

Ignoring his pile of clothes, Nathan grabbed a beer out of the dorm-size fridge (the six-pack a housewarming gift from his old roomies) and sat down at a rickety kitchen table with the stack of papers. The top page in the stack was blank but slightly discolored, a stain marring a portion of the sheet. He was dying to find out what he'd just discovered. Whatever it was, someone had thought it was important enough to hide it away.

The tabletop on which he'd set the papers was small, with a drop-down leaf on each side. He pulled up one side so his long legs could slide under, and he scooted his chair closer. He straightened the stack of papers and laid the top sheet over, as if opening a book that was missing its binding. The second page wasn't blank. It was covered from top to bottom in looping cursive, black ink, with the occasional red mark in the margins. Scrawled across the top were the words *Chapter One*.

He knew immediately he was looking at a manuscript—an early draft of a book. But there was no author name. The smeared handwriting directly underneath the discoloration he'd noticed on the top sheet was barely legible. Leafing through the stack, he had to go down a dozen pages before the stain was gone entirely.

Maybe he should just put this back where he'd found it. He could ask Frank or Virginia about it in the morning. He felt guilty, reading something someone had taken so much care to hide away. But as he read through the first paragraph, and then the second—or what he could make out despite the stain—the story drew him in. His guilt was quickly replaced by curiosity.

He read slowly, the beautiful handwriting foreign to his eyes. There was a melody to the rhythm of the words. While the red marks indicated a lack of grammatical skill—something he'd personally experienced in his creative writing courses—the author's style appealed to him. He tried to ignore the distraction of the editorial marks. He could picture the setting and began to see the characters develop. Was this a love story? A mystery? The story would have to evolve more before he could be sure. It wasn't a modern-day setting—which wasn't a surprise, since he'd found the manuscript hidden away in an old desk, probably long forgotten.

He remembered Frank mentioning he'd taught creative writing in his younger years, before leaving academia to help Virginia run the bookstore. Did he put the manuscript there for safekeeping? Given his previous occupation, he certainly could have done some editing for authors.

When Frank initially warned him to be careful of the desk, he'd said it was a favorite of Virginia's. In that case, maybe Virginia knew something of the manuscript. Maybe she'd even *written* it.

He felt certain no one had read this manuscript in a very long time.

The texture of the paper felt different, heavier. The black ink flitting across the pages had a hushed, mellow quality to it. Even the red slashes faded to pink in places.

Perhaps his new employers knew nothing of the old manuscript.

Nathan read on, transported to another time and place.

The story followed four young women as they embarked on a hot, dusty road trip to Washington, DC, during the summer of 1963. Nathan knew from his studies that the '60s had been a time of extensive cultural shifts in America, and he could feel these playing out within the dynamics of the small group of childhood friends, maturing now into women with pointedly different views. Two of the young women had left home against their parents' wishes. Nathan began to assign labels to each of them as he read, based off the author's vivid characterizations and lively conversations during long hours on the road and at picnic tables outside of roadside motels: an outspoken feminist, a twenty-two-year-old Vietnam War widow, a preacher's daughter, and a flower child. He appreciated the way the author wove two men into the story and how their presence impacted the group. The jovial, charismatic man intrigued the women, while his more introspective, brooding sidekick held back. One man was black, the other white, which subtly introduced racial tensions into the already complicated storyline.

Eventually, the grumbling of his stomach pulled him out of the story. He didn't want to quit reading, but if he didn't get something to eat and use the bathroom, he wouldn't be able to concentrate.

The time on his phone read 11:16 p.m.

No way . . .

It hadn't been much after 5:00 when he lugged that last load of clothes up the narrow wooden stairs to his new apartment.

Six hours?!

No wonder he was starving.

On top of that, Frank expected him to be downstairs by eight the next morning. With less than a month until Thanksgiving, they needed to get their holiday promotional plans figured out. It was make-or-break time, and Nathan needed to be sharp.

With a sigh, he gathered up the manuscript, using a gas receipt he'd stuffed into his pocket earlier in the day to mark his place, and tucked it all back into its hiding spot. He doubted anyone would have noticed if he'd left the stack on his kitchen table until he could get back to it, but that didn't feel right. He liked the air of mystery that the hiding spot lent to the story.

Once his discovery was safely stowed away, he pulled a baggie of leftover meat and cheese slices out of the fridge, thankful his mom had thought to send it with him when he left Whispering Pines that morning. He dug through the small box of groceries he'd brought over from his old apartment, sure there was at least one sleeve of Ritz crackers in there somewhere.

He ate, took a quick shower, tried to arrange the still-to-be-unpacked boxes from his old place so that he at least had a pathway from bed to bathroom to kitchen to stairs, and laid down. He needed to be in good shape for his first full day on the job tomorrow.

His body was tired from the move and the late night at the Halloween party the night before, but his mind raced with the story he'd found under the desk. His imagination picked up where his reading left off. He slept, but it wasn't a restful sleep. Dreams shifted, first focusing on the story itself and then on the fame he found when *he* brought the story to the world, as if he'd been the one to pen the novel. There were book signings, personal appearances, even a movie deal. The actor cast to play the hippie girl looked an awful lot like Grace, with smooth, straight hair skimming her waist. He agonized while he watched her tall, lithe body lean in to kiss the quiet, sullen stranger, duped into believing the man wanted a world of peace and harmony, as she did. Since Nathan was the orchestrator of this dream, the scene shifted, and suddenly *he* was the one about to be kissed, holding his breath as the Grace look-alike bent toward him . . .

Beep! beep! beep!

Instinctively, he reached for his phone, intent on killing the sound that pulled him away from her. He kept his eyes shut tight, grasping for the vision, but it swirled away, leaving only a black void.

He covered his head with a pillow, groaning into the fluff.

I can't even get lucky in my dreams.

The jangle of a bell below snapped his eyes open. It was dark. He was cold, disoriented.

More noises were coming from below—foreign sounds.

He fumbled for his lamp, but his fingertips grazed a cold, flat surface. No lamp. Finally, reality seeped in, and he remembered he wasn't in his old apartment, sharing a room with a guy who regularly consumed too much alcohol and snored like a freight train. He was on his mattress, on the floor of his new apartment above the bookstore, shivering in the cold. The soft blue blanket he'd thrown over himself the previous evening didn't hold up against the chill. With another groan, he tossed off the thin covering and scooted to the edge of the mattress, placing bare feet on the scuffed hardwood, his knees nearly even with his chin. He needed to get his bed frame set up.

Who's downstairs?

Frank had said to expect him about eight. It was only seven. Nathan stood and went to the window overlooking the deserted street in front of the bookstore. Sure enough, Frank's white sedan was there, parked in its usual spot under a cone of light from a nearby streetlamp in front of the vacant building next door. He'd glanced into that building the day before and noticed a FOR SALE sign on the floor. It looked like it could have been empty for a long time. Nathan's new boss always left the spots closest to the bookstore open for potential customers. He needed to go out and move his car, too. It was now *his* job to fill the front spots with paying customers.

Time to get to it.

CHAPTER 3

Gift of Collaboration

"Good morning, Nathan."

"Morning, Frank."

Nathan grinned at the older man as he set his laptop on the sales counter next to a cash register that looked to be older than *he* was. Frank wore a white button-down dress shirt, brown dress pants, and polished loafers, the same outfit he seemed to wear every day. Nathan suspected the older man considered this to be "casual dress," since he was minus a tie. The man's thinning hair, white with streaks of gray, was neatly combed, and Nathan caught a whiff of aftershave, mixing in with the comforting scent of piles and piles of books.

Nathan had finger-combed his own longish hair, only taking the time to brush his teeth and throw on a black polo and khakis and passing on the rest of his regular morning routine in an effort to get downstairs early to impress his new boss. Now he regretted not squeezing in that haircut his mom had suggested the previous day.

"Were you able to get settled upstairs yesterday?" Frank asked.

"Got a good start on it. I still have to unpack, but at least most everything is up there. Hey, I was going to let you know there's actually a bunch of stuff in that little desk upstairs. Do you maybe want me to transfer the things out of the drawers and into a box so you can take it home, now that I'm living up there?"

Nathan didn't specifically mention the manuscript, waiting instead to gauge Frank's reaction.

"Really? I didn't realize Virginia still had things in her desk up there. She used to treat upstairs like her own personal office and break area. When our daughter was younger, she'd hang out up there after school. We've never actually used it like an apartment before," Frank explained. "Why don't you ask her about it when she comes in?"

"I'll do that," Nathan said. "I'm surprised to see you already this morning."

Frank flicked his gaze to the old Timex on his left wrist. Nathan doubted the man was late for anything. "I *am* early, aren't I?" the older man acknowledged with a chuckle. "Sorry about that. Did I wake you?"

"No, I was up. Kind of. Do you always come in this early?"

"*I* do, but not my Ginny. I'll pick her up midmorning. She likes to sleep in these days, but I don't want her driving, and I can't seem to keep her away from this place."

Nathan shook his head in amazement. "That is so cool that she still likes coming here, after all these years. I hope someday I'll find work I love that much."

Frank looked up from the paperwork he'd pulled out of a large, battered brown leather briefcase he'd opened on the counter—the type of briefcase Nathan had only ever seen in older movies. "I hope you do, too, son, I hope you do. In the meantime, I brought doughnuts to celebrate your first *official* day here." He nodded toward the white box sitting on the end of the counter.

The mention of sugary bombs of carbohydrates to start the day caused a rumble in Nathan's stomach. Not a bad way to start.

***

They spent the first part of the morning discussing possible options for the upcoming holiday season. Frank referenced an old, tattered notebook he pulled out from under the counter beneath the cash register. Nathan watched as he flipped to a page earmarked with a sticky note.

"We can start with what we've been doing the past few years," he said, running a finger down the list. The finger was misshapen, the knuckles swollen. Nathan wondered if Frank had arthritis.

He also wondered what the odds were that he'd get Frank to shake things up a little. Since he was here to breathe new life into the old bookstore, the holidays seemed like the perfect time to try some different ideas. It might be the *only* time to try something new. He knew, deep down, there was little hope of keeping the doors open if business didn't pick up.

He bided his time, listening to the litany of things the Fisks had tried before. Nothing sounded too exciting, but he needed to keep an open mind and be careful not to say something that would offend Frank. This bookstore was his life. Or, at least, his *wife's* life.

Nathan nodded along, finally piping up. "I like that you kick things off with a big event on Small Business Saturday, the day after Black Friday, instead of trying to compete with the big guns, head to head."

Frank nodded. "Yes, the concept seems nice, but traffic the past two years has been disappointing."

"What have you done to advertise?"

Frank didn't reply. Thinking he hadn't heard the question, Nathan asked again.

The older man frowned. "Son, you have no idea how expensive advertising has gotten. I can't afford either print or radio."

"I understand," Nathan conceded, careful not to sound patronizing. "But there are other options these days. Do you do any social media? You know, like set up events on your Facebook page, post about it on Instagram, anything like that?"

Again, Frank said nothing—but this time, Nathan knew the man heard him.

"I'm going to guess, based on your expression, that you maybe haven't tried that approach. I know you have a website, at least."

Frank nodded, suddenly more eager. "Our daughter Karen set that up for us a couple years back. She showed Ginny how to keep it up when she knew she couldn't . . . uh . . ." His voice trailed off.

Nathan was painfully familiar with why Karen could no longer help with the store's website. Wanting to steer clear of any conversation about that whole debacle—which, regrettably, involved his own parents—Nathan nodded in understanding but didn't prod.

Frank eventually gave a grim smile. "We may need you to bring us up to date with that social media stuff, young man."

"Not a problem, Frank. That's one of the reasons you hired me. Got a spare sheet of paper in that notebook?"

Frank flipped to the back and tore out a sheet.

Nathan picked at the rough edges of the paper, considering how blunt he dared be with his new employer. What the Fisks had been doing around the holidays hadn't been working. That much was painfully clear from the tattered notebook sitting between them.

"Frank, we may need to come up with some fresh new ideas if we want to start turning things around for you."

Frank met Nathan's eye. "I'm willing to at least *listen* to your ideas. But a few things will be non-negotiable. Virginia looks forward to them every year, and since this could very likely turn out to be our last holiday season here, I want her to enjoy herself."

Nathan sighed, wishing Frank wasn't so pessimistic about things, so stubborn. He'd need to convince the man he could help them turn things around. Ever since agreeing to come work for the Fisks, he'd been reading up on the resurgence of small independent bookstores. Their nimbleness to respond to changing readers' tastes and habits could be an advantage against the larger chains who, due in part to their sheer size, were slower to adjust.

But that only worked if the independents were willing to swivel.

***

After debating their options for a couple of hours, Frank scooped up his briefcase, made his way around two tables of books set between the store entrance and the counter, and unlocked the front door. He spoke as he walked. "I normally use Monday mornings to update my paperwork. Can you occupy yourself for a bit? Help anyone who might stop in? Your mother will be in tomorrow to pick up my financials for the third quarter—and you know she's a stickler for accuracy."

Jess's small ownership interest in the bookstore was what led to Nathan's new job. He was painfully familiar with his mom's attention to detail and her high expectations. He'd been fighting to live up to those expectations his whole life. He always felt he came close to meeting *her* expectations, just not those of his father. Seeing how things were now, maybe his father should have worried more about his *own* behavior.

Nathan nodded. "Would you mind if I start by doing some rearranging of this front area? Maybe make a little more room for the trick-or-treaters on Tuesday night?"

Frank glanced around the sales floor with a shrug. "Sure, go ahead. Just don't be surprised if Virginia has her own opinions on that when I bring her back here before lunch. Now you're wading into *her* domain, young man."

Nathan nodded again. No time like the present to try to start proving himself.

They'd already agreed to prepare a flyer about their upcoming holiday season and attach it to candy bags, to be given out to any little kids that stopped in on Halloween. Nathan would work on that tomorrow morning after they'd had a chance to share some of their ideas with Virginia. For now, he'd start making some of the physical changes he'd been itching to implement ever since he'd first visited the bookstore.

His time at Barnes & Noble had taught him the importance of the front displays. There, at the big retailer, those front tables were important real estate, often tied up by the big publishers and well-known authors. Here, he wouldn't have those same constraints.

There tended to be some degree of predictability as to what buyers were interested in, depending on the season. October was a good month for selling horror; shorter days, longer nights, and the commercialization of Halloween all helped. But as soon as the calendar flipped to November, tastes quickly changed: There'd be the inevitable renewed interest in the classics. Grandparents would be searching for a new series for their tweens. Friends would be browsing for the latest bestsellers or, occasionally, a beautiful hardcover edition of a personal favorite for gift exchanges.

Nathan took a moment to look around. He needed to get to work while things were quiet. He wanted to surprise Virginia. First things first. There were too many tables crowded into the front space. One, if not two, needed to go.

"Got any tubs around here?" Nathan called to Frank, now seated at the cluttered desk in a back corner of the store.

Frank glanced his way, his eyeglasses perched on the end of his nose. "What do you need tubs for?"

"Just need to do some rearranging."

"There are a few downstairs."

"I'll go grab them," Nathan replied, making his way toward the basement stairs.

Flicking the light on, he made his way down. He'd been down there the previous summer with his mom to help the Fisks clean up after a rainstorm. He recognized the smell first: Old paper and even older walls. It smelled musty. Little seemed to have changed in the months since the storm. Stacks of old books rested on tables in sagging rows. He was excited to spend time down here later, exploring. Frank had mentioned Virginia's desire to help up-and-coming authors, and Nathan suspected there were diamonds hidden amongst the mediocre in the piles down here.

But today wasn't the day for that. He had plenty of work to do upstairs.

***

An hour later, the little bell over the front door jingled again. Nathan, his back to the door, glanced up in dismay. He'd made a mess in his efforts to rearrange the tables. He needed at least another hour before he'd have things looking better.

"Oh *my*, what do we have here?"

Nathan cringed at the sound of Virginia's voice. This was even worse. He'd assumed their first customer of the day was finally stopping in. Frank hadn't even left to pick Virginia up yet. He was still at his desk, working on financial reports for Jess.

Well, now the real *work begins.*

Nathan stood up from where he'd been piling books into a tub on the floor, brushing his hands off on his pants before extending one to Frank's wife. "Morning, Virginia. I'd hoped to have this put back together before you got in today. I wanted to surprise you."

Virginia clasped Nathan's hand and pulled him in for a quick hug. "I am so glad to see you, Nathan," she greeted him. "Even if you've already messed everything up." The wink she gave him meant she was probably kidding.

At least he *hoped* she was kidding.

Frank had made his way to his wife's side by now, fairly quick for an old man. "Virginia, we talked about this. I don't think it's a good idea for you to be driving," he said as he helped his wife out of her knee-length, rose-colored wool coat.

"You've made yourself abundantly clear on that point," Virginia replied with more than a hint of frustration in her voice.

Nathan watched the older couple interact. He suspected Frank meant for his comment to sound stern; however, his tender actions spoke louder. Virginia switched her black purse from one hand to the other as she pulled her arms out of her sleeves with Frank's assistance. Frank tossed the coat over his arm and Virginia leaned in to place a quick peck on his cheek, using her thumb to wipe away the bright smudge of lipstick she'd left behind.

Frank glanced out the large plate-glass windows, and Virginia scoffed.

"Oh, relax, dear. Mabel dropped me off. When I couldn't find my set of keys, I gave her a call. You do realize that as soon as my new glasses come in, I'm planning to start driving myself again, don't you? I can't be expected to ask for rides every time I want to go somewhere."

Now Frank patted the breast pocket of his button-down. "I thought you might try to drive this morning," he said with a knowing nod.

Virginia waved a dismissive hand at her husband. "Enough about us old codgers and our failing eye-sight," she said, turning back to Nathan. "What exactly are you doing to my bookstore? I thought it looked quite nice."

Frank took Virginia's coat back to another corner of the bookstore where a small alcove had been set up with four comfortable chairs, a small sink and coffee area, and a coat tree. Nathan watched him go, feeling like he'd been left to the wolves.

He turned back to face Virginia, debating how best to respond. He didn't want to get off on the wrong foot with her. Frank had already warned him that his wife could be quite territorial when it came to her store—*her* store, he'd called it—and she wasn't big on change.

"It did look nice, Mrs. Fisk. I just thought I'd get a jumpstart on our holiday displays, maybe switch out one or two of the bigger tables for a smaller one between the door and the counter before tomorrow night—you know, so there's room for any little trick-or-treaters and their parents."

Virginia didn't reply immediately. She eyed Nathan for a moment and then looked around the store, crossing her arms and tapping her foot, as if deep in thought. She nodded her head slowly. "You know, I've been telling Frank for years that we had too much clutter in here. I like that this area is more open with that large table out," she said, motioning toward the rectangular table Nathan had already collapsed and wrestled over to the top of the stairs.

Frank must have overheard—his grunt at her comment was hard to miss. Nathan bit his lip in an effort not to laugh.

"And by the way, please don't ever call me 'Mrs. Fisk' again. Call me Ginny, or *Virginia* if you must, but Mrs. Fisk was my mother-in-law. We don't rest on formalities around here."

Nathan nodded. He hoped he'd avoided stepping on his first land mine on the job.

"Well, come here then, and I'll show you where we house the children's books, and together we can decide on the table display for tomorrow night. Maybe we can entice the little kiddies to convince their parents to buy them a *ghost* story."

Nathan did as she asked. Frank had already shown him the kids' section earlier, but he knew better than to try to take the lead this morning. He could sense Virginia was setting some ground rules to remind him she was still in charge. Frank caught his eye and raised one eyebrow at him, his silent communication clear.

I told you so.

***

The rest of the morning passed quickly, and Nathan had to admit that Virginia did have a flair for displaying books. She strategically placed things at eye-level for the kids and elevated the center section of the table to display adult horror books, choosing those that Nathan knew to be books that sold well but with covers that weren't too scary for the little ones to see. She was looking to attract young and old readers alike, and doing a decent job at it, too.

A few people stopped in but did more browsing than buying. Nathan knew Monday mornings were seldom busy in retail, but he was glad to see at least a little foot traffic.

He eyed the front window. It currently boasted an autumn theme, complete with bushel baskets of apples and bright-orange pumpkins. There were cookbooks with comfort foods on their covers, American history books, and a handful of current bestsellers. It fit the season, but if Nathan was going to help the Fisks increase traffic, the front display would need more *oomph*.

"Your window display looks nice, Virginia," Nathan said, hoping the compliment would make Virginia more open to the suggestions he was about to make. "It's very *fall*-ish."

"Why, thank you, Nathan. I thought the apples were a nice touch."

"That front window is a beauty, what with its heavy wooden framing on the outside. I like the red paint. Eye-catching."

"The red was your mother's idea," Virginia replied. "It works well for Christmas, Valentine's, and even summery displays."

Good call, Mom, Nathan thought.

"What would you think about adding a Halloween theme to the window display, see if we can't draw more people in tomorrow? When I grabbed a coffee at the bakery down the street, the woman at the till told me things get busy down here on the thirty-first. She said most of the stores hand out treats."

"But, Nathan, Halloween is *tomorrow*," Virginia reminded him with a slight shake of her head "We couldn't possibly change out the window display that quickly!"

If I tell her I can do it, I better be able to pull it off, he thought, bothered more than he'd care to admit by the expression of doubt on her face.

"If you give me the green light, I can get it done. I've got some ideas, and my Grandpa George *loves* Halloween. He has a room in his basement full of decorations he's been collecting for years. He has way too much at this point—not that he'd ever admit to that. I bet he'd let me borrow a few things."

Virginia strode over to the front window hesitantly.

"It couldn't be too scary. I don't want to scare the children. And it would have to come down on Wednesday morning. I'm not one to decorate the window for Christmas until closer to Thanksgiving, but we can't have ghosts and goblins out *after* Halloween."

Nathan nodded, relieved to hear her giving in. "I completely agree with all of that. What do you say? Do you trust me to create an amazing front window?"

Virginia's face lit up with a wide smile. "You are going to be a fun one to have around, aren't you, Nathan? I love that you're already breathing some fresh air into this place. I suppose the next thing you're going to suggest is that we all dress in costume for Halloween?"

Nathan shoved his hands in his pockets and rocked back and forth on the balls of his feet. He graced Virginia with his full-wattage smile—the one that usually helped him convince his mother to do whatever he wanted her to do. "Well, now that you mention it . . ."

"You *are* a handsome one, aren't you," Virginia replied with a twinkle in her eye. "I bet that smile of yours has those college girls falling at your feet."

If only, Nathan thought, thinking of one college girl in particular.

"Frank will be the tough sell on the costume idea," Virginia went on. "I, on the other hand, am always looking for an excuse to dress up. Back in my younger years, I enjoyed theater nearly as much as my books."

Nathan wasn't surprised. Virginia had a flair for the dramatic.

"I can dress up the window for Halloween, then?"

Virginia held her arms wide. "Be my guest. But you'll have to work fast. And depending on whether or not I like it, I may even let you help with the *Christmas* display."

"Thank you, Virginia. I won't disappoint you."

Her eyes twinkled. "See that you don't."

***

"Hello?"

"Hi. Grace?"

"Hi. Who is this?"

Nathan cringed. It'd taken him the whole drive over from the bookstore to his college campus to work up enough nerve to call her. It would have helped if she'd have recognized his number, or at the very least his voice.

Guess she didn't bother to attach my name to my number when she sent me a text at the Halloween party.

"Grace, it's Nathan. Julie's cousin?"

"Oh, *hey*, Nathan. What's up?"

At least she didn't say "Nathan who?"

"I was calling to take you up on your offer," Nathan replied, trying to sound relaxed—even though he was anything but calm.

"I'm sorry. What offer?"

"To help me brainstorm ideas for the bookstore?"

There was a rustling noise on the other end of the line.

"Sorry about that," Grace said. "I'm heading into a night class, and I almost dropped my phone. Sure, I remember talking about your new job at the bookstore. Did you start today then?"

"I did. But I'm actually on my way to class now, too," Nathan replied. He'd pulled into an empty spot in the school parking lot just before he'd called her. It wasn't nearly as hard to find a parking spot at 6:30 in the evening. "We're trying to figure out some cool events for the holidays to bring more people in. I thought you might have some ideas."

"Fun! But, hey, I have a test, so I can't talk now. How soon do you have to decide what to do?"

"Can you hold on a sec?" Nathan grabbed his backpack from the passenger seat and shoved the keys to his dad's Lexus into his jacket. He got out, locking the doors behind him. Other students would probably mistake it for a teacher's car. The Lexus was sweet, but not a typical ride for a college kid. He was only driving it because his pickup wasn't reliable.

Not like Dad needs it these days.

He put his phone back up to his ear. "Okay, sorry, you there? We're handing out flyers tomorrow, along with treat bags for the kids. There's a big downtown Halloween deal where kids can trick-or-treat at the different stores."

"That soon, huh? I'd love to help you out, but I need time to think. Can you keep your flyer vague for now? You know, names and dates but not much for details? Are you doing anything the weekend of the eighteenth?"

Nathan, caught up in a small wave of students heading toward various evening classes, stopped in his tracks, causing others to have to weave around him.

"The eighteenth?"

"Well, I know Julie is always bugging you to come to spend a weekend over here, and an old friend of hers is coming that weekend. His name's Ben. She met him a while back—out at Whispering Pines, I think."

"Oh, sure, I met Ben. He seemed like a good guy. Are they dating?"

"No, not really. It's pretty casual, but Julie wants a bunch of us to go out. Maybe you'd like to come, too?"

Someone bumped into Nathan from behind. "Sorry, dude," the guy said, shooting him a look over his shoulder that said he really wasn't sorry and why was Nathan standing there like an idiot in the middle of the narrow sidewalk?

Nathan started moving again. If he didn't hustle, he'd be late for class.

"Nathan? Are you busy that weekend?" Grace asked again.

"I work until four on Saturdays, and we aren't opening on Sundays until after Thanksgiving. Is that too late to come?"

"No. Actually, that would be perfect. Julie's going to be thrilled. I'll try to come up with some ideas for the bookstore between now and then. Just plan to spend the night. It'll get late. Hey, I gotta run, but we'll see you soon, okay?"

"See ya then," Nathan agreed just before she ended their call.

He broke into a light jog. Class started in three minutes, and he'd catch hell from his professor if he was late. Not that some cranky old teacher was going to ruin his mood after Grace's invite.

CHAPTER 4

Gift of Decorations

"Nathan, do me a favor, will you, dear? I need something out of my little desk upstairs. Do you mind running up and grabbing it for me?"

Nathan snapped his fingers at her request. "Shoot, Virginia, I meant to ask you about that desk. When I was moving in, I noticed there were things in the drawers. Do you want me to box the stuff up for you so you can take it home? I wondered if you'd forgotten about it."

Virginia shook her head. "No, I knew it was still up there. It's all remnants from my theater days. Having it here comes in handy once in a while." She beamed. "Like today."

"Sounds good. I'll go grab whatever you need," Nathan agreed, ready for a break from scooping candy into little baggies. "What am I looking for?"

"My crystal wand."

"Your . . . what?"

"My crystal wand. I can hardly be Glenda the Good Witch without my wand. What would the children think?"

It wasn't taking Nathan long to learn it was better not to even ask. To say Virginia Fisk was unique would be an understatement. "Be right back."

Nathan took the narrow wooden stairs two at a time. Maybe he should throw his costume on quick while he was up here. The downtown event was slated to start at four o'clock and go until eight. He was pleased with how his front window display turned out, and excited to see if it would help to pull people into the store.

The midnight-blue velvet cape he'd found in his grandfather's costume closet was draped across his mattress. The silvery-white stars that ran along the lapels and hem would glow bright white in the black light he'd rigged up. He'd left a spot in the front window where he could stand and wave to passers-by. He'd try to wear the long white beard and wig, too, but they made him itch like crazy.

Virginia wouldn't allow any scary costumes, but Nathan had to admit her idea that they all dress up as characters out of classic children's books was a good one. He changed into his darkest jeans and a silvery tunic (also borrowed from George's costume closet). He slipped his cape on, hoping his ensemble looked good. There wasn't a long mirror in his apartment where he could check.

He stopped at Virginia's desk, wishing he'd thought to get something *he* could use as a wand. It would have helped in his Dumbledore getup. But, he reasoned, what kid wouldn't recognize the famous wizard from the *Harry Potter* series? Maybe there was a large book downstairs that he could use as a prop instead. Every good wizard had a spell book.

Other than the bottom drawer he'd accidentally knocked open on Sunday, he hadn't dared look in any of the other drawers in Virginia's desk. Now, as he searched for her wand, he could see they were all stuffed full. It didn't take him long to find what he thought he was after. He pulled out a long, clear glass cylinder infused with glitter. It had to be Virginia's "wand." He had to admit—it did look like the wand the Good Witch of the South would carry. Lots of small white boxes and a few masks like ones you'd see at a masquerade ball filled the drawer where he'd found the wand.

He closed the drawer, not wanting to snoop in Virginia's things, now that he'd found the wand. He spared a glance at the bottom drawer, thinking again of the manuscript he'd found there. In the craziness of the past two days, he hadn't had a chance to read any more of it, nor had he asked Frank or Virginia about it.

Something told him Virginia would have the answers.

***

"I *love* what you did with the front window," Virginia said, accepting her wand from Nathan with a smile. "Thank goodness for your grandfather and his decorations."

Nathan laughed. "Us kids always loved playing downstairs in his costume closet. It inspired many one-act plays."

"And was that where you found your wizarding costume?"

Nathan walked over and set his purple pointed cap and the white wig and beard down on the front counter. "Yep. I had my pick of costumes. But I thought this would fit with the theme in the front window. I'm going to stand up there and try to catch people's eye, motion them into the store."

Virginia gave a little squeal. "The littles are going to *love* that!"

"The littles?"

"Ginny has always called small children 'littles,' " Frank explained as he stapled their flyers to the treat bags.

"Honey, you need to go put your costume on," Virginia directed her husband.

Nathan caught the exasperated look Frank gave her. "Dear, you know I think this is silly."

"I know you do, Frank, but humor me."

Sighing, Frank set the stapler down and popped a Tootsie Roll into his mouth. He grabbed a bag from under the counter and headed to the back.

Virginia turned back to Nathan. "I know I shouldn't manipulate him like that, but it's the quickest way to get him moving. He has it in his head that I've become a tad bit fragile, like someone he needs to handle with kid gloves. I'm not sure where he gets that idea, but who am I to argue?"

Nathan shrugged. Watching the two interact was going to be entertaining—and probably educational.

"Say, Virginia, can I ask you a question?"

"Of course."

"I know you love books and you love this store. Have you ever written any books yourself?"

He could see the question caught Virginia by surprise. She set her wand down carefully, so it wouldn't roll off the counter, and picked up another flyer to fold.

"Why in heaven's name would you ask me that, Nathan? Is that something *you* would like to do? You know, write books for a living? I've always liked to help new authors find readers. I could help you, too, if you like."

Nathan wasn't sure if she was intentionally trying to deflect his question, or if the manuscript he'd found actually belonged to someone else.

"No," Nathan said—but then paused. It was true he'd toyed with the idea himself, and maybe Virginia could get him started . . . but he pulled his mind back to his original reason for asking the question. "Well, actually, I *might* like to try that someday. But I found something."

"Whatever do you mean, you *found* something?"

Nathan glanced toward the bathroom, but Frank hadn't come back out yet. For some reason he couldn't explain, he wanted to keep this between himself and Virginia for now.

"On Sunday night, when I was moving in, I found something in that old desk upstairs."

"You mean in the desk where you found *this*, dear?" Virginia asked, fingering her glass wand. "Whatever were you doing going through my old junk?"

Nathan shook his head. "Oh, no—I wasn't snooping through your things, Virginia."

His reassurances left a puzzled look on her face. If *she* hid the manuscript in the secret compartment, maybe it was so long ago that she'd forgotten about it.

Maybe it's not even hers . . .

Nathan started again. "Honestly, I bumped into the desk when I was moving my things in upstairs. A drawer popped open, and when I tried to close it, it jammed. But"—he held his hands up to her—"I didn't damage anything."

Virginia waved her hand at his reassurances. "Don't worry about hurting that old thing, Nathan."

He shrugged. "The bottom drawer wouldn't close. I realized the drawer itself had a false bottom, and I'd jarred it loose. A bunch of papers fell out onto the ground."

Virginia raised an eyebrow. "Oh?"

"I wasn't sure what I'd found at first. I couldn't help but read a bit of it. It's actually an old manuscript, and someone had to have hidden it away in that secret compartment. Probably a long time ago."

Memory dawned in Virginia's eyes.

"For heaven's *sake*, Nathan. I'd forgotten all about that old thing! Yes, I admit I dabbled a bit with the idea of writing a novel, but it was just silly."

From what Nathan had read so far, he didn't think it was *silly* at all.

"Why do you say that?"

Virginia sighed. "I had this ridiculous notion that, just because I loved books, I could *write* books, too. You see, back then, Frank and I were newly married. It was the '70s. Karen, my daughter, was about eight. Frank saved us. Literally. He came into my life during a dark time, and he guided me back to happiness. He inspired me to start doing all the things in life I'd always dreamed of doing. Even opening my store," she said, glancing around the bookstore, her eyes reflecting her love for the place.

Nathan nodded, encouraging her to continue.

"We first met when I was working at the county library. Frank facilitated a weekly creative writing course at the library, trying to guide a small group of would-be authors to write the next great American novel. Initially, I thought it would be a fitting tribute to Frank if *I* wrote an amazing book and dedicated it to him, for all he'd done for us."

Virginia sighed, lost in her memories now.

"But I was foolish to think that. I had a friend take a look at it and, honestly, she was less than encouraging. After all the time I'd put into writing it, stealing time away from Frank and Karen to work on my secret project, I came to accept it simply wasn't to be. Finally, I admitted to myself that I had no future as an author. I set my book aside and focused on helping people who *did* have the talent to write books." Virginia shook her head sadly. "You know, I never even *told* Frank I wrote that manuscript. I wanted it to be a surprise . . ."

The older woman sighed, then got back to folding the flyer she'd held, forgotten in her hand, while she reminisced.

Nathan wondered if he'd accidentally stumbled on the one thing

Virginia most regretted; he felt a twinge of regret at stirring painful memories. But he'd read enough of the manuscript to know it was good. It was *really* good.

"Virginia, what did your friend say that made you think you didn't have the talent to write a book?"

Virginia took another flyer off the stack and began folding it. Nathan waited.

Finally, she pushed the paper to the side. "That is an excellent question, Nathan. She read my manuscript, marked it up with her nasty red pen, and then said she thought I was wasting my time. No publisher would be interested. Well, maybe not in so many words—but that was how I took it. You see, she worked with Frank at the university. She was also an instructor in his department, but she taught the underclassmen. She focused more on proper grammar and such. I'd wanted her to polish it up a bit before I started searching for someone to possibly publish it. Back then, remember, that was our only option."

Nathan nodded. The option to self-publish would have still been far in the future.

He thought back to all the red markings on the manuscript he'd found. "Did her edits bother you that much?"

Virginia stood a bit straighter. "I wasn't a simpering little female, Nathan. I could handle criticism. But don't be so quick to judge. Until you've personally poured your heart and soul into writing something for months on end, you can't appreciate how difficult it can be to accept the notion that drafting a manuscript is only the first step in the battle."

He cringed. She was right—he didn't have any idea how that felt.

"No, the edits themselves weren't the problem. I knew I was far from an expert. It was the fact she quit about two-thirds of the way through. She apologized but explained she didn't feel the book itself merited all the additional work it would take to make it, oh, what did she say . . . 'even close to viable.' A few years later, I realized that I should never have listened to her, but by then it seemed too late for my book."

"Why?" Nathan asked.

They both glanced back at the click of a door. Frank came out of the bathroom, wearing his own Halloween getup.

"We'll talk about this later, Nathan. Please, promise me you won't say a word about this to Frank?" Virginia pleaded, catching and holding Nathan's eye.

He could see how important this secret was to her. "Of course, Virginia. Not a word."

Frank joined them at the counter, placing his street clothes on the shelf underneath. Nathan looked him up and down, unable to hold back his laughter.

"Woman, I don't know how I let you talk me into these charades," Frank said, shaking his head at his wife as he tried to blow a wayward piece of straw away from his face.

"You have to admit, you do make an amazing scarecrow, Frank," Nathan said, petting the stuffed black crow sewn onto the shoulder of the battered old flannel shirt the older man wore.

"Frank, dear, *The Wizard of Oz* is a classic. The kids will love you!"

Ignoring his wife, Frank glared in Nathan's direction. Nathan pulled his hand back from the crow and hustled to take his post in the front window.

The littles *were* going to love this.

***

Nathan's idea to stand in as part of their Halloween window display was a hit. Kids passing by loved it when he waved at them directly, and they'd pull their chaperones inside, anxious to see what treats they might find.

Turning off the overhead lights directly above the front window allowed the black light he'd set up to work its magic on the stars lining the front of his wizard cape. He'd wanted to set up the fog machine he found in his grandparent's basement, too, but realized the moisture would be hard on the books. The plywood silhouette of a castle directly behind him—glowing with a purple haze from a cheap spotlight with a colored bulb he'd picked up at the hardware store—did the trick instead.

He found himself already planning how he could improve the display for next year. But first, he had to make sure there would *be* a next year for the store.

He grinned as he saw a familiar "little" heading his way down the sidewalk—a waddling Toucan Sam bird with a colorful striped beak—followed closely by his mom and Seth. His baby sister pulled up at the sight of him when he waved at her from the window. Her eyes grew wide, and her bottom lip began to tremble; she was clearly confused by what she was seeing. Jess burst into laughter as Seth caught the little girl up in his arms and rested her on his hip, giving Nathan a wave as they made their way to the door. The bell above the door jingled as Seth pulled it open, letting Jess pass in front of them. Nathan stepped away from the front window to greet his family. Harper refused to look in his direction now, arms tight around Seth's neck.

"Well, hel-*lo*, Jess!" Virginia said. She stepped away from a young boy and his parents after thanking them for stopping in and suggesting the miniature police officer pick up a treat bag from the nice scarecrow man.

Nathan grinned as the father stopped to pick up one of the books Virginia had expertly displayed, flipping it over to read the blurb on the back. In addition to handing out plenty of treat bags and flyers to the kids, they were managing to make a few sales.

"And who might this sweet little one be?" Virginia asked, the white sparkles of her poufy gown and glittering tiara catching Harper's eye. The young girl's arms fell away from Seth's neck as she turned toward the older woman.

"Virginia, this is Harper, my youngest," Jess said. "And you've already met Seth."

Nathan had to admit his mom's way of introducing his baby sister was starting to feel almost normal. He watched as the toddler reached for the wand in Virginia's hand, her mouth forming a tiny *O*. Virginia must have been aware that Jess had adopted Harper, as she didn't show any hint of surprise.

"It is a pleasure to meet you, Miss Harper," Virginia said, handing Harper her wand.

"Be careful, honey," Jess warned the young girl as Harper took the wand

and held it up to the light, giggling as the glitter inside sparkled as if truly magical. She gave it a little shake, holding on so tight her knuckles were white. She *probably* wouldn't drop it.

Nathan slipped his hat, wig, and beard off, setting them aside so Harper could see it was him and not a big scary wizard. He held out his hands to her, and while she grinned at him—now that she could see who he was—she stayed in Seth's arms, waving Virginia's wand in his direction.

"Good luck getting this thing away from her when it's time to leave," Seth warned before wandering over to visit with Frank, Harper still on his hip. Frank finished bagging up the novel for the trick-or-treater's dad and smiled as Seth and Harper approached.

Jess eyed her oldest up and down. "You got that from Dad's closet, didn't you?"

"Recognize it, do you? Yep. And the castle, too," he said, motioning toward the front window. From here, the unpainted plywood back and braces were evident. It looked much more impressive from the street view.

"I'll have to send him a picture of it," Jess said. "He'll get a kick out of seeing his precious decorations put to good use." She turned her attention back to Virginia. "I *love* your costume. You look so pretty."

"Well, thank you, Jess. This old thing has been hanging in the back of my closet for quite some time, just waiting for another excuse to be worn. I have to admit—the children seem to enjoy it. I've had my picture taken with so many little trick-or-treaters tonight, I've lost count."

Jess clapped her hands together. "That's wonderful! It has to be a good sign. Maybe business will pick up a bit now, heading into the holidays."

Nathan appreciated his mother's head for business. She also had a vested interest in seeing this bookstore survive. Plus, he knew she cared for it far beyond her ownership interest. She was a book lover herself—but even more than that, she'd become immensely fond of the Fisks.

"We can only hope," Virginia said, glancing back at her husband, who was now holding Harper while Seth made motions toward the tin ceiling he'd helped Frank fix the previous summer. She fiddled nervously with her tiara. "We need to get Frank to drop this ridiculous notion of closing the store. I can't let that happen. *We* can't let that happen, Jess. I'm not ready."

Jess reached out and clasped Virginia's hand as the woman let it drop back down to her side. "I understand, Ginny. Nathan and I will do what we can to help prevent that from happening. You need to trust us. And you need to take care of yourself. If you push too hard and wear yourself out, Frank will walk away from this. You do realize that, don't you?"

Virginia smiled in a way Nathan was starting to recognize as the older woman's attempt to get someone to go along with what she wanted. He was beginning to suspect Virginia wasn't nearly as frail as people tended to think.

"Of course, Jess, dear. I'll play my part. Now, how is Harper enjoying her first Halloween? And where in heaven's name did you find that *adorable* little bird costume?"

Chapter 5

Gift of Encouragement

Nathan decided Tuesday evening was a success. They'd generated plenty of traffic and handed out nearly all of their flyers, which included dates, along with vague details, for their upcoming, loosely planned holiday events. He also had plenty of pictures he could post to the store's social-media accounts. While his window display had helped to bring people in, Virginia had been the true star of the evening. Customers gravitated to her, and children were awe-struck by her costume and wand.

They'd want to figure out how best to capitalize on their success, and more ideas were already starting to form, but he needed time to think about them before mentioning them to the Fisks. He'd pitch them to Grace and Julie first, see what they thought. After seeing the Fisks dressed up for Halloween, he was pretty sure he had a built-in Santa and Mrs. Claus at his disposal, even if they didn't realize it yet. Virginia's white gown would be the perfect start, and Frank could use George's wizarding wig and beard.

As promised, Nathan spent Wednesday morning switching the front window display back to Virginia's original fall theme. She wasn't ready for him to move to a Christmas theme yet; he was okay with that, since he needed time to plan something spectacular. He'd gotten lucky with George's stash of Halloween-related decorations, but, unfortunately, his grandfather didn't have a similar room in his basement geared toward Christmas. Maybe Seth had things he could repurpose from his architectural salvage store instead.

***

Nathan spent the next couple of weeks splitting his time between class and the bookstore. He was, without a doubt, learning more at the store every day. Virginia still hadn't said anything more about the found manuscript. He didn't pull it out again and held off on asking her about it. It was in her court.

By his third week on the job, he was feeling more comfortable with things. He wasn't scheduled to work Wednesday afternoon or Thursday, since he had classes. School felt like a nuisance, with his impending spring graduation and the fun he was having at his new job. While he knew his failure to plan for his long-term career drove his father nuts, Nathan wasn't inclined to look too far down the road. For now, he was enjoying his time working in the bookstore, although a tiny seed of an idea was starting to wiggle its way into his brain. He didn't feel the need for stellar grades or a hard-hitting job search for his "forever job" right now. He just wanted to finish up with his degree, help the Fisks get their quaint little shop back on more solid footing, and see what else might come his way.

Besides, no one believes in "forever jobs" anymore.

***

By Friday afternoon, Frank had made sure Nathan knew the basics of keeping the store running in his absence. It promised to be a cool, overcast weekend and Frank had plans to go duck hunting with buddies. Based on his reluctance to leave despite the fact he'd be late if he didn't get on the road soon, Nathan suspected Frank was worried about more than just the store.

"I've got this, Frank. We'll be fine here," Nathan said, attempting to reassure the man. "Go, have fun. I wouldn't have taken you for a hunter, but you don't have to worry about leaving us for a couple of days."

"I don't care much about the hunting, and I've never cared for duck, but it's a tradition. We've been doing this November hunt for fifty-some odd years. We started as a bigger group, but life happens. The dogs have been replaced many times over, and even a few of the wives, but the core group of guys has been doing this forever. I only wish I didn't have to leave

Virginia alone, now that Karen isn't around to check on her."

Nathan envied Frank's part in a group like that. He hadn't had that type of friend network—not since they moved from their old neighborhood as kids. He'd never felt like he fit in after that. Maybe his upcoming weekend with his cousin and her friends could be the jumping-off point to some deeper connections.

"Virginia will spend the rest of today here with me," he told Frank. "I'll give her a ride home when we close up shop, and I'll pick her up in the morning so she can spend the day here tomorrow, too. She mentioned going out to dinner and a movie tomorrow night with a girlfriend. And even though I'm heading out of town when we close tomorrow, my mom is only a phone call away, should Virginia need anything."

"I appreciate that, Nathan." Frank scooped his keys off his cluttered desk, glancing at his watch. "I know I really shouldn't worry but . . ."

Nathan held up a hand. "Frank, stop. Virginia will be fine. You are only going for a couple of days. I don't think you give her enough credit. She's a tough lady."

Frank looked skeptical, squinting in Nathan's direction. "Less than a month on the job and you think you already know my wife better than I do, huh?"

Nathan lowered his hand. "Of course not. I'm sorry if I said too much."

With a sigh, Frank shifted his keys into his left hand and extended his right to Nathan. "I'm the one who should apologize. Your being here has put a spark back in Ginny's eyes. She loves this place, and I'm starting to think maybe you really can help us make it work again for us. For *her*. Never mind my ramblings. Her health issues this past year scare the dickens out of me, that's all."

Nathan shook Frank's hand then placed his own on the older man's shoulder, using it to turn him toward the door. "I get it. I do. Now get out of here before Virginia gets back with her tea from the bakery, or she'll be mad. Go kill something with your buddies."

***

"My heavens, how did you finally get him out of here?" Virginia asked when she came back to the store, carrying a cardboard holder with two cups. "I thought he'd never leave!"

Nathan laughed and stepped forward to take the carrier from Virginia. "I just had to remind him you were perfectly capable of a weekend on your own. You two might benefit from a little time apart, don't you think?"

"Believe me, you are preaching to the choir. I have a full weekend planned. Frank hasn't left my side for *months*."

"You know, I'd be fine here on Saturday by myself. You don't have to come in."

Virginia unwound the silk scarf she'd wrapped around her hairdo before leaving to get her afternoon tea from the shop a block over. Nathan knew she'd visited her beautician the previous afternoon, and now her always-neat white hair was in some type of fancy bun-thing. He thought he remembered his mom or sister calling it an "updo." Her eyes seemed extra sparkly, too— maybe from the cold.

"Oh, I'll be here tomorrow. But I may not be much help to you."

Her comment surprised him. "What are you up to, Virginia?"

Virginia took a sip of her tea before responding, wandering to the front window and letting her hand trail over some of the books displayed there. "Our little talk a few weeks back has gotten me thinking. You've cost me *sleep*."

"Our little talk?"

"Yes," she said, raising her paper cup in his direction—or maybe she was lifting it toward the ceiling. "About the manuscript you found."

So she hadn't put it out of her mind after all. Between working at the store and trying to keep up with homework, Nathan hadn't had a chance to read any more of the secret manuscript he'd only just recently learned had been penned by Virginia herself. He was itching to get back to it, even hoping to take it along with him for the weekend. Maybe he'd even let Grace have a sneak peek at it, but he felt he needed to get Virginia's permission to do that first.

"I just can't stop thinking about it," she continued. "I hadn't thought about my book in *years*, but your finding it has stirred everything up again.

Maybe I made a mistake when I gave up on it so easily based on one person's comments. It turned out the woman I asked to help me with the edits was jealous when Frank married me. I didn't know that until later, when she got tipsy at her going-away party and confessed all. But, then again, maybe it *is* just rubbish. The book, I mean. Honestly, I can only remember the high points of the plot. I think tomorrow would be the perfect time for me to read through it again. You know, with Frank gone and all. Get reacquainted with the storyline."

"I think that's a great idea," Nathan said. "And I think you might be surprised at how good you were. Should I run upstairs and get it for you now?"

Virginia shook her head. "No, not yet. I still have to place my last book order today so that we have plenty of new inventory for the upcoming season. Tomorrow will be soon enough."

Nathan thought he saw a flicker of fear in her eyes, giving him pause. He hoped he hadn't made a big mistake mentioning that old manuscript. What if he'd gotten her hopes up about something that would ultimately lead to disappointment . . . again? Maybe he should have kept his mouth shut.

But if he were honest with himself, he knew it would have been wrong to stay quiet. That book deserved to see the light of day. It was good. *Really* good.

And maybe he could help Virginia realize a long-deserted wish, too.

***

The next morning, Nathan was packed and ready to go. Julie had texted him expressing her excitement that he was coming. Her friend Ben should get in by four, she said, and they'd wait for Nathan before heading out for a Saturday night on the town.

He couldn't help but wonder if *Grace* was excited that he was driving up to see them, too.

But first things first. Today was the day Virginia was going to rediscover her story. Nathan brought the stack of papers downstairs with him and set it on the corner of the sales counter before leaving to pick her up.

He pulled up to the Fisks' home, admiring the quaint two-story. It had been dark the night before when he'd given Virginia a ride home. If the Fisks had a garage, it was in the back, accessible through the alley. The home was a pale yellow with white trim and a graceful front porch. Three orange pumpkins added a splash of color to the gray wooden steps, a stand-in for colorful flowers he suspected once flowed from the now-empty window boxes.

He parked at the curb and got out, intending to escort Virginia from her front door, but the woman must have been watching for him. Before he could round the front of the Lexus, she was already halfway down the stairs.

"Morning, Virginia."

"Good morning, Nathan. Thank you for the ride. I think Frank took my keys with him, that scoundrel. Now that my new glasses came in, I certainly could have driven."

Nathan opened the car door for her, glancing at her face and wondering why she wasn't *wearing* her new glasses.

Once Virginia settled in the passenger seat, he got back in and pulled away from the tree-lined boulevard, tires crunching on the leaves piled against the curb. He noticed her shiver, so he flipped on her seat-warmer. *Perks of Dad's Lexus.*

"I've got your manuscript ready for you to read this morning, if you're still interested in rereading it while Frank is out of town."

She nodded at his mention of the book, her pale hand coming up to fiddle with her hair. She offered him an apprehensive smile and then turned to stare out the window of the Lexus. The blue veins of her hand and deep-red nail polish stood out in stark contrast with her snow-white hair. Nathan could sense her nerves, could feel the anxiety rolling off of her. He wondered again if reminding Virginia about her old manuscript had been a terrible idea.

"Look, Virginia, don't be nervous. If you decide you want to take your book and hide it away again, I'll keep your secret. No pressure. You've been reading first-time novels by new authors for decades. Pretend you didn't write this one. Go into it with the same cautious optimism I bet you give all newbies. Didn't you tell me once that it's been your mission to help share new talent with the world? Maybe we could pretend the author's name is . . . Autumn . . . hey, what was your maiden name?"

Virginia laughed out loud, some of the tension dissipating. "What are we going to do with you, Nathan?"

***

Virginia's stomach turned over at the sight of it, just lying there. Her finger traced the faded outline of the tea stain on the top sheet, her mind drawn back to that long-ago day when little Karen accidentally bumped the desk where Virginia had sat contemplating whether or not to throw her mess of a story into the trash and get back to focusing on the demands of raising a young daughter and building a life with her new husband. Her confidence was already low, and when the tea sloshed onto the sheets she'd worked so hard on, she'd taken it as a sign that she was being ridiculous to even consider putting her words out into the world. Her mother had drilled it into her head that pursuing the arts was a frivolous waste of time.

Now, when she gazed upon the decades-old stain, she knew the truth. It had been a mistake to allow the disbelievers to dissuade her. In hindsight, she knew neither her mother nor her editor "friend" had her best interests at heart, those many years ago.

Nathan couldn't possibly know what this stack of papers he'd found represented to her. It was so much more than a half-edited story. Young Nathan . . . puttering around in the store she'd spent the better part of her life nurturing, his whole life ahead of him. Plenty of time to pursue all of his heartfelt desires. She, on the other hand, was no longer sure what each day would bring, or how many years she even had left.

When she was Nathan's age, her hopes and dreams for the future knew no bounds. The youngest of four girls in a well-to-do family, and always her father's obvious favorite, Virginia used to envision a life full of art, the written word, and love. Real life would test her commitment to all three.

Her mother had ranked wealth, community standing, and polite etiquette as her top ambitions in life, and felt it was her duty to instill similar mindsets in her girls. Only one of Virginia's sisters had done as their mother wished. Virginia and her other two sisters all fell short.

Because Virginia and her mother, Helen, were opposites in so many ways, they were destined to a life of constant disagreements and disappointing each other.

Perhaps if her father—born into a wealthy family, a successful businessman in his own right—had been able to curtail his wife's harsh ways with their daughters, they would have enjoyed a happier family unit. But in a home where he was outnumbered by females five to one, he left the majority of child-rearing to his wife, swooping in to spoil them on occasion but seldom taking an active role in their day-to-day. In the end, his loving nature wasn't enough to counteract his wife's ruthless expectations.

Virginia, somewhat insulated during her earlier years from the forcefulness of her mother's will by the buffer provided by three older sisters, grew up with a head full of fairy tales. Her innocence and naïveté were nearly her undoing.

"Virginia? Are you all right?"

Nathan's question snapped her back to her bookstore.

"What was that, Nathan?"

"I asked if you wanted me to start the coffee."

She placed her handbag on the counter, stepping away from her old manuscript. Seeing the physical evidence of her quite literally *faded* dreams, written so long ago, stirred up both old and new feelings of excitement . . . with a fair amount of dread mixed in. She needed to boost her confidence before she once again flipped back that top sheet and read the words she'd written.

"Yes . . . please go ahead and start the pot so we have something to offer our Saturday morning customers. But I'm actually in the mood for a slice of coffee cake to go along with a cup of coffee. I'll run down to the bakery for some. What can I pick up for you?"

Nathan filled the coffee pot with tap water and poured it into the reservoir. He had suggested a Keurig so customers could always get a fresh cup, but Frank didn't see the need.

"I'm happy to run down there for you, Virginia. It's cold this morning."

Virginia buttoned her wool coat against the chill. "Thank you, but I could use some air. Should I surprise you with a treat?"

"Sure, thanks."

Virginia pushed through the front door, enjoying the familiar tinkling of the bell overhead. She'd miss those little details the most someday. She hoped that time wasn't anytime soon, although Virginia knew that if Frank had his way, they'd either sell or lock the doors permanently and head south. She'd been able to hold him off so far because it still felt as though she had work to do. She honestly didn't know if she'd ever be able to walk away from it. Besides, she'd never pictured herself as a snowbird, leaving the snowy climate of Minnesota for heat and humidity during the winter months.

If pressed as to why she wasn't yet ready to give up on her little bookstore, she wasn't sure what the answer to that question might be. Seeing that yellowed manuscript, sitting on the edge of the scuffed wooden countertop, had her wondering.

Maybe her old friend Mabel could help. They'd confided in each other through the years; their friendship had been slow to build, but it eventually reached the level of utmost trust. They held each other's deepest secrets in strictest confidence. Every woman needed at least one friend they could trust, no matter what. Mabel was that friend for Virginia.

"Good morning, Ginny," Mabel greeted her as she pushed her way into the hometown bakery. Virginia inhaled the welcoming scent of fresh-brewed coffee and bread baking in an oven somewhere in the back, noticing that only one table was open. "I'm surprised to see you this morning. I thought Frank was off on his annual weekend duck hunt. Don't you have that boy watching your place for you on weekends now?"

Virginia laughed at Mabel's reference to Nathan. *That boy.*

"Yes, Nathan is proving himself to be a great help at the store. I know I don't usually come in on Saturdays, but there was something . . . *special* I wanted to work on today when Frank was gone."

Mabel slipped the white apron she wore up and over her head, hanging it on a hook behind the counter. Virginia knew her friend, now in her early sixties, would have started her day by 4:00 a.m.

"It's been a busy morning," Mabel said, rolling her shoulders and pulling her hairnet off, fluffing her short, steel-gray curls. "I'm lucky I have Tansy to help."

"Tansy? Your niece? I thought she was living in Minneapolis these days?"

"She was . . . is. But she called and asked if she could come for a visit. That brother of mine has never been much of a parent to her, so of course I said yes. Some nasty business about a fight with a boyfriend, kicked out of his apartment, needing a little time to get back on her feet."

Virginia watched as Mabel poured two cups of strong black coffee, placed two pieces of her famous coffee cake on white plates (served on Saturdays only, making it a special treat), and came out from behind the glass-fronted cabinets, juggling it all like a pro.

"And I welcome the help. Tansy's making a delivery now, but she should be back any minute. Baby shower across town. Now, what were you saying? You have me curious about what you might be working on, now that Frank finally gave you some space. Is it an early Christmas gift?"

Virginia laughed, the last of the tension she'd felt in her shoulders ever since Nathan mentioned the manuscript again this morning ebbing away in the presence of her good friend. She'd welcome Mabel's thoughts about her long-hidden secret.

"You might say it's a very long overdue Christmas gift. I wrote something for Frank—a book—nearly forty years ago, initially planning to surprise him with it. Remember, he used to teach creative writing."

"Of course, I remember you telling me about your early days with him. Did you get very far with it, or is it just the beginnings? What was it about?"

Virginia wrapped her fingers around her coffee cup, still feeling chilled, despite the warm scented air of the cozy bakery. She suspected the chill was nerves rather than temperature.

"I had a full rough draft written. It's a fictional story, modeled after the bedtime story Frank used to tell Karen in front of the fireplace. It was about the power of friendship."

"It's a children's book, then?"

"No," Virginia said with a slow shake of her head. So much time had passed, the details were fuzzy now. "Frank's story had a childish bend to it, certainly . . . Karen was only about eight when he used to tell it to her . . . but I gave it my twist." Virginia picked up her fork and sectioned off a bite of cake, pushing it around the plate but not eating it. "Honestly, so much time has passed, I've forgotten much of it. I'd planned to read it today, with Frank gone, but now I'm not sure I want to."

Mabel nodded but said nothing more until she'd polished off her own piece. Pushing her plate away, she crossed her legs and looked Virginia in the eye. "I can't believe you wrote a book and never said a word about it."

Virginia understood Mabel's surprise. The women seldom kept secrets from each other.

"Only Karen knew I was spending extra time writing, but she was young and paid little attention to what I was up to. Only one other person ever read those words until now, and she was . . . less than encouraging."

Mabel nodded. Virginia could tell that she understood.

"Now *that boy*, Nathan, has read part of it, too. He thinks I should do something with it, claims it 'needs to see the light of day.' So that's my plan for this beautiful fall Saturday. Sit down with a cup of tea, tune out everything else, and revisit the world I created back when our marriage was brand new, and I still had time to at least *consider* chasing my dream of becoming a published author."

Mabel dabbed the sugar crystals off her lips with her napkin then sipped her coffee as Virginia explained how Nathan had come to read part of her manuscript. Virginia took the first bite of her favorite breakfast treat, giving Mabel time to process.

"Why did you never tell me you wanted to be a writer?" she finally asked.

Virginia shrugged. "I never told *anyone*. Not even Frank."

"But why not?"

"I don't honestly know. Part of me always thought I'd get back to it someday when Karen no longer needed me. But, of course, that time came and went long ago. I was probably just scared. And now it's too late."

Mabel set her white stoneware cup down hard enough that the dregs of her coffee lapped over the sides, seeping into a paper placemat. "Do you actually believe that?"

Virginia sighed. Mabel seldom took a harsh tone with her—and when she did, it was because she was calling her out for making excuses or rationalizing.

"Mabel, I believe it. I do. I'm much too old to start something as demanding as an author career at my age."

"Bullshit."

Virginia choked on the coffee she'd just sipped from her cup. She could count on one hand the number of times she'd heard Mabel curse.

"Mabel!"

"What? You are trying to use your age as an excuse to shove that book back into a drawer and pretend it never existed. You haven't even reread it yet. That's baloney."

"I heard you the first time, dear. Why do you feel so strongly about this? And why in heaven's name do you think I should do anything *but* hide that old thing away again?"

"Because I think the time has finally come for you to prove your mother wrong, once and for all."

***

As Virginia walked back to her store, swinging a white paper bag stuffed with a sandwich and fresh cookie for Nathan, she couldn't stop smiling. Mabel's words struck right to the heart of the matter. In a brief, twenty-minute conversation, her friend had been able to pinpoint the cause of her pain and reluctance. She'd vowed never to let her mother's dire warnings about pursuing her love of the arts hold her back—but, despite her best intentions, her mother had been winning all of these years.

She has been stifling me my whole life, and I allowed it to happen. She's still doing it, and she's dead, for heaven's sake!

Maybe, *just maybe*, there was still time for her to do something with her book. At least, Mabel seemed to think there was. And she was right more times than not.

Nathan was finishing up with a customer when Virginia walked in.

Based on the size of the bag the young woman carried out, he'd been able to help her pick out a decent stack of books.

"Maybe I should stay away from here more often."

Nathan chuckled. "I may have charmed her into buying a couple more than she'd intended."

"Huh." Virginia looked back over her shoulder to see if she could get a better look at the woman, but she was gone. She turned back to Nathan, smiling coyly. "Did you get her phone number?"

"Ginny, now you're starting to sound like my mother. No, I didn't get her phone number. I'm—" Nathan hesitated. "I'm too busy to date right now."

"Does that mean you don't already have a girlfriend? I guess I assumed you must, with that smile of yours."

"No girlfriend at the moment," Nathan assured her, reaching for the bag she still held in her hand.

She handed him his lunch. Virginia may be an old, happily married woman, but she wasn't blind. Nor had she ever been immune to the charms of handsome men. The fact Nathan wasn't dating anyone did surprise her, regardless of whether he'd ever mentioned a special someone. She'd have to figure out why he was single. Maybe she could help line him up with someone. He'd be a catch.

"I know I said I'd bring you a treat, and it's still early, but I picked you up lunch." She slid the manuscript from where it still lay on the counter. "Now, if you don't mind, I think I'll take this old thing, go curl up in a chair over there, and give it a read."

***

Less than an hour later, Virginia called Nathan over to the store's reading nook. He could hear her distress.

Not a good sign.

He hurried back to her.

"What's up, Virginia? Have you gotten very far?"

All but a couple of pages were still neatly piled on the small table next to her armchair. She clutched the other sheets tightly in her hand. Nathan suspected they'd be crumpled when she relaxed her fingers.

"No, I haven't gotten *far*. I can barely read this scribble!"

"You can't read your own handwriting?" Nathan asked. He cringed when she shot a glare at him.

"Don't sass me, young man. Normally I can read my handwriting just fine. It's just that this is too faded and rather cramped. It's going to take me *days* to get through this, if I can even do it at all. My eyes aren't as good as they used to be."

"Would you like me to run you back to your house so you can try it with your new glasses?"

Virginia tossed the sheets she'd held back onto the pile next to her and slumped in her chair, deflated. "I'm afraid that won't be enough. Maybe I'm being silly. Who cares about some dumb old rough draft I scratched out when I wasn't much older than you?"

Nathan glanced toward the front of the store, glad there were no customers about at the moment. He pulled a tufted ottoman over so they could sit eye to eye.

"Virginia, do you remember why you wrote this in the first place?" he asked, motioning toward the stack of papers.

"Yes, I already told you *why*. I had this silly notion that, since Frank taught creative writing back then, I could surprise him with a book I wrote and specifically dedicated to him. My way of thanking him for coming into our lives at such a critical juncture and turning the dark days bright again. Books have always been a mutual love for both of us."

Nathan nodded, her words again striking a chord with him. Maybe he was as much a romantic as Virginia. He needed to convince her not to give up on her book this time.

"If there was some way, any way at all, I could help you turn *that* into the book you've always wanted to hand to Frank . . . would you at least consider it?"

Virginia focused on something over Nathan's shoulder, her eyes taking on a faraway look. He waited, not wanting to push any more than he already had over the past few days.

"Nathan, my feelings on this are all over the place. Honestly, when I first saw it sitting there this morning, I was *sure* this was all a big mistake. But I talked to Mabel about it. The owner of the bakery. You see, she and I go way back. She tried to help me realize I was letting fear hold me back. She buoyed my spirits. But now, when I can't even *read* the dang thing, I don't know what to do."

Nathan nodded, not immune to the frustration she felt.

"Do you trust me, Virginia?"

She chewed on her bottom lip and seemed to consider his question.

"I do trust you, Nathan. But you are starting to sound like your mother. I heard her ask Frank the same question when she first came to see us, after Celia died and Jess took over for her. You are every bit as tenacious as your mother."

"I'll take that as both a 'yes' and a compliment."

Virginia sighed. "What do you propose, young man?"

Nathan rubbed the palms of his hands on his jeans. He knew what the next step had to be, and he also knew he probably didn't have time to take it on right now. But maybe Grace and Julie could help him this weekend.

"What if I typed up the manuscript for you? I've read enough of it to know this should not be hidden away. Not again. You need to do something with it. *We* need to do something with it, if you'll let me. In this day and age, you don't need to find a publisher. I could help you self-publish it."

Nathan could feel his excitement building. He sensed Virginia was close to getting on board.

"Typing all of that up will take a long time, Nathan," Virginia said, casting a doubtful glance at the stack of papers by her elbow. "We are going to get busier in here soon with the holidays, God willing . . . and don't you have finals coming up?"

"I do. But I have an idea. I think I can get some help with the typing. It would be so cool if you could give this to Frank for a Christmas present this year."

"Lord, child, that is insane! Nobody can pull a whole book together in a little over a month!"

Nathan laughed. "I've heard it's possible, Virginia, but I suppose we don't have to be in that much of a rush. When's Frank's birthday?"

"February fifteenth. That's still not enough time. Our anniversary is in August . . . maybe I could give it to him for an anniversary gift?"

"I'm honestly not sure how long it takes, but maybe we could pull it together by Valentine's Day."

Virginia shook her head, but at least she was smiling. "This all feels crazy to me. I tell you what. Let's take it one step at a time, please. If you think it won't be too much of a burden to type it up, you do that, and then I'll give it a read. I'm still not a hundred percent convinced we have a viable story here. Do you *see* all the editorial scribbles all over this thing? Let me read it, and then we'll decide whether or not to move ahead with it. Fair?"

"Fair. Now, if you don't mind, I have typing to do."

Chapter 6

Gift of Frosty Mornings

"Hey, cuz," Julie greeted Nathan, waving him through the door after she'd buzzed him into their building. "How was the trip?"

"It's an easy drive. Sorry I'm later than I thought I'd be. We had a customer come in ten minutes before closing, and the guy was in *no* hurry."

"I hope you at least made a good sale," Grace said, strolling into the kitchen, likely straight from the shower given the towel hiding what Nathan knew to be a curtain of straight, pale-blond hair that hung nearly to her waist. The friendly hug she offered Nathan left him flustered. Or maybe it was how amazing she smelled . . . like summertime.

"He didn't leave empty-handed," Nathan managed to say once his brain would again form a cohesive sentence. He stole a glance at Julie to see if she noticed, but if she thought he was acting weird, she gave no indication. "Where should I put my stuff?"

"Here, I can throw it in my room," Julie said, taking his duffle bag. "Do you want me to take your backpack, too?"

"Nah. I might need it."

Julie carried his bag a few short steps down the hall and set it down just inside a doorway. "Tell me you didn't drive all this way to stay in and do *homework*."

Grace saved him from having to reply. "What time is Ben supposed to get here?" she asked, unwinding the towel from her hair. Wet strands fell around her shoulders, instantly wetting her shirt. "I need to get ready."

Julie pulled her phone out of her back pocket as she came back into the tiny kitchen. "He thought they'd get here about six. Originally it was four, but he got stuck at work, too. So pretty soon. Ben's not usually late."

Grace turned to her. "Did you say 'they'?"

"Yeah. Oh shoot, did I forget to tell you Ben's bringing his friend Denny along? I think you'll like him. He is *hot*."

Grace groaned out loud. Nathan groaned in his head.

"Julie, I told you to *stop* trying to set me up. I am so *not* interested in guys right now."

"What makes you think I was trying to set you up?"

"Oh jeez, I don't know, maybe the 'hot' comment might have tipped me off? Just don't go getting any ideas—and don't put any ideas in his head, either."

Julie opened the fridge. "Nathan, want anything to drink? We've got water, Diet Coke, or beer."

"I'll take a beer, thanks."

Maybe it'll help settle my nerves, he thought as he accepted the drink.

While he was relieved to hear Grace wasn't interested in Julie setting her up, he felt deflated at her comment about no interest in guys.

I'm going to end up stuck in the damn friend *zone again.*

Maybe he'd have to try a little of that charm Virginia claimed he possessed to win Grace over. Because now that he was back in the same room with her, he was afraid this little crush he'd been nursing for over a year wasn't going to fade away anytime soon.

The apartment door slammed open and bounced off the wall. All three of them jumped.

"Zoey, what the—?"

"Oops, sorry! Didn't mean to slam the door open," the girl apologized. She shut the door and then looked around the kitchen. "Hey, Nathan. Julie mentioned you might come this weekend. Good to see you. It's been awhile. When did you get contacts? You look good!"

Nathan blushed. "Hi, Zoey. How've you been?"

"I'll be better once finals are over. I was planning to drive home yet tonight, but now I can't. I got called into work today, so I didn't get my paper done. I'm going to have to do homework all day tomorrow instead."

Zoey had been Julie's best friend all through high school, so Nathan had seen her around, mostly at Whispering Pines. He smiled at her running commentary. She'd always been chatty.

Julie opened the fridge a second time, pulled out another beer, and handed it to Zoey. "Here, you look like you could use this. I thought you had that date thing back home tonight, too."

Zoey took the beer and screwed the top off. "Had to cancel. I guess I'm going to have to give up on the idea of getting back together with Trevor. He's pissed at me for canceling, *again*. And he's right. Neither of us has time for a long-distance relationship."

"Yeah, I'm never doing one of those again," Grace chimed in, using her towel to squeeze water out of her still-wet hair. "I gotta finish getting ready if we're leaving soon. Hey, Zoey, Julie has a hot one for you tonight. Who needs Trevor?"

Nathan watched Grace head back to a small bathroom and shut the door. He was beginning to regret making this trip.

***

"Oh my God, I'm so glad you got us out of there," Nathan said with a laugh as he climbed out of the front passenger side of the Uber they'd used to get back to the girls' apartment. He opened the back door so that Grace could climb out.

"I could have made it home by myself, Nathan. You didn't have to leave. You came all this way to see your cousin. I feel bad you cut your night short."

Nathan thanked the guy for the lift and slammed the door, joining Grace on the sidewalk. She'd given him the perfect opening to tell her he'd also been anxious to see *her*. He opened his mouth to say the words, but Grace's phone went off, and he snapped it shut as she dug in the small purse slung over her shoulder.

"That's Dad's ring tone," she whispered just before answering.

He followed her into their brick three-story apartment building as she talked to her dad, Grant. Nathan had met Grant a few times over the past couple years. He seemed like a decent guy. Nathan thought it was cool that Grant, a writer, had recently published a book. Maybe he could pick his brain about the whole self-publishing process if Virginia decided to move ahead with her manuscript.

"Dad says hi," Grace threw back to him over her shoulder before continuing with her phone conversation.

Once inside the girls' apartment, Nathan shrugged out of his jacket, hung it off the back of a nearby chair, and grabbed his backpack. He didn't want Grace to feel like he was eavesdropping while she visited with her dad, so he crossed over to the living room and turned on a lamp next to the couch. Sitting down, he pulled out his laptop and Virginia's manuscript, thinking he'd try and knock out a page or two while Grace was still on the phone. He'd gotten a couple of hours of typing in earlier when there weren't any customers around. After rereading the beginning, he was more determined than ever to convince Virginia to get this book published.

He got lost in the story again as his eyes flew over the words, his fingers dancing over the keyboard. Grace came in and flicked another light on, settling into a recliner with a backpack down at her feet. Gone were the sexy jeans and boots she'd worn to dinner. Now she was in gray sweats and a pale-pink sweatshirt, hair caught up in a high ponytail and glasses perched on the end of her nose, but still looking no less sexy to Nathan.

"What are you working so hard on?" she asked, looking curiously at the stack of papers next to his laptop on their coffee table.

"Oh—sorry!" Nathan sat back on the couch, trying to look relaxed and at ease. "You were talking to your dad, so I thought I'd get a little more of this typed up."

Grace leaned over and picked up the top sheet, holding it closer to the lamplight. "What is this? The handwriting is so pretty, but it's faded."

"Would you believe me if I said it might be the world's next number one *New York Times* bestseller?" he joked.

She looked at Nathan over the top of her glasses, set the sheet back on the pile, and leaned back in the recliner, tucking her bare feet underneath her bottom. "Do you expect me to believe *you* wrote that?"

Nathan laughed, relaxing for real this time. "What, you don't think my handwriting looks like that?"

"Well, I *suppose* it could . . . but I doubt it."

"You're right. I haven't written in cursive since grade school. And I could never write like that. But looking at this now, I kind of wish I could. Virginia wrote it."

"Virginia? Is that somebody from school?"

Nathan shook his head. "No. She owns the store where I work now. Her and her husband, Virginia and Frank Fisk."

"*She* wrote that? What is it exactly? And why do you have it?"

Nathan used his pen as a placeholder and then flipped the pages he'd already typed back onto the stack. It now looked much as it had when he first found it, the stained sheet back on top.

"It's a long story. Actually, it's a *romantic* long story, so you probably wouldn't be interested."

Grace pinned him with a hard look. "What's *that* supposed to mean?"

He'd been joking around, but now he worried he'd ticked her off. "You know, based on your earlier comments, it sounded to me like you had no interest in romance."

"What comments?"

Yep, she's not finding any of this funny.

He tried again. "You said something to Julie when I first got here about having no interest in men. Look, I'm sorry. I shouldn't have brought it up."

Grace pushed up out of her chair. "Oh. That's right. I did say something like that. But I actually said 'guys,' not *men*. And I probably should have said 'boys,' because any I've dated recently—including Connor—have acted like they were twelve. Do you want something to eat?"

"Ouch!" he said, watching her leave the room.

So . . . his name's Connor.

"I'm sorry if you've had some tough luck in the dating world lately," he called after her. "Trust me, not all guys are jerks. In case you haven't noticed, I happen to be a pretty great guy."

"Oh, I noticed," she said, laughing.

He barely caught her words as she slammed cupboard doors. *Don't read anything into that,* he counseled himself. The girl was clearly bitter about something that had nothing to do with him.

She came back into the room, carrying a bag of chips and two bottles of water. "Sorry, we're out of beer. And what's with that fufu food they served us for dinner? I'm starving."

"Yeah, I could have used a burger instead of Thai food, but it was fun."

Grace handed him one of the waters and sat back down. She took a handful of chips and set the bag on the coffee table between them. "Help yourself."

"What has you so bitter when it comes to guys?" Nathan asked, unable to help himself. He wanted to know what he might be up against—if, that was, he'd ever be able to get Grace to notice him in that way.

"I got burned by a guy I met last spring. He goes to college down in Texas now, Austin, I think. He made me think he wanted to try to have a long-distance relationship, but it was a farce. I flew down there to see him in mid-October and it was a *disaster*. Suffice it to say I'm not opposed to romance—I've just never actually dated anyone that had the slightest clue what the word even means."

Nathan *did* understand why she felt that way. If the guys she'd dated were anything like some of his buddies at college, they were clueless.

Grace shrugged. "But, come on, you sent me off on a tangent. You have me intrigued. I want to hear this long, romantic story behind that stack of papers you have there."

He took a drink of the water and then, not wanting to chance a spill on the manuscript, set it on the carpet next to his feet. He told Grace how he'd stumbled onto the sheath of papers when he knocked into the antique desk and the drawer bottom fell out. He tried to articulate how the story itself sucked him in, hours flying by as he read the chapters.

"I'm typing it up because she can't read it anymore."

"What do you mean? She can't read her own handwriting?"

"She's older, and you saw how the ink has faded. Plus, she doesn't like to wear her glasses."

Grace pushed the sleeves on her sweatshirt up and drew her knees up to her chest, wrapping her arms around her shins and grasping her hands together. "How old is she?"

Nathan shrugged. "I guess I have no idea. Sixty, maybe? Frank talks about retiring sometime soon, but I don't know if that's because of their age or Virginia's health. She's had some trouble with her heart."

"Why do you think she hid it away so long ago? Was she afraid it wasn't good enough?"

"I think so. Even now, Virginia seems more than a little scared when she talks about maybe doing something with it. I think part of her wants to shove it back in that drawer and forget I even found it. But I'd hate for her to do that. Her husband, Frank—he's crazy about her. They've been married a long time, like almost forty years, and I can tell she's crazy about him, too. He was the reason she wrote it in the first place. He used to be a creative-writing teacher, and she's always loved books. It's what brought them together."

Grace smiled at him but said nothing. He began to feel self-conscious, unable to read her expression.

"What?"

"Nothing," she said, dropping her feet back down and taking a few more chips out of the bag. "Keep going."

"Not much more to tell. I offered to help Virginia finally turn this into a real book that she could give to Frank as a gift. He doesn't know anything about it. She's unsure. It's been so long since she's even read it, she wants to do that first. Then she'll decide. And that brings us to tonight. The quicker I get this typed up so she can read it, the better. If I can convince her to do this, to turn this stack of papers into an honest-to-goodness book she can hand to her husband, it'll mean the realization of a dream she thought died a long time ago. She's spent her career helping other authors get their books out into the world . . . I think it's her turn now."

"Oh, we *so* have to help her do this!" Grace said, sliding forward so she was sitting on the edge of her chair, excitement shining in her eyes.

Nathan was surprised by her enthusiasm. When the rest of their group had suggested checking out an off-campus house party—not everyone was twenty-one yet, so bar-hopping hadn't been an option—she'd begged off, claiming she had a headache.

"Like . . . now?" Nathan said. "What about your headache?"

Grace waved off his concern. "I might have just said that to avoid going to a party full of noisy and drunk frat guys."

He laughed as she shivered in mock horror, then said, "I was so glad to have a legitimate excuse to ride home with you. I'm not much of a partier. Besides, you shouldn't take an Uber by yourself."

He half expected her to take offense at his statement, but she only nodded. "How can I help?" she asked, glancing toward Virginia's manuscript.

"For now, why don't you start reading? See if you agree with me that this is worth pursuing. I already have this chunk typed up, so go ahead and start from the beginning. If you catch up with me, maybe you can take over on the typing for a while, and I can start doing some research on the next steps."

Grace nodded, accepting the pages he handed to her. "I suppose someone else made all these red corrections? An editor, maybe? Has the whole *thing* been marked up like this?"

"No, only half. I'm sure it would be a good idea to have someone go through it all again. I can maybe help find someone to do it."

"Dad knows lots about this stuff, too. We can call him tomorrow."

Nathan grinned. "I was hoping you'd say that."

Grace pulled her lamp closer as she began to read. Nathan picked back up where he'd left off. They continued on that way, each rising to take a bathroom break or stretch, but neither seemed inclined to quit. The only sounds were the clicking of the keys on Nathan's laptop and the *tick-tock* of a clock somewhere in the apartment.

When Grace caught up with him, she again offered to help with the typing.

"If you're sure you don't mind, I *could* use a break," Nathan said, rubbing his eyes. "Do you want to switch spots?"

Grace stood and reached into a basket at the end of the couch, pulling out a blanket. She came and sat beside Nathan, signaling for him to move farther down on the couch.

"You look exhausted. Since this is technically your bed for the night, why don't you lay down? Use that pillow and this blanket. Just stick your feet behind me and stretch out. It's a deep couch. I need to sit forward, anyhow, so I can type."

Nathan hated to sleep while she worked, but she was right—he could barely keep his eyes open. But who was he kidding? He'd never sleep if she were sitting that close to him.

He took the blanket from her. "Are you sure you don't mind? If I fall asleep, wake me up when you want to switch off again."

Grace assured him she would, and he did as she'd instructed, stretching out behind her. He was careful to stay as far back against the cushions as he could, so his legs wouldn't awkwardly rub against her backside as she bent forward toward his laptop. Convinced he'd never fall asleep lying so close to her, he tried to force his muscles to relax. The tapping of the keys reminded him she wasn't paying him any attention, and at some point, he drifted off.

***

Grace quietly shut the laptop and then stretched her head from side to side. Nathan was right. Virginia's story *was* extraordinary. She was a talented writer. But according to Nathan, Virginia had never written any other books. What a sad waste of talent. Maybe there would still be time for Virginia to do more writing, if that had always been her dream.

It was so sweet of Nathan to encourage Virginia to do something with her manuscript. Even if the woman decided not to turn it into a finished book, she'd have assurances from at least Nathan and Grace that it was terrific.

A soft snore caught her attention, and she glanced back at Nathan, sleeping soundly on the couch behind her. He'd turned around while she'd been typing, his face now up against the cushioned back. The blanket had puddled at his side. She gently covered him back up with it and stood, careful not to wake him. At the muffled sound of giggling from out in the hallway, Grace sprinted on tiptoes to the apartment door, opening it quietly and signaling to the foursome headed her way to keep it down.

It was nearly three in the morning, and their arrival was the only sound in the hushed corridor. The rowdy group did a *relatively* good job quieting down, although it was apparent they'd all had fun.

Once everyone was inside the kitchen, Grace tucked the manuscript and laptop safely away into Nathan's backpack and took it into her room with her. She didn't think anyone would bother it but didn't dare take that chance. She considered trying to get through the last few chapters herself, but she'd reached her limit. So instead, she crawled into her bed and flipped off her lamp. Her roommates, Julie and Zoey, could get their other two visitors settled without her. Based on the whispers and giggles coming from the kitchen, they weren't quite ready to settle down for the night yet.

***

Nathan woke to a mostly quiet apartment the next morning.

So much for closing my eyes for a few minutes.

Nathan thought he remembered hearing Julie's laughter at some point during the night, but he could recall little else after turning the keyboard over to Grace.

He swung his feet off the couch and searched for his phone. It had slid to the floor, the battery dead now. Based on the light coming through the patio door, he should probably get going on his homework. But his laptop and backpack weren't where he'd left them. All three of the bedroom doors were closed. The clock on the kitchen wall revealed it was only ten minutes past eight.

Based on the competing snores coming from the bedroom just off the kitchen, he suspected Ben and his buddy were in there. He knew Grace's room was on the left because he'd spotted a framed photograph of her and her dad when he'd used the bathroom the night before. He hated to wake her; hopefully she wouldn't mind.

He rapped his knuckles lightly on Grace's door, and it opened a crack. Grace peeked out, yawning and rubbing at one sleepy eye, wearing the same sweats she'd had on the night before.

"Hey, morning, Nathan. You're up early."

He felt a twinge of guilt for waking her. He had no idea how long she'd stayed up, typing on Virginia's manuscript.

"Sorry about that," he whispered. "You don't happen to have my backpack in there, do you?"

She opened her door farther, stretching as she did so. "I do. I brought it in here for safekeeping. Those guys were still pretty wound up when they got home last night. I didn't want to chance anything getting spilled on Virginia's stuff or your computer. Did you talk to them?"

Nathan spied his backpack leaning up against the wall. "Nah. Slept like a baby. I think I heard Julie at some point, but they must have kept it pretty quiet. Everyone else is still sleeping."

Grace glanced at the time on her phone, lying on her bedside table. "Want to go grab some coffee down the street? I've got a lot to do today, too. Might as well let the rest of them sleep. We can bring something back for them to eat later."

"Sure, that'd be great. I could probably use a shower, but my other stuff's in Julie's room."

Grace nodded, heading for the bathroom. "We keep a few extra toothbrushes on hand. Never know who might stay over. Brush your teeth, and I promise you'll feel at least half-human again. We can shower later."

She rummaged in the vanity under the sink and handed him a brand-new toothbrush and travel-size toothpaste. "I'll go change quick."

Nathan brushed his teeth and finger-combed his hair. He should grab his cap out of his car on the way to the coffee shop. Despite his initial reservations, he was glad he'd driven over yesterday. Getting time alone with Grace, first last night and now this morning, was amazing. Catching up with Julie and Zoey over dinner and getting to know Ben and his friend Denny had been fun, too. Based on the hand-holding he'd noticed between Julie and Ben, he suspected those two were more than friends.

He let Grace use the bathroom, and then they slipped quietly out of the apartment, Grace giggling at the snores coming out of the far bedroom. She led the way down the stairs, her long ponytail swinging behind her through the hole in the back of a baseball cap. She pulled on the quilted, ivory-colored jacket she'd grabbed on the way out the door. Nathan couldn't help but watch her long legs, ensconced in form-fitting black yoga tights as she jogged down the stairs. Army-green duck boots completed her outfit.

A fresh coating of light snow met them outside, but the clouds had moved on. The sky was a brilliant blue, interrupted only by the golden globe of the sun. Their breath puffed out into the quiet morning air. Not surprisingly, the sidewalk was empty of all but fallen leaves coated in a dusting of snow as they made their way to the coffee shop. Their shoulders bumped as they walked along, each lugging heavy backpacks. They walked in silence, lost in their thoughts, Nathan thankful for a bit more one-on-one time with Grace.

He considered asking Grace how she was feeling. She'd been critically ill when their families first met, but following a successful bone marrow transplant and months of rest and recovery, she seemed perfectly healthy now. When Julie first mentioned to him that Grace was going back to college and they were rooming together, he'd asked his cousin about Grace's health. Julie's response consisted of assurances that Grace was healthy, coupled with a warning to never ask *Grace* about her illness. She'd confided to Julie that she hated dwelling on that dark time.

Nathan stole a glance at Grace's face as he opened the door for her to enter the coffee shop. Her cheeks were pink and her eyes bright. He took Julie's advice and didn't ask.

They ordered coffee and doughnuts, settling into a corner table overlooking the street.

"Sorry I fell asleep last night. I didn't mean to. How long did you type?"

Grace rummaged in her backpack for something, then pulled out a thick black notebook. "Until about three. I tried to get it all done for you, actually, but you were right. Some of the handwriting was hard to read, and it was slow going. There's still a few chapters to go."

"Only a few? God, you type faster than I do," Nathan said, sipping his scalding coffee. "Thanks for your help. I should be able to finish that up after I get home tonight. Virginia will be *thrilled*."

Grace nodded as she flipped open her notebook. "Promise me you'll email me the last little bit? I can't wait to see how it ends. But we also need to talk about ideas for your holiday events at the bookstore. Remember, you asked me to brainstorm?"

She tapped her finger on the open page in front of her. Nathan looked down and laughed at what seemed to be a long list of ideas.

"May I?" he asked, motioning toward her notes.

She handed him her notebook and then bit into her doughnut as he read her list. Her handwriting reminded him of Virginia's, graceful and artistic. It made his chicken scratch look juvenile. He quickly scanned her notes, liking what he was seeing, and handed them back to Grace.

"Those are some awesome ideas. I especially like the one geared toward helping kids with their gift-giving. And, of course, I love the local author event. Virginia is a sucker for promoting new authors."

Grace smiled, referring to her notes. "I checked, and there are five weekends between Thanksgiving and Christmas," she said. "Is the plan to do something big each Saturday?"

Nathan started in on his pair of doughnuts, not sure if it was hunger or Grace's smile making his stomach skip. He attempted to stay focused. "That's what Frank and I discussed. We need to capitalize on this time if we're going to save the store. I have to help him change things up a little. He didn't feel like they've brought in much additional traffic in the past couple years. Gotten kind of stale, you know? I'll have to loop Virginia in, too, because she has a few things she loves to do every year, but she was pretty open to my ideas for Halloween. She'll be easy to work with."

"And don't forget, she'll be busy working on her book—*if* she decides to do something with it."

Nathan nodded. "I sure hope so. Plus, she won't want Frank to know that she's working on her manuscript. That might get a little tricky. She might have to hide away at home more."

They talked through the things Grace had dreamed up. Nathan liked what he was hearing.

"In this day and age," Grace explained, "you need to find ways to connect with people. To make the store a fun *destination* instead of simply another place to buy books. If people want a book, they're probably going to order it quick online—especially in December when everyone's so busy. But if you give them a fun reprieve in the middle of the hectic holiday season and help them check things off their "to do" list, they'll not only appreciate it—they'll tell their friends."

"That makes total sense. I thought of something else, too. Last year I waited too long to do some online shopping and, with shipping taking longer in December, I got stuck. What if we capitalized on that advantage, maybe even play up the fact they don't have to worry about shipping deadlines if they shop at Book Journeys?"

Grace nodded as she popped the last bite of her doughnut into her mouth. "Love it!"

"Any chance I can convince you to come help at any of these?"

"Well, I was kind of thinking we could talk to Dad and see if he'd be willing to come for the author event—if you decide to do one. His book is starting to gain some traction."

"That would be awesome! I talked to him at the Halloween party, tried to get a sense of whether or not he'd be open to something like that, but he seemed a little gun shy." He finished off his first of two doughnuts and set the plate aside, more interested in Grace than his breakfast.

"Yeah, he hates being the center of attention. But he's had to do other meet-and-greets lately, and once he gets there and starts talking to people, he enjoys it. Besides," she said, grinning, "Dad will do pretty much anything I ask him to do."

Nathan didn't doubt that. *He'd* do pretty much anything she asked him to do, too. He wondered if Grace knew how lucky she was to have such a strong relationship with her dad.

Grinning back, Nathan continued, not willing to let thoughts of his own father spoil his mood. "I'll talk to Frank and Virginia, get their buy-in. If they're good with it, I'll call you. Then maybe you can talk to Grant about it first before I call him."

"Deal," Grace agreed, glancing at her phone as it vibrated on the table. "Looks like the party animals are up and hungry." She showed him her phone.

Bring food!

Nathan laughed. "You probably know this, but my cousin is not a joy to be around when she's *hangry!*"

"Ah, yes, the dreaded anger that stems from hunger. We better take the crew food *and* coffee. But I hope some of these ideas will help you turn things around at the bookstore."

"I really do, too," Nathan said. "I'm really coming to love that place. It would be a shame if they were forced to close their doors."

Grace shoved her notebook into her backpack and downed the last of her now-cold coffee, eyeing Nathan curiously. "Are you thinking about staying on there . . . you know . . . after you graduate?"

It's like she can read my mind, Nathan thought.

He glanced out the window, considering how much he wanted to share with Grace. He'd initially taken the job with the Fisks because he'd liked the idea of applying some of what he'd learned at Barnes & Noble at their much smaller store, to help them bring in more business. He knew his mom loved Book Journeys, so it felt natural to want to help. But now, he was starting to see himself possibly playing a bigger role there, once college was in his rearview mirror. He hadn't shared this idea with anyone, though. It felt too new, too *unformed* to discuss just yet.

Grace's phone pinged with another text. She rolled her eyes and showed him the screen.

Hello?!

Nathan stood, hoisting his heavy backpack onto his shoulder. "I'm not sure *what* I'll do. But for now, the rent's cheap. Come on, we better go feed the animals."

***

Nathan knew it was now or never. He'd been wanting to ask Grace out for months but hadn't gotten up the nerve. Now, as they walked back to the apartment, through the last of the fallen leaves littered across the sidewalk, it was time. He couldn't very well ask her on a date in front of an apartment full of people, and they only had a block to go.

Taking a deep breath, he reached out and caught Grace by the hand. She had the bag of pastries in her other hand, and he held the drink carrier full of coffees.

"Can you hold up a sec?" he said, dropping her hand after lightly tugging her to a stop.

Grace turned toward him, the sun bright in her face. She raised her hand to block the glare. Despite its brightness, the sun offered little warmth this time of year, and her cheeks were red from the brisk morning air. "What's up?"

He looped his thumb through the strap of his backpack, trying to hide his nerves.

"Any chance we can do this again some time?"

"This?" Grace asked, confusion on her face.

"I had fun last night. Can we see each other again?"

"Sure. Remember, I'll come to the bookstore if you have that author deal. Finals will be over then. And maybe I can sneak over for another weekend deal, too."

She's going to make me come right out and say it.

"I meant besides that. Could we, like . . . you know . . . go out some time?"

Grace suddenly dropped her hand and shuffled her feet, moving to stand shoulder to shoulder with Nathan, facing away from the sunshine.

"Last night was fun," Grace said. "And this morning was great. You're a fun guy, Nathan. But . . . I can't date right now. It's not you. Really. It's me."

And here it comes, he thought. *The friend zone.*

"Can we keep this as friends? You know, get through finals and all? School and the bookstore will take all your time between now and Christmas . . . or even New Years. I'll help at an event or two when I can, and we'll see how it goes. Okay?"

Better than nothing, Nathan thought, resigning himself to be patient. Again.

"Sure, forget I even asked. Thanks again for all your help, Grace."

But her gentle rejection took some of the shine off the morning.

CHAPTER 7

Gift of Gumption

Sunday morning dawned bright but cold. Virginia planned to spend the day at home, reading a new novel that had just come in. She might recommend it for their January book club but wanted to read it first. A glance at the digital clock on the stove told her she was getting up fashionably late. After an enjoyable dinner the night before with her friend Barbara, she'd come home to an empty house but a mind she couldn't quiet.

She missed Frank.

She made herself buttered toast and tea, then took a seat in the breakfast nook overlooking their backyard. When Frank wasn't at the bookstore, he could often be found back there, puttering around with his perennials. He'd readied them for winter's slumber, so there was little color now.

Frank was a practical, steadfast man. They say opposites attract, and it certainly applied to their relationship. Virginia loved color, theater, the arts, and visiting. Frank was content to stay in the background, taking care of the business aspect of their store and all the other more practical aspects to life. He indulged Virginia, and she knew she'd brought excitement to his existence. Perhaps more than he'd preferred.

She nibbled at her toast—not because she was hungry, but because if Frank were here, he'd be sure she ate something for breakfast. She didn't have much of an appetite these days, but even with him away, she didn't want to disappoint him.

She supposed she was silly to let Nathan try to encourage her to do something with that old manuscript. She'd given up on that dream long ago. Mabel wasn't far off when she accused Virginia of giving in to pressures from her mother when she hid that rough draft away and tried to put it out of her mind so many years ago.

After all, wasn't that the way of most mother-daughter relationships? Can daughters ever really live up to their mother's expectations? *She'd* never been able to. And she hated that the cycle was now repeating itself. She'd come to be sorely disappointed in *her* daughter, too.

Karen had been a delightful child. For a while it was just the two of them, before Frank came into their lives. She'd left her first husband, something nearly unheard of back then. But his drug use and hippy ways were creating an unsafe environment for a newborn. Virginia and Karen got out; her ex, succumbing to his addictions, did not. Despite being nearly destitute, Virginia and her daughter found ways to survive.

Before Frank stepped in to turn her world around, there had been Celia.

Celia was a close friend of her mother's, although Virginia never understood that relationship. Earlier, when Virginia foolishly ran off with her starving artist, herself not yet twenty years old, her parents disowned her. Later, when everything fell apart and Virginia found herself widowed, penniless, and the mother of a newborn, Celia stepped in. She offered her a place to live and helped her get on her feet.

Virginia shuddered to think how their lives might have turned out if not for Celia. Celia helped her survive. Then Frank slowly infiltrated her life and allowed her to *thrive*.

Now, would Nathan, Celia's great-nephew, be the next person to offer her a lifeline?

Experience had taught her that regrets are terrible thieves of joy. In recent years, she'd come to regret allowing her mother back into their lives after she'd married Frank, convinced now through the value of hindsight that her daughter's grandmother had been a terrible influence over Karen. The two, her mother and her daughter, had formed a close relationship. Right or wrong, Virginia now shouldered the burden of guilt for many of her daughter's missteps in life. She knew this was yet another common dynamic of mother-daughter relationships.

It was too late to save Karen. Her daughter had done things Virginia could still barely fathom. Stealing from unsuspecting clients to fund a lifestyle of privilege? Fair or not, Virginia blamed her own mother for whetting Karen's appetite for the finer things in life.

But was it too late for her to give Frank the one gift she'd been too afraid to give him?

With a sigh, she nibbled on the corner of her cold toast. She knew Frank loved her, but she worried she was becoming a burden to him. Had she allowed herself to give up too soon, not only on her book but on genuinely living her life? Had she given in to the aches and pains caused by her advancing years, the disappointment over Karen's failures, the weight of her regrets?

Her mind jumped back to the last time she'd visited with Celia. The older woman had invited her over for tea, a month or so before she died. They reminisced about the years Virginia and baby Karen lived in Celia's basement. They'd become close back then, Virginia benefiting from the wisdom of the older woman and Celia enjoying having a little one around, never having had children of her own. Virginia suspected now that Karen would have grown into a completely different type of woman if *Celia* would have been her daughter's role model instead of Helen, Virginia's mother.

With another, heavier sigh, Virginia stood and gathered up her breakfast dishes.

"When did I let myself become such a pathetic old woman, dependent on others, frail in both mind and body?" she asked the empty kitchen. Her dear friend Celia would not have approved. *That* woman had never given in to the inconveniences of old age. She'd stayed active and independent until the very end, truly *living* until her early nineties.

Virginia reminded herself she was nowhere near that old yet. Her mother had lived even longer than Celia. She needed to get back to this business of living, not just existing.

Nathan wanted to help. He had the energy and unvarnished optimism of youth on his side. She made a decision right then. She'd take him up on his offer and give the love of her life a Valentine's gift he'd never expect. And if she was going to do this, she needed her strength back. She needed to start eating again; she needed to get some exercise. Just as the doctor ordered.

Decision made, she cleaned up her breakfast mess and checked the freezer. She'd pop a frozen roast into the oven so Frank would come back to a home-cooked meal.

Wouldn't that surprise him!

But it was too early to start dinner yet. First she'd get dressed and go for a walk around the block. Frank would hate the idea of her going out alone, but she was done being coddled.

For the first time in a long time, Virginia was excited to have something new to look forward to instead of fearing a bleak, downward slide to the end. As she stepped out onto their front porch, she smiled up at the sparkling blue sky. She'd be fine on her walk.

After all, Celia was likely still watching over her.

***

Nathan squeezed in a couple more hours between Sunday and Monday night to finish typing Virginia's manuscript—the time he should have used doing homework. He was feeling pressure, falling behind in his classes, but helping Virginia with her book held so much more appeal than his schooling at the moment.

He supposed most college seniors felt the same way—excited to get on with their life, little motivation left to push through with the last of their classes. He'd graduate in the spring. At this point, what did it matter if his GPA slipped a bit? It wasn't like he planned to enter some competitive fight for a job somewhere. At least not right away. He was committed to helping Frank and Virginia turn the bookstore around. Little else mattered to him these days.

He didn't see Virginia again until Tuesday morning, and even then he wasn't able to speak to her alone until Frank made a run to the post office.

"Thank goodness!" Virginia said as the door closed behind the older man. "I thought he'd never leave."

Nathan laughed. He'd noticed that Frank seemed to be hovering around Virginia even more than usual all morning. He said as much to her.

"I know. Frank is such a worrywart. I think he senses something's up. He wasn't too pleased with me when he got home on Sunday and found my sneakers next to the back door."

Nathan clicked off his laptop and closed the cover. He'd been entering their planned events on the calendar tab of their website after getting Frank and Virginia's buy-in on the ideas he'd brought back from his weekend with Grace.

"Is he that much of a neat freak that he gets mad if you don't put your shoes away?"

Now it was Virginia's turn to laugh. "No, that wasn't it at all. You see, the only time I wear sneakers is when I go on walks, and I got out of that habit a while back when my heart started giving me trouble. Foolish on my part. My doctor has been on me to get walking again, but I didn't listen. I was afraid exerting myself would be dangerous. But, of course, that isn't true."

"Ah. I see. Frank didn't like you going for a walk when you were home alone this weekend."

"Exactly."

Nathan looked closer now at Virginia. Something about her seemed . . . different. Maybe it was how she was acting, talking.

"You seem different today, Virginia."

"You are an observant young man, aren't you?" she noted, walking toward the front of the store and looking through the front window, up and down the street, then returning to him. "I decided something on Sunday. Actually, I made a few decisions. And I have your aunt to thank for that."

"My aunt? You mean Renee or Val?" Nathan asked, surprised Virginia even knew his mom's two sisters.

She shook her head. "No, I guess she would be your great-aunt. Celia Middleton."

"Ah." Nathan knew Celia had been part owner of this bookstore before his mom, but he wasn't sure where Virginia was going with all of this.

"Don't look so confused, Nathan," she said, smiling. "Celia was an amazing woman, as you know, and kept busy up until she was in her nineties. I'm nowhere *near* that old, but I'd already resigned myself to feeling, and *acting*, old. All this business with Karen, my own mother's death last year, and then my heart issues . . . it all had me resigned to the notion that I was washed up. Celia would have been appalled with me."

Nathan started to protest, but Virginia raised her hand to stop him.

"Don't try to make me feel better, Nathan. We both know it's true. Now, our only problem is that Frank's worried. He senses I'm up to something. He's watching me like a hawk, which is going to make our mission that much more difficult."

Nathan grinned. He suddenly felt like he was in *Mission: Impossible*. "Our mission?"

"Yes. That is if you still want to help me get my book published?"

Nathan raised his hand, and she slapped it a high-five.

"Absolutely! I told you I wanted to help, and I meant it. I even recruited some help this weekend."

Virginia's eyes widened and she wrung her hands. She found a chair and sank into it with a sigh.

"I hope you don't mind?"

She shook her head. "No, no, of course not. This is all just a tad bit overwhelming. Plus, I'm sore from getting my walk in for three days in a row. Bit stiff. I supposed it's fine if you want to let someone else help. If I'm going to do this, I need to get comfortable with letting other people read my work."

Nathan turned and nearly jumped up to sit on the counter but thought better of it. He found another chair and sat in that instead, so he was once again eye-level with Virginia. He wanted her to see this as a partnership.

"Good. And I'm happy to report that my friend Grace loved what she read. She helped me type a bunch of it up on Saturday night."

She gave him a sly look. "I thought you said you didn't *have* a girlfriend?"

"Who said she was my girlfriend?" Nathan asked, wishing Virginia's comment had been more accurate. His early-morning talk with Grace came rushing back.

"I guess you didn't say it, but I assumed . . . oh, never mind. I'm prying now. Sorry. That was kind of her to help."

"She's a kind person. And she's smart. She helped me with some of those ideas we talked about for your events between now and Christmas. She loved your story. Her dad is an author, too. Remember I said I thought I had someone we could bring in for that author event? That someone is her dad. Grace said he might be able to help us with your book, too."

Virginia's hand fluttered up to her chest. "Oh, goodness. It *is* getting real. I'm scared."

Nathan understood—he was nervous, too. He didn't want Virginia to end up disappointed. They were all going to need to keep the faith. They had lots to learn.

She settled her hand back into her lap. "Remember, Frank can't know anything about this."

As if she had to remind him.

***

Nathan called Grace later the following week.

"She wants to do it, Grace. Virginia wants to turn her manuscript into a real book and give it to her husband for Valentine's Day. His birthday is the very next day after that, too."

"That's *great*, Nathan! Did you finish typing it up so she can read it?"

"I did, thanks to you. I'll email it to you so you can read the ending. I'd still be working on it if you hadn't gotten so much of it done the other night. We *both* appreciate it."

"Not a problem. I'm just happy to help. What about the other things we talked about—you know, to try to bring in more business over the holidays?"

"Yep, they were up for some of those ideas, too. We're already busy getting things planned. Did you happen to mention an author event to your dad yet?

"I haven't talked to him since you left, but I will when I'm home. I'll leave after class tomorrow. We're visiting his sister's family for Thanksgiving."

"Sounds good. Have fun. Let me know what Grant says, and then I'll call him if he doesn't flat-out tell you no."

"Will do. Are you heading home tomorrow, too? For Thanksgiving?"

"I'm not. I have a lot to do to get the store ready for the Friday and Saturday after Thanksgiving, plus I'm behind on school work. Mom wasn't happy with me when I told her I might not be able to make it, but she seemed to calm down when I told her the Fisks invited me to come over to their place for dinner."

"I'm sorry you won't get to spend it with your family, Nathan."

Nathan shrugged, then realized Grace couldn't see him. "It's all right. I'll see them all at Christmas. Probably before that, even. Mom wants me to help the Fisks turn this place around as much as *I* do. She gets it. It all takes time."

"Well, have fun, don't work too hard, and I'll let you know what Dad has to say about your author event."

"Thanks, Grace. Tell him hello for me, and eat lots of turkey."

Nathan hung up, feeling a momentary twinge of regret that he wasn't close to *his* father. He wondered what they served for Thanksgiving in prison.

CHAPTER 8

Gift of Happily Ever After

*N*athan stood on the Fisks' front porch, a bottle of pinot noir in one hand, his other resting on their door knocker. He hesitated, wishing for a moment that he was standing at his own grandparents' door. He'd never celebrated Thanksgiving without them. When he'd talked to his mom earlier, she'd been taking a pumpkin pie out of the oven. His favorite. Here he just felt like an intruder.

Ridiculous, he chided himself. *They invited me.*

He knocked. He heard clicking heels approach and the door swung inward.

"Nathan, how *wonderful* to see you! Come in, dear."

He stepped awkwardly across the threshold and into the warm, welcoming scent of roasting turkey. He breathed in deeply, reminded himself to relax, and handed the bottle of wine to Virginia. Jess had suggested he bring the wine, and based on the smile Virginia offered him as she took the bottle, his mother's advice had been solid—as usual.

"I was just finishing up the table and Frank has been busy in the kitchen," Virginia explained, spinning on her heel and leading Nathan farther inside.

For some reason, he'd expected their home to look like something out of the seventies. He should have known better. Pale gray walls and white trim along with a shiny wooden floor set the stage for modern furniture and tasteful décor. The only nod to more traditional furnishings was a handsome wooden cabinet against a far wall, under a set of open stairs. The glass-fronted piece was dark wood with rich scrolling. The shelves inside were bursting with books.

Following Virginia, he glanced into a dining room to his left. The table was set precisely how he would have guessed Virginia would prepare a holiday table: fresh flowers, fancy dishes, and more silverware at each place setting than he'd know how to use. He was sure she'd leap at the opportunity to teach him which fork was which.

"I'll set this in the fridge to chill before dinner," she said, her fancy dress swirling as she continued toward what Nathan assumed was the kitchen, a cloud of perfume mixing in with the cooking smells.

Frank greeted Nathan as he followed Virginia into a warm and inviting kitchen, then turned back to his wife. "Ginny, dear, you've been on your feet since seven this morning. Why don't you go lie down for a bit? That way you'll enjoy dinner. I'm sure Nathan is willing to help me get everything on the table."

Virginia turned away from the refrigerator, the wine now chilling inside. Nathan expected her to insist she wasn't tired—she didn't *look* tired to him, and Virginia never liked to miss out on things—but instead she said, "Maybe you're right, dear. It *has* been a busy morning. If you gentlemen are sure you've got this, I'll go rest for thirty minutes." She leveled a raised eyebrow at them both, adding, "But don't carve the turkey without me."

"We wouldn't dream of it, dear," Frank assured her, reaching for the can opener and a can of black olives.

As Virginia passed Nathan on the way out of the room, she winked at him, looking wide awake. She was up to something, and Nathan suspected he knew what it was: another excuse to work on her manuscript, away from Frank's ever-vigilant watch.

***

"Here, let me get that, Frank," Nathan said, eyeing the golden-brown turkey nestled in the oven as the buzzer went off. "You have your hands full mashing those potatoes." As Frank handed him the oven mitts, Nathan noticed a bead of sweat trickle down the older man's forehead; he seemed relieved.

Compared to the size of the bird he'd watched his grandfather carve for their crew in years past, the one crackling in the Fisks' oven looked child-size, like something you'd find in a miniature toy kitchen set. He supposed it didn't take nearly as much food to feed three as it did twenty.

"We'll let that rest for a few minutes," Frank said, nodding toward the turkey Nathan had set on the kitchen island. "Can you cover it with that tinfoil again? Seal it back up. And then would you mind grabbing the sweet potatoes and green-bean casserole out of the fridge? Set those in the oven now that there's room."

Nathan, happy to have something to occupy his hands, removed the smaller dishes from the refrigerator and set them on the counter, pulling the plastic wrap off before placing them into the oven.

"Don't you use a beater on those?" he asked, noticing Frank using a hand masher on his now-drained pot of boiled potatoes. Val, his aunt, always used a beater, although she was probably working on twenty pounds of potatoes versus Frank's much smaller kettleful.

Frank added a pat of butter and a splash of cream before continuing with his vigorous task. "Ginny would skin me alive if I tried that. She insists this is the only way to prepare mashed potatoes *properly.*"

Nathan grinned. Frank tended to joke about Virginia's high expectations when his wife was out of earshot.

He helped Frank with the many last-minute details of pulling their Thanksgiving meal together. He did as the older man asked, realizing for the first time how much work was involved. He owed his grandmother, his aunt Val, and everyone else who helped with their family holidays a thank-you for their many years of doing this. He'd never realized the coordination and hard work involved.

"It feels different this year," Frank said, placing the cover on the mashed potatoes to keep them warm.

"Thanksgiving?"

Frank nodded, removing his glasses and cleaning the lenses with a dishtowel. "This is the first year without Karen and her husband here."

Nathan set the jar of green olives he'd just managed to twist open down on the counter and turned his full attention to Frank. They'd danced around the topic of what had happened between his father and Karen, the

Fisks' daughter, but had never really discussed it in depth. He'd wondered when they would get around to talking about this.

"I imagine it does feel weird," Nathan said, leaning against the counter, palms face-down on the surface. "I couldn't help but wonder whether Dad would get a turkey dinner today. It's not like he spent the last couple of Thanksgivings with all of us, anyhow. He usually claimed he was working, or some other excuse. But still . . ."

Frank nodded as he put his glasses back on. "I'm sorry, Nathan. I'm sorry for whatever part my daughter played in your father's downfall. I've wanted to talk to you about this, but it never really felt like the right time to bring it up."

Nathan nodded. "Yeah, once in a while it feels like the elephant in the room. Like we're dancing around something important."

"Come on, we can take a ten-minute break," Frank said, hanging the dishtowel back on a cupboard knob. "Let's sit down."

Nathan followed him into the living room and took the chair opposite Frank. He liked the idea of putting a time limit on their discussion. Get things out in the open and then move on, hopefully never speaking of it again.

Frank kicked the footrest up on his recliner with a sigh. Virginia probably wasn't the only one who'd been on her feet since early morning.

"As I'm sure you already suspected, we are incredibly disappointed in our daughter's behavior. We suspected she wasn't happy in her marriage, but she never gave any indication that she was unfaithful. I don't think her husband was all that surprised, but as parents, you never want to think ill of your kids."

Nathan almost corrected Frank. Not all parents thought as highly of their children as Frank suggested. Nathan had grown up listening to harsh criticism from his dad, never feeling like he measured up.

"Being unfaithful was bad enough, but when you add in everything else . . . it is completely inexcusable."

Nathan considered how best to respond to Frank. His father was far from innocent in the whole mess. After all, look where he was spending his Thanksgiving. Nathan fiddled with a loose thread in the armchair and stared at a silent football game playing on a small television in the corner of the room. Frank gave him time to gather his thoughts.

"I won't lie . . . when everything blew up with Dad, we felt blindsided. Mom, of course, was crushed, but since she was the one who pulled all the pieces of what was happening together, she'd had more time to come to terms with it all. My dad is a bastard. He cheated on Mom for years—not just with your daughter. *And* he's a criminal. He put my mom in the nearly impossible position of raising Harper, my half-sister, when another woman he'd slept with got pregnant but wasn't capable of raising her. And Dad couldn't do it—raise Harper, I mean—from his jail cell. It was all a big damn mess that he created all by himself but couldn't clean up."

Nathan pulled his eyes away from the game back to his host. He hated seeing the pity in the older man's eyes.

"How do you think your mom is holding up?"

Nathan couldn't help but grin, despite the seriousness of the topic. "Mom's tough. Dad screwed her over enough through the years—by that point, I don't think she loved him anymore. How could she? I'm just proud of her for getting her life back on track so fast, and for taking Harper. It would have killed me to know I had another sister out there, somewhere, and that she might not be safe. Harper's biological mother is a flake, to put it lightly. What Dad saw in her, I'll never know."

Frank sat with that for a moment, then asked, "Do you approve of the man your mother is seeing now?"

"You mean Seth? Yeah. I do. He's a good guy. It was weird when I found out they were dating. I mean, it's hard to think of your mom dating *anyone*, you know? And Seth is younger, too. But he's cool."

"I know he was a big help to *us*," Frank said. "Helping us fix the ceiling and a couple other issues over at the bookstore gave things a nice little facelift. I agree—he seems like a decent man. Trust me—sometimes it isn't the first relationships, or even the first marriages, we find ourselves in that'll carry us through to our golden years. Take Ginny and I, for example."

If Frank was about to share more on their relationship, he was cut off by a loud buzzer from the kitchen. He snapped the footrest down on his recliner and pushed up out of the comfortable chair, trying but failing to stifle a soft moan at the effort.

"Come on, kid, duty calls. You don't by chance know how to make gravy, do you? That was always Karen's job."

Nathan stood, shrugging at his boss's question. "No, but how hard could it be?"

***

It turned out gravy was harder to make than expected. *Too* hard. Nathan would add "delicious gravy" to the list of things to thank Val for when he next saw his mom's youngest sister. If Virginia was disappointed there was no gravy to top Frank's fluffy mashed potatoes, she didn't let on. She hooted when Frank described the gooey mess Nathan made from the turkey drippings.

"Come on, then," Frank directed, using the carving knife in his hand to point his wife and Nathan, carrying the turkey on a hefty white platter, toward the dining room table. "Let's eat before everything gets cold."

Frank stood at the end of the table, Virginia seated to his left and Nathan to his right. He asked Nathan to light the tall white tapers flanking the fresh flowers, and Virginia filled their wine goblets while Frank carved into the bird. His knife easily sliced through the golden skin. Frank took his seat, offered up a quick prayer of thanks, then picked up his fork. By now, Nathan was famished, and he began heaping his plate high with the many mouthwatering dishes. He ate a forkful of stuffing, sighing in delight at the familiar taste.

"Oh child, it's delightful to see you tear into this meal. Frank worked so hard. It's fun to see someone enjoy it."

Nathan stopped, embarrassed when he noticed his hosts had filled only their salad plates. Uncomfortable at his social faux pas, he set his fork down and took a nervous sip from his wine glass. Frank laughed, took one bite of his lettuce salad, then set the small plate off to the side and motioned to the large bowl of potatoes at Virginia's elbow.

"Enough of this rabbit food," he joked. He plopped a generous mound onto his plate and exchanged his small fork for his largest one. "What do you think of the stuffing, Nathan?"

Nathan relaxed. "It's amazing. It reminds me of my aunt's."

Virginia grinned. "I bet it's the same recipe. You know, when I was a little girl, I used to *hate* stuffing." One glance at the scoop Virginia added to her plate as she spoke told Nathan she didn't hate it anymore. "I love it now," she said, the candlelight twinkling in her eyes. "Nathan, you remember me telling you I lived with your great-aunt when I wasn't quite as old as you, don't you?"

"Sure," he replied just before shoveling in another forkful of the tasty brown stuffing.

"Back then, I never went home for any holidays. Celia always invited us to her family dinners, but I never wanted to intrude. She'd have a houseful, I told myself, and she didn't need two more at the table. But Celia always insisted on sharing the leftovers. Back then, I didn't have much money for food, and I'd never have dreamt of throwing away anything she gave me. So I ate the leftover stuffing and fell in love with it. It was one of many recipes I asked her to share with me. It's *still* my favorite."

"No wonder this tastes like home," Nathan said, accepting the bowl Virginia passed back to him and helping himself to seconds. "Mom and Val probably use Celia's recipe, too."

"I'm sure they do, dear," Virginia agreed, cutting a dainty piece of white turkey breast with her knife and fork.

The conversation continued to flow as they enjoyed their Thanksgiving meal together. Frank and Virginia finished well before Nathan but insisted the boy take another helping of nearly everything. They kept him talking, too, asking him about holiday celebrations from his childhood. Eventually, he pushed his chair back a few inches from the table and set his napkin to the side.

"That was amazing, but I can't eat another bite. I hope you know how much I appreciate you two inviting me over. I would have had to settle for a turkey pot pie today if not for your invite. You're probably getting sick of me, between the bookstore and now inviting me into your home."

"Think nothing of it, Nathan, dear. But Frank does have one last surprise up his sleeve for you today," Virginia announced, pulling a dainty teacup closer. "Of course, if you're too *full* . . ."

Frank joined in on his wife's ribbing. "Guess I'll give it to old Bert when I take him his plate. What he can't eat, he can feed to his squirrels. Ginny and I can't possibly eat all of it."

Nathan grinned at their blatant teasing. "All right, I'll bite. What are you two up to?"

Frank glanced at the teacup his wife was tapping and stood. "I'll go get the coffee."

Virginia watched her husband leave the room then smiled back at Nathan. "Frank and I feel bad we kept you from your family today."

Nathan started to interrupt but stopped at Virginia's expression.

"We *do* feel bad. It's never fun to be away from family for big holidays. You're missing yours because you committed to helping us save the bookstore. I thought the least I could do was call your mother to find out about your favorites. Even though dinner with us is a pale substitute for dinner with your loved ones, we wanted it to be nice."

"Is that why you had so much stuffing?" Nathan asked, laughing.

"We may have thrown in an extra bag of dried bread crumbs, yes. But she also warned us that it wouldn't feel like Thanksgiving for you if you didn't have a piece of pumpkin pie."

Frank returned, a silver coffee pot in one hand and an extra-large piece of pie on a dessert plate in the other. He set the plate in front of Nathan with a flourish, filled his wife's cup with coffee, set the pot down in a space between half-filled serving dishes, and again left the room, returning again a minute later with two more plates, the slices on these much smaller than Nathan's generous helping.

"How did you know not to put whipped cream on mine?" Nathan asked, eyeing the dollops of white cream on the two smaller slices. Before they could respond, he nodded. "Wait. Mom told you, of course."

Nathan figured the small fork laid diagonally above his plate was the dessert fork. He grasped it readily. He could never be too full for pumpkin pie. He took a greedy bite, savored it for a moment, then motioned to the two of them with his fork. "I've been doing most of the talking tonight. Why don't you guys tell me more about how you two met?"

Frank shook his head as he took a careful sip of his steaming coffee. "Oh, we don't want to bore you with the story of us two old fuddy-duddies."

"I beg your pardon!" Virginia cried, clinking her delicate china cup down onto its saucer. Nathan watched in amusement. "First of all, never *ever* lump me in with whomever you are calling an old 'fuddy-duddy.' And second of all"—she turned back to Nathan—"ours is a timeless love story for the ages."

Frank stared at his wife in surprise, then burst into laughter. "My dear Ginny, forever the dramatic one!" Frank dabbed at his eyes with a linen napkin as he continued to laugh.

Nathan glanced Virginia's way. The woman was staring pointedly at her husband.

Frank made a visible effort to rein in his amusement. "My apologies, dear. I will refrain from calling you a fuddy-duddy in the future. Why don't *you* share our story with Nathan, then? You have a better memory for details."

Virginia pursed her lips at her husband. Nathan suspected she was trying to decide whether or not to let him off the hook. He watched a look pass between the two and was perceptive enough to see it for what it was—the gift of grace, earned through a near lifetime of loving each other despite the odds.

"Forgive me if I've told you some of this before," Virginia said, turning her attention back to Nathan. "But I hate to leave out any of the good parts."

From the corner of his eye, Nathan saw Frank's shoulders twitch, but the man kept his enjoyment over his wife's storytelling theatrics quiet.

"I had my fair share of mishaps and made some poor decisions at an early age," Virginia began, reaching over to fill Nathan's coffee cup and then filling her husband's and her own.

Nathan took it as a sign to take his time and enjoy his pie.

"Truth be told, I might have made a greater number of poor decisions than most young ladies back in those days. Most girls did as their mothers asked. *I* did the opposite. Eventually, I'd come to realize many of my mistakes were born of a rebellious nature, spurred on by my mother's disdain."

Nathan might have laughed at the number of words it took Virginia to come out and say she'd screwed up to spite her jerk of a mother . . . if he wasn't able to relate through the pain he'd also endured because of how his father treated him.

"Mother wanted me to focus on finding a wealthy husband who would take care of me and mine instead of pursuing my passion for creating art and writing poetry. If he was well-to-do, Mother didn't care if he was as boring as a log or as homely as the back end of a donkey."

"Would your mother have lumped me into either of those two categories, dear?" Frank asked, still making an obvious effort not to laugh at his wife's embellishments.

Virginia paused, glancing at her husband. "No, Frank. You know she had reservations about you from the start, since you didn't hit her *well-to-do* threshold in the first place."

"Ouch," Nathan said with a laugh, but then nodded his understanding to encourage Virginia to continue. He took another bite of his pie—despite his now achingly full stomach.

"You can guess what happened next. I fell madly and passionately in love with a flamboyant artist. When Mother refused to even have him over for dinner, I packed my bags and stole out in the dead of night, knowing she'd be devastated to be disobeyed by yet another daughter."

Nathan glanced at Frank to gauge his reaction. He'd heard enough of their story before tonight to know Frank wasn't the passionate artist Virginia mentioned. Frank seemed unfazed, although less jovial now, sipping his coffee and listening to his wife. Nathan doubted he'd forgotten any of the details, despite his earlier claim.

"Did she come after you?" Nathan asked, imagining how his parents would have reacted to something like that; it would have been ten times worse for Virginia, back when women didn't have as much say in how they lived their lives.

"She couldn't be bothered," Virginia answered, resignation reflected in her expression. "Mother was hard, difficult, but not stupid. She knew I'd never change my ways until I learned some hard lessons. And Nathan, my boy, did I ever. I married the man. I've never been quite sure how I convinced him to marry me. He didn't believe in any structured institutions, be it the law, organized religion, or marriage. He did love me in his own way. But he suffered. At the time, I thought it was all the drugs . . . but looking back now, I suspect he was mentally ill. Maybe if I'd have known, I could have gotten him help. But it was all I could do to survive and keep our newborn daughter alive. The partying got so bad, I had to leave with my baby. My sister took me in. He fell into such a deep depression after we left him. He never recovered. In the end, he overdosed. No one called it a suicide, but I've always suspected it wasn't an accident."

Virginia had fallen into a near trance-like state as she spoke, reciting the painful events of her past, seeming to travel back to that time. The chiming of a grandfather clock somewhere pulled her back to the dining room table. She shook her head as if to dispel the painful memories.

"Pardon me for such a depressing talk, but to understand the joy Frank brought to my life, I felt it was important for you to know more of my background. However, before Frank saved me—saved us—your dear aunt Celia stepped in."

Virginia went on to remind Nathan how Celia, a childhood friend of Virginia's mother, took the young widow and her baby in after her estranged husband's funeral. The sister didn't have the means to support Virginia long-term, so Celia gave Virginia free housing and helped with food until she could get on her feet. She even helped her land a coveted job at the local library.

"While I'd always enjoyed reading, and played around with my poems, my work at the library was where I truly came to develop my second love . . . books."

"And that's when she started chasing me," Frank added.

"You were quite the catch back then, dear," Virginia said, a teasing tone creeping into her words, one Nathan had noticed her use before when addressing her husband. "I, on the other hand, came with a lot of baggage. As you can imagine, it took a Herculean effort on my part to get this handsome and studious creative-writing teacher even to notice me, a frumpy, husbandless librarian."

Frank stood up, shaking his head. "Trust me, dear, Nathan knows you well enough by now that he'd never accuse you of being *frumpy*."

Virginia smiled up at her husband, appreciative of his compliment.

"I suppose 'frumpy' might not be exactly the right word. But we were as different as night and day, my Frank and I. It took over a year of helping him with the classes he offered at the library before he even realized I was single. And another year before he asked me out. We were friends first."

"I was a bit hard-headed back in the day," Frank acknowledged, picking up the bowl of mashed potatoes and basket of rolls.

Nathan moved to stand as well. He didn't want Frank to feel he had to clear the table himself.

"Sit down, Nathan. We can help Frank in a minute. First, he needs to take a plate over to Bert next door. He'll be waiting for Frank and his dinner. It's something Frank started years ago when we first moved in. Pity for a lonely old bachelor. Something I saved Frank from becoming through my tenacity."

"That you did, dear, and I'm eternally grateful," Frank agreed as he left the room, only a shadow of sarcasm in his tone.

Nathan could hear Frank rattling around in the kitchen. "Are you sure he doesn't need my help?"

"I'm sure. We can finish our coffee, and then the three of us can get this mess cleaned up, lickety-split. Now, where was I?"

Nathan felt awkward picking the story back up without Frank, but he said, "Explaining how you won Frank over."

"Ah, yes," Virginia said, grinning at her memories. She went on to explain how Celia would watch her daughter, Karen, so she could go out on dates with Frank. Eventually, she introduced Frank to Karen, and the little girl quickly had Frank wrapped around her little finger.

A door closed.

"Finally!" Virginia said, raising her hands toward the ceiling. "I've been *dying* to talk to you about my manuscript!"

Nathan loved this woman's style. She knew exactly how to handle her husband and what to expect out of him. He supposed years of a loving marriage allowed for that type of thing, although he'd never witnessed synchronization like that with *his* parents. Or love.

He voiced a concern he'd been nursing. "Virginia . . . you aren't having second thoughts about turning your manuscript into a book for Frank, are you?"

Virginia set both her elbows on the table—something her deep-seated manners probably rebelled against—and cupped her chin, leaning forward toward Nathan. "Of course not! Now that I've had a chance to read through it, I'm more excited than ever. There is quite a bit of rubbish in there, and I have work to do before I can turn it over to a real editor to help me, but I'm up for it if you are."

Nathan grinned. "I am *totally* up for it. I'll call my friend Grace tonight and see if her dad might know an editor. I have another idea, too, someone at school who might help, but I'm not sure yet. If you're willing to keep working on the manuscript, I'll keep trying to figure out the other pieces."

Virginia rubbed her palms together with the glee of a child. "Won't Frank be surprised?"

"He'll probably be shocked," Nathan agreed. "The fact you started this so long ago makes it even more special. But you didn't finish your original story. How did you finally get Frank to the altar? Once he developed a relationship with Karen, did things move faster?"

Virginia sat back in her chair, her expression curious. "That's *exactly* what happened, in fact. Did Frank tell you that?"

"No, not in so many words. But we did talk a bit more about Karen while you were back in your room, *resting*." He paused, struggling with how best to articulate his observations of Frank. He could see the surprise steal across Virginia's face. "Don't worry. We needed to talk about it. Based on what he said, I can sense how deeply this mess with Karen has affected him. I don't think he'd be so disappointed in her if he didn't care about her in the first place."

Virginia sighed. "In the early days of our relationship, I worried about how Frank would feel about Karen. As it turned out, I think it was Karen who spurred Frank on to take the next step and marry me so we could become a real family. Celia hosted a small garden wedding for us in her backyard. Not long after, Frank and I bought this house, and this is where we raised Karen. Together."

"Did Frank get along with your mother?"

"Yes . . . as well as anyone could, given Mother was such a difficult woman. Frank can be much more diplomatic than me, and he thought I needed to have at least *some* communication with her through the years. Frank lost his parents when he was a young adult, you see, and he wanted more for me. For us."

"Did he encourage you to let your mother and Karen spend time together?" Nathan asked, thinking it would have been a logical next step if Frank had wanted Virginia to repair her relationship with her mother.

A door opened, signaling Frank's return from delivering food to their neighbor.

Virginia stood and set her linen napkin on her plate, signaling the official end of their holiday meal. "You are an astute young man, Nathan. I suspect you've also come to the conclusion that Frank regrets that particular decision, given how things turned out. But I've never blamed him. He's always had our best interests at heart. Now, enough reminiscing. I can hear Frank loading the dishwasher. Let's go give him a hand."

CHAPTER 9

Gift of Impromptu Invitations

*G*race picked up on the second ring. "Hey there," she said, panting slightly. "Happy Thanksgiving, Nathan!"

"Hi, Grace. Happy Thanksgiving," he repeated as he backed out of the Fisks' driveway into the quiet, dark street. It was only five o'clock, but the sun had already set. He tossed his phone on the seat next to him while keeping an eye on the dashboard. He liked the backup camera and Bluetooth features of his dad's car. It'd be hard to go back to his 1997 pickup truck. Maybe he wouldn't have to. It wasn't like Will needed his wheels again anytime soon. "You sound out of breath. Did I interrupt something?"

"No, I just lugged my stuff up to my apartment. Those stairs are tough with a big load."

Nathan navigated the corner, droplets sprinkling his windshield as it started to rain. He glanced at the outside temperature on his dash—thirty-one degrees.

"I thought you were spending the holiday with your dad?"

"I did. We had fun over at my cousins', but I needed the weekend to study and finish a big project. Who sets a due date for a group project for the Monday after Thanksgiving? I don't even have *class* Monday, but we still have to submit it online. How are *your* classes going? Are your finals going to be tough?"

Nathan grimaced, feeling what was becoming a familiar surge of guilt. He hadn't put much effort into his classes since he'd started at the bookstore. He admitted as much to Grace.

"I guess I can understand that," she replied. "You're passionate about helping them get the bookstore business up. But don't tank your grades."

"I know. I've worked pretty hard up until now. I'll be careful. And you probably want to get going on your homework now, so I won't keep you."

He turned onto Main Street. The Fisks didn't live far from their store. He noticed each streetlamp now bore either a gold star or a red-and-white candy cane, their bright Christmas bulb lights reflecting off the now-wet pavement. The town was ready for the next holiday before this one was even over.

"But I wanted to let you know Virginia's excited about her manuscript, now that she's had a chance to reread it. She even snuck off for a pretend nap while Frank and I were putting the final touches on dinner today so she could work on it. Frank is clueless. She still intends to keep this a surprise for him."

"Aww, that is so sweet."

Nathan parked at the far end of their block, careful to leave all the spots in front of the store for what he hoped would be a busy Black Friday morning. He was thankful there were no time restrictions on the street parking, or he'd have to park two blocks down at the only city lot and lug his leftovers through the drizzle.

"They make a pretty cool couple," Nathan agreed. "In a way, they remind me of my grandma and grandpa, but not my folks."

He could hear Grace sigh through the phone. She'd met his parents. Even his dad, but only briefly, that first summer out at Whispering Pines. It was then he realized he'd never been told the story behind why it was just Grace and her dad. He wondered what had happened to her mom.

"Will the bookstore be busy tomorrow?"

It wasn't the right time to ask about her folks. "We can only hope. I need to make some tweaks to our Christmas display in the front window tonight and get some other things ready. It might be a late night . . . and an early morning. But honestly, we made a bigger marketing push for Saturday."

"Why not advertise for Black Friday?" Grace asked.

"Black Friday is tough. Frank said very few people get downtown that day, at least early on. But the day after is Small Business Saturday. Everyone downtown does something unique to try to draw people away from the big box stores."

"Sure, I've heard of that," she replied. "Pick your battles, right?"

"Right. Are your roommates home?"

"Nope. Just me this weekend. They're hanging out with family. But you knew Julie was gone, at least. Even though you couldn't go home, don't you guys usually all get together?"

He tapped his fingers on his steering wheel and eyed the brightly lit banner strung across Main. He'd watched them hang it earlier in the week, but it hadn't been lit up until tonight. Must be on a timer. Something about the holiday lights and Grace's comment made him feel homesick for the noise and laughter he knew he was missing out on.

"Yeah . . . usually."

"Oh, Nathan, I'm sorry. I shouldn't have reminded you."

He reached for his phone, got out, and opened the door to the backseat, threading his fingers through the plastic bags that held what would likely be the sum of his meals for the next few days. He missed his family, but it had been a fun day. And now there was work to be done.

"Don't apologize. I had fun today with the Fisks. Hopefully this weekend will be the beginning of a busy holiday season for the bookstore. It'll be fun to see all the people."

Nathan slammed his car door and walked back to the dark storefront. Icy rain pelted him in the face. He had so many more questions for Grace about getting started on this project for Virginia, but he needed to get inside.

"Hey, I have to get going, Grace, but can I call you later this weekend? I wanted to start planning the next steps for Ginny's book, but I only just realized how much work I have tonight."

"Ginny?"

Nathan laughed. "Sorry—Virginia. Frank calls her Ginny all the time, and I guess I'm starting to see her like that, too. She was as excited as a little kid tonight when she brought up her manuscript."

"I love it," Grace replied. "Sure, call me later. I brought it up with Dad earlier today, but there were so many people around, we didn't get into any details. I'll get some advice from him soon, though, so I'll know more by the time you call back."

Nathan carefully set some of his bags of leftovers down on the wet pavement, inserted his key in the fancy lock of the heavy front door to the bookstore, and clicked it open. "That's great. Find out if he knows any good editors we could get on short notice, would you?"

"Sure. Good luck tomorrow!"

The tiny bell clanged above his head as he pushed into the hushed, dark interior. He loved the smell of this place, a unique combination of the vast shelves of books mixed in with a slight musty smell most old buildings sport, plus three large bowls of pine-scented potpourri Virginia had set out around the store to "freshen things up" in anticipation of holiday shoppers. He didn't need to turn on the lights to find his way back to the stairs leading up to his apartment; there was enough light through the large, plate-glass window in the front to show him the way.

As he walked by one of the bowls, the heavy smell of pine took him back to Whispering Pines, the resort his aunt Renee now owned and where his family now gathered for many of their events.

He missed them.

***

Nathan groaned at the incessant chirping of his alarm. It felt like he'd barely slept. It'd been after midnight by the time he'd laid down. He'd gotten things ready downstairs, but then Grace's comments about his classes shamed him into doing some homework before turning in.

He reached over and fumbled with the switch on the lamp next to his bed. *Click.* Nothing. The bulb must be burned out. He lay there in the dark, the only sound the now-familiar creaking of the old building, and he flipped through the upcoming day's activities in his mind. Frank had warned him it might be quiet for the early-morning hours—most shoppers hit places like Walmart and Target first thing, wanting to snatch up the early-morning Black Friday specials—but that it might pick up closer to noon. When Nathan had suggested opening earlier than usual, Frank had laughed. "Not worth it, kid."

Nathan got out of bed, throwing his comforter up over the rumpled sheets. Good enough. He glanced out his window overlooking the street, but all was quiet. Frank was right. Downtown looked deserted, but Nathan suspected things were hopping around town by seven in the morning on Black Friday.

He padded over to his small fridge, carefully so he wouldn't stub a toe on something, thinking a piece of pumpkin pie would be as good as anything for breakfast. He pulled the door open, surprised the interior was dark.

Ugh.

Was the power out instead of one burned-out bulb?

Back to the window he went. Now he noticed the streetlamps weren't on in the early-morning dawn. The problem looked to be widespread based on the darkness outside.

He sent Frank a text and got an immediate response.

Yep. Dark over here, too. We won't open until the lights are back on.

Nathan sighed. This wasn't how he'd pictured the start of their holiday season.

***

Last night's drizzle had turned to ice at some point after Nathan went to sleep. Local news on his phone app reported a few power lines down and slick roads, but they thought they'd have electricity back on by eleven.

His stomach grumbled as he worked on his laptop in the gloom downstairs, ready to open the doors and get this party started the moment the lights clicked back on. He hadn't dared open his fridge again to take out a piece of the pie; with the power off, he didn't want the food inside to spoil. What he wouldn't give for a big cup of strong black coffee and a doughnut right now.

This weekend they were doing what Frank and Virginia always did to kick off the holiday shopping season, but next weekend . . . next weekend, they would hold one of the events Nathan and Grace dreamed up. He checked his planning notes and continued to refine things, hoping it would be as fun as he imagined. He'd noticed some interest when he'd posted about their plans to social media over the past couple of weeks.

The front door rattled. Nathan glanced up to see Frank balancing an armful of goodies as he struggled to unlock it. He jumped off his stool and rushed to help. Frank held a drink carrier in one hand and a large, orange box in the other.

"I smell coffee, and that box looks suspiciously like doughnuts. Did you read my mind?"

Frank laughed. "After all our decadent eating yesterday, I figured you might be hungry. Funny how stuffing ourselves never seems to hold over until the following day."

"Where did you find this?" Nathan asked, taking the box from Frank.

"Power is only still out downtown," Frank reported, setting the coffee on the counter and pulling off his gloves. "I drove over to the bakery out by Walmart. Don't tell Virginia. She hates it when I buy from anyone other than Mabel. But I didn't see that I had a choice today. What a mess it is out that way. The roads are still slick, and there are fender-benders left and right in the chaos."

Just as Nathan took one of the cups, the lights flickered and then glowed. A humming announced various systems turning on. Hopefully that would include the heat. It had cooled off to sixty-three degrees inside, and Nathan had been contemplating putting on his gloves when Frank arrived.

"And we're back in business!" Frank said, clapping his hands together.

That one simple motion reminded Nathan of Virginia the night before, clapping in excitement over her book. He wondered if he'd ever find a girl and be with her long enough that they'd pick up on each other's mannerisms. At this point, it wasn't looking good.

***

Once the glaze on the streets and sidewalks melted off, foot traffic picked up downtown. Nathan was proud of their festive window display and enjoyed watching people stop to take it in, pointing at the toy train as it made its rounds through a forest of books.

Earlier, when he'd first suggested the focal point of the window be an elaborately decorated Christmas tree, Virginia loved the idea and insisted she had the perfect box of vintage ornaments they could use. She claimed she'd rediscovered the box when cleaning out her mother's home. Her only concern was putting them on anything but the freshest of real trees.

Frank flat-out refused even to consider bringing a real pine tree into their historic building. "Virginia, dear, think about it. To be effective, you'll need to leave the lights glowing on it all day long. Between that and the warm air constantly blowing out of these vents to counteract these leaky windows, the thing will be dry as a tinderbox by the middle of December," Frank argued, pointing to the fancy black-iron scrollwork masking two large heating vents that stretched from the bottom of the window trim to the floor.

"We'd probably want to leave the tree lit up all night, too," Nathan added, but when Virginia spun on him, hands on her hips and lack of appreciation for his comment evident on her face, he bowed his head and busied himself with a table display.

Let Frank and Virginia battle it out themselves, he thought.

"But Frank, Mother would roll over in her grave if she knew I was placing her precious handmade German glass baubles on a tree made of metal and plastic."

Frank made a scoffing sound, his stance now a mirror image of hers. "Ginny, you didn't care what your mother thought of anything you did when she was alive. You don't expect me to believe you care what she thinks now that she's *dead,* do you?"

Nathan watched the older couple out of the corner of his eye, wondering if he was about to witness his first big blowup between the Fisks. He figured they must fight at home sometimes, because who doesn't, but he'd never personally witnessed more than a little squabble between them.

Virginia relaxed her stance, appearing to consider their options. "We could change out the tree halfway through the month, so it stays fresh."

"It's not going to happen, dear. We can't risk the fire hazard. What if the thing went up in flames while Nathan here was sleeping upstairs?"

A look of horror passed over Virginia's features. Nathan shivered.

"All right. You win, honey," Virginia caved. "But if I can't have a real tree, can I at least have pink lights? I hear you can order them online in LEDs, so they stay cool. And for heaven's sake, let's spend a little extra to get a *decent*-looking artificial tree. The one we've used in recent years looks cheap, and it's too small."

"I hate pink."

"Yes, dear, I know it isn't your favorite color, but you must let me win a point or two in this little debate of ours. Otherwise, what would be the fun in arguing?"

Frank shook his head and made a dismissive gesture with his hands. "Fine. Order your pink lights. Better here than on the tree at home next to my television set."

Nathan watched Frank walk back to his desk in the corner of the store, apparently leaving the rest of the planning for the most important window display of the year to the two of them. He couldn't help but wonder if Virginia had an issue with an artificial tree or if it was all a ploy to get her pink lights.

The woman knows how to get what she wants.

The hoot of a train whistle pulled Nathan back to today. He smiled as a little girl stood outside, pointing at the miniature train as it wound its way around the base of the Christmas tree.

To satisfy his wife, Frank had splurged on an attractive, five-foot-tall, *life-like* tree. Nathan had constructed a broad base for their display by pushing two tables together. He loved how it had all turned out—like something straight out of an old movie.

The tree, covered from top to bottom with Ginny's mother's priceless ornaments and dripping with carefully applied silver tinsel, twinkled in the glow of pink and white Christmas lights. A crowning silver star reached the upper edge of the grand window. Around the base of the tree, nestled in mounds of white linen meant to mimic snow, was a carefully choreographed mess of wrapped and partially unwrapped gifts, bright wrapping paper providing bursts of jeweled colors. Throwback toys—tubes of Lincoln Logs, an Etch A Sketch, a beautiful baby doll, and more—all poked out of the boxes. And, of course, there were books—plenty of gorgeous, hardcovered versions of recognizable classics, meant as a reminder that books make the perfect gift.

The train had been Karen's when she was growing up. While it brought a tear to Virginia's eye when Nathan first turned it on and it made its virgin trip around the piles of gifts, she'd insisted that every proper holiday window display required a toy train.

The little girl outside must have agreed with Virginia's assessment. She tugged at the hand of the older woman standing behind her, pulling her into the store.

Mission accomplished.

***

Business was steady throughout the afternoon and evening on Friday, even if it fell short of stellar. Frank said he felt like it was similar to years past, which bothered Nathan. The point was to increase business, not merely *maintain*.

Virginia came and went throughout the afternoon, doing downtown Christmas shopping of her own.

"You realize you are spending every penny that we are earning here today, don't you, dear?"

"Frank, what do you expect me to do? You know I can't resist the lure of all the delightful little shops around here. It's important to support the downtown district and all of our small, local businesses. We don't want any more buildings sitting empty around here like the one next door. That's been an eyesore for years. Besides, I won't have time to shop tomorrow—I'll be working here all day."

"You don't have to keep all the other businesses open single-handedly," Frank teased.

Frank had gone home for a nap midday, suffering from a headache, but he was back now and insisted he was feeling better. Nathan had enjoyed helping shoppers pick out gifts, and was even seeing some slight improvement in his gift-wrapping skills. Frank and Virginia insisted they offer free wrapping to their customers; they always had and they always would.

"It's the little things, Nathan," she'd told him when he'd asked if it was necessary.

And he had to admit—customers did seem to appreciate the extra effort.

By the time they flipped the sign on the door from OPEN to CLOSED, Nathan's feet throbbed, the papercut on his thumb stung, and he was starving.

"You did good today, kid," Frank acknowledged, clapping Nathan on the shoulder in a fatherly-like gesture. "And I appreciate you giving Ginny time to get some shopping done—and me resting to get rid of that blasted headache. Now, get some rest of your own and enjoy some of those leftovers. Maybe even have a beer. You deserve it."

"Sounds good, Frank. I could use another piece of that pie."

"Rest up, kid. Tomorrow is another day. And it'll be a busy one."

I hope so.

***

A decent meal and sound sleep revived Nathan. He was back downstairs by eight the next morning, restocking shelves and getting the coffee going. Frank had told him today was a particularly special day to Virginia. Every year, she treated the Saturday after Thanksgiving as "Customer-Appreciation Day." She had a go-to menu that always included decadent pastries in the morning from Mabel's bakery, delicate finger sandwiches throughout midafternoon, and hearty chili later in the day.

"We don't necessarily make a ton of sales, but Virginia sees it as her chance to give back to our many faithful customers for buying their books from us for years."

Nathan *did* understand the wisdom in giving back to customers; he was just worried that it might not be a practical approach in bringing in *new* patrons. They'd get through this weekend, though, and he'd keep pushing to make next weekend's event as successful as possible at bringing in the new.

He'd just finished helping a man pick out two current bestsellers as gifts for his daughters when the bell over the front door jingled. He thanked the man for his business and, glancing toward the front of the store, was surprised to see Seth standing there.

"Hey, Seth! What brings you around? I thought Mom said you were spending the day out at Whispering Pines with her and everybody else?"

Seth strode toward Nathan, meeting him halfway with a warm handshake and slightly awkward hug, glancing around the store at the same time.

"You all by yourself?"

The sound of a door shutting and Frank's voice provided the answer: "No, Frank's here, too." The older man made his way over to stand next to Nathan. "Great to see you again, Seth. I wondered what time you'd pull in."

Nathan looked between the two in confusion. "You knew he was coming?"

"Sure did. Seth's here to pick you up."

"Pick me up?"

Frank nodded, crossing his arms in front of him—something he often did when he was serious about something. "That's right. Virginia and I appreciate all of your help over these past few weeks, and especially yesterday, handling most everything here yourself from morning to night. We felt bad that you couldn't enjoy Thanksgiving with your own family. So back when Ginny talked to your mom to find out a couple of your favorite foods, and Jess mentioned the family get-together today out at that resort of yours, we knew we wanted you to be able to go enjoy yourself."

"But that's ridiculous, Frank. Today will probably be busier than yesterday. I can't just leave. We have a full day planned."

Frank shook his head. "You *can* 'just leave.' Don't forget—I'm still your boss. If I say you go, you go. Besides, I'd like to take tomorrow off and watch a little football. I know we have to be open on Sundays now through Christmas, but we don't all three have to be here for that. It'll be a trade-off. We'll work the store today, and you hold down the fort tomorrow to give Ginny and me a day off. How's that sound?"

Nathan again glanced between Seth and Frank, conflicted.

"I just talked to your mom," Seth reported. "Val's already baking, and I guess they need some taste-testers. Besides, Lizzy will be there, and she wasn't happy when you missed Thanksgiving. She says she hasn't seen you in months."

Nathan was the oldest of the grandchildren; Lizzy, another cousin, was the second oldest. He flashed back to his conversation with his mom the morning after the Halloween party out at Whispering Pines. She'd been worried about Lizzy. Nathan had promised to check in on her, but he'd forgotten. It *would* be good to talk to her.

Frank turned away with a wave. "Go. Have fun with your family today. We managed by ourselves for decades before you came along. We can manage one more day."

Suddenly the prospects of Val's baking and spending time with his family sounded like a great idea. It would be fun to catch up with Lizzy. Maybe he could even get some advice from her where Grace was concerned.

He smiled. *Whispering Pines . . .*

It would be good to be back.

CHAPTER 10

Gift of Joyful Preparation

*A*s Seth backed his loud diesel pickup out of a parking spot in front of the bookstore, Nathan asked him the question that had been weighing on his mind.

"How do you think Mom's holding up?"

"I think she's found her groove," Seth replied. "She misses you and your sister, but Harper keeps her busy."

Nathan sighed. "I need to catch up with Lauren. See how she's weathering those freshman classes. I remember feeling overwhelmed at first by the sheer size of some of those auditoriums where they hold the lower-level classes. It's always a culture shock, coming from classes of thirty kids where the teachers all know you. In college, you're just a number. It gets better the last couple of years, but it takes a while."

Some of the comments Lauren had made at the Halloween party concerned Nathan. She'd only stayed for an hour and then headed back to the duplex early, saying she already felt behind with her course work.

I should have called both Lizzy and Lauren.

He'd let his new job, new apartment, and his relationship with the Fisks consume him. This unexpected trip out to Whispering Pines would give him the chance to check on both his cousin and his sister.

"Yeah, college was a struggle for me," Seth said, nodding. "I barely made it through. Let's hope Lauren handles it better than I did."

"How does she seem to you?"

"Lauren? Tell you what, Nathan, why don't you judge for yourself? Remember, I've been an old bachelor all my life. Judging the mental state of women isn't my forte."

Nathan looped his hand through the handle above his passenger-side window to steady himself as Seth's three-quarter-ton truck banged over an occasional pothole in the streets. The pickup could haul heavy loads, but it didn't offer a comfortable ride.

"I'd hardly call you old, Seth. Are you even forty yet?"

Seth's grin answered the question before he even spoke. "Not quite—but don't remind your mother of that. It still bugs her that she's got a few years on me."

"But you have a daughter, too. Doesn't that give you some clue as to what makes girls tick?"

"Not even a little. Kaylee's a teenager now. I can't pretend to understand what's going on in that head of hers anymore. When she was three, maybe, but not these days."

Nathan sighed. Women were a mystery.

They rode in silence for a bit, country music playing on the radio, and Nathan considered Seth's words. While the idea that his mother was dating still felt weird, she smiled more now than she had in years. A big part of that was thanks to Seth.

"I know Mom jokes that your age bugs her, but she seems happier with you around. Thanks for that."

Seth didn't reply immediately. He merged onto the interstate in the direction of their family resort.

"Your mom's great, Nathan."

"She is. She's always been great. But Dad put her through hell. She deserves so much better. Just . . . don't screw this up, okay?"

Seth took his eyes off the road for a second, meeting Nathan's.

"You can trust me to take good care of your mom, Nathan."

Nathan nodded, then turned his attention to the scenery rushing by, chewing on Seth's response. Trusting anyone where his mom was concerned wasn't easy. But Seth seemed like the real deal. His mother probably didn't think she needed to be *taken care of,* but he appreciated Seth's comment. And spending time with the Fisks was showing him that sometimes romance can survive the trials life inevitably provides. He'd take Seth at his word, and hoped his mom had made a better choice this time around.

"So enough of this relationship talk," Seth said, filling the awkward silence inside the cab that the music wasn't minimizing. "What did you think of that Viking's game?"

*****

Nathan couldn't help but grin when the old wooden sign for Whispering Pines came into view. As Seth navigated the turn off the main road onto the gravel that would take them to the resort, he glanced over and said, "What's so funny?"

"Nothing. I just always love coming here, even in the winter," Nathan replied with a shrug. "It's so cool that Celia gave the resort to Renee, and that now Mom and Harper live out here, too. It would have been fun to grow up out here."

As the heavy pickup bumped across the pitted gravel, Seth nodded in agreement. Another pickup was making the same trek right in front of them, and Seth slowed a bit. "That'd be your uncle. Jess said Lizzy was particularly anxious to see you."

Nathan could see the pickup in front of them had two people in the front and three in the backseat—probably all three of Ethan's kids. He was anxious to talk to Lizzy, too. The two oldest cousins had always been close, often tasked with keeping the younger crew in line. Lizzy was also in her senior year of college, and he hadn't had a chance to talk to her about her plans yet for after graduation. He was also anxious to see Julie. After his recent weekend visit over to her and Grace's apartment, he should probably talk to her about Grace, too. He needed to find out what the deal was with her, and he knew Grace and Julie were tight. Maybe between Lizzy and Julie, he could figure out what to do about this fascination with Grace that he couldn't seem to shake.

Both pickups pulled into the lot of the old lodge and parked next to each other. A few other vehicles were already there, including a patrol car.

"Looks like most of the gang's here," Nathan said, reaching for his door handle as the pickup's diesel motor sputtered and shut off. "Hey, Seth, thanks for the ride. Your showing up was a nice surprise, and it'll be a fun day."

Nathan jumped down to the gravel and slammed his door just as Lizzy climbed out of her dad's truck.

"Nathan!"

He grinned at her as she headed in his direction.

"I can't *believe* you weren't at Grandma and Grandpa's on Thanksgiving!"

"Hello to you, too, Lizzy. What's got you so wound up?"

His cousin stole a glance back over in the direction of her dad's pickup, where doors were slamming. Nathan followed her gaze and saw his uncle, Lizzy's two younger brothers, and the woman Ethan had brought to the Halloween party.

She turned back to him and whispered, "Dad brought a date!"

"A date?"

"Yeah, can you believe it? Pretty gutsy, huh? I didn't even know the woman existed, although it sounds like my brothers think she walks on water."

If Lizzy was just finding out about Ethan's dating, Nathan understood his cousin's reaction . . . he'd felt a mess of reactions, too, when his mom told him she was dating Seth.

He grabbed Lizzy's shoulders and looked her in the eye. "Elizabeth, it's not that big of a deal. Your folks have been divorced for a while now. It was bound to happen sooner or later."

He was surprised at the intensity of her reaction when tears flooded her eyes.

"Whoa! Look, I *promise* this isn't the end of the world." He squeezed her shoulders, trying to reassure her. Lizzy wasn't prone to tears. He remembered Seth's earlier comment about not understanding women. Normally he felt the same, but in this case he got it.

Lizzy dashed the moisture away, glancing around, probably making sure no one else noticed.

"I suppose. It just felt like an ambush this morning when we picked Brooke up on the way over. I had no idea."

Nathan looked over at the woman standing beside Ethan's truck. "Your dad brought her to Renee's Halloween party. You didn't know?"

The scathing look she shot him provided her answer. "And that's not all. Now my psycho mother tells us she's getting married. *Again*."

"Really? Okay, that might be a little tougher to take. Do you like the guy?"

Lizzy hung her head and kicked at the gravel. "Not even a little."

Nathan took his cousin's upper arm and spun her toward the front door of the lodge.

"It sounds like this is a job for Val's Christmas cookies."

***

Finishing off a cup of coffee to cut through the sugar rush from the five or six cutouts he'd eaten while "helping" Lizzy and Julie frost cookies, Nathan glanced around the busy main room at the lodge. He had to admit—it was great to see so much of his family again.

His two cousins had run back to the duplex to grab a five-pound bag of sugar Jess forgot to bring over earlier; before they left, Nathan had quietly admitted to them both that he'd been wanting to ask Grace out, but that she seemed reluctant. Lizzy had only met Grace once, so she didn't have much input, other than to agree with Julie's suggestion that he should date other girls if Grace wasn't interested.

He'd just gone back to the kitchen for another cup of coffee and was mulling over their advice when his mom walked in.

"Did you leave any to freeze?" Jess asked, coming to stand next to him, her forearms leaning on the large island. "I saw you sneak a few."

Nathan motioned toward the multiple sheets of yet-to-be-frosted cookies. "I was doing quality checks, Mom. Imagine what a waste all this would be if they weren't any good."

"What's the verdict? Will Santa approve?"

He scooped another cookie—this one frosted—off a tray set aside to allow the frosting to harden before the treats went in the freezer for safekeeping. "I don't know, Santa, you tell me."

Jess laughed in surprise as he stuck the head of a snowman cookie in her mouth. She bit it off and wagged the remaining half of the cookie at him. "Shh! Nathan! There are still young ears around."

Shrugging, he looked over his shoulder, relieved to see Val's boys—the only ones still young enough to believe—were occupied and hadn't heard him.

"It won't be long before you have to watch what you say around Harper, too."

"Sure, but she isn't even one yet. By the way, where *is* my little terror of a baby sister? I haven't seen her since Halloween."

"Upstairs with Lauren. Why don't you check in on Lauren, too, see how school is going? She might be more open with you."

Nathan nodded and grabbed up one last cookie to sample on the way up to see his two sisters. "I'd planned to do just that."

As he turned to leave, Jess stopped him. "Wait, before you go—how are things going at the bookstore? Are Frank and Virginia getting used to having you around?"

He nodded as he munched and swallowed. "You were right, Mom. They are quite the couple. It's funny to watch Frank pamper Virginia—and to watch *her* manipulate him to get pretty much anything she wants." He paused to take another sip of coffee. "But don't get me wrong—I know she's crazy about him, too."

"Ah, yes, they do go back and forth. I can't imagine how awful both Virginia and Frank must feel about their daughter Karen. She screwed up *so* badly," Jess said in a wistful tone as she brushed cookie crumbs off the island into her hand. "Scratch that. I do *kind* of know how they feel, since your father screwed up, too. Have the three of you talked about that at all?"

"We did. On Thanksgiving. It was nice to clear the air."

Jess walked over and dumped her hand over a trash can, then rubbed her palms together. "How *was* Thanksgiving, by the way? Did Frank's cooking hold a candle to Val's?"

Nathan laughed. "It was close. By the way, that reminds me. I owe Val and Grandma a thank-you. I never realized how much work it is to pull together a holiday meal like that until I helped Frank."

"I'll have you know, *I* helped some in that department, too," Jess said, but the twinkle in her eye told Nathan she knew her contribution was usually limited to setting tables and doing dishes. And bringing pumpkin pie.

"Yeah, you just keep telling yourself that, Mom."

The incessant pinging of the oven timer pulled Jess across the kitchen. She picked up mitts and slipped them over her hands, then fumbled to kill the annoying alarm with the unwieldy edge of the mitt. She pulled one tray out, its cookies golden-brown, and popped another one into the oven. Nathan could see this process would go on for hours.

"How do you feel about the foot traffic at the store?" Jess asked as she slipped a mitt off to reset the timer.

"I'd term yesterday 'steady,' at least once the ice melted outside and shoppers found their way downtown. I called Frank to check in a few minutes ago, and he reported they ran out of Virginia's finger sandwiches by 1:30, so I'd say that's a good sign. Today is her annual 'Customer-Appreciation Day.' Frank was open to most of my ideas, but he wouldn't hear of mixing things up today."

Val hustled back into the kitchen area from somewhere. "Thanks for switching those out, Jess!"

"Not a problem, sis," Jess replied, then turned back to her son. "So did you plan something for *next* weekend, then? I would think you need to hit every weekend hard at this point."

"Yeah, you guys should stop over next Saturday. We're going to have specials all day. Some giveaways—because who doesn't like free stuff?—*and* a fancy cocoa bar. It'll be free for everyone—unless they want to leave a small donation. Our only real ask is that they jot down their email address. Grace and I talked about how helpful it would be to have a mailing list."

"Wait, Grace? As in Grant's daughter, Grace?"

Nathan nodded, hoping his mother wouldn't notice anything in his expression. Why did he always get flustered when her name came up? "Yeah, Julie's been inviting me over to their apartment, and I finally went. Grace helped me brainstorm ideas we could try at the store during the holidays. She had some good ones."

"I'm not surprised. Grace wanted to help with our retreat planning in our early days of that business venture, too."

Slamming of cupboard doors interrupted. Val had a tendency to make lots of noise when she was irritated.

"Val, do you need some help?" Jess asked.

"Only if we want to be done with this baking before ten tonight," Val shot back.

Both Nathan and Jess laughed when they saw the smudge of flour across Val's forehead. She just scowled at them.

Jess turned back to her son. "Duty calls. Why don't you go check on your sisters?"

***

Nathan had to straddle a baby gate spanning the landing at the top of the stairs. Now that their baby sister was walking, he knew the gate was a necessary inconvenience.

"Hey, bro," Lauren greeted him from where she sat cross-legged on a blanket on the floor, surrounded by baby dolls and books.

"Hey, yourself," he said, scooping up Harper when she crashed into his legs. "Na, na, na," she babbled, using her chubby palms to squeeze both Nathan's cheeks. He pulled her hands down, laughing, and gave a playful pinch to Harper's baby-plump cheeks in return.

Lauren grinned. "Who can resist those cheeks?"

"Hers or mine?"

"Definitely hers."

Nathan picked up one of the dolls. "Wasn't this yours? I can't believe you kept it all these years."

"How could I possibly give her away?" Lauren asked with a pout, eyeing what Nathan knew had been her favorite doll. "I'd have given *you* up before I let her go, big bro."

Nathan handed the doll to Harper, then got down on the blanket, too.

"How's school, sis? Those freshman English and Science classes can be a bitch."

Harper toddled on unsteady legs toward the large windows overlooking a view of the partially frozen lake below. "Bi, bi, bi . . ."

"Careful. Mom will *kill* you if 'bitch' becomes her new favorite word."

Nathan leaned back on the palms of his hands and stretched his long legs out in front of him, crossed at the ankles. "I'm a little rusty around kids. I was talking Santa downstairs, and Mom reminded me of the same thing."

"Yeah, sometimes it's hard to transition from hanging with college kids to ten-and-under."

"So, spill. How's it going?"

Lauren sighed. "Pretty good, I guess. I'm not having too much trouble with my classes."

Nathan smoothed a corner of the rumpled blanket. "Always the brain."

If he expected to get a rise out of her, it didn't work. He kept quiet, seeing if she'd share more.

"Does it bother you, Nathan?"

"Does *what* bother me?"

"That whole nasty business with Dad."

Nathan pulled his legs up and wrapped his hands around his shins. "Hell yes, it bothers me."

"Me, too. Sometimes it feels like everyone else has forgotten about it. About Dad. No one talks about any of it anymore. They've been able to move on."

Nathan pondered how to respond.

"I suspect that makes it easier, especially for Mom. To move on, I mean. And no one else wants to make her feel bad, so they don't bring it up either."

Lauren nodded, and brother and sister watched their newest family addition slap her hands against the window as if she could touch a bird as it flitted past.

"I couldn't help but wonder what they fed him in prison on Thursday," Lauren admitted.

"Hopefully nothing more than he deserved," Nathan replied, unable to keep the bitterness out of his voice. He'd wondered the same thing.

Footsteps pounded up the wooden stairs. Jess, shorter than her son by eight inches, caught her foot as she tried to step over the baby gate.

"Careful, Mom."

Jess caught her balance, then stood facing the three of them with her hands on her hips.

Nathan caught the look of concern in her expression. "What's wrong?"

"We just got a call. Well, *Matt* technically got the call."

Since Matt was the county sheriff in addition to being their aunt's husband, calls he received often meant trouble.

"And?" Nathan prodded.

"There's a bad fire. We're afraid it might be at Uncle Ethan's place. He and your grandfather just took off."

Nathan pushed up off the blanket and stood. Lauren followed suit.

"At their *house?*" he asked, alarmed.

"No, no, I'm sorry. At Ethan's fourplex. The one Celia left to him."

"Oh, God, that's terrible!" Lauren said. "Is anyone hurt?"

Jess shrugged. "We don't know much yet. But I wanted you guys to know what's going on. Elizabeth and the boys are pretty upset."

"Well, yeah," Nathan said, hurrying over to pick up Harper. "Let's go downstairs."

***

It was agonizing, waiting. Matt sent word that the fire *was* at Ethan's fourplex, but he didn't give any other details. After an hour, Lizzy couldn't take it anymore and started trying Ethan's phone, but he wasn't picking up.

Finally, Nathan could tell his cousin reached someone. She walked toward the front, quieter portion of the lodge, her phone pressed to her ear. He, along with the rest of the family, waited for her to come back with a report.

When she came back, her expression looked slightly relieved. "Dad said the firemen were able to put it out. There was lots of smoke, and he could see flames when he first got there, but he doesn't know how much damage there was yet. He's more worried about the people who rent from him. Two ambulances left the scene with their lights and sirens on. Older people live there. He and Gramps are going to the hospital now to see if they can find anything out."

Nathan gave her what he hoped was a reassuring smile and watched as his mom hugged her oldest niece. "Think positive thoughts, honey. And maybe a few prayers that no one was seriously hurt."

Lizzy nodded her head, tears dragging mascara down her cheeks and onto Jess's white blouse. "Thanks, Aunt Jess. I've been trying to do that ever since Dad rushed out of here. Now I have to find Brooke. Dad asked me to update her."

She brushed impatiently at her face, glancing around for her father's date. Nathan could see she was less than thrilled with her assignment.

"Do you want me to update Brooke for you, honey?" Jess offered.

Lizzy shook her head. "Thanks, but I'll do it. I was really ticked when we first got here, and I'm still not thrilled Dad brought her, but the fire kind of puts things in perspective, you know? I guess maybe I was being a *tad* bit immature earlier."

She shot Nathan a sheepish look, and while he was tempted to tease her about her earlier temper tantrum, he decided to let it go. Now wasn't the time for jokes, and he didn't have to act juvenile either.

The next few hours were difficult as they waited for more news. Everyone pitched in to help get the baking finished up. Staying busy helped calm the nerves.

Lizzy arranged cooled cookies inside plastic containers and Nathan was supposed to then transport them to one of the two large chest freezers. While Lizzy stacked, the two cousins got a chance to visit and catch up.

Nathan had thought he got lucky with the easier job, until he realized there was very little room *left* in the freezers. He was juggling a stack of loaded containers, trying to hold the freezer door open and rearrange things to make some room, when a hand reached over him to brace the lid of the chest open.

"You look like you could use a little help."

Nathan glanced over his shoulder, nodding his thanks to Seth.

"Val would've killed me if I dropped all these," he said, now better able to make room for the additional cookies.

"What time did you want to head out?" Seth asked. "I'm sure Ethan will be back out to pick up Brooke and the kids, but it might be a while yet."

Nathan rubbed his icy hands together as he straightened, and Seth closed the lid. He thought about the homework he had waiting for him at the bookstore. "Yeah, it's getting late. Maybe we should get going."

Seth nodded and turned back toward the kitchen. "Let's go say goodbye. Your mom will keep us posted."

***

Seth and Nathan were just climbing into Seth's truck, the night cold and dark around them, when Ethan pulled into the parking lot, his tires crunching on the gravel. He pulled under the cone of light cast by the only streetlight and tapped his horn in greeting. The lodge door burst open and Nathan watched Brooke rush over to Ethan's pickup.

Nathan and Seth got back out of their vehicle, but Nathan took Seth's lead and hung back, giving Ethan a minute. The lodge door opened again, and this time Lizzy and her two younger brothers rushed out. Nathan cringed as he watched Lizzy pull up short at the sight of Brooke in her dad's arms.

"Great," Nathan murmured. He hurried to his cousin's side and put what he hoped was a comforting arm across her trembling shoulders. He bent down to whisper in her ear. "Relax, Liz, your dad is back now. Safe. Remember what you said about perspective? Don't worry about any of the other crap. You'll figure that out later."

Lizzy nodded, but her lips remained in a tight line. He hoped he'd been able to defuse a potential scene, but he could still feel the tension radiating from her body. He squeezed her shoulder and stepped away—she'd had a day full of difficult surprises, and she'd need time to come to terms with it all.

"Thanks, Nathan," Lizzy whispered back.

Finally, Ethan turned from where he'd been talking to Brooke and took a step toward his kids. Lizzy rushed into his open arms, hugging her dad. Then she held an arm out, motioning to her brothers. Both boys stepped down off the sidewalk to the gravel next to their dad's truck, and the four of them formed a tight knot. Brooke stood off to the side, looking uncomfortable.

Nathan turned back toward Seth's truck and noticed him giving Brooke a smile and slight wave. *He probably knows how she feels,* Nathan thought. *Like a bit of an outsider around this big, loud family.*

They'd all done what they could to help, but it was time to go. He felt drained from the day's unexpected twist.

***

"Thanks again for the ride, Seth," Nathan said as Seth pulled onto Main, driving slowly. "It was fun to see everybody. I still can't believe Ethan's building burned today. Keep me posted on any updates, will you?"

"Of course."

The dark street was deserted, even though it was barely nine o'clock. The downtown area was experiencing some revival with the influx of two new boutiques and the reopening of the old movie theater, but the only bar hadn't yet found a way to cater to a younger, hipper crowd. Their clientele, unfortunately, consisted mainly of career drinkers who started early and were nearly asleep on their stools by this time of night.

"I'd ask if you wanted to go grab a beer," Seth said, nodding toward the flickering neon sign advertising Grain Belt Beer, "but I've got an early morning tomorrow."

"Good, because a nightcap in that place isn't an uplifting way to top off the day."

Seth laughed. "Let me guess. The place smells like the inside of a pack of cigarettes, your shoes stick to the floor, and old peanut shells crunch when you walk."

"And you never want to order a draw because washing the glasses probably consists of nothing more than a swipe of a dishtowel."

Seth pulled to the curb in front of the bookstore. "Wow."

"What?"

"Your window display looks great."

Nathan snapped off his seatbelt. "Thanks! It did turn out pretty great.

I know a Christmas tree is cliché, but honestly, this one reminds me of the pine trees out at the resort."

"Did *you* set all that up?"

Nathan shrugged. "For the most part. Virginia helped. She has a flair for that kind of thing, and she already had those cool ornaments. She wanted a real tree, but Frank put his foot down on that one."

"Good call on Frank's part. I've seen what fire can do to old buildings like this, and given what Ethan's dealing with right now . . ." His voice trailed off as he stared at the festive display.

"If you guys hear anything more, remember to keep me posted, okay?" Nathan reminded Seth, opening his door and jumping down to the pavement.

"You got it. Maybe we'll see you next weekend. Your mom said you have a big event planned?"

"Well, in my *mind* I'm hoping for a big event. We'll see if I can pull it off."

Nathan shut the door and waved as Seth backed away from the curb and drove back down the street in the direction they'd come. The stench of diesel fuel hovered then dissipated. He fished his keys out of his jacket pocket, stopping to survey their window display.

The twinkling tree stood out in stark contrast to the darkened interior. Strands of tinsel swayed, likely nudged by heated air inside and shimmering in the glow of the pink and white bulbs encasing the Christmas tree from top to bottom. Virginia's ornaments were like nothing Nathan had ever seen. Growing up, his mom had always decorated their trees with simple, color-coordinated bulbs interspersed with homemade ornaments, compliments of Nathan and Lauren.

These ornaments were much fancier. Virginia had said some were mercury glass. Each was unique. Her father had given her mother one every year on their anniversary. Nathan had been deathly nervous he'd accidentally break one while arranging them on the tree as Virginia directed their placement, pointing him here and there, but she'd assured him not to worry. She didn't believe in keeping beautiful things tucked away, hidden from the world.

He supposed that made sense. When she'd initially said it, he'd considered challenging her on that particular point. Hadn't she hidden her beautiful story away for years? But he let it go.

His eye traveled from ornament to ornament, forgetting for a moment that he was standing on a nearly deserted street on a Saturday night. There was a nutcracker in a bluish-silver hue, standing five inches tall and looking somehow regal, as if he offered protection against an imaginary foe. A more intricate, soft-pink ballerina, stood poised on a lower branch, as if ready to pirouette across the bottom half of the tree. He also liked the bells hanging near the center; he could almost hear the clear chiming sound the cluster of three silver bells would make, if only they were real. But his favorite ornament of all was a small angel near the top, looking down at him. Incredibly thin strands of gold, woven into a mesh that sparkled in the light, made up her wings. The angel's gown was a flowing white, her hair golden like her wings. In one hand she held a tiny silver book; her other hand was raised, palm outward, as if dispensing a blessing.

The passing of a car on the street snapped Nathan out of his thoughts. He probably looked like a nutcase, standing there staring at the window like he was, all alone. Or a potential thief casing the joint. He'd better get inside. But there was no mistaking the calmness he'd felt settle over him as he stood there for a moment, appreciating the simple beauty of Virginia's ornaments.

It reminded him that the holiday season was so much more than shopping and presents. If you just slowed down and allowed the magic and the beauty to seep in . . . those were the things that made this time of year special. He'd do well to remember that when trying to best serve their customers.

What would your old roommates think of you now, standing in front of a freaking window display in the dark, contemplating the meaning of Christmas?

But he already knew the answer to his question. They'd think he was a total dork.

Or maybe that he was growing up. Besides, he had a job to do—responsibilities to the Fisks to help turn this place around. He couldn't worry about what other people thought.

He remembered Grace saying he needed to offer customers an *experience*.

After one last glance at the pretty scene he and Virginia had created, he shoved his key in the old door lock and clicked it open. His practical mind told him to get upstairs and put in a few hours of studying for his upcoming finals, but the characters hanging on the Christmas tree spurred his imagination.

Maybe Virginia wasn't the only one able to write a story.

Maybe he had a few in him, too.

CHAPTER 11

Gift of Kind Gestures

*L*ater that week, Nathan sat in his Thursday-night class staring at the paper lying on the desk in front of him. Enough blank areas on the page stared back at him to put his overall grade in Literary Theory at risk.

I shouldn't have wasted my time sketching out that silly story.

Virginia's vintage ornaments had inspired an idea that blossomed in his brain as he stood on the sidewalk in front of their window display the night of the fire. He'd tried to forget about it, but when he couldn't quiet his mind, he'd given up and started penciling it out. Instead of studying in his spare minutes, he'd messed around with a short story. Now he'd probably end up doing the same thing that Virginia had done with her old manuscript so long ago—shove it in a drawer and forget about it for who knows how long.

If he wasn't careful, his focus on the bookstore—and lack of focus on everything else he should consider important—could be the downfall of his college career.

At least Frank seemed optimistic about things at the store. He'd called Nathan to check in on Sunday. Nathan could hear football playing in the background as Frank reported on their Customer-Appreciation Day. Apparently, having ran out of food, Virginia was horrified that she'd underestimated how much food they'd need, but delighted at all the foot traffic.

Since then, Nathan had split his time between helping customers and preparing for this coming Saturday. But considering how tonight's test was going, he should have made more time for studying. He tried to concentrate. Despite so many of his classmates having already dropped their test sheets on the professor's desk and left the room, the clock on the wall said he still had nearly ten minutes.

He scribbled a half-baked answer to another question, hoping for once that he'd channeled enough of his dad's gift for bullshit to satisfy his professor.

"You're going to have to wrap it up, Mr. Rand. You've got five minutes."

A glance around the room showed him he was the last one still working on his test.

What's the use?

He couldn't do justice to the final essay question in five minutes. He stood with a heavy sigh, scooping his backpack off the floor and his test off the desk.

"Do you want to talk about it?" his teacher asked when he handed her his test.

"What do you mean?"

"Nathan, I've had you in at least four classes, and I've been your advisor for the past two years. You've never been the last one to finish any test," she said. Looking down at the paper he'd passed to her, she added, "And from the looks of this, 'finish' might be too generous of a word."

He shook his head as he shrugged on his backpack. "Guess I just wasn't feeling it tonight."

"Not feeling it. Is that the way this works? You give up if you're 'not feeling it'? That's not like you, Nathan."

Nathan suppressed another sigh; he knew Ms. Sullivan well enough to know she would never let him off the hook that easily. As his college advisor, she'd helped him out when everything fell apart with his dad and he started slipping in a few classes; but ever since he'd gotten through the worst of that, she'd been pushing him.

"I've got a new job," he offered.

She held up her hands with a questioning look on her face, as if to say *Welcome to the club.* During his advisor meeting the previous spring, she'd scoffed at him when he balked at taking eighteen credits so he could still graduate at the end of four years. She seldom shared personal tidbits about her own life, but that day she'd confided to him that after teaching all day, she'd often put another eight hours in at night, writing novels, because that was her dream. "If you want it, you have to work for it," she'd said to him more than once.

She wasn't done pushing him.

"And *I'm* trying to wrap up this rough draft so I can let my pain-in-the-ass editor work on it over the holidays," she replied sardonically, motioning to the mess of papers on the desk in front of her, "but that doesn't mean I don't have to keep up with my other responsibilities."

He nodded. "I'll be better prepared for the final."

"See that you are, Nathan. I've always thought you had real potential. Now isn't the time to let things slide. You need to be *all in.*"

Nathan grinned at her comment, appreciating both the off-handed compliment and the warning laced within it. He knew if push came to shove, she was in his corner. He took two steps backward and spun toward the door.

"Yes, ma'am."

As he walked back toward his vehicle, he mentally ran through his days between now and finals. He'd better buckle down.

And what was that his professor said about an editor?

***

Nathan was nervous. There were four weekends between now and Christmas, and he had to make them all count. Next weekend they were bringing in three different authors, and his time before then would be mainly spent getting the word out in advance.

But first, they had to get through this weekend.

When he and Grace first started brainstorming on how they could make a trip into Virginia's bookstore more of an experience, they'd come up with what they'd dubbed an "immersion shopping experience." They'd started with the premise that often the type of people who like to *give* books as gifts also enjoy *reading* books themselves. December was a busy month for everyone; what if they came up with a way for customers to relax while shopping in their store?

"I love the bookstore, but I hate shopping," Nathan had said, sitting across from Grace in that coffee shop and absently doodling in his notebook. "If I could hand someone my list and let them do all the shopping for me while I kick back and relax, I'd love it."

"So . . . do that for your customers, then," she'd said.

"Do *what*, Grace?"

"Let someone hand you a list and do their shopping for them."

Nathan set his pen down. "I just said I *hate* shopping. To be clear, that is the exact opposite of 'I want to do everyone else's shopping for them.' "

"It's just a simple mind-shift, Nathan. What is it you like about working in bookstores?"

Her question caused him to hesitate. He remembered looking away from the distraction of her pretty face, out the window, to a swirl of fall leaves dancing down the sidewalk. "It's fun to help customers find the perfect book. And I like the books themselves, of course. I love figuring out the best way to display great books so that customers see them, pick them up and read the back blurbs, and then buy them."

"Isn't that just helping them shop?"

He looked back at her. "I guess. What are you getting at, exactly?"

"Imagine this. A frazzled mother walks into your bookstore. She has her two kids with her, and they're whining because they've been shopping with her for hours already and they're bored. How could you help that mother?"

"I don't know, give the kids something to keep them busy so she could shop in peace?"

Grace took Nathan's notebook and flipped it around to face her and held out her hand for his pen. She began writing. "That's a start. But she's almost done with her Christmas shopping and is down to the last three people on her list, but they are *tough*. She never knows what to get them, and she wants to finish. She came into the bookstore because they all like to read, but she has no idea what kinds of books they like. Glancing around your store, she feels overwhelmed. One last complaint from one of her bratty kids and she's likely to turn around and go home and just give up on getting her Christmas shopping done early for once."

"Jeez, Grace, you make it sound hopeless."

Grace laughed. "Not at all. I think it's important to put yourself in your customers' shoes. Give them what they need."

From there, they'd derived the concept behind this weekend's event. Nathan just wished Grace had been able to come over for it, but she was too busy studying for finals. At least *one* of them would have decent grades this semester.

He slid his tub of extra supplies underneath the table where they'd set up their hot chocolate bar, making sure the red tablecloth hung to the floor to camouflage the storage area. He also checked to make sure the big silver coffee urn was plugged in. Today he'd filled it with cocoa he'd prepared upstairs in his kitchen using the recipe he'd gotten from his aunt, Val.

A stack of festive red paper cups and black lids stood at the ready next to white ironstone mugs. Customers would have their pick, depending on whether or not they wanted to take their cocoa with them when they left. Glass canisters lined the back of the table, filled with different flavors and shapes of marshmallows, peppermint sticks, and caramels. He had canisters of whipped cream in the fridge that he'd set out in a bowl of ice when they opened, because who didn't like a dollop on top of their cocoa? Well, *he* didn't, but he knew most people did. The jar of maraschino cherries and shaker of sprinkles would provide the perfect finishing touch.

"Here you go, Nathan. Folks can drop their freewill offerings into this," Frank said, handing Nathan a clear, rectangular plastic container with a slit in the top and a festive TIPS BRING GOOD CHEER label. The box already contained a handful of dollar bills, compliments of Frank. "Nothing like a little peer pressure to prime the pump of people's generosity."

Nathan set the box in the rear righthand corner of the table, pulled the plastic wrap off a tray of small cookies, and went to check on Virginia's progress on the sign.

Frank unlocked the front door. It was showtime.

"That looks great, Virginia," Nathan said, grinning at what she'd added along the bottom of the black chalkboard sign: *Share a Cup of Joy!*

"Do you have the profiles ready?" she asked, grinning back.

"Yep. Right here," Nathan said, pulling a stack of paper out of his backpack.

"Tell me again how this is going to work?"

The bell over the shop door rang out, announcing their first customer.

"How about I show you instead?" Nathan said with a wink, turning to the front of the store. He was a bit surprised when it was a young woman he'd seen in the store before. "Hey, good morning! It's good to see you again. We've got just the thing to warm you up."

The woman's cheeks were flushed. "A cup of coffee would be great. It is *cold* out there."

"I actually might have something better than that—at least if you like chocolate," Nathan said, motioning over to his hot chocolate bar. "We're just adding the finishing touches, but you're welcome to a cup of cocoa if you like."

He walked her over to the refreshments. He remembered talking her into purchasing more books than she'd intended on one of his initial days at the store; it had greatly boosted his confidence. "Amanda, right?"

"Right. Your cocoa bar is so *cute*," she said with a giggle, staring at the selection.

Nathan grinned back and then explained about the freewill offering. "But only if you want to. We plan to donate it to the Salvation Army. There are so many needs this time of year and never enough resources."

"What a kind gesture," Amanda said as she looked over the table of goodies. "Which cup should I use?"

"That depends. You're welcome to use either. We're trying something new this weekend, and since you're our first customer of the day, you can be our guinea pig if you like. Unless you're in a hurry?"

"I'm not in a hurry, but I do have quite a bit of shopping to do today."

"Holiday gifts?"

She grimaced. "Christmas gifts. I've barely started."

"Perfect. I'm guessing since you're here, you might be thinking *books* for at least one person on your list?"

"Two. My grandma, for one. She *loves* to read. Books are the only thing I ever get her. She doesn't want anything else. Says her apartment is cluttered enough as it is. But she's always happy to make room for one more book.

And I need something for a guy, too. About my age. Our age, actually," she said, motioning between herself and Nathan.

"A b— . . . a friend?" Nathan asked, nearly saying *boyfriend* but stopping himself for some reason.

"No, my brother. We're twins."

Virginia must have been eavesdropping, because she approached them with two of the profiles Nathan had printed out, a clipboard, and a pen.

Nathan took the items from her. "Thank you, Virginia."

The customer looked at the sheets. "What are these?"

"This is a special service we're offering to our customers this weekend, free of charge. If you'd like, we can do your shopping for you, while you relax with a book and a cup of cocoa over in our reading nook," Nathan explained, pointing toward the four comfortable wingbacks in the corner of the store.

She smiled, incredulous. "But how will you know what I need?"

"This is designed to help get us started." Nathan held up the clipboard. "We'll pull together our best suggestions for you, and of course you get to make the final selection. Then we'll wrap everything up for you and send you on your way, with names crossed off your list and your batteries recharged from cocoa and a little reading time." He handed her the clipboard.

Amanda seemed to warm up to the strange idea far faster than he could have hoped. "What a great idea! Should I fill a sheet out for each of them? Are you sure there isn't any extra charge for this?"

"No charge. You'd be doing me a favor, going through this with me so I can see how well it works. Make your cocoa, take a seat over in one of those chairs, and fill out the forms. Then I'll shop for you while you relax with a good book. We've set some suggested reads out on the coffee table over there, but help yourself to any of the other books you've wanted to check out."

She beamed. "That sounds great."

The front bell rang again. This time when he glanced up, it was his mother walking in with Harper on her hip. Virginia was already making her way over, cooing at the baby.

"Go ahead and help them," Amanda said as she filled one of the white mugs with cocoa from the urn.

"No worries. It's just my mom and sister. But let me get the whipped cream out," he said, making his way back to the small fridge in the reading area. He'd forgotten to set it out when they opened. Once he had the cream set out and his first customer settled in a chair with her clipboard and drink, he made his way back over to where his mom was visiting with Virginia. "Hi, Mom. Hey there, Harper," he said, reaching for the baby. She tumbled into his arms.

"Hi, hon," Jess greeted him back. "It looks *great* in here! I love the front window."

"Thanks. We like it, too."

"She's cute," Jess said, more quietly this time, nodding her head back toward the reading nook and the woman Nathan had been helping.

"What?"

"That girl. She's cute. And Virginia said she's stopped in more than once, but didn't buy anything the last time when you weren't here. We're guessing she's here as much to see you as to buy books."

Nathan glanced back to where the girl was filling out one of his sheets. *Good old Mom, always trying to set me up.*

"Don't be ridiculous. She's here to buy gifts for her grandma and brother."

"Whatever you say, Nathan," Virginia replied with a knowing grin.

"Okay, now you're just making it awkward. Come on, Harper, let me show you the train," he said.

He balanced her on his hip while he plugged the train in. He laughed when she clapped her hands in amazement. Trying to ignore his mother's comments about their customer, he set Harper on her feet and crouched next to her, capturing one of her chubby hands so he could pull her back from the display if she got too close.

"Look, but don't touch."

If the nearly one-year-old understood the warning, she ignored it, grabbing for a corner of white linen. Lucky for Nathan, she wobbled a bit in her excitement, missing her target. He scooped her back up into his arms.

"Harper," he said in a tone she wasn't used to hearing from him.

Her bottom lip started to quiver.

"Look, here comes the train again," he said, hoping to distract her as the engine clickity-clacked across its plastic track in their direction. It worked. Nathan pointed out the various ornaments, sparkling on the Christmas tree in the window.

Then he heard his mom say, "Ethan has his hands full, but I'm hopeful things will work out all right."

He strode back to where Virginia and Jess stood talking. "Do you have more news from Uncle Ethan?"

"Ethan's friend got to go home from the hospital, so *that's* good news."

"Oh, good. Rex, right? Lizzy was really worried about him."

Virginia glanced over Nathan's shoulder. "Why don't you give that little princess to me, Nathan. I think our customer might be ready for you to do some shopping for her."

Sure enough, he could see Amanda heading his way.

Virginia grunted at Harper's weight when Nathan passed her on. "My, you've grown, child. Let your brother get some work done now."

***

After scanning the profiles Amanda handed to him, Nathan quickly thought of a book for her twin brother. The guy wasn't much of a reader but loved gaming. *Ready Player One*, a science-fiction novel, would be a safe bet. He'd get input from Virginia for ideas for the grandmother.

"I can't thank you enough for helping me find this," Amanda said twenty minutes later. I think you might have discovered a book my brother will *actually* read. He's been dating this girl who loves books, but he'd rather game. Maybe this will give him something to talk to her about."

"I take it you like the girlfriend?"

Amanda shrugged. "I've only met her twice, but she seems way more decent than some he's dated. I figure I better encourage the good ones."

"That one's been a big hit," Nathan said, nodding to the book she held in her hand. "And do you think one of these might work for your grandmother?"

Amanda leaned closer to inspect the three novels Nathan had laid out for her on the counter. All were beautifully embossed hardbacks. "These are gorgeous. And they look like a set. Are they a series?"

"No, but they are all considered classics. I'm sure your grandmother has probably already read them, but maybe not recently. These would look great on a bookshelf or coffee table, and they're large print. You mentioned on your sheet that the print couldn't be too small."

Amanda picked up the book closest to her, running her finger across the gold-embossed title that stood out handsomely on a deep-burgundy background. "This would match her living room, and she's told me before that *To Kill a Mockingbird* is one of her all-time favorites, so the sequel would be perfect. But I like the looks of this navy one, too. *Wuthering Heights*. Bet she hasn't read that one in a long time. Her birthday is in March. Maybe I'll come back for it if she enjoys this large print."

"Perfect. We'll be here. If this is gone, I can always order you in another one."

"And it'll give me another excuse to stop by," Amanda said, looking expectantly at Nathan.

Virginia's earlier comment floated back through his brain.

Maybe I should ask her out, Nathan thought. That was what she was hinting at . . . wasn't it? But then he remembered everything he needed to get done in the next few weeks. *Yeah, right, like I have time for that. Maybe I'll ask if she does come back in March.*

"Can I wrap these two up for you, then?" Nathan asked, smiling back at her.

He thought she might have looked disappointed for a second, but then her smile was back. "Yes, please. Oh, and by the way, I loved the book you recommended to me last time."

Nathan stacked the two books she was purchasing and set the other options he'd pulled for her to the side. "*Little Fires Everywhere?* I've heard good things about it, but I haven't had enough time to read lately."

She nodded. "I get it. Do you work a lot?"

"Quite a bit. Plus, I'll be graduating in June," he replied, stooping down to rummage for two white boxes under the sales counter.

"Oh, sure. I never had time to read for fun either until after I finished school."

Nathan rang up the sale and placed the books in gift boxes. "Which paper do you prefer?"

She pointed to the traditional red-and-green roll. "That one for Grandma and the plain brown paper for the gaming book."

"You got it," Nathan said, handing change back to her.

"Excuse me a minute. I want to put this in the freewill box. The cocoa was excellent, by the way. And so was the service."

He smiled at Amanda as she walked away, still debating whether or not he should ask her out. He tried to focus on his wrapping, but his mind went back to his conversation with Julie and Lizzy out at Whispering Pines. Julie seemed surprised at Nathan's interest in Grace; apparently Grace hadn't mentioned anything to Julie about their conversation on the way back from the coffee shop. He wasn't sure how to take that. But both his cousins encouraged him to start dating other girls if Grace wasn't in a place where she wanted to go out.

"She's been through a lot over the past few years, what with her health problems and everything. I know her main focus right now is school. She feels like she's behind since she missed so much when she was sick. I think you need to accept that she isn't interested in dating anyone right now, not just you."

Lizzy had echoed Julie's advice.

Maybe they were right.

Amanda patiently waited for him to finish wrapping her gifts once she'd dropped money in the donation box. As Nathan adhered the last piece of tape to the brown-wrapped box, he looked up and caught her eye.

"So, Amanda . . . I know you said this one's for your brother. I nearly asked you earlier if you were shopping for a boyfriend. Do you mind me asking if there *is* a boyfriend?"

"No," she replied, her simple answer less than clear.

"No, you don't mind, or no, you don't have a boyfriend?"

"Both. I don't mind you asking, and there is no boyfriend," she added, sending a shy smile his way.

Come on, ask. What do you have to lose?

"Any chance I could get your number and give you a call sometime? Maybe we could grab a movie or dinner sometime after the holidays."

"Thank *God*," Amanda said, her smile growing. "I thought I was going to have to ask *you* pretty soon."

Nathan grinned back, relieved to not be on the receiving end of a flat-out rejection again. He tore off a corner from a scrap of wrapping paper and handed it to her, along with a pen. She jotted something down, folded it in half, and handed the slip of paper back to him, their fingers briefly brushing.

"Thanks again for all your help today," she said with a small wave before she turned and headed for the door. "I'll be sure to let all my friends know to come here for cocoa—and a helping hand with their shopping, too!"

"Thank you for stopping," Nathan said, wondering whether or not he'd just made a mistake by asking out someone other than Grace. Despite his cousins' advice, *Grace* was still the one he wanted.

CHAPTER 12

Gift of Lessons Learned

*T*heir experiment with creating an immersion shopping experience was a big hit. Both Saturday and Sunday were busy, and few people left the store empty-handed. When Sunday night came, Nathan was about to lock the front door at closing time when Frank came in off the sidewalk.

"I have to hand it to you, Nathan, your little 'personal shopper' idea seemed to work pretty well this weekend," Frank said as he came through the door.

"I think so, too. But I'm surprised to see you. You didn't have to come down here on a Sunday afternoon. I could have closed up shop."

Frank glanced at his wrist. "Ten after five. I don't see anyone else pulling up. I think we'll call it a day. I just wanted to come down and get a count on our freewill offering. I saw quite a few twenty-dollar bills in there earlier." He shuffled around, seemingly unable to speak what was really on his mind, then said, "Virginia's been in her room most of the afternoon. I'm worried she might not feel well, even though she keeps insisting she's fine . . . I thought maybe some good news related to the donations might cheer her up, you know, draw her out of her room. Did you count the money yet?"

Nathan barely heard Frank as he stared at the cocoa bar.

Where the heck is the money box?

Frank locked the door and flipped the sign to CLOSED, then glanced Nathan's way when he didn't reply.

Nathan tore his gaze away from the cocoa bar, ice settling into his veins.

"Is something wrong? You look pale as a ghost," Frank said, making his way toward Nathan.

Nathan strode purposefully over to the table, pulling up the long tablecloth to look underneath. It wasn't there either.

"Frank . . . did you put the donation box somewhere?"

Now it was Frank's turn to look confused. "No. I just got here."

"Where the hell did it go?" Nathan asked. His mind felt as though it wasn't quite firing on all cylinders. He was sure the box had been there a few minutes ago. Now there was a large open space on the tablecloth where the box had sat all day.

Frank pulled his jacket off and tossed it onto the sales counter on his way back to the table. "Don't worry. A big box like that can't just disappear."

Nathan continued to search. He looked in the reading nook and under the sales counter. He even checked in the bathroom. Nothing.

How could I be so irresponsible?

He'd been working the store alone for the past three hours, and he knew for a fact the box was still there when Frank left earlier in the afternoon.

"I don't know, Frank . . . I don't see it anywhere. Do you—" He gulped, then tried again: "Do you think someone took it?"

"Let's not jump to any conclusions. A box that size would be difficult to carry out of here unnoticed. Come over here and sit down. Tell me what you can remember as far as customers in here since I left."

Nathan followed Frank back to the wingback chairs. Rubbing his face, Nathan took a seat, struggling to remember the sequence of customers he'd helped.

"Business was steady . . . I think I was wrapping packages when you left. At one point, a man came in with two young kids, needing help to find a gift for his wife. He couldn't make up his mind, even though I pulled out some great options for him. While he was deciding, I kept a close eye on his kids because they were having a hard time keeping their hands off the train. I vaguely remember someone else stopping in around that time—a middle-aged woman, I think—and I told her I'd be with her in a minute . . . but she mustn't have had time to wait. I remember hearing the bell above the door, and when I looked that way, I could see the back of her jacket as she left. But I didn't even notice her walk over to the cocoa bar."

Frank reached over and patted a reassuring hand on Nathan's knee. "All right. That might be helpful. Just relax, Nathan. We'll figure this out."

"Who would steal a freewill offering box? I am *so* sorry, Frank."

Frank rubbed at his temples in silence, as if attempting to eliminate a deep ache.

"You feeling okay, Frank?"

Nathan watched as the man rolled his shoulders and tilted his head from one side to the other. "Can't seem to shake this headache this week. But I'll be fine. Now, Nathan, think. Did you ever step away, for even a minute, while you were here by yourself? You know, to use the bathroom or anything? I have to do it all the time, so I'm not judging you."

Nathan let his eyes wander around the bookstore. Had he stepped away? Ran upstairs or downstairs for something? He knew he hadn't used the bathroom since Frank left.

Then he groaned. "I *did* . . . at one point, when there was no one in here, I ran upstairs quick to grab my laptop. I wasn't gone more than two minutes. I didn't hear the door open or anything, and you'd think I would hear the bell, but all was quiet."

Frank nodded, pushing to his feet. "We should probably check around to see if anything else is missing. Then I think I'll call Nick, my buddy on the force. He might have some ideas."

Nathan hated the thought of bringing in the police, but he agreed they probably needed to.

He went immediately to the sales counter, where he'd been working when Frank first came in. The cash drawer was closed. It was impossible to keep it locked during the day; instead, there was a hidden button one needed to push to open it. Nathan held his breath as his index finger sought out and pushed the button now. Had they hit the cash drawer, too? The air rushed out of him in relief when the drawer slid open with a *ding*. The cash and customer checks were still there.

"The cash drawer looks okay, Frank," Nathan reported to the older man, who was rifling through his cluttered desktop.

"Nothing seems to be missing over here, either," Frank replied. "Think I'll give my buddy a call now before it gets too late. Why don't you balance out the cash drawer, make sure it's all there?"

Nathan nodded and picked back up where he'd left off when Frank first came back. The credit card receipts, cash, and checks in the drawer came to within thirty-eight cents of the sales receipts. Acceptable at the culmination of a busy weekend.

A knock on the door not fifteen minutes later announced the arrival of the man Frank had called. Frank let the uniformed man in, again locking the door behind him.

"Nick Williams, this is Nathan Rand, my employee. Thanks for getting over here so fast. As I said on the phone, I'm afraid someone might have stolen our freewill offering box."

After shaking Frank's extended hand and nodding a greeting in Nathan's general direction, the man said, "You caught me just before I went off duty, Frank. When did you notice the box was missing?"

Frank glanced once again at his Timex. "Probably twenty minutes ago or so now. I stopped by to help Nathan wrap things up after a busy weekend, and I was curious how much we'd been able to collect. I was hoping to count the money so that I could report back to Virginia. That's when we noticed it was missing."

"Show me."

Frank walked the man, looking official in his blue uniform, back to where they'd set up their cocoa bar. Nathan stood by awkwardly, not knowing what to do. Frank gave the man some background on their weekend and a very rough estimate of how much money might have been in the box.

"We set it up here because we didn't want people to miss it," Frank explained while Nathan looked on. Another wave of guilt swamped him. It had been *his* suggestion to set the cocoa bar up in an area not far from the front door.

"And you've checked all over in here?" Nick asked, scanning the room from where he stood.

Frank nodded.

"We've looked all over on this main level, but not upstairs or downstairs yet," Nathan chimed in. "Want me to go check?"

"Tell you what. Why don't *I* take a look? You stay here with Frank. Point me toward the stairs, would you?"

The officer was gone for a bit, checking first upstairs and then downstairs. He returned empty-handed.

"That's quite the basement you've got down there, Frank. A person could get lost in all those little rooms. And what the hell are you going to do with all those books? You've got enough down there to open another store."

"Tell me about it," Frank agreed. "You've met Virginia. She's never been able to pass on a book that intrigued her, even if there was little chance we could turn around and sell it. There were a dozen years there where she thought she had to buy up at least ten copies from every new author she discovered."

Nick grinned, but then shrugged. "Unfortunately, I didn't find anything upstairs or downstairs that might help us figure out what happened to the money. Have you looked outside?"

Frank and Nathan's blank looks gave him his answer.

"Give me a few more minutes to check around the perimeter of the building, and then we can discuss what happens next."

They watched as Nick pulled a flashlight from his belt and flicked it on. The man had long sleeves on under his uniform, but no jacket.

"Do you want to borrow my coat, Nick?" Frank offered.

Nick laughed. "I'll be fine, but thanks. Unless it's below zero, I don't do coats."

As the door closed behind the man, Nathan pushed away from the sales counter. "How do you know that guy?" he asked Frank.

"His dad is one of the guys I duck hunt with every year."

Nick wasn't gone long, and he wasn't empty-handed this time. This time he was carrying the missing donation box.

"Let me guess," Frank said. "It's empty."

Nick walked over and set the clear plastic box on the sales counter with a heavy sigh. "Sorry about that, Frank. It was lying upside down in the alley, nothing else around it. I hate to say it, but this was probably a quick crime of opportunity. Someone probably saw the chance to grab the box quick and slip away unnoticed. These types of cases are nearly impossible to solve. But why don't you guys walk me through your afternoon on the off-chance something jumps out that might give us some answers."

For the next twenty minutes, Nick asked questions, and Nathan did his best to answer them. He hated the interrogation, but he understood it was necessary. He was a relatively new employee at the bookstore, and now money was missing. He deserved the tough questions for his carelessness alone.

The officer finished scribbling in his small notebook and once again shook Frank's hand. "I'm sorry this happened to you, Frank. You guys were trying to do a good deed, and someone took advantage of that. I'll do a little digging, but don't hold your breath. Be sure to give me a call if you notice anything else unusual." The officer glanced at Nathan before adding, "And try to be more diligent in the future."

Nathan nodded respectfully to the police officer. His guts felt like they were tied up in knots.

I wonder if this is how Dad's victims felt.

CHAPTER 13

Gift of Miracles

Frank left, disappointment etched on his face. Nathan knew the man would hate having to go home and tell his wife the money they'd collected had been stolen. He'd even offered to call her to break the bad news himself, since he felt responsible, but Frank assured him that wasn't necessary. "It's not your fault," Frank kept reminding Nathan.

But it happened on my watch. I am responsible, Nathan thought once he was alone in his apartment, miserable over the turn the weekend had taken.

Grace's comments about finals shamed Nathan into attempting to spend the rest of his Sunday evening studying, but it was a struggle to concentrate. He had one week of classes left before the tests. He'd groaned when he checked his grades. They'd slipped more than he thought while his focus had been on the bookstore. In the far recesses of his mind, he could see his father smirking at him, reminding him he'd never have what it takes. He'd prove his old man wrong. He could be a success in both school and the business world. Not everyone had to be a *doctor* to be successful.

Or a criminal, he amended.

It was late by the time he turned in. He didn't have class again until Tuesday, so tomorrow he'd split his time between work and studying. He was only scheduled to work in the afternoon, but he still set his alarm for 7:00 a.m. Now wasn't the time to sleep the day away.

The next morning, his cell phone rang as he was climbing out of the shower. He was surprised to see it was Frank calling. Normally his boss would be driving over to the store by now.

"Hey, Frank, what's up?"

"Good morning, Nathan. Did I wake you?"

Nathan propped the phone between his ear and shoulder, tightened the towel around his waist, and loaded his toothbrush with paste. "Nope, I was up. Too much to do. Is everything all right?"

There was no response.

"Frank?"

"Look, Nathan, this headache isn't getting any better. My vision is a bit blurry this morning, too. I think I better go in. Would you mind opening for us?"

Nathan set his toothbrush down on the sink. The tone of Frank's voice was concerning.

"Of course. Don't come in at all today. I can handle it. But do you need me to give you a ride to the clinic?" He thought of Ginny's new glasses. "Virginia hasn't been driving much."

"Thank you, but no. She gave me quite the talking to last night. She's concerned about this blasted headache of mine and insists it's her turn to take care of me. I think I'm going to have to let her do just that. At least for today."

Despite his concern, Nathan couldn't help but grin. Virginia was living up to her new mission of getting her independence back. Ironically, it seemed to be coming at Frank's expense. The tables were turning and now Virginia was stepping up to take care of her husband.

"She's more than capable of doing that, Frank," Nathan confirmed. "Go try to figure out what's going on and don't give this place a second thought."

***

Nathan was surprised when Virginia showed up with lunch slightly before noon.

"I thought you were busy with Frank today," Nathan said, shutting the top of his computer. He'd immediately broken down the cocoa bar after coming downstairs earlier, then spent most of the morning restocking shelves and freshening up the store after their busy weekend. Only two people had stopped in since he'd opened the doors. With little else to occupy him, and his mind still riddled with guilt over the stolen money, he'd decided to try to get some studying in again.

Virginia's appearance was a ready distraction, as his mind still couldn't focus. She joined him at the sales counter, setting a computer bag down on the floor and pulling off her gloves.

"We spent the better part of the morning at the clinic. Mostly waiting, but they also ran a few tests. They aren't sure what's causing Frank's headaches. It might just be a bad sinus infection. We picked him up some medication, and I got him settled on the couch with a remote and snacks. He's ornery, of course"—a hint of a smile touched her lips—"so when I suggested I might come here, he was all for it. He mentioned you had lots going on today, so maybe I could relieve you for a couple hours."

Nathan got down off the stool he'd been perched on and motioned at a nearby chair, thinking Virginia might want to sit. She waved off his suggestion. He'd do well to remember she was tired of being coddled.

"I hope the medication clears it up for him . . . It's rare for Frank to be out of commission with anything, isn't it?"

Virginia nodded but said nothing as she wrung her hands.

"Say, Virginia, did Frank mention anything to you about what happened yesterday afternoon? You know, with the donation box?"

Virginia's hand came up to smooth her hair—something he'd notice her do before when she was either nervous or upset. "Yes. Yes, he did. That is certainly unfortunate. You never know what drives people sometimes, do you?"

Nathan was a little surprised by her response. She didn't seem overly upset about the missing money. Concerned and disappointed, yes, but not terribly *upset*. He'd expected her to be angry. Maybe her concern over Frank's health was overshadowing everything. That would be understandable.

"I'm sorry I let that happen . . . I feel terrible about it."

Virginia wandered over to gaze at the Christmas tree in the front window. The noisy train had become bothersome, so it wasn't switched on. "Nathan, as you grow older you will come to learn that there are many things outside of our control. If you let those things bother you too much, it will negatively impact how you feel about the world. It's Christmas time. There are people out there, right now, barely scraping by. We were collecting that money to give to people in need. While I'd never condone this type of behavior, I'm choosing to believe that whoever took that money is very desperate right now. Wouldn't you *have* to be desperate to steal a donation box? I, for one, refuse to dwell on it. Our hearts were in the right place when we collected it. Maybe fate intervened to get it to someone in desperate need."

Nathan came over to stand beside Virginia, still struggling with the guilt. Was she right? Should he dig deep and *try* to find a measure of empathy for anyone desperate enough to steal money meant for charity?

No—it was still wrong.

His gaze fell upon the nutcracker ornament. "I feel like that guy is keeping an eye on things for us. If only he could talk."

Virginia stretched to touch the nutcracker's silvery boot. "This one was always my favorite. He always reminded me of my father. He was a quiet man, always in the background, watching. I knew he kept us safe. My mother was the opposite in so many ways. I never really understood their relationship. I guess I never will. And now this little guy reminds me of Frank. *My* protector."

Virginia gave the vintage ornament a light poke, sending it swaying slightly on the branch until it began to slide down. Taller than Virginia, he reached up and more firmly anchored the ornament to the tree.

"You're as bad as my baby sister, Ginny. Do I have to tell you to 'look but don't touch,' too?" Nathan joked as he glanced over at the older woman.

She mustn't have seen the humor in his comment; she only offered him a wan smile in return.

***

Virginia appreciated Nathan's help and admired his youthful optimism. His quick reflexes saved the nutcracker from what would surely have been a fall that ended in mercury glass splintering everywhere.

She needed to pull herself together.

Frank's health had her scared to death. She knew she was probably overreacting. Hopefully whatever had him feeling so miserable could be easily treated. She prayed that was the case.

When he wasn't yet home from the bookstore the evening before, she'd been worried sick that something had happened to him. They'd argued earlier in the day about him driving when he was suffering from such miserable headaches. She realized the irony of her not wanting Frank driving; but she'd envisioned him, hurt in his crumbled car somewhere.

Oh, how she hated the impact their aging bodies were having on their day-to-day existence.

She'd breathed a sigh of relief when his headlights shone through the front window. When he told her about the missing money, clearly expecting her to be upset, he didn't understand why the bad news came as such a relief to her. When she'd tried to explain how worried she'd been, he insisted she stop fussing. He'd be fine in a day or two.

It wasn't until later, when Frank was snoring softly next to her and she couldn't sleep, that her mind made a surprising connection. She seldom allowed herself to think back to the darkest days of her life: when she'd been terrified she'd fail to keep her newborn baby girl safe and fed. Back then, the man snoring beside her was a stranger. At nineteen years old, she'd ran to escape a tyrannical mother, only to find herself living under a tyrant all the same.

Their home was little more than a commune frequented by drug addicts and criminals. It hadn't started out that way, but Bryce—her artist boyfriend turned courthouse husband—loved his drugs more than he ever loved her.

One night, while baby Karen slept in a dresser drawer next to her side of the mattress, set directly on the floor in their tiny bedroom, she could hear Bryce and another man talking just outside her door. The man was arguing with her husband, insisting he consider selling their baby, that there were people out there willing to pay good money for children and that Bryce was a shitty father anyhow and little Karen would be so much better off. Virginia remembered lying there, petrified of the slurred conversation outside. She prayed they'd go away and forget all about their drunken scheming by morning. Thank God she'd slid the deadbolt in place that night when she'd gone to bed. Worried things were spinning out of control, she'd installed it earlier that very day. She heard their voices trail off, down the hallway, and she was desperately grateful for answered prayers. Bryce didn't come back that night. She eventually slept, awaking to the weak sunlight of another day.

That was when she knew she had to take Karen and leave. Anywhere would be safer than where she was at that moment.

She packed their meager belongings in the early light of dawn, nursed the baby, and quietly snuck out of their tiny room, Karen swaddled against her body. She remembered it like it was yesterday, that gut-wrenching, tiptoeing walk down an empty hallway. Beer cans, used syringes, and someone's soiled pants littered the floor. The only way out was through a common living area. As she'd feared, the scattered sleeping mats and two couches were all occupied by both men and women in various states of consciousness.

Virginia made it out that day and never looked back. She knew she needed to get to her sister Shirley's apartment, but Shirley lived an hour away. Her childhood home was close by, but Virginia knew her parents would never let her through the door. While her father would have wanted to, she doubted her mother would have allowed it. Besides, Virginia didn't want to hear "I told you so." With her tiny baby strapped to her body, Virginia faced a real dilemma. She couldn't walk to Shirley's; it was too far. It was December, and the temperature was below freezing. She had no money for a bus or taxi. She didn't even know who she could call for help. Her world for the past year had shrunk down to encompass only Bryce's circle of friends, and there was no one in that group she trusted.

What happened next would forever alter her view of so many different aspects of life. She did the unthinkable. Not because she wanted to. It broke her heart even to consider stealing from someone else. She'd been raised to know the difference between right and wrong, and taking anything that didn't belong to her was unquestionably wrong. But the alternative was worse. She couldn't go back to the place she'd been calling home with Bryce. She couldn't go to her parents. But most of all, she couldn't let her baby freeze to death.

She wandered down the busy downtown sidewalks, hoping for a miracle. Karen started to fuss with hunger and cold; the thin wool coat she'd pulled on before leaving the house wasn't enough protection against the elements.

Suddenly a young boy was at her side, pulling on her sleeve.

She pulled back in surprise. She'd been so intent on her dire circumstances, she hadn't even noticed the boy until he touched her. The child was well-dressed. He couldn't have been more than four years old.

"Ma'am, can you help me? I can't find my momma," the little boy stuttered, visibly shaking.

With a stabling hand on the baby bundled across her stomach, Virginia got down on one knee to face the child. "Where did you last see your mother?"

The boy's eyes darted from side to side, filling with tears. "Don't know! We were waiting for a carriage ride. Momma knows I love the horses. But then lots of people came by, and a man offered me a candy cane, and when I turned around, Momma was gone. The man offered to help me find her, but he was big, and he was scary! I ran. Just like Momma told me to. But now I'm lost."

Virginia listened in horror, realizing the boy might have just avoided a terrible fate by running. She thought back to the conversation she'd overheard the night before. Was the world full of horrible people preying on children?

She offered her hand to the young boy. "What is your name?"

"Louis," he muttered, wiping at his wet eyes with his free hand.

"Come on, Louis, I'll help you find your momma."

Together, Virginia and the little lost boy started down the street in the direction he thought he'd come from, Virginia again praying for a miracle— this time for Louis. At one point, she led him to a bench and ordered him to be quiet while she tried to again nurse Karen. She'd eaten so little and had nothing to drink all day that she knew the baby was receiving little sustenance, but it calmed the infant for a bit nevertheless. Just as she was tucking Karen back into place against her skin, Louis popped up off the bench, pointing down the street to where a small knot of people gathered.

"Momma, I can see Momma!"

Taking the small boy by the hand again, Virginia hurried toward the crowd. As they neared, a woman not much older than her broke away and ran in their direction, a young girl on her heels.

"Louis Jacob!" she yelled, arms outstretched. "Where did you go? You scared me!"

Louis tugged at Virginia's hand to run to the woman, and she released him. His little legs pumped as fast as they could, and the woman dropped the shopping bags and purse she'd been carrying and scooped him up into her arms. The young girl hugged the woman's legs, the three of them forming a tight unit on the sidewalk in front of Virginia.

Virginia approached slowly, unsure of what to say to the woman. She'd managed to help Louis, but now Karen's squirming little body reminded her of her own problems.

It all happened quickly. Virginia saw the woman's purse lying on the sidewalk, the contents strewn on the concrete. It must have popped open. Virginia knelt and began to tuck things back into the bag, her fingers wrapping around a black wallet.

She'd prayed for a miracle. Was this it?

Not daring to reconsider—she knew her conscience might win out— Virginia tucked the black leather wallet between Karen and her own body. She then snapped the woman's purse closed, got to her feet, and extended it to her.

"Excuse me," Virginia said. "You dropped this."

The woman raised her face from where it had been tucked against her son's neck as she spun him in a slow circle of relief. Her eyes locked with Virginia's and she lowered the boy back down to stand on his own feet.

"How can I ever thank you? I was so scared I'd lost him forever." The woman accepted the purse Virginia handed back to her, looped it over her wrist, and then clasped Virginia's hand in hers. "You are like a guardian angel."

Virginia attempted to smile back at the well-meaning woman, praying she wouldn't read the guilt that was racking her body, reflected in her eyes. She needed to get away before the woman checked her purse.

"Happy to help, ma'am," Virginia said, averting her eyes from the intense stare of the mother and down to the little boy. "It was nice meeting you, Louis. Now be careful and stay close to your momma in the future."

She turned away then, hoping to distance herself from the shameful situation and find a way to her sister's. Would the wallet even contain any money?

"But I'd like to thank you properly," the woman said, laying a hand on Virginia's forearm. "Can I give you some money or something for your trouble?"

Virginia turned back to the woman and caught her hand as it reached for the snap on her purse.

"Of course not," Virginia said, in what she hoped to be a calm and friendly tone. "Please enjoy the rest of your day, and have a very Merry Christmas."

The woman smiled and nodded her thanks again, and Virginia spun on her heel, fighting the urge to break into a run in the opposite direction of the kind woman and her small family.

Virginia remembered thinking, over and over, *What have I done?*

But then little Karen squirmed in discomfort against her heart. She'd prayed for a miracle, and when one presented itself, she'd accepted it. She'd never again assume the line between right and wrong was always black-and-white.

***

Now, as she stood in her little bookstore that she'd worked so hard to open and maintain, she considered whether or not to tell Nathan what she'd done so many years ago. While she'd rationalized her actions at the time due to the severity of her dire circumstances, she'd never told another living soul what she'd done. Only the other woman knew—or at least probably suspected—that she'd stolen the wallet that long-ago day.

She'd seen the confusion on Nathan's face when she'd made light of the stolen money. Would he understand that sometimes someone could be desperate enough to cross the line, and it didn't *necessarily* make them a terrible person? Would he think less of her if she told him how she'd come to learn this? She knew he was still bitter about the crimes his own father had committed. He probably wasn't in the best frame of mind to accept her early mistakes either.

"Wasn't that food you had in your hand when you came in a little while ago?" Nathan asked, clueless to her inner turmoil. He turned away from the Christmas tree and headed for the grease-stained bag on the sales counter.

Virginia laughed, tucking away the memory of her most shameful moment for the time being.

Sometimes a personal experience is the only way to learn the toughest of life's lessons.

"Yes, dear. Take all you want."

CHAPTER 14

Gift of Nice Surprises

Virginia reported that Frank's headache subsided after taking his new medication. Nathan hoped he was on the mend.

He'd done his best to get some studying in, and as he sat in his Literary Theory class for one last lesson before finals the following week, he forced himself to pay attention. The end was in sight. It would be a relief to wrap up his second-to-last semester before graduation.

He closed his notebook, the page in front of him covered with more doodles than notes, and stowed it in his backpack as his professor wrapped things up. Half the class had already cleared the room when she asked him to wait a minute. Bracing himself for what would probably be another lecture, he hung back. Once the other students were gone, he approached her desk.

"What do you need, Ms. Sullivan?"

"Take a seat, Nathan," she said, motioning to the desk right in front of hers.

He did as she asked, fighting his irritation at the extra attention she seemed to be showing him. He hadn't done *that* bad on his last test.

"Are you doing all right, Nathan? You started strong in this class, but for the last month or so you seem to have lost your focus."

Here we go, he thought. *Lecture time.*

"I'm fine. Probably just a case of senioritis."

Ms. Sullivan sat back in her chair and gave him a tired look. "You do know that isn't really a thing, don't you? And remember, I've asked you more than once to call me Michelle."

Nathan sighed. "I *do* think senioritis is a thing, even if it's not a real word. But don't worry. I've been studying more this past week, and I'll do fine on your final. I'm just busier this past couple of months because of that new job I told you about. And I *enjoy* it. Have you ever shopped at Book Journeys? It's this great little bookstore run by an older couple, the Fisks. I've been studying up on trends in the industry, and I'm trying to help them keep their doors open. It would be a shame to see another independent bookstore close. Plus, Virginia and Frank are great people."

Ms. Sullivan appeared surprised by Nathan's explanation. "I *do* know the Fisks. At least Frank. Believe it or not, he taught my freshman creative writing course way back when. I didn't know he owned a bookstore. I learned a lot from him."

"Wow," Nathan said, equally surprised. "Small world."

"Wouldn't he be about retirement age by now? I graduated from college, oh, thirty years ago."

"He'd like to retire, but his wife, Virginia, loves the bookstore and isn't ready to give it up yet."

"Oh my gosh, I'm going to have to check out their store. I'd love to stop in and say hi to Mr. Fisk."

Nathan bent to pick up his backpack. "That'd be great. We need all the new customers we can get. Tell your friends about it, too. I need to help them drum up more business, or I'll be out of a job before I even graduate. And that would suck, because I'd like to help them keep this going for Virginia's sake."

"Hey, maybe when I finally release my first book, they'd stock it in their store."

"How's your writing been going? What's your book about?"

She grinned, seeming to have forgotten the initial reason she'd asked him to stay after class. She went on to tell him just a bit about the murder mystery series she'd been working on for at least five years. "I've got three books ready to go, and the fourth is with my editor now."

Nathan stood and looped his bag over his shoulder. "Way to get it to your editor before the holidays. I'm sure the Fisks would be happy to stock your book in their store. Virginia loves to help new authors. Hey, now that you mention it, I'm trying to help Virginia figure out how to take an old manuscript she wrote and turn it into a book for her husband. You know, help her 'realize a lifelong dream' type of thing. Kind of like you. She has a draft, but we need a professional editor to take a look at it, help her polish it up a bit. Do you know anyone?"

"Sure. I could refer you to my editor, but she's pretty booked up. Might take six months or so to get on her calendar."

Nathan's temporary excitement plummeted. "I was hoping to help her get it pulled together in time for his birthday in February. Maybe I'm being totally unrealistic."

Ms. Sullivan regarded Nathan, chewing her lip in thought. "Maybe. Maybe not. I've done some editing for authors in the past. Do you want someone with lots of experience, or would you take a chance on me?"

"Seriously? You've graded my papers. I know from personal experience that you're both tough but helpful. Would you be willing to consider editing Virginia's book?"

She shrugged. "I don't see why not. I don't have much for plans over the holidays. I'm not going to make it home to my folks this year. Flights are too expensive. Tell you what—talk to Mrs. Fisk, see if she might be interested in me helping her with her book. If she is, get me a copy of the first couple of chapters, let me know how long the manuscript is, and I'll work up a quote for you. Maybe we can come up with something that will help us both out."

"You really don't have anything else to do over the holidays?" Nathan wished he could take back the words as soon as he'd said them—they sounded so much harsher out loud than in his head. "I'm sorry . . . that didn't come out right."

She sighed at his apology, but tempered it with a grin. "Unfortunately, I really don't. I've been single for a few years—" She wriggled a bare ring finger in his direction. "Divorced, no kids, and no family close by. But don't feel sorry for me. A little quiet time after the craziness of semester end sounds wonderful to me at the moment."

Nathan grinned, feeling as if a weight was lifting off his shoulders. "Good thing I was slacking off. If you hadn't pushed me, we wouldn't have stumbled on a chance to help each other out."

Hand on hip, she bit back a laugh. "Get out of here. And *study.*"

***

Nathan couldn't believe his luck. Finding an editor had been his biggest hurdle in helping Virginia turn her manuscript into an actual book for Frank. This weekend would be their author event, and he'd planned to sit down with Grace's dad, Grant, and pick his brain about everything they'd need to get done to make Virginia's dream a reality. Having a possible editor lined up would prove to Grant that he was serious about this.

He was thankful Grant had agreed to be one of their featured authors. They'd scheduled Grant for late afternoon on Saturday. Grace's latest text had assured Nathan she was trying to figure out a way to attend, even though she had lots of studying to do for finals.

In addition to Grant, whose novel was science-fiction, Nathan had also lined up a guy who both wrote and illustrated children's books and a woman who wrote romance novels. He hoped the variety would pull lots of customers in throughout the day.

Despite Virginia's assurances that she didn't blame him for the stolen donation money, Nathan felt driven to prove himself by delivering a first-class event on Saturday. He'd even wrestled the four wingback chairs out of the back area of the store and ordered in folding chairs for a small audience. He planned to have each author take a seat in front of what he hoped would be eager fans for a short question-and-answer session in addition to a book signing. He'd ordered refreshments and hit social media hard all week.

By Friday morning, he couldn't think of anything else he could do to make Saturday the best event possible. He'd confirmed, again, with all three authors. It was out of his hands now.

Virginia was excited about the scheduled event. Nathan had been sure to clear everything through her. He valued her experience, and he wanted her to enjoy the day, too. Frank was staying out of their way, quietly going about his usual routine. When he left to run an errand, Nathan was glad to have a minute alone with Virginia.

"I might have exciting news," he said as he watched Frank drive away.

"More exciting than tomorrow's event?" She was loading a fresh roll of wrapping paper onto the dispenser.

He grinned in anticipation. "I think I found you an editor for your book."

The paper she'd been loading slid off the dispenser rod and rolled to the floor with a thud.

"Oh my, I'm so clumsy!"

"Here, let me get that," Nathan said, scooping the paper off the floor before it could unroll. Was Virginia flustered at his mention of an editor? He'd expected more excitement, but he understood that it could be nerve-racking to hand her book over to someone new—especially after her terrible first experience with editing. "Don't worry, Virginia, she's my professor at school, and she's cool. She knows Frank, in fact. She was his student years ago. She writes, and she's done some editing on the side."

Nathan had a momentary twinge, worried she might have decided not to do anything with her story. But when she met his eye, she wore a confident smile.

"That sounds perfect, Nathan. When can I meet her?"

"How about Saturday? I mentioned the author event, and she wanted to stop by."

Virginia took the paper roll from him and locked it in place with a definitive *click*.

"I can't wait. Just make sure she doesn't mention my book to Frank."

***

Nathan stared out the tiny window of his apartment through the gloom of dusk. It was only three o'clock in the afternoon, but the sky boasted an ominous dark smudge on the horizon. If he could alter the path of the bank of clouds rolling toward them by sheer will alone, they'd be rushing away in the opposite direction. Disgusted, he realized this new development could derail his best-laid plans.

If there's one thing you can count on regarding the weather in Minnesota in December, it's that you can't count on anything!

Capturing Wishes | 161

He'd kept an eye on the forecast all week. The cynical part of him had doubted the weatherman's initial prediction of warmer-than-usual temperatures and no precipitation. Now they were predicting the first winter storm of the season.

Resigned to the fact he couldn't control the weather, he searched his apartment for his laptop. Maybe he could squeeze in some studying.

It has to be here somewhere . . .

His phone pinged with a text, distracting him from his search.

Can you send me the address for the bookstore?

"I hope this weather doesn't screw up her plans," Nathan said out loud, his words filling the quiet space. He'd been looking forward to seeing her. He typed the address back to Grace, warning her if she was coming in the morning to keep an eye on the weather. He didn't want her to get caught out on the highway in anything.

His phone pinged back:

Not a problem!

Unsure how to take her response, Nathan gave up on his search of his apartment, wondering if maybe his laptop was downstairs after all. He'd thought he'd left it upstairs, but maybe not. Heading back down, he marveled at how dark it was outside already.

Virginia was sitting near Frank at his desk, sipping her afternoon tea.

"Hey, have either of you seen my laptop this afternoon?" he asked, taking the last bunch of steps two at a time.

"My heavens, child, if I did that, you'd find me in a heap at the bottom of the stairs!" Virginia said with a laugh.

Nathan grinned back. It was good to see Virginia looking more relaxed, now that Frank was feeling well enough to work again. He repeated his question.

"No, I didn't see you with it today," Frank said, glancing toward the sales counter.

Virginia shook her head.

"It's got to be here somewhere . . ."

Nathan stooped down to peer under the counter. The shelf underneath was a catch-all for most everything. But his laptop wasn't there. He heard the bell above the door signal a customer. Careful not to bang his head, he stood to greet the arrival—and was shocked to see Grace standing in the doorway.

"Nice tree," she said with a smile, nodding toward the front window display.

"Nice surprise," Nathan shot back, grinning as he rounded the counter and headed her way. "Why didn't you tell me you were coming tonight?"

He stopped a few feet from her, their conversation on the sidewalk outside of her apartment suddenly playing over in his head as he took in her pink cheeks and windblown hair. She was wearing the same jacket she'd had on that day. He'd played off her rejection like it hadn't been a big deal, but seeing her show up early, as a surprise, had his heart racing.

"It was a last-minute decision. I was meeting with my study group in the library at school, and my friend got a text from her dad telling her to keep an eye on the weather. When I saw there was a possibility of snow overnight, I thought maybe I should come *now*. I hate driving on snow or ice on the highway. This way I'd be sure not to miss your event tomorrow. I'm so proud of Dad—I *had* to be here."

Nathan noticed the large duffle bag on her shoulder and reached for it. "Here, that looks heavy."

She handed it to him. "Thanks. I *might* have overpacked. I brought some textbooks . . . I have to find some time to study."

The scrape of a chair behind him reminded Nathan that introductions were in order.

"Well, I'm glad to see you. Come on, let me introduce you to the Fisks."

Nathan set Grace's bag on the counter and she followed him back to Frank's desk. Virginia was standing next to Frank, eyeing Grace with curiosity. She gave Grace a welcoming smile and then smirked at her husband as if they shared a secret.

Just like Virginia and my mom, Nathan thought.

"Frank, Virginia, I'd like you to meet Grace. Grant Johnson's daughter. He's one of our authors at the event tomorrow. Grace is my cousin Julie's roommate and a friend of mine. She's also the one who helped me come up with some of the ideas for the holiday events for Book Journeys."

Grace pulled off thick wool mittens and shook hands with the Fisks. "It's great to meet you both. Nathan has told me so much about you."

"It's nice to meet you as well, dear," Virginia said, clasping Grace's outstretched hand with both of hers. "And thank you for helping Nathan with ideas to drum up more business. We are certainly having fun trying some new things this year."

Grace glanced between Nathan and the smiling Virginia. "You are more than welcome, Virginia. I hope they helped."

Virginia released Grace's hand and checked the dainty diamond watch on her wrist. "Well, Frank, my heavens, look at the time. If we're going to have baked chicken tonight, homeward we must go. Nathan, would you mind closing up tonight? It's been awfully quiet this afternoon. Hopefully there won't be any more customers, and you can catch up with your friend."

Nathan wondered if Virginia thought he wasn't on to her charade. She was no more worried about getting home to get a chicken in the oven than she was likely to skip tomorrow's author event. Her mind was manufacturing something between himself and Grace that, unfortunately, didn't exist. But he'd let her have her little fantasy . . . for now.

"I wish you wouldn't 'hope' we'd have no more customers today—that would mean I'm not doing a very good job bringing in new business for you. But I can certainly handle things here until close. Get some rest. Tomorrow will be busy for all of us. And cross your fingers that it doesn't storm."

Frank had gone back and retrieved both Virginia's coat as well as his own. "Let's leave these young people to catch up without your less-than-subtle insinuations making things awkward for everyone, dear."

"Oh, Frank, whatever do you *mean?*" Virginia replied, donning her wool coat with Frank's help.

"Sorry," Frank mouthed over her head to Nathan and Grace. "Get your purse, dear. Call if you need anything last-minute for tomorrow, Nathan,

and if not, we'll see you in the morning. Have a nice evening."

"Night," both Nathan and Grace replied, waving after the pair.

The door shut behind them, a few errant snowflakes swirling in at their exit.

"They're sweet," Grace said. "What a cute couple."

The flakes of snow bothered Nathan.

"Was it snowing when you came in?"

"Not yet, but it smelled like snow. It looks like it's starting to come down now."

Nathan walked over to the large front window, peering around the side of the Christmas tree to gaze outside. Light snowflakes danced in the cones of light cast by the streetlamps.

"Your front window looks even better in person than it did in the picture you sent me," Grace said. She'd come up behind him and was crouched low, so she was eye-level with the track. "Does the train work?"

"It does. But the noise got annoying, so I don't usually turn it on anymore. Want to see?" Nathan flipped the switch and the train powered up, clicking over its tracks. He knew the whistle would blow when it had made one full turn.

Grace squealed in delight. "It reminds me of the train my grandpa used to have set up in his basement!"

Before she could say more, the front door opened again. Nathan was surprised to see Amanda and another girl come through the door. He smiled at Grace and raised a finger as if to say he'd be right back.

"Welcome back, Amanda. Out braving the snow this afternoon?"

"Hi, Nathan," Amanda said before glancing back over her shoulder toward the street. "It isn't bad yet, but I hear there's a storm coming. We thought we'd stop in and do some more Christmas shopping now, just in case the weather is worse tomorrow. You're still open, aren't you?"

"Of course, come on in. Anything in particular I can help you with?"

"Maybe. My friend liked the idea of getting some help with gift ideas, and I told her how helpful *you* were last weekend. Why don't we look around a little and then maybe see if you have some ideas?"

"Sounds good," Nathan said, giving them some space. When they headed to the New Release table to the left of the front door, he made his way back to Grace where she'd been standing near the front window on the opposite side of the door, watching.

"I'm sorry. This might take a little while. Do you want to run upstairs to my apartment and study, or grab a chair back in the corner down here? We could go get something to eat after they leave."

Ignoring his question, Grace grinned at him with a mischievous glint in her eye. "You have a fan."

"What are you talking about?" Nathan shot back, uncomfortable under Grace's knowing smile.

"That girl. She likes you. It's so obvious."

And does that bother you? Nathan wondered.

But of course, he'd never come out and ask her that. He'd felt a twinge of guilt when Amanda had first walked in, since he'd asked for her number but hadn't called her. But she was acting perfectly normal, so he'd thought he was off the hook.

"Don't be ridiculous. 'That girl' is just a good customer. Where do you want to sit?"

Grace walked over to her bag and unzipped it, pulling out a massive textbook and a small laptop. "If you don't mind, I think I'll grab a folding chair over here. You can give me a tour later."

***

While his two customers continued to browse the shelves and Grace got settled in the reading nook, turning two metal chairs toward each other as a makeshift desk, Nathan checked around again for his laptop. He still couldn't find it. It had to be upstairs. He'd check again when he gave Grace the tour.

Speaking of Grace, it suddenly dawned on him that he had no idea what her plans were for the evening. Did she want to stay here . . . with him? She'd brought her overnight bag. Her dad lived an hour away, and he didn't know if she knew anyone else that lived close. He thought of the small red couch upstairs. Grace wasn't much shorter than he was, and she might not fit on it either.

He'd have to figure it out later. Amanda and her friend were making their way back toward him.

He smiled. "Who are you shopping for today?"

CHAPTER 15

Gift of Openings

"*I* think they were disappointed I was here," Grace said as Amanda and her friend left with a small stack of books each. She was still seated in one of the uncomfortable metal chairs, and her voice carried as the door shut behind his customers.

"Grace! Be quiet, they'll hear you," Nathan warned, crossing over to lock the front door and flip the sign to CLOSED. It was ten minutes until five, and the snow was starting to come down harder. There'd be no more customers tonight.

He was afraid she was right, which, from her teasing tone, meant maybe she didn't care that someone else was interested, either. He'd do well to remember that. But Grace was here now, and he should enjoy her company.

"Are you hungry?" he asked.

"Famished."

Nathan checked outside. "I wonder if they'll still deliver a pizza. Or do you want something else?"

"Pizza would be great."

He made a call. The weather wasn't shutting them down yet.

"They'll be here in forty minutes or so. How about that tour while we wait?"

Grace gathered up her things. "Sounds great. Where should we start?"

Nathan started on the main floor—not that there was much she hadn't already seen from her vantage point in the reading nook. He showed her the different sections, including the table he'd dedicated to the authors scheduled to speak at the event the following day. He watched her smile light up her expression when she picked up one of her dad's books. The spaceship crossing in front of a brilliant moon, or some faraway planet, was eye-catching.

"I like his cover."

Grace groaned. "I do, too, but he didn't decide on this one until *after* he made me look at hundreds of possibilities with him."

She flipped a few pages into the book, running her finger over the dedication.

"I noticed that. Pretty cool that your dad dedicated his novel to you."

"I was touched," Grace agreed, her eyes moist when she looked up. "He's been my rock. I'm lucky to have him." She scoffed at herself, looking back down. "*That's* an understatement. Or a cliché? I don't know, Dad's the writer . . ."

She was rambling, embarrassed by the sudden show of emotion. To spare her, Nathan picked up another copy of Grant's novel, flipping it over to look at the back cover. The man in the picture looked back at him, a serious expression on his face. "Grace . . . you've never mentioned your mother. Why is it just you and your dad?"

Grace set the book back down on the table and wandered over to the glowing Christmas tree. "I suppose it's not something I talk about very often. It all happened so long ago. She died when I was little."

Now Nathan felt terrible. How could he not have known that? He'd assumed her parents had split at some point. "I'm sorry, Grace. I had no idea."

Grace glanced his way, her face solemn, then back at the tree. She seemed to be studying the small ballerina.

"These ornaments are beautiful . . . I loved to dance when I was little."

Nathan came to stand beside her. "Virginia found a box full of these ornaments when she cleaned out her mom's house a few months ago. Her mom died last summer."

"She was lucky to have her mom for so much of her life," Grace said, tucking a long strand of hair behind her ear.

An errant strand of silver tinsel on the floor caught Nathan's eye. He picked it up, draping it back on a needle of the tree. "Unfortunately, they weren't close."

"But Virginia seems so nice. That surprises me."

"She makes it sound like they were very different from each other. Anyhow, regardless of what she claims, I can tell these ornaments are special to her. I'm sure her mom was important to her, too, even if they were always arguing. Do you still like to dance?"

Grace reached out and gently removed the pale pink ballerina from the tree, holding it in her hand. "Not so much. My mom had just dropped me off at dance class. I was seven. She walked me in, kissed me on the cheek, and said she'd be back in an hour. She always came back. But that day, it was Dad who came. I knew right away . . . something was wrong. He pulled my dance teacher to the side, talked to her, then scooped me up into his arms, breaking down in sobs right there in front of everyone." She glanced up at him, seeming embarrassed, and said simply, "Drunk driver."

Heartbroken for his friend, he wiped away the sole tear that coursed down her cheek and pulled her into a hug. There was only one tear. She stayed there, in his arms, for only a minute or so, still clutching the ornament awkwardly to her chest. She pulled back, took one last look at the graceful dancer, then put her back on the tree.

"It was all a long time ago now. And Dad's been great. I couldn't ask for a better parent. Anyway, I didn't much like dance after that day. Dad wouldn't let me quit right away, but when the winter session was over, I begged him not to sign me up again. Going to that studio every week was too painful."

Nathan wondered if Grace's mom died around the holidays, but he decided not to ask. Part of him was jealous of her close relationship with her dad. He'd never felt that with his father. But at least both of his parents were still alive. He couldn't imagine growing up without his mom. Not even without his dad, admittedly.

"Enough of this depressing stuff." Grace sniffed, a smile back on her face. "You were right. This store *is* amazing. I love the variety of books you have here. And this old building . . . it's great."

"It is pretty cool, isn't it? Come on. I'll show you the basement before the pizza comes. Then we can take the food upstairs so you can see my apartment. The stairs are back here."

He led her back to the door to the basement, flipping on the light. "Watch your step. These stairs are old, a little rickety."

They descended, each keeping a hand on the smooth wooden handrail.

Looking around the large room at the bottom of the stairs, Grace gasped.

"I know, right? There are as many books down here as there are upstairs. And there are even more in those smaller rooms back there," Nathan said, motioning to the dark spaces beyond the reach of the light. The rooms farther back must have separate light switches. During the day, windows offered enough light that he'd never had to turn any on beyond this main area.

Grace was wandering down one of the aisles created by long rows of tables, her hand trailing over the various piles of books. "What *is* all this?"

Nathan shrugged. "Stock they didn't sell, I guess. Bookstores can sometimes return unsold books, but apparently the Fisks didn't do much of that. Virginia joked once that returned stock reflected poorly on authors and she hated to do that."

"A girl could read for a whole year straight and never get through even a portion of these."

"But it would be a fun year," Nathan joked, heading over to one of the tables and picking up a book. "I wonder how many of these were written by brand-new authors. I bet quite a few. And some of these might have been the only books they ever published."

Grace meandered over to another table. "Unfulfilled dreams."

"Probably too many of those down here. I've been trying to think of something we might be able to do with all of these old books."

"Besides throw them away?"

He laughed. "Now that you mention it, I *have* lugged entire garbage pails full of wet books out of here."

"Ugh, that sounds *awful*. And heavy."

"It *was* nasty. The first time I came here with my mom to meet the Fisks, it had stormed the night before. When we got here, Virginia was upstairs alone. Frank and their daughter, Karen, were down here, cleaning up a mess from the heavy rain."

"Water and paper don't mix. Did all of this get wet?"

"No, thank God. That might have killed my back. Just stuff back there," Nathan said, motioning back to a darkened doorway. "I think Frank's got most of the books cleared out of there now, just in case it happens again. In fact, I should probably check."

He took two steps back toward the next room, then jumped at a pounding sound from upstairs. "God, that scared me," he admitted with a nervous laugh. "That would be either a late customer or our pizza."

"I'm hoping pizza. I'm starving. How 'bout you?"

***

"I like your apartment," Grace said from her cross-legged position on the floor, an open and nearly empty cardboard pizza box between them.

Nathan stuffed the crust of a slice into his mouth and looked around, nodding as he ate. "Me too. It's the first time I've lived alone. I'm not sure I could ever go back to having roommates."

"Bad history there?"

"Nah. Just enjoy having some space to myself. You know, no one leaving dirty dishes in the sink or empty beer cans in the bathtub."

Grace laughed. "I can't say I've ever had roommates do *that*, but yeah, I can see what you mean. Don't get me wrong, Julie and Zoey are great, but I grew up as an only child. So sometimes the drama of an apartment full of girls gets to be a bit much. There were four of us, but one girl moved out. She was another friend of Zoey's. Things got better when she left."

Nathan looked around his tiny apartment. He'd thrown his comforter up over his unmade bed when they'd come upstairs with the pizza, embarrassed over the mess. Grace assured him not to worry about it; he hadn't been expecting company.

He still wasn't sure if she planned to stay the night.

She must have noticed him glancing between his bed and the couch. "Hey, Nathan, I hope it's okay, me just showing up like this. I guess I didn't think through the whole sleeping thing. Maybe I should go to a hotel. You don't have much room for me here. I don't want to intrude."

Nathan shook his head adamantly. "No. I'm glad you're here. I'd probably be a nervous wreck right now, worried this snow was going to ruin things for tomorrow, if you weren't here to distract me. You can take my bed. I've got a sleeping bag. Neither of us will fit on that little thing."

Grace slapped a hand on the small red couch behind her. "It's pretty, but it's not very big. It looks like something you'd find Santa sitting on, talking to little kids."

Nathan looked up suddenly, eyes bright. "Hey, I like that idea! I've been trying to convince Frank to dress up as Santa Claus the last Saturday before Christmas. I could haul this downstairs and put it by the tree. I wish I could get my hands on a decent Santa suit. This would make the perfect bench!"

"But then you'd lose your one little spot of color up here," Grace pointed out.

"What? You don't like my décor?"

"I'm not sure I'd call this 'décor,' " she said, looking around at Nathan's hodgepodge of furniture and bare walls.

"Do you think you could do better?"

Grace laughed at the challenge. "I *know* I could help you jazz this place up."

He grinned slyly. "I thought you said you had homework."

"I do—and you probably do, too—but it wouldn't take much."

Nathan closed the now-empty pizza box and got up off the floor, crushing the box so it'd fit in his embarrassingly overflowing garbage. "What do you suggest?"

"What do you have that could go up on the walls?"

He shrugged. "Not sure. When I first moved in, Virginia mentioned I could use anything from the basement or her little storage closet downstairs to make the place homier. I just haven't bothered."

"Let's go look," Grace suggested, tossing her empty water bottle in the garbage. "Sounds more interesting than Economics."

Nathan groaned. "Anything sounds more interesting than that."

***

An hour later, Nathan's apartment walls were no longer bare. Together they'd dug up a stack of old posters from the storage closet, along with empty plastic frames.

Grace adjusted the corner of a large frame filled with an old book promotion ad for *Gone with the Wind*. It sported a bold graphic of a majestic Southern plantation in the light of a hot summer sun. He'd opted for that one over a poster advertising a book with a bleak, cold landscape on the cover. "This way I can *pretend* it isn't ten degrees and snowing outside when I'm up here," he'd said.

Grace stood looking at the plantation hanging above the red couch. "Have you ever actually read *Gone with the Wind?*"

"No. I watched the movie, but frankly, my dear, I don't give a damn."

His weak attempt at mimicking the voice of Rhett Butler had them both dissolving into a fit of laughter.

"You have to admit, this looks so much better," Grace insisted, scanning the room. "Now if you just had a little holiday cheer up here, it'd be perfect."

Nathan plopped down on the couch. "I think this red is all I need. There's enough Christmas downstairs in the store."

"Don't be a Scrooge. Do you have anything we can set out?"

While Nathan didn't care one bit about bothering with holiday decorations for his apartment, Grace was enjoying the process. And he was enjoying spending time with her. "I think I saw an old Christmas-tree box in the basement. But who knows—it could be moldy, given the water problems down there."

Grace reached out a hand to pull Nathan up off the couch. "Come on, let's go check it out!"

Nathan let her pull him up, but he didn't immediately release her hand, her actions bringing him close. He was in her personal space, but he held his ground, waiting to see how she'd react. Not one to back down from much, Grace didn't step back either. She held his gaze for a minute.

"Are you going to lead the way?" she finally asked.

He smirked and stepped around her, discretely exhaling the breath he'd been holding once his back was to her. It felt a bit like they were playing a game. And he liked this game.

They went back down to the basement, snapping on lights to chase away the shadows. Nathan thought the Christmas-tree box was in the small room in the northeast corner of the basement, but he'd only been in that room once. He crossed the large downstairs room and stopped at the portal to the next room, reaching in along the wall, feeling for a light switch. When he couldn't find one, he pulled out his phone and shone a light beam on the wall. The switch was a bit higher than usual. He flipped it, and light flooded the room.

"What was *that*?" Grace asked. Something in her tone caught Nathan's attention.

"What was what?"

She pointed. "There. In the corner. When the light came on, that stack of boxes was swaying a little."

"I doubt that."

Nathan walked over to the boxes in question. He pushed at the top one. It felt empty. The whole stack seemed to be nothing but empty boxes, but they blocked a view of the corner of the room. He grabbed hold of the lowest box and dragged it a couple feet toward the middle of the room so he could look behind it.

"That's strange . . ."

There, behind the boxes, was a narrow door he'd never noticed before.

He tugged on the door, but it didn't budge.

"Where does *that* go?"

He glanced over his shoulder to where Grace still stood in the doorway between the main room and the back section of the basement. "I have no idea," he admitted with a shrug. "I never noticed it before. The knob feels like it's locked."

"From the other side?"

"Yeah. It doesn't make any sense."

"*Now* do you believe me that those boxes moved?"

Nathan used his foot to slide the empty stack back in front of the previously hidden doorway. "Not unless you think someone just went out that door and locked it behind them. Which, of course, is ridiculous."

"If you say so," Grace said, still eyeing the boxes. She crossed her arms over her chest, rubbing her hands up and down as if to warm up. "Little creepy if you ask me."

"Don't let your imagination get the best of you. Come on. I don't see that tree box. Maybe it's over in the other room across the way."

But he made a mental note to ask Frank about the door in the morning. It was weird if the door locked from the *outside*. He couldn't help thinking about the stolen donation jar . . .

Could that door give someone easy access in and out of the building?

He didn't want to scare Grace, so he let the subject drop.

Sure enough, the box he was remembering was in a different room. Wording on the outside of the cardboard box, which didn't appear to have any water damage, mentioned a three-foot Norway spruce. His apartment could handle a tree that small if it made Grace happy.

He followed Grace up the basement steps, carrying the tree and turning off lights as they went. At the top, he pulled the basement door closed and discreetly threw the deadbolt. As far as he knew, this door was never kept locked. But until he found out what the deal was with that door in the basement, he was going to *start* locking it.

Twenty minutes later, the little tree was set up on the end table next to Nathan's red couch.

"It needs decorations," Grace pointed out.

Nathan extended his empty palms. "Sorry, fresh out of lights and tree decorations."

She plopped down onto an area rug on his apartment floor and pulled her backpack closer. "Well, I guess that's that. I'll call Dad and ask him to bring some old stuff from home with him in the morning. You can't have a naked tree. Guess we've adequately stalled long enough. I better get going on some studying. How about you?"

"I suppose. You know, Grace, you've proven yourself to be almost as good at procrastinating as I am—at least when it comes to studying for finals. And you aren't even a senior yet."

"But now the sooner we get started, the sooner we can call it a night."

Nathan lifted his backpack off the kitchen floor and set it on his small table.

That's when he remembered—he still hadn't been able to find his laptop. The hidden door in the basement stole into his brain.

"No way . . ."

Grace glanced up from a notebook. "What did you say?"

"Oh . . . nothing. I need to find my laptop. I can't remember where I put it."

Grace's eyes went back to the notebook in her lap. Nathan's again scanned his small apartment, searching for possible hiding spots. That was when he remembered checking his email just before falling asleep the evening before.

Sure enough, tucked under the edge of his bed . . . was his computer.

And you thought someone came through that door in the basement and took the thing like an evil elf.

CHAPTER 16

Gift of Pink Christmas Lights

It was several hours later when Grace asked, "Do you have any coffee?"

Nathan glanced at the clock in the bottom righthand corner of his computer and then at his guest, sitting at his kitchen table. "Grace, it's almost midnight. You can't drink coffee *now.*"

"God, Nathan, you sound like an old mother hen. I *need* coffee. I'll be up for hours yet."

Nathan set his computer aside. It was then that he heard the wind howl. "I can go down and make a pot. Man, I think that storm they threatened has arrived. It could screw everything up."

"Don't think like that. A little snow and wind can't shut down Minnesota shoppers on a Saturday in December."

Nathan grunted. "Mother Nature can shut Minnesota down any time she chooses. Let's hope tomorrow isn't one of those times. I'll be back."

As he stood, Grace did the same, stretching.

Nathan had to look away. Her presence in his tiny apartment was distracting him from his studies. While she'd been head down, deep into the books for the past hour, he couldn't keep himself from glancing her way. He'd never have guessed she'd end up here, in his apartment . . . just the two of them on a stormy Friday night.

Get a grip, bud. How many times does she need to reject you before you get it? Friends, remember?

"I'll be back," he said again.

"Can I come, too? I need a break."

"Suit yourself," he said, heading for the stairs.

"I think you need a cup of coffee, too, crabby-pants."

The bulb above the stairs had burned out a week ago, and he hadn't gotten around to changing it yet. It didn't matter. Light from the Christmas tree and the street beyond cut through the darkness, making the stairs visible enough. He'd become so accustomed to the layout of the store; he didn't turn on any lights as he weaved his way through tables of books, back to the reading nook. There he flipped a small lamp on next to one of the chairs; the soft glow gave him just enough light to allow him to fill the reservoir on the coffee pot with water and add coffee grounds to the old machine.

"Decaf or regular?"

"You're kidding, right? Decaf is a *waste*," came Grace's voice, but he couldn't see her in the semidarkness.

He sighed but did as she asked. Seconds later, water began to gurgle. "This old thing is trusty but slow. It'll take a few minutes."

Another screech of the wind drew his eyes to the plate-glass windows up front, the gusts causing the panes to rattle in their frames. He could see Grace's silhouette, standing near the twinkling Christmas tree.

"Oh, wow . . . check out the snow *now*," she whispered, as if awed by the power of the recently arrived storm.

Beyond the window display snow swirled, danced, and shot horizontally, pushed by a wind strong enough to rattle the street sign on the corner. The illuminated MERRY CHRISTMAS banner, spanning from one side of Main to the other, looked to be in danger of pulling loose.

He saw her wrap her arms around herself and shiver. The front window, never airtight, couldn't completely block the vicious wind. He nearly put his arm around her as he came up next to her, but held back.

"What were you saying about a little snow and wind?" he joked.

A banging sound above them drew Grace's eyes upward.

"Don't worry, that's just the furnace. Old buildings make all kinds of noises—especially on a dark and stormy night," he teased.

But Grace's face didn't reflect fear in the pink and white twinkling light. It reflected wonder.

"Oh my gosh . . . look at that."

"What?" he asked, following her gaze upward.

There, all across the tin ceiling, were tiny points of light; it was as if they were gazing up at the stars instead of a crappy old ceiling . . . as if the ceiling had melted away and they could see up into the velvety darkness of a summer night, instead of the howling blizzard outside.

He was struck with an idea.

"Hold on a minute," he said, dropping to a knee.

He pulled the fabric back that draped down from their table display in front of the window to the floor, rummaging around underneath. When he set up the window display, he'd used old throw pillows to create mounds of what looked like snow around the tree and train tracks. There were still a couple of spare pillows underneath the table, along with some other supplies he hadn't ended up using. As he fumbled in the darkness, his finger tangled in an extra string of Christmas lights he'd forgotten was there. He pulled those out, set them aside—he'd wrap the extra lights around the little tree upstairs later—and continued his blind search for the pillows. He finally found two throw pillows he'd known were there. He laid them out on the floor between the window display and a table full of books. There would be just enough room. He stretched out on his back, his head on one of the pillows, facing the ceiling. He tapped on the back of Grace's calf.

Grace laughed when she looked down. "You're crazy."

"Come down here. The coffee will take a while. The ceiling looks pretty cool with the Christmas tree lights reflecting off the tin like this," Nathan said, pointing up.

She dropped down beside him so that they were both stretched out on their backs, looking up. Nathan could feel the tickle of her hair on his cheek. He didn't brush it away. There was room for them both on the floor, but not much to spare. She was close.

"Okay, now make a wish," he said softly.

"Make a wish?"

He pointed toward the ceiling again. "Yeah, make a wish. You know, like you're supposed to do when you see the first star in the night sky."

He could feel Grace wiggling next to him, probably trying to get comfortable. He could feel her warmth despite the chill coming off the hard floor.

"Done," she declared.

"What did you wish for?" he whispered back, careful to keep his eyes trained on the ceiling instead of her face, although he knew she'd be beautiful in the soft glow of the Christmas tree's lights.

"I can't tell you that. Then it won't come true."

Nathan readjusted the pillow under his head. "Hmm . . . I know that's *normally* the rule, but it doesn't apply at Christmas time. Everyone knows that."

Out of the corner of his eye, he could see Grace tilt her head to look at him. He did the same, catching her eye. She watched him calmly for a second or two before replying. He could feel his pulse speed up. Maybe his little stargazing suggestion was a bad idea.

"Why are the rules different at Christmas?"

"Think about it, Grace. Little kids are encouraged to ask Santa Claus for whatever it is they want for Christmas. Most times that works out pretty well for them. We shouldn't quit asking just because we grow up."

The corners of Grace's mouth slowly lifted, her face relaxed in the soft light. Just as Nathan could feel himself starting to angle toward her, she broke eye contact and again looked back up at the ceiling. Nathan took a deep, steadying breath and did the same.

"I like that idea, Nathan. Kind of like . . . like capturing wishes . . . but for grownups. All right, I'll play along. I wish this storm would subside so Dad can make it over here tomorrow and your author event can happen, just like you planned. I know how hard you worked to pull it all together."

Nathan smiled to himself, trying to not let anxieties about tomorrow rise up. "While I appreciate the sentiment, Grace, I'm afraid we can't control how long this storm lasts. Try something else. Something *you* want. For *you.*"

She was silent for a long moment. Nathan wished he knew what she was thinking. He picked out a particularly bright point of light above his head and concentrated on it, breathing in and out in an attempt to relax and enjoy the moment.

"All right. Here it goes. I wish you'd ask me again."

The point seemed to grow a little brighter as her words registered.

Maybe this wishing business is actually working.

He turned onto his side and propped his upper body up on his elbow. "Ask you again . . . ?"

"Yes. Like that morning, on our walk back from the coffee shop." Now she angled her head, catching his gaze.

Heart pounding.

"That's a wish I'd love to grant. Grace Johnson, could we go out sometime? Like . . . on a date?" As he again voiced the question she'd already turned down once, he felt far more confident. He leaned over her, and she gave a slight nod just before he gave her the briefest of kisses. He laid down flat again.

"Now it's your turn," Grace said. "What do you wish for?"

Nathan captured her hand in his, threading their fingers together.

"I already got my wish."

***

After three more hours of studying, still wired from his captured wish, Nathan made a makeshift bed for himself on the floor of his apartment, doubling up an extra comforter and then using a sleeping bag on top of it. Grace didn't want to take his bed, but he'd insisted.

His alarm went off at seven, as it did most mornings. But it was darker than usual. A glance at the window revealed snow-encrusted panes. Not a good sign. He glanced toward his bed and was surprised to see Grace was already sitting up, papers spread around her and a computer in her lap.

"Morning. Aren't *you* the early bird—how long you been awake?" Nathan asked as he crawled out of the tangled sleeping bag and stood, the floor ice-cold on his bare feet. He walked over to the window. The upper right corner of the glass wasn't iced over, allowing him a glimpse of the street below.

"I've only been up for an hour or so," Grace replied, pushing her glasses up onto the top of her head. "I've got good news and bad news. The good news is the storm's over. The bad news is they closed the interstate."

Nathan plopped down on the edge of his bed, causing her papers to shift. "I guess not all wishes come true."

"Oh no, don't be such a Negative Nelly. Or . . . a Negative Nathan?"

He smiled grimly. "Sounds pretty negative to me."

She shook her head. "Plows are out, and they're hoping to have the highway open again by ten. It sounds like some vehicles were stranded out there, making for a big mess."

"Main is a mess, too," he said, motioning to the window. "But Frank told me once that they usually plow that pretty fast when it storms. We might still be able to pull this off today."

Grace piled her papers together and shoved them in her bag. "Got any more of that coffee?"

"Sure. Why don't I go make another pot, and you can jump in the shower if you'd like?"

***

Nathan pulled socks on and jogged down the stairs, the floorboard at the top creaking as it always did. He headed toward the coffeemaker but stopped halfway across the store. They'd forgotten to put their pillows away.

Virginia would've never let me live that down if she came in and saw that!

He started the coffee, then went to stash the pillows back under the front window display. He picked one up, but paused when he heard something roll away.

"What the . . . ?"

It was the nutcracker ornament, now staring up at him from the floor. He knelt for a closer look. He picked it up carefully, turning it over, relieved to see it wasn't damaged—which was surprising, given it had to have fallen six or seven feet. He'd have thought the old glass would shatter on the ground. It was a good thing he hadn't put the pillows away after all.

"That was close."

He'd have hated to tell Virginia her favorite ornament was ruined. He must not have secured it to the branch as well as he thought a few days earlier. This time he crimped the wire hanger tight to the tree when he hung it back up.

Looking around the store, he started down his mental "to do" list for the author event. Thank God they hadn't scheduled anything to start in the morning; but he'd still like to open the doors by ten if he could.

The coffee pot chimed, finished brewing. Then the store's telephone rang.

Next the bells on the tree will start ringing.

"Merry Christmas. This is Nathan, and you've reached Book Journeys. How can I help you?"

"Nathan! Nathan, is that you, dear? I can hardly hear you."

Nathan held the earpiece away, worried he might have just blown an eardrum. "Virginia, is that you? Is everything all right?"

As he listened, Nathan's worry over all that he needed to get done in the next two hours evaporated, replaced with grave concern for Frank. Virginia explained how Frank could barely get out of bed this morning, his head was hurting so badly. Her voice cracked with emotion. She wanted to take Frank to the hospital, but their driveway and the street were too full of snow.

"Do you think you need to call an ambulance? They'd have to have procedures for emergencies like this."

Grace must have heard him on the phone as she tiptoed down the stairs, a concerned look on her face. *"What's wrong?"* she mouthed.

Nathan covered the mouthpiece with his hand. "Frank's really sick," he whispered. He returned his attention to what Virginia was saying. "All right. Keep me posted. Don't worry about anything here. We'll be fine. Grace is here, remember? I'm sure she'll help me if you can't make it in."

He hung up, saying nothing as he walked over to the coffee pot, pulled out two clean mugs, and poured. He handed one to Grace, then sipped his, wondering what he could do to help Frank and Virginia, and cursing the storm that still threatened to ruin everything with what it left behind.

"Is there anything we can do to help?" Grace finally asked. "How far do they live from here?"

"Not too far. A mile, at most."

"Why don't we run over there? Shovel their driveway out? At least that way, once the plow comes through, they could get their car out."

Nathan set his coffee cup in the sink, unable to finish the bitter brew. "Grace, we can't get our cars out yet either."

She rolled her eyes. "I meant we could literally *run* over there. You know—as in, use our feet?"

Now he looked at her more closely. "Hey, we *could* do that. But your hair's wet from your shower."

Grace gulped more of her coffee, gasping at the heat of it, and dumped the rest down the drain, her cup rattling against Nathan's. "Give me five minutes and it won't be."

As she sprinted up the stairs, he checked the time. Grabbing Frank's old notebook from under the sales counter, he dashed off everything he should do before he opened the doors. Five minutes later, he'd checked off two of the items, then followed Grace upstairs to change. He'd tape a note to the outside of the door when they left, just in case they couldn't make it back in time to open.

***

Jogging a mile on a normal day would have taken them ten minutes, tops. Slogging through snowdrifts ranging in depth from mere inches to thigh-high made for slower going. Luckily, Grace had boots and warm winter gear in the trunk of her car.

Dressed in layers against the biting cold, they headed in the direction of the Fisks' neighborhood, passing the bakery on the way. Virginia's friend, Mabel, and another woman were outside, trying to shovel off their sidewalk. He'd waved a greeting, feeling bad he didn't have time to stop and help. Mabel wasn't much younger than Virginia. But the other woman, whoever she was, looked to be about their age. Frank needed them more.

Twenty minutes later, as they rounded the corner to the Fisks' street, Nathan sighed with relief when he heard the unmistakable sound of heavy equipment. A street plow was already making its slow trek in their direction, sending a plume of white snow twenty feet in the air.

He stopped so they could catch their breath, motioning toward the plow in case Grace hadn't noticed it yet.

"Thank *God*," she said, bending over with her hands on her knees, gulping in air. "I think it's a solid *two* miles over here, not one."

"It did seem longer on foot," Nathan conceded.

Then he remembered: the Fisks' garage and driveway butted up against a back alley, not the street out front. He could see their home now, a cheerful splash of yellow against the vivid white of fresh snow and a brilliant blue sky. There wasn't a car in sight, meaning their cars had to be in the garage. He doubted the plow would head down the alley yet. An ambulance might be Frank's only option. But first, Nathan would have to clear a path out from the house to the street. Right now the snow looked pristine, lying thick across the front of their house, not a sidewalk in sight.

Nathan jogged across the partially plowed road, Grace not far behind. He waded through the snow, consistently as high as his knees, to where he thought the pathway to their front porch lay hidden. Their feet thundered up the wooden stairs, past two large pots filled with tree toppers and red berries.

"Thank God the snow is powdery, and not wet and heavy," Nathan said, his breath crystalizing over his shoulder to Grace.

At the top of the stairs, he banged on the red door. When he heard nothing from inside, he tried again. Grace reached around him to ring the doorbell. He was about to try to peek through a window flanking the door when they heard footsteps.

The brightly colored door swung inward, and Virginia stood there, dressed in a simple outfit topped with a ratty, heavy wool sweater.

"Oh, Nathan, you are a sight for sore eyes. How*ever* did you get here? I'm so worried about Frank. He's miserable again, only this time it seems worse."

She stepped back so they could enter. Grace and Nathan stomped the snow off their boots.

"We thought we'd come over and see how we could help . . . maybe clear snow so you could get the car out, take Frank in to get checked," Nathan explained, still breathing heavy. "But I forgot about the alley. How long does it usually take them to clear that out?"

"It can take a while. They clear the streets first. But I made a call this morning. I have a friend whose son works for the street department. She called him, and they promised to make us a priority."

Nathan shook his head and smiled. "That would explain why there's a plow on your street before Main."

Virginia shrugged, the smile on her face not quite reaching her worried eyes.

"Is there a shovel in the garage?" Grace asked.

She nodded. "It should be open. There's an old snowblower in there, too, but it can be a bit finicky. I don't know if you'll be able to get that beast started."

Footsteps echoed above them.

Virginia glanced over her head. "He's up. I need to run upstairs and check on him."

Then there was an ominous thud, as if something heavy had hit the floor upstairs, followed by the sound of breaking glass. Nathan kicked his boots off and was up the stairs in a flash, rushing ahead of Virginia. He took the stairs two at a time, inhaling sharply when he saw Frank crumpled in the hallway ahead, motionless, in slippers and a robe. A broken lamp was on the floor next to him, probably knocked off a nearby table.

"Frank? Frank, are you okay, buddy?"

Frank's face was ashen, and he gave no response. Nathan knelt next to his friend, tempted to roll him from his side to his back, but stopped; he didn't want to risk causing Frank any more injuries. Virginia reached the top of the stairs, one hand over her mouth in horror. Grace was behind her, probably making sure Virginia didn't have trouble on the stairs.

"Virginia, do you have a phone up here? I think we better call nine-one-one."

Frank must have heard this. He rolled to his back with a moan, making a feeble waving motion.

Virginia pointed to an open doorway. "In there, next to our bed."

Nathan ran into the room and picked up the extension, thankful for Frank's resistance to taking out landlines. Grace popped in, grabbed a pillow off the bed, and disappeared out into the hallway again. He made the call, explaining the situation. The operator promised to get someone over there as quickly as possible.

Frank's eyes were open when Nathan joined them again in the hallway. Glass from the broken lamp was now safely out of the way.

"You are all . . . overreacting," the older man was saying in a shaky voice. "I got a little dizzy . . . must have fainted. I need some rest, maybe some food so I can take something for this blasted headache."

Nathan was limp with relief, after the panic he'd felt over Frank's slack features, but he knew Frank needed medical care. Something was wrong.

"Grace, do you mind staying here with Frank and Virginia? I'll go try to clear the steps and path to the street for the ambulance."

Frank tried to sit up. "Ambulance? That's ridiculous. I don't need an *ambulance*."

Nathan helped him get to a seated position but then met and held Frank's eyes, a serious look on his face. He lowered his voice. "Frank. You collapsed. Virginia is worried sick. You don't want anything to happen to *her*, do you? I've never seen her so upset. We need to get you some help and figure out what the hell is going on with your head. All right?"

As Nathan had expected, mention of Virginia's well-being caught Frank's attention like nothing else would. Frank conceded with a nod.

Confident now that Frank would be all right—at least for the moment—he ran back down the stairs, leaving the Fisks in Grace's capable hands.

***

By the time the wail of sirens rose in the distance, he'd managed to clear a path from the doorway nearly to the road. He used the shovel in his hands to wave down the emergency vehicle. While the plow hadn't completely cleared the street yet, it had made enough passes that the ambulance could get close. They cut the siren as the ambulance pulled to a stop in front of Nathan, but the lights kept flashing, the yellow and red pulses reflecting off the snow and neighboring houses like some sort of parody of Christmas lights.

A woman wearing an EMT uniform got out of the passenger side and approached Nathan. He gave her a quick explanation of what was happening, and she hurried around the back and flung the doors open. Her partner came around from the other side, and together they pulled a gurney out. Nathan offered to help them carry it through where the snow was still deep, but they asked him to step aside, assuring him it wasn't their first snowbank. They made their way inside, and he stayed to clear the rest of the path to the ambulance.

Just as he finished, and was leaning on the shovel to catch his breath, the door to the house next door opened and a man stepped out onto the front stoop. "What's going on? Did something happen to Frank or Virginia?"

Nathan suspected this was Bert, the old neighbor Frank had taken Thanksgiving dinner to a few weeks back.

"Frank's having a bit of trouble, and we wanted him to get checked out," Nathan hollered back, trying to keep his voice reassuring. The guy looked to be at least ninety years old.

Bert, if that's who he was, waved and then disappeared back into the house.

Man of few words.

A flurry of activity on the porch drew Nathan's eye. The EMTs carefully descended the steps with Frank on the stretcher, an oxygen mask on his face, eyes closed. He hurried to Frank's side, whispering assurances to the man, unsure if Frank could even hear him.

Once Frank was loaded into the back and one of the EMTs jumped out, Nathan pulled her to the side. "Is he going to be all right?" he asked quietly.

The woman glanced toward the house before answering. No one else had come out yet. Nathan guessed Grace was helping Virginia grab jackets and probably her purse so the woman could ride to the hospital with her husband.

"He's stable. He was initially sitting up and talking when we got to him," the woman explained, "but he drifted off. The oxygen is just a precaution. As soon as his wife gets down here, we'll take them in, let the doctors give him a more thorough exam. I understand he's been seeing a doctor lately?"

"Yes, that's right. I work for Frank. He's been gone quite a bit for doctor visits and some bad headaches. But we thought he was on the mend."

The opening and closing of a door ended their hushed conversation. Nathan hurried to Virginia's side to take her arm, giving Grace a thankful smile. "You go ahead and ride over with Frank. Would you like me to go get my car and come over, too, if they've plowed Main?"

"No, no, that isn't necessary, Nathan. Thank heavens you were here when Frank collapsed—and to clear the *snow*! But you've done what you can. Do you think you'll be able to handle the events at the bookstore today? I suspect I won't be able to make it over there."

They'd reached the ambulance where the EMTs were ready to get moving. "Don't give it another thought, Virginia. Everything will be fine. If you find out anything, please give me a call. Leave a message if I can't pick up. And if you need anything today, just let us know, and one of us can get it to you. All right?"

Virginia nodded, transferring her hand from Nathan's arm to the female EMT's. They'd set a step stool down on the ground and helped Virginia safely enter the back of the ambulance. Nathan caught her eye, trying to express confidence, as the doors slammed shut between them.

Not a minute later, the rescue unit was speeding away, lights and sirens flashing.

CHAPTER 17

Gift of Quick Decisions

*B*y noon they were ready. Jess came early to help when she heard about Frank. Grant got in earlier than they'd expected, too. Nathan appreciated the help.

Thank God for parents.

"Hey, Dad!"

Grace hurried to help with the door as her father fought to maneuver through it. He was carrying a heavy box, most likely full of extra copies of his books. Nathan took the box, setting it on the sales counter in the middle of the store. Once Grant's hands were free, he hugged his daughter.

She rubbed the stubble on his face. "This is new, Dad. I *like* it. Pretty hip. You've never had a beard before."

"You don't think it ages me twenty years?" Grant asked his daughter, rubbing the palm of his hand up and down his right cheek. "I was surprised at how gray it is."

"You look distinguished. Now all you're missing is a tweed blazer," Grace teased, tugging at the sleeve of his black dress shirt.

Grant squeezed Grace's shoulder and then walked over to where Jess was arranging Christmas cookies on a crystal platter. "Tell me you have an extra one or five of those for me," he said to Jess. She placed one last cookie on the tray and then came around to stand next to Grant, arms extended. He caught her up in a friendly hug.

"It's so good to see you, Grant. It's been months! I like the new beard, too. I bet this new look of yours attracts the ladies."

Grant released her, scoffing at her comment. "If it's not *Grace* trying to set me up, it's *you*."

Grace and Jess wiggled their eyebrows at him.

"How were the roads for you?" Jess asked.

Grant snagged a reindeer cookie off the platter and bit off a leg before replying. "No lunch," he said in the way of an explanation as he held up the now half-eaten cookie. "They weren't great, but I'm glad I was able to get here. I'm just sorry I won't get a chance to meet the Fisks. I hope Mr. Fisk will be all right."

"I do, too," Jess said, frowning. "Nathan said he's been suffering from bad headaches lately, but then the pain became unbearable this morning. I didn't even know he'd been ill."

"Sorry, Mom, that's my fault. I should have told you. But he seemed to be getting better." Nathan checked the time. "Hopefully we'll start to get some traffic. We scheduled our first author for two o'clock. I called her, and she assured me the street in front of her house had been cleared, and as soon as her husband finishes snowblowing the driveway she'll be over. The second author is supposed to talk at three, but I haven't been able to reach him yet this morning. He lives over in Aitkin, so he's going to have a tough drive. Hopefully he'll make it on time."

"And what time do I go? Was it four?" Grant asked.

"Yes. But it's great you came early. Do you mind mingling with our customers throughout the day, signing some books if they want to buy one?"

"Not at all, Nathan, that's why I'm here. Well, *and* to see my beautiful daughter and all of you. But duty calls . . . an author's work is never done."

"Speaking of an author's work, I appreciate your willingness to help Virginia with her manuscript," Nathan said, grinning at Grant.

Jess set the artfully arranged cookie tray on the corner of the countertop, then turned back to her son and friend. "Did you say 'Virginia's *manuscript*'? What do you mean?"

Nathan glanced around, but there were no customers in the store at the moment. "Mom, that's another thing I didn't have a chance to mention to you . . ."

"Didn't I just talk to you a couple days ago? It's not like you haven't had plenty of chances to update me on what sounds like lots of things going on," Jess scolded her son, but there was no heat to her words.

"I couldn't because when I talked to you, Frank was never out of earshot. He wouldn't have appreciated me mentioning his headaches to you. He doesn't like anyone to fuss over him. And as far as Virginia's manuscript goes, she might not appreciate me saying anything to you about that, either, as it's supposed to be a surprise. Come to think of it, I didn't tell you about the missing money, did I?"

Jess threw her hands up in exasperation. "Seriously, kid? *What* missing money? It sounds like we have some serious catching up to do."

Nathan shrugged, trying not to feel too guilty. Things had been crazy lately.

"While there's this lull before the first author talk, why don't we all sit down, grab some coffee, and let Nathan bring everybody up to speed on things?" Grant suggested. "I might have to try another one of those cookies, too."

They grabbed refreshments and each took a seat on a folding chair in the reading nook. Nathan felt a little silly, like they were old ladies sitting down to tea and gossip, but nevertheless he explained to his mother how he'd stumbled across Virginia's manuscript, accidentally slamming into her old desk the day he moved in upstairs.

"I can tell from the look on your face that you liked her story," Jess said, fascinated.

Nathan liked that he'd always shared a love of reading with his mom.

"I *loved* the story, Mom. I had to convince Virginia not to shove it back in that desk drawer and forget about it again."

"I understand why that was her first reaction," Grant said. "*Writing* a book is one thing. Letting someone else actually *read* what you wrote is a whole different level of scary. Thanks for that background on the manuscript, Nathan. It filled in some gaps for me, too."

Jess shook her head. "Wait. I still don't see how Grant and Grace are involved with something Virginia wrote."

Nathan went on to describe Virginia's struggle to read the faded manuscript, his offer to type it up for her, and Grace's fast typing skills.

"I got sucked into the story," Grace chimed in. "Once I started typing, I couldn't quit. I kept going until three in the morning."

Nathan grinned as he thought back to the weekend he'd spent with Grace. *I forgot to tell Mom about that, too,* he realized, but he knew if he brought it up, the conversation might get sidetracked again. Instead, he summed up Grant's involvement. "Since Grant's already published his first book, Grace asked him if he could help Virginia figure out how to self-publish her book. She wrote it initially, way back when, as a gift for Frank. Now she wants to give it to him for a birthday present. Better late than never, right?"

"Wow. That's crazy. So where are you at in the process?"

"Well, Jess, I think if we can find someone with some editing experience to go through it, that'll put us over the biggest hurdle," Grant replied. "I haven't read it yet. Nathan, if you could email me the electronic version you typed up, I'll read through it, too. I'm no editor, but I might be able to help if there are some plot holes, that type of thing. I need to figure out what genre the book is so we can get a cover created and a few other things. Then we'll get it uploaded to a print-on-demand service, and eventually get an honest-to-goodness book in Virginia's hands to give to Frank."

Jess shook her head in wonder. "You make it all sound so easy . . . I thought it usually took *years* to publish a book."

"Not anymore, and not if you do it yourself," Grant replied. "Besides, we don't have years. We barely have months. According to Grace, our drop-dead date is Valentine's Day."

"You're kidding. Is that realistic?"

Grant shrugged. "Realistic? Probably not. Possible? Absolutely."

"Oh, Grant, that reminds me," Nathan burst in, excited. "I talked to my professor, and she's done some editing for other authors. I told her the story, and she offered to help. She was going to try to stop by today so that we could talk about things some more. I'll be sure to introduce you if she makes it."

The bell over the front door jingled, and three women Nathan didn't recognize entered the store. He stood to welcome them. The women headed for the table setup of Book Journeys' three featured authors. He let them browse, gathering napkins and now-empty coffee cups.

"At least with Frank gone today, we might be able to talk more openly about the book and make some progress on Virginia's behalf."

"You still need to update me on the missing money, Nathan," Jess said before he could walk away again. "Was it a *lot* of money?"

Jess, with her interest in the bookstore, would naturally be concerned. Nathan couldn't help but wonder if she thought immediately of his father, her ex-husband, at the mention of missing money. He regretted mentioning it.

"No, Mom, it wasn't anything like before. Last Sunday afternoon, someone snuck in here and stole the donation box we set out for freewill offerings at our cocoa bar. I'm still really upset about it. We'd planned to donate the money we raised to the Salvation Army. Who *does* that?" But even as he said it, he thought of Virginia's rationalizations that someone may have desperately needed it.

Jess reached out and discreetly squeezed Nathan's hand. "Sounds like you've been dealing with quite a bit, son."

He smiled reassuringly at her. "Nothing I can't handle, Mom."

***

And handle it he did. The day went off without a hitch. All three authors made it on time for their sessions; there were at least fifteen customers for each talk, and they seemed excited to meet Grant and the other two authors; Jess and Grace were kept busy wrapping books purchased as Christmas gifts and keeping the holiday treats and coffee stocked.

Grace had an idea to take a large piece of construction paper, cut out some quick snowflakes and glue them to the front, and fold it in half like a big greeting card. Across the front of it, she penned the words *Get Well Wishes.* Many of the customers attending the author talks knew Frank, and they were sorry to hear he was ill. People signed the card for him throughout the day. Nathan knew Frank would be both moved and embarrassed by the sentiments.

Virginia called twice during the day. The first time she reported they were running more tests and had given Frank something to ease the pain. He'd been sleeping most of the day. The second time she called, she didn't have anything new to report, but Frank was awake, and they were curious about how the talks had gone.

"Nathan, you have no idea how much we both appreciate your help today. What would we do without you?"

Nathan assured her he'd enjoyed the day and was relieved to hear Frank seemed to be doing better.

By six, the store had cleared out. All the other stores downtown closed for the evening, so Nathan flipped the sign on the door. Grant and Grace were visiting back on the folding chairs, and Jess was stowing the few remaining cookies into a plastic container.

"I don't know about the rest of you, but I'm starving. Anybody have time to go grab a bite to eat?" Nathan asked.

Before anyone could answer, there was a light tapping on the door. Nathan's professor, Michelle Sullivan, was there.

"Nathan, I'm so sorry!" she apologized when he let her in. "My street didn't get plowed out until half an hour ago. Did I miss everything?"

"Hi, Ms. Sullivan . . . Michelle. Afraid so. But I'm glad you stopped by. I've got some people I want you to meet."

He made introductions, letting everyone know Michelle was the professor who had offered to help with the editing of Virginia's manuscript.

"But where is Frank? I was hoping to get to meet his wife, too."

"I'm sorry, Michelle . . . Frank is actually in the hospital. He's been having some trouble, and Virginia is with him, so neither are here today."

"Oh my gosh, I'm so sorry to hear that! I hope it isn't something serious. Although, if he's in the hospital, maybe it is. Will he be all right?"

"They're running lots of tests," Nathan explained, hesitant to share too much. "We should know more soon."

"What a shame. Poor Frank. I'll just stop back another day. I won't be able to start working on her book until I finish grading finals, anyway." Michelle paused and gave Nathan a look that spoke volumes.

"Don't worry. I studied for *hours* last night," Nathan joked.

It was true: he *had* studied for hours. Just not on her subject . . . yet.

"I'll call before I stop next time. Again, I'm sorry I missed everything today, Nathan. I should probably get going," Michelle said, pulling her gloves back on. "I know you're closed."

Grant stepped forward before Michelle could turn and leave. He extended a hand to her. "Hi, I'm Grant Johnson, a friend of Nathan's. I'm planning to help turn Mrs. Fisk's manuscript into a book as well. We were talking about grabbing dinner somewhere before we all head home. Would you like to join us? Maybe we could start formulating our game plan around Virginia's book."

Nathan thought Michelle seemed tempted by Grant's offer. She likely lived alone, since he knew she was a divorcée. "That's a great idea," he said. "Come on, join us. If your street just got plowed, you've been stuck at home all day."

Michelle shrugged. "Sure, why not?"

Jess reached for her coat. "Great! Have any of you been to the Italian place a couple blocks down? Virginia told me once that their lasagna is to *die* for. And we could walk. I need to get home before too long, so going someplace close would work best for me."

Nathan hadn't been to the restaurant. He'd checked out their sample menu posted in the window, but their prices scared him off—he was a college student still, after all. Tonight was different. It had been a crazy couple of days, and today had been a success, even if they hadn't had quite as many people stop in as he'd hoped due to the weather.

Plus, Grace had agreed to go out with him. He had lots of reasons to celebrate.

***

Normally the restaurant required reservations, especially on a Saturday night, but tonight they got lucky. When Jess called to inquire about a table, they'd just had a cancellation. The group spent the next hour enjoying good food and getting to know each other better. Virginia was right: the food *was* excellent. By the time they'd finished, and their plates were cleared away, they also had a rough plan pulled together for getting Virginia's book done by Valentine's Day.

"I just hope all this business with Frank doesn't have her second-guessing herself again," Nathan said, voicing the concern that had been niggling the back of his mind.

Grace, who'd only just met the Fisks the day before, but who'd been with Virginia after Frank collapsed, nodded. "She did seem freaked out when they were getting ready to take Frank away in the ambulance. She might want to wait with the book."

Jess wrapped her hands around the cup of tea she'd ordered in place of a nightcap. "You're right, she might. But, just between us . . . what if she puts it off, and then something happens? She'd regret it forever. I love the idea of her finally being able to give Frank such a heartfelt gift after all these years."

The reality of that possibility quieted the group for a moment.

"Her face lights up when she talks about giving him her book," Nathan said, hating to think about her disappointment if, God forbid, something happened to Frank before she had a chance to hand him the novel.

"What if the five of us make a pact?" Grant suggested, looking around the table. "Virginia's already done most of the work by writing it. It's not like there's a ton of pressure to turn the thing into a bestseller. It's meant to be a gift. I like the idea of helping her do this."

Michelle, who'd been relatively quiet throughout the meal, weighed in. "I like the idea, too. A long-lost manuscript, a chance discovery, a romantic backstory, and then a concerted effort of a bunch of people who barely know the couple, all coming together to help the author accomplish a lifelong goal. The whole thing seems like the basis for a great story."

Grant laughed. "I like the way you think. A story within the story."

Michelle blushed, sipping at her white wine.

"If Virginia says she needs to stop working on it for a while, do we tell her we'll do it for her instead?" Nathan asked, a bit uncomfortable with the idea.

Grace sat forward. "Nathan, remember what we talked about last night? About how we should still wish for things, even when we're grown up? Especially at Christmas?"

Nathan tried not to blush. He'd never forget their conversation on the floor of the bookstore under their makeshift stars, but that didn't mean he wanted the three older adults at the table to hear about their evening.

"It sounds to me like this is Virginia's wish," Grace went on. "To finally give her husband the story she wrote for him so long ago. And together we can make that happen. I think that even if Virginia says to stop working on it right now, we do it anyhow. Surprise her, too."

Nathan nodded, seeing the merit to her proposal. "I like it, Grace. Is everyone in? Do we do this now, with or without Virginia's input?"

Two wine glasses, one glass of beer, another of water, and a cup of tea were all raised and clinked in unison.

"I like a group that can make quick decisions," Michelle said, grinning around the table at her new acquaintances. "Thank you for including me, Nathan."

"Maybe your holidays will be a bit busier than you'd initially hoped," he said, smiling back with a wink.

Everyone looked pleased. Frank would finally receive his book, and Virginia could focus on helping her husband heal.

It would be their own manufactured Christmas miracle.

CHAPTER 18

Gift of Reasonable Explanations

Something woke him. He opened one eye, then shut it again against the darkness.

"Nathan!" came a hushed but urgent whisper from above.

"What?!" he said out loud, sitting up now, the sleeping bag pooling down at his waist.

Grace giggled, then asked quietly, "Sorry, did I scare you?"

Nathan flopped back down onto his back, his head only partially hitting the pillow. "Ouch!"

"Sorry, Nathan. I didn't mean to scare you. But I heard something!"

And that would explain why she's whispering . . .

A memory flooded in, one of his dad telling the story of how, late one night, his mom had thought she'd heard someone in the house. His dad had grudgingly headed downstairs to check, he'd managed to step on the cat halfway down the stairs, and they'd both tumbled to the bottom. His dad dislocated his shoulder, the cat escaped without injury . . . and an errant screen door was the guilty party, slamming in the wind.

Good thing I don't have a cat.

Nathan reached up and turned on the small lamp next to the couch.

Then he heard it, too: like a drawer or a door sliding closed.

He suddenly couldn't remember if he'd locked the door at the top of the basement stairs after he'd hauled two tables back down that he'd brought up for the author event.

He kicked off his sleeping bag and reached for the hoodie he'd tossed to the side when he'd laid down hours earlier. From the corner of his eye, he saw Grace crawl out of his bed. His mouth went dry when he saw she was wearing a thin T-shirt and tiny shorts. She'd already been in bed, reading, when he came out of his shower the night before, so he hadn't noticed. She caught him looking and hurriedly pulled on a pair of sweats and a sweatshirt she scooped off the floor. He couldn't be sure in the dim light of the lamp, but he thought she'd turned pink.

"What are you doing? Stay here. I'll go look," he said, trying to sound braver than he felt. If there was someone down there, it might not be smart to barge in on them unarmed.

Grace dug in her purse, pulled something out, then came around the end of the bed. "Forget that. I'm not staying up here alone." She showed him a small canister she held in her hand. *"Mace,"* she mouthed.

Okay, not a bad idea.

"All right, but stay behind me."

Nathan walked as softly as he could to the top of the stairs, slowly opening his door and listening while he tried to peer down into the darkness below. He maneuvered around the squeaky area on the top step, motioning for Grace to do the same. The enclosed stairs blocked most of his view until he reached the bottom and could peek around the corner.

All looked as it should in the soft glow of the perpetually lit Christmas tree in the front window. The heat must have kicked on: the delicate tinsel dripping from the branches was swaying on an invisible stream of air. The front door was closed, the deadbolt flipped horizontally as he'd left it.

He'd taken three steps onto the floor of the bookstore when the classic opening chimes of "Jingle Bells" rang out. He spun on his heel in a panic, back toward the apartment stairs, and banged into Grace. She dropped something, and he held his breath, worried her Mace might spray out.

"Oh my God, Nathan, relax, it's just my alarm," she hissed, a slightly hysterical note to her whisper. She scooped up her dropped phone and the holiday tune cut off. An eerie silence descended again. He could see now that she still held the can of Mace in her other hand.

"Damn, Grace, you gave me a heart attack! Why did you have your alarm set for three in the morning?" he uttered, spinning back around and hurrying to the light switch on the wall next to the front door. "After all that racket, if someone . . . or some*thing* was down here, we've managed to scare them away by now."

Grace met his eye from where she still stood, not far from the base of the apartment stairs, a phone in one hand, a can of Mace held at the ready in the other, and her long hair in a tangled mess where it had half-escaped her ponytail. She grinned. Then she burst out laughing. "Sorry . . . I thought I set it for *eight*, not three. The numbers look almost the same if I don't have my contacts or glasses."

Nathan didn't see the humor in any of it. He'd blown any chance he'd had at playing the strong, macho man, protecting her from some unseen intruder. But Grace's laugh was infectious. He finally grinned back before making a loop through the store, checking for anything unusual. Now that the lights glowed brightly from the tin ceiling above, his hesitancy was gone.

Besides, the store *felt* empty—other than the two of them, of course.

Grace followed his lead and did a similar sweep, starting from the other direction.

"There's nothing here," Nathan said after they'd swept through twice.

"But there was . . . right? You heard it, too, didn't you?"

He looked around one last time, feeling a bit like they were standing in the middle of a fishbowl when he glanced at the darkened street outside. "Yeah, I heard . . . *something*."

He shivered despite his assurances to Grace that, if anyone *had* been in the store, they were gone. He flipped the overhead lights back off, preferring the dim light from the tree.

"Let's go back up. It's three in the morning, too early to stay up. And before you even suggest it, no, I'm not going to crack open the books to study for finals at this ungodly hour."

As he walked back toward the staircase leading up to his apartment, Grace stopped him with a light touch to his forearm.

"What about the basement?"

He paused, remembering the secret door they'd found in that back room on Friday night. Maybe "secret" was too strong of a word, but he'd never noticed it before.

He nearly begged off. It was likely no one had used the old door for years. On the other hand, maybe this was his chance to prove to her he wasn't afraid of the dark or things that go bump in the night. Just because it was an old building, full of creaks and groans and unique sounds, didn't mean there was anything to be scared of, hiding behind a stack of books.

Or in the basement.

"I can go down and check, make sure that door we found is still shut tight. You should stay here. Or, better yet, go upstairs."

"Uh, no thank you. I'm coming with you."

Nathan shrugged, secretly relieved not to have to go down into the depths of the old building alone. "Suit yourself."

He grabbed a large metal flashlight from under the sales counter. He probably wouldn't need it, but it felt better to have something solid in his hand. He turned the doorknob and opened the door to the basement stairs, dismayed to discover he *had* forgotten to lock it.

Relax . . . that doesn't mean someone was up here.

He turned on all the lights as they made their way down to the basement. The tables he'd hauled down earlier were still leaning up against a far wall, just as he'd left him. Nothing looked disturbed. He walked back toward the room housing the mysterious door, hoping Grace couldn't see his legs wobble a bit, knees shaky. She hovered close behind him, her breath on his neck.

I'm not the only nervous one.

He flipped the switch on the flashlight as they approached the black hole of the entrance to the far room. But nothing happened.

Great, dead battery.

At the doorway, he reached inside, higher up this time, and flipped on the light.

He took an involuntary step backward, pressing up against Grace as she struggled to peer over his shoulder. He was taller than her when she wasn't wearing high heels.

"What?" she asked, finally managing to peek under his arm. "Oh, no," she gasped. "That's not good."

No . . . not good at all, he thought, scanning the small room to make sure they were alone as he held the dead flashlight in front of him like a weapon.

The narrow door, locked tight from the other side the night before, was ajar, jutting into the room. The boxes he'd set in front of the door lay on their sides, jumbled across the pitted brick floor. They'd likely made little sound when they scattered, empty as he knew them to be.

"Maybe we should go upstairs and call the police," Grace whispered, her failed effort to stay quiet echoing dangerously loud in Nathan's ears.

That was when they both heard it—a shuffling sound . . . beyond the door.

It feels like we're in one of those budget horror movies—two idiots about to walk blindly into the swinging axe of a serial killer.

Nathan might have laughed at the thought if he wasn't so terrified. Grace moved in closer behind him, her hands on his waist now, virtually no space between them.

This is ridiculous, Nathan scolded himself. *There has to be a logical explanation for all this.*

He made a decision. "Come on. If somebody wanted to hurt us, they'd have already done it. Give me your phone."

He heard her take a deep breath. "All right, then," she said, her voice at a normal volume now, similar to Nathan's, all the whispering over. She handed him the phone with the flashlight turned on.

"Better than nothing."

He reached back to grasp her hand, wanting to keep her close. Just in case. He pulled the door open enough for them to pass through, clueless as to what they might be getting into. He'd half expected the door to lead outside, into the cold, but it didn't. Nathan had to duck slightly as they passed through the narrow door.

They stopped to listen. Dead silence.

They'd entered another room, this one also full of boxes. The containers were old, discolored in the weak glow of the light beam. Some bulged under the weight of their hidden contents. A few had even split open, spilling out their secrets. The room, at least near the mystery door, was long and narrow. The phone's light didn't penetrate far. The floor was dusty, disturbed here and there.

"Probably mice, or rats," Nathan said, pointing.

"Maybe that's all we heard," Grace suggested. "I don't see anyone."

"I don't see anything either. Should we go back? Or do you want to keep going?"

Nathan could feel her hand pull up in his, as if she'd shrugged, but he couldn't make out her expression in the gloom. Tempting as it was to turn back, he wanted answers.

"Let's just go a little further," he suggested.

They walked slowly on. A tiny, dirty window covered with bars allowed in a smudge of light. They could still hear scurrying sounds, but if there were rodents down here, they stayed hidden behind boxes. Finally, they came to the far end of the mysterious room. Here, someone had constructed a wall of a different material than the rest—rough wood instead of concrete blocks. Nathan pushed against the splintery surface, but there was no give to it, and no other obvious way out of the room aside from the way they'd come.

"Weird," Grace whispered. "This room must be part of the Fisks' basement, after all. I thought at first it might belong to the building next to the bookstore, but not if there isn't another door."

Nathan agreed. *Time to head back.*

They weren't going to get any answers down here tonight.

Nathan was careful to lock the door at the top of the basement stairs.

***

"Should we call someone?" Grace asked again once they were safely back in Nathan's upstairs apartment. Having not thought to put on shoes when they'd heard something downstairs, they both tossed their now-filthy socks into the trash.

"Not tonight. If there was someone in the bookstore, they're long gone. Maybe it was nothing. These old buildings make a lot of noise. I know we thought we heard something, but . . ."

"What about the basement? Those boxes were stacked on top of each other, and that door was shut tight last night. How do you explain that?"

He didn't have a quick answer for Grace. He'd been wondering the same thing since they'd turned around and made their way back upstairs. Maybe he'd loosened the door when he'd tugged on it the night before. Something, maybe suction from the old furnace, might have pulled the door open, and that could have knocked the empty boxes down. Heck, maybe there was even a raccoon or something in that hidden room they'd ended up in, and the animal was able to push the door open after Nathan had dislodged it when he'd tugged at it the night before. There had to be a reasonable explanation, and it didn't *have* to include someone sneaking around in the dark, going somewhere they shouldn't have been.

At least he'd keep trying to convince himself of that.

Grace looked over at him from where she'd crawled back under his covers. "I hate putting you out of your bed, having to lay down there on that hard floor, Nathan . . . do you want to switch spots? Or lay on the other side of the bed? There's room for us both."

Nathan ran nervous fingers through his hair, not sure if she was implying something or just wanting to be nice.

She must have read the emotions playing across his face.

"Come on," she laughed. "I'll take these extra pillows and lay them between us. Don't worry. I'm not some sex-starved coed, waiting to jump your bones."

He laughed too. *Being nice . . . with a touch of sass.*

"If you insist," he said jokingly.

Keeping his sweats and hoodie on, he climbed into his bed, lining the pillows up between them himself. Once they were both settled, Grace turned off the bedside lamp. They both lay there quietly, listening to the night sounds of the old building. He wondered if she was as aware of him as he was of her. No one else was around. He remembered his dream the first night in his apartment after he'd read the beginning of Virginia's book— Grace leaning in to kiss him . . .

"Did you pay any attention to what was in those old boxes, in that back room we found?" Grace asked.

Nathan, flat on his back with his right arm bent under his head, glanced her way, but couldn't see anything other than her silhouette in the darkness.

Guess her mind is on a whole different path than mine.

"Nah. I was more worried about someone jumping out from *behind* the boxes. Why, did you look?"

"Kind of, but you had my phone, and it was pretty dark. It didn't look like books, though. It would be kind of fun to look through them. You know . . . when it's daylight."

Not a bad idea, Nathan thought. *Maybe it would help us figure out what's going on.*

"Why don't we check it out in the morning? We don't open the store until noon on Sundays. I wonder if the Fisks even know about the room?"

"Wouldn't that be something if they didn't? Haven't they owned this place for, like, forever?"

"Practically."

He could hear Grace roll over. When she spoke, he could tell she was facing the other direction. "Okay, sounds like a date. I better get my beauty sleep."

It didn't take long until her breathing evened out. Nathan jumped when he felt a cold foot touch his.

He'd never be able to fall asleep. Not with her so close.

CHAPTER 19

Gift of Sugar Plum Fairies

*H*e woke to "Jingle Bells."

"Oh my God, Grace, turn that off." He felt like he'd just drifted off, then gotten yanked from the heaviest stages of sleep. He slammed a pillow over his gritty eyes. "Grace!"

When the cheerful instrumental continued, he raised a corner of the pillow to peak over at his weekend guest's side of the bed. There was nothing but rumpled blankets and a pillow.

"Sorry!" came her voice from the direction of his tiny bathroom. "Be right out!"

He felt around in the blankets for the source of the irritating noise. When he found her phone, he picked it up to turn the alarm off.

What monster uses a Christmas carol as an alarm?

He regretted his actions immediately. There, on Grace's screen saver, was a smiling picture of her with some tall guy, his arm draped casually over her shoulders. Was this the guy she'd flown down to Texas to visit? The one she'd mentioned when he visited their apartment a few weeks ago? He'd assumed, based on her comments about being done with men, that the jerk was out of the picture.

Maybe not.

"Give me that," Grace said, yanking her phone out of his hand. "Just push this button to turn off the alarm."

Once the music stopped, she tossed her phone back onto his plaid comforter, the one he'd had ever since he was in middle school. She was dressed for the day, but a towel hid her hair. She didn't seem to notice his upset over the picture. Suddenly, he felt as naïve and clueless about women as he'd been in middle school.

"I'm starving," she said, opening his small fridge to gaze inside. "If you have some eggs and cheese, I could make us omelets."

He tried to resist glancing over at her phone again to look at the picture, but he couldn't. This time, he only saw it for a second before the screen went black.

"Nathan, do you want me to make omelets?" she asked, sounding impatient. She shut the fridge door and turned toward him when he didn't answer. "Is something wrong?"

"Course not," he said quickly, swinging his legs off the side of the bed. He headed for the bathroom. "An omelet sounds great. If you don't mind, I'm going to shower quick."

He shut the door behind him with a *click* and leaned back against the door, disgusted with himself. He'd gotten his hopes up again. After her comment the first night here, in front of the Christmas tree, and her joke about a date in the basement—not to mention their *kiss*—he'd thought they might be at the beginning of something more than just a casual friendship. Now he just felt confused, possibly used.

I bet she was feeling bad about that dude, and thought she could waltz right in here and let me boost her confidence. She can think again.

He tossed off his clothes and climbed in the shower, turning the water scalding hot to try to rinse away his frustrations. When that didn't work, he flipped the handle to COLD, gritting his teeth as ice-cold water sluiced over his body. He finished up, brushed his teeth, then cursed when he realized he hadn't remembered to grab any clean clothes in his haste to get Grace out of his sight earlier.

Screw it, he thought, wrapping the towel around his waist.

He left the small bathroom, walked over to his dresser, and pulled out underwear, jeans, and a rust-colored Henley. He opened his closet door to block Grace's view from the kitchen before dropping his towel. Once dressed, he shut the door, made the bed they'd slept in but not really shared, and joined her in the kitchen, doing his best to still look nonchalant.

She smiled at him as she slid half of a huge, hot omelet sprinkled with melted cheese onto a plate in front of him. A smaller plate was piled high with toast.

His heart skipped a beat. Maybe he'd been too quick to judge. Maybe Grace hadn't thought to change out the picture on her phone. He could sulk the rest of the morning, or he could enjoy himself.

"This looks good, Grace, thank you."

"You're welcome. Sit."

He did as she ordered, downing half a glass of orange juice while she slid the other half of the omelet onto her own plate, turned off the burner on his tiny stove, and joined him at the table. He took a bite of his eggs and nearly groaned.

"You made *this* with what was in *there?*" he asked, shocked that she'd been able to create something that tasted so good with the junk in his cupboards. "How did you learn to make these?"

She laughed, taking a big bite. "I didn't have much choice when it came to cooking. If I didn't help Dad out sometimes, we'd have had to settle for cold cereal or peanut butter and jelly sandwiches *way* too often."

They enjoyed their breakfast, comparing notes on upcoming finals and how much they still needed to study beforehand. Nathan did his best to put Grace's phone screen out of his head. He finished his breakfast first.

"You cooked, I'll clean up," he said, carrying his dishes over to the small sink and filling the reservoir with dish soap and hot water.

Grace nodded, popped the last bite of her omelet into her mouth, and then drained her juice glass. She stood and took her dishes over to Nathan. "I suppose I better be on the road by early afternoon. One, maybe."

"At least the roads should be clear," Nathan said, reluctant to see her go with so many unanswered questions as to where they stood.

If anywhere . . .

"I wonder if Frank had a good night?" he said, changing the subject.

As if on cue, his phone rang. Grace gave him a little finger-wave as she grabbed her discarded overnight bag and headed back to the bathroom. Nodding her way, he answered his phone.

"Hey, Frank, feeling better?"

"Hello, Nathan. It's Virginia. I'm on Frank's phone."

He thought she sounded exhausted. "Are you at home?" he asked.

"I was. My friend Mabel came up to visit Frank last night. You know, Mabel from the bakery?"

"Sure. Her and some other girl were out shoveling when we ran over to your house through the snow yesterday morning." He was a bit distracted by the sound of Grace brushing her teeth. He turned away from the bathroom door, giving Virginia his full attention.

"That was probably Tansy. She's Mabel's niece. Had some trouble with an ex and came to stay with Mabel for a while. Anyhow, when visiting hours ended last night, Mabel gave me a ride home. Frank insisted I get a good night's rest instead of trying to sleep in one of those uncomfortable chairs in his hospital room. I drove back over this morning."

While the highways would be clear by now, Nathan hated the idea of Virginia walking on the snow-covered sidewalks and driving on the icy roads in town by herself.

"How did you get your car out of the garage?"

"Well . . . about that."

Nathan could picture Virginia's late-model Lincoln, hung up on a snowbank behind her garage. "Did you get stuck?"

"Oh no, the nice young man who lives down on our corner came through with his snowblower and cleared away what the plows weren't able to get out of the alley. I just *might* have clipped the bumper on the track for the garage door as I was backing out—darn ice. Be a dear and don't mention that to Frank, would you? I may need you to take a look at it for me sometime soon. Make sure the door will still go up and down."

Nathan laughed. He should have known Virginia wasn't going to let a little ice hold her back.

"Anyhow, I thought I'd give you an update on Frank." She went on to explain that, unfortunately, they were still trying to determine what was going on with him. "I know you have finals coming up, and if you don't have time to work today, you go right ahead and leave the store closed. Our customers will understand."

Nathan thought that was a terrible idea. The customers might *understand*; however, this close to Christmas, they wouldn't be able to wait if they were gift shopping. They'd buy their books elsewhere if Book

Journeys was closed—even its best customers. He had a ton of studying to do, but he could juggle.

"I've got things handled here. You take care of Frank, okay?"

"All right. Thank you, Nathan."

"Say, Virginia, I was wondering if you knew anything about . . ."

He stopped when he heard her address someone else.

"I'm sorry, Nathan. The doctor just stepped in, and I need to speak to him. Can I call you back later?"

"Of course. Call me if you need anything."

Nathan slipped his phone into his pocket, sorry he hadn't gotten a chance to ask Virginia about that strange door in the basement or the weird room. Though she might not have been able to answer in her worried state.

He finished cleaning the kitchen. Grace came out of the bathroom, hair done and makeup on.

She smiled at him. "What do you say we go check out that room?"

***

"As far as dates go, I have to admit—this is a first for me."

Nathan laughed as he led the way down the basement stairs for a third time that weekend. The basement had a different feel during the daytime.

"What, your old boyfriend didn't take you down into a musty old basement to dig through boxes in a sealed room before?"

"Not hardly."

He let it go, not wanting to think about what kinds of dates she'd gone on with the guy still smiling up from her phone. He thought about Frank and Virginia, and how there was a man Virginia thought she loved before Frank—and now, look at the two of them, forty years later. Not that he was looking for anything like that at this point in his life, but . . .

You just never know.

This time, the empty boxes in the back room sat exactly where they'd left them.

"It seems like the bookstore ends about here, don't you think?" Grace asked, looking above and behind her, motioning with her hands. "I'm still not sure if that other room is part of this building or the one next door."

Nathan stepped over to their mystery door, examining it in the natural light streaming through the two windows tucked up against the ceiling of the room. The wooden door was narrower than most, the hinges heavy with corrosion. The side of the door facing into the room where he'd thought the Fisk basement ended was painted gray, making it blend in with the surrounding walls. The paint was thick, peeling off in places to reveal an aqua color. The edge of the door and the other side remained what was probably the original aqua paint. The doorknob itself was black and oblong-shaped, marred with a big dent on the aqua side, as if something had banged hard against it.

"Come on. We should be able to see in here better now," Nathan said, ducking into the mystery room.

Grace started to follow, but hesitated at the threshold. "Do you think we're trespassing?"

"It's possible. But the building next to the Fisks on this side is vacant. Virginia said something about it sitting empty for years. And Frank said it was all right to park in front of it. Can't remember if he even told me what used to be in here. I think some corporation bought it, maybe for a downtown revitalization project that has yet to materialize. I doubt anyone would care if we look around."

Grace shrugged and entered the room, apparently satisfied with Nathan's justification.

There was an old broom to the right of the door, its wooden handle sliced with what looked to be chew marks, its bristles sparse and frayed. Nathan used it to brush debris away from the small window to let more light in. Grace coughed when a cloud of stirred dust floated her way. Waving her hand in front of her face, she walked away from the cloud, then knelt in front of one of the split boxes. Nathan set the broom down and watched as she folded the cardboard flaps back.

"What's in that one?"

She shook her head. "Looks like a stack of old fabric. Dishtowels, maybe? We probably should have worn gloves down here . . . maybe even masks. There're mouse droppings in this box, on top."

"This date just keeps getting more and more romantic all the time," Nathan joked.

Grace laughed as she pulled a piece of cloth out of the box, pinching it between her index finger and thumb.

Nathan shrugged. "Maybe there's something better in some of these other boxes."

They each peeked into the various boxes, moving slowly, worried something might leap out of one. No telling what kinds of spiders—or worse—were lurking.

"Bingo!" Grace finally said, folding down the top of a box that had been taped shut.

"Find something good?"

"*Oh*, yes," she confirmed, rising from her knees and lifting a large piece of some kind of red fabric out of a box. "I think I just found the perfect Santa suit for someone to wear on that red couch of yours for the kids before Christmas."

He watched as the fabric unfolded, revealing a heavy velvet coat in a rich burgundy-red, trimmed in creamy white fur. When Grace held it up, it reached to her knees.

"Wow," he said, taking the coat she handed to him. "This sucker's heavy. Looks old. I think this is real fur."

Grace was already digging in the box again. She pulled out what looked to be a short pair of pants, made out of the same burgundy velvet. Holding them at her hips, she did a little jig.

"This is *not* your everyday Santa suit," Nathan pointed out, taking the pants from her to free her hands. "Tell me there are cool old boots in there, too."

"Not sure," came her muffled reply as she reached farther into the large box that stood as tall as her waist. Without looking up, she held up a red hat, trimmed out with the same white fur and a white ball on the tip, smashed to a flattened state after who knew how long compressed in the box.

Just as Nathan took the hat from her, she squealed and jumped back, running right into him.

"Oh my God," she cried, pointing toward the inside of the box. "I thought for a minute that something had crawled in there and died! But maybe it was . . . like . . . a fur coat or something."

Nathan shifted the bundle of red velvet over to her and looked for himself. Sure enough, the bottom half of the box looked to contain some sort of dead animal, but he could see now that it was probably bear or mink fur.

Yeah, right, like you'd know the difference, he thought.

He pulled it out slowly, not entirely convinced all of it belonged on the cape or whatever it was he was holding.

"That is *gorgeous*," Grace declared, shifting the red bundle to her hip and feeling the trim on the piece Nathan now held. "I think it's a cape. Look at this fancy braid, where the trim attaches to this satin. These gold and green strands make an intricate rope."

Nathan glanced back over his shoulder, into the box. "And there's the boots!"

He let the heavy cape drape over his one shoulder while he stooped down to pull out a set of thick-soled, lace-up boots. He set them on the floor then took out the last few things from the bottom of the box: a pair of brown leather gloves and a wide leather belt, black with a large gold buckle.

"This has to be the prettiest Santa suit I've ever *seen*," Grace said, her free hand stroking the fur on the deep red jacket she held. "Maybe it even belonged to the *real* Santa, once upon a time! It's nice enough to be the real deal."

Nathan snorted. "Yeah, if you *believe* in that sort of thing."

"You really need to work on your holiday spirit," Grace teased, a sparkle in her eye. "But what do we do with it now? I hate the thought of stuffing it all back in that box. It's a wonder nothing's happened to it. It's not like a cardboard box offers that much protection, even if it was taped shut."

Nathan nodded. He felt the same. "Should we take it upstairs, see if we can find out what the story is with it?"

"But it's not ours."

Glancing around the room, Nathan struggled with their dilemma. "I know it's not *ours*, and I'm not suggesting we *steal* it or anything . . . I think that, somehow, this suit was forgotten or lost along the way. We could research these buildings—the bookstore and the one next door, I mean—and try to track down who the rightful owner of it is. Heck, maybe Frank or Virginia already know."

Grace slowly nodded. "You're right. Why don't we take all this upstairs, where it won't get dirty? But . . ."

Nathan eyed her curiously when her voice trailed away. "What?"

"I wonder if there are any other treasures in these boxes?" she asked, grinning.

He laughed. "I see. You want to snoop some more."

"Kind of."

Nathan shrugged, put the red Santa hat on his head, handed Grace the belt and gloves, and picked up the boots. He maneuvered around her, heading back toward their aqua-colored door. "Let's go, then."

"Ho, ho, ho!" Grace said, close at his heels.

***

Ten minutes later, they were again searching the mystery room. They'd draped the Santa suit across the wingback chairs he'd moved back into the reading nook upstairs. Nathan needed to open the store in an hour, and Grace had hoped to be on the road before long, but they couldn't resist poking around a little more.

Nathan still found it hard to believe the aqua door was the only way in and out of the room. While Grace made her way through another stack of taped boxes, he shimmied his way behind the boxes piled near the outer wall. The mottled light streaming through the small, barred window above let him see there was a narrow gap there, and he was able to pass through going sideways. He kept a close eye on the wall itself, running his fingers along the icy concrete bricks as he went. Many of the boxes rested on wooden pallets, suspending them six inches off the ground. The black streaks marring the lower third of the wall was probably mold, and Nathan doubted six inches was enough to protect the boxes' contents from moisture damage.

He kept inching his way down the wall, passing directly under the window. He had to stop when his path was blocked by several old windows stacked against the outer wall. The windows extended a foot over Nathan's head and numbered at least ten. He couldn't just move them out of the way. His only option was to shuffle back the way he'd come.

Suddenly the piles of boxes and other manner of discarded junk seemed to close in on him. He'd never been comfortable in tight spaces. He thought he felt something on his foot and glanced down to see a small brown mouse scurry down along the wall in the same direction he needed to go. Biting his lip to keep from screeching, he took a deep breath—hoping he wasn't inhaling black mold—and hurried after the mouse. He didn't want it running past Grace.

But if it did, she was oblivious. She was emptying the contents of a box onto the taped top of another one. "Check these out, Nathan."

She pulled out what looked like a small wooden box from a white gift box and held it up for him to see. Then she tipped the box over, holding the lid shut and twisting a small golden ring on the bottom. When she turned it back over and opened the lid, a tiny ballerina, no more than an inch tall, spun in a slow circle to a chiming rendition of a familiar tune.

"How did you know it was a music box? And what is that song?"

"Technically, I'd call it a jewelry box. My grandma used to have one. It was almost identical to this except it played a different song. The box sat on her dresser, and she kept her wedding ring in it after Grandpa died. If I was very careful with it, she'd let me wind it up. This song is from *The Nutcracker*. I used to dance to it in my ballet recital when I was little. Something about sugar plum fairies," Grace said, smiling at the memory. "There must be twenty of those white boxes in here."

Grace's discovery had Nathan scanning the room again. "I wonder where all this stuff *came* from?"

"Maybe an old department store? There's a pretty wide variety of things. Have *you* found anything?"

Nathan motioned toward the stack of old windows that had hampered his progress. "I walked back behind this tall row of boxes, checking out the outside wall in case we missed anything, but then these windows blocked my way. I had to come back around this way."

Still curious, he made his way toward the pile of windows again, this time from the inside of the room. He had to step around a few things, including a pile of what looked to be old magazines that had spilled out of the bottom of a split box. On the far side of the windows stood a foldable screen, blocking the wall behind it. He folded it out of the way.

"Um, Grace . . . I think I found another way out."

"Really? Hold on a sec."

Grace hurried over to him as he eyed the dented steel door in the outer wall. They'd missed it earlier, in the dark, the boxes and folding screen completely hiding it from view. But the sound of tearing paper, Grace's yelp, and a ripple of crashes had him spinning back toward her.

"Eww, *gross*," she complained—but she didn't look hurt or even upset, sitting on the filthy floor, surrounded by scattered magazines.

Nathan picked a nasty spider's web out of her long ponytail. "Guess you might need shower number two before you hit the road."

"Not a bad idea," she agreed, grinning up at him before picking up one of the magazines. If the condition of the ripped cover was any indication, it was the one she'd slipped on. "Look. This magazine is dated August 18, 1961."

She handed the mutilated magazine to Nathan. He looked it over, then picked up another one off the floor. "Oh, wow, cool. Check this one out. Mickey Mantle and Roger Maris, two of the greatest baseball homerun hitters who ever lived. Together on the front cover of *Life*. Good thing you didn't tear *this* one. Did you know Roger Maris was from Minnesota?"

"Hibbing, right?"

Nathan handed the magazine to her, impressed. "Yeah. Are they all from around that year?"

Grace thumbed through the stack that had escaped the box. "Yeah, the early '60s."

"Wonder if that's how long this stuff's been down here? Nearly sixty years . . . here, get off that gross floor, I want to show you something."

Grace took Nathan's hand and he hoisted her up. She brushed her bottom off with her free hand and let him lead her over to his discovery.

"Oh, *wow*, can you open it?"

"Haven't tried," he said, reaching over to snap the deadbolt. It spun easily in his hand. He shoved on the door. It creaked open an inch or so, allowing a blast of icy air to enter and sunlight to flood the room. "Probably a big snowbank out there." Nathan pushed harder, grunting, but the door was stuck. "Maybe we can run out back to the alley when we're done down here, see where this comes out. We'll know it's this door, now that I was able to push it out over the snow a little."

He pulled the door shut again, locking it. The room, cold before, was now frigid. They'd have to go up soon, but he was still curious about the door placement: one into the basement of the bookstore and one leading outside. It seemed like there should be one more from the building next door. Nathan still doubted the room belonged to the bookstore.

Thinking he might find another door, now that they could see better, Nathan continued along the walls, Grace following him. They reached the strange wooden wall, but there was no opening in it. Same with the other inner walls of the room: no openings in those concrete blocks, either.

"I bet there used to be a door there," Grace said, pointing back at the wooden wall. "Someone must have boarded it up for some reason."

"If they did, they created a time capsule in here."

"Speaking of time, I hate to say this, but I better get going. If I don't put in a solid ten hours studying today, I'm not going to do well on my finals," Grace said, pulling out her phone to check the time.

"And now you need to shower again, unless you want to wallow in sixty-year-old spiderwebs and dust."

"Good point," she said, following Nathan out of the room.

When they got back into the bookstore's basement, he searched for something he could jam under the doorknob of the small door from this side. It was highly unlikely anyone still had access to that old room from outside, but he didn't want to take any chances. And he didn't like how loose the deadbolt had felt when he opened the outside door he'd discovered. A metal chair with a cracked black leather seat stood against the outer wall. He jammed that under the doorknob. For extra protection, Grace helped him wrestle a castoff dresser in front of it, making it nearly impossible to dislodge the chair.

"That should do it until we can figure out the deal with that room," Nathan said, brushing off his hands.

Grace turned to leave, but Nathan caught her hand. He knew that once they got upstairs, there was lots to do and she had to get going.

She looked at him in confusion. "What?"

"I just wanted to thank you for coming this weekend. It was great to have your help yesterday, and I know your dad was glad to see you. *I* was glad to see you. It was a fun weekend."

Grace gave him a timid smile, as if unsure where this was going. She met but didn't hold his eyes, looking down at the hand he didn't hold, as if checking her nails.

He thought then that maybe he needed something, some assurance that she'd come because she wanted to see him, not just to get away from the bad memories of some other guy. He stepped closer—slowly, because she looked like she might dart. Leaning forward, he kissed her softly, to test her reaction. She allowed it, but leaned back soon after their lips met.

"Can I call you?" he asked.

"Of course," she replied immediately. "We have lots to figure out about Virginia's book."

He sighed inwardly. Not exactly the topic he'd had in mind.

"I guess we do. Come on. We better get going then," he said, leading the way across the larger room, stacked high with old books.

He paused at the base of the stairs and turned back to her. He was about to ask about the picture on her phone's screensaver, but he stopped himself at the last second.

Do I really want to know?

Instead, he decided to end their weekend on a more positive note. He plastered what he hoped was a relaxed smile on his face. "Thanks again for the fun weekend. And that incredible Santa suit you found might even be enough to entice Frank to dress up like Father Christmas, if he's feeling up to it. Didn't I tell you, on that first night when you were admiring my red couch, that I *wished* I could get my hands on a decent Santa suit?"

She smiled back, no longer looking timid or unsure. "I guess some wishes *do* come true . . . when the timing is right."

CHAPTER 20

Gift of Truthful Conversations

*F*rank was still in the hospital on Monday morning. Nathan wanted to visit him before opening the store. Since there was a good chance Virginia was missing her daily tea from Mabel's bakery, he decided to pick her some up before heading to the hospital. He'd bring both Frank and Virginia a pastry, too. Anything from Mabel's would beat hospital food.

He was about to go out the front door and take the sidewalk to Mabel's when he remembered—they'd never checked the alley after leaving the basement on Sunday morning to see where that door came out. Grace had hurried off once she'd washed away the dirt and cobwebs, promising to call after she finished with finals. He'd had a busy day with customers at the store, and then he'd forced himself to do a little more studying.

Speaking of finals . . .

Today was the day. Jess had agreed to cover for him this afternoon so he could take his first test. He was so behind; he needed to buckle down, and fast. With so much going on, no wonder he'd completely forgotten about the door leading out into the alley.

Instead of going out the front, he decided to use the backdoor and walk through the alley. While the front of the bookstore was level with the street, the ground sloped away in the back, so stairs were needed to get down to the alley. He opened the back door to find the stairs still piled high with snow from Friday night's storm. A plow had made a pass through the alley, but snow still piled high alongside the buildings. He picked his way carefully in the direction of Mabel's, watching for the newly discovered door. He had to go beyond the edge of the bookstore and two-thirds of the way down the back of the building next door before he saw it.

The snow was still vaguely swept away where he'd pushed it open a few inches. But it wasn't simply snow blocking the door; there was also an old cart in the way, a battered metal garbage can without a lid sitting inside. Based on the depth of snow inside the can, no one had used it in a long time.

Why, then, were there faint wheel tracks in the snow, as if the cart had been moved? Snow partially filled the tracks; someone must have moved it before the last storm, but it couldn't have been much longer ago than that. The buildings hugging this alley would have provided moderate protection from the storm's flurry of snow, keeping the wheel tracks from being completely obscured.

The hair stood up on the back of his neck when he saw faint footprints as well.

Someone had been back here. Had someone used the door to get into that room?

. . . and then into the bookstore?

He tugged on the handle of the door. There was a little give, but it was locked. The area around the handle and lock bore lots of scratches. He had no way of knowing if these were from simple wear and tear through the years, or something more concerning.

Nathan glanced around as if he'd find the answers, but of course all was quiet on the still, cold Monday morning. A car drove by the end of the alley, the tires crunching on the icy street, but then all was quiet again.

"Get a grip, dude," he muttered to himself.

***

The Fisks were happy to see Nathan when he rapped on Frank's hospital room door. Virginia stood and took the drink holder from him, and he set a white bakery bag on the tray next to Frank's bed.

"Tell me you have a blueberry muffin in there for me," Frank said, eyeing the bag greedily.

Nathan laughed. "Matter of fact, I do. Figured you could use a break from hospital food. Is it okay for you to eat it?"

"Hell yes," Frank said, snatching the bag off his tray and peeking inside.

Frank must have been tired of more than just the hospital food. Nathan had never heard him utter a single cuss word before.

"Thank you for this, dear," Virginia said, holding up a paper cup with her name on it and a greeting from Mabel, penned on the side.

Nathan took the cup holder from her, handed Frank his cup, and threw away the empty holder before pulling up a chair. He'd already drained half of his vanilla latte during his drive to the hospital. Frank talked about the tests the doctors had been running and his frustration over the lack of answers. Virginia apologized for leaving Nathan to handle the store during its busiest time of the year.

"Don't worry. Mom rearranged her schedule so she can fill in when I have to go to class this week. And anyway, I'm done on Thursday. We have the week covered. Once I'm done with finals, it'll be clear sailing."

"You two are such a blessing," Virginia said, offering Nathan a tired smile. "Now, tell us more about this past weekend. Was it a success?"

Nathan relayed more details about the author event on Saturday. He was pleased about the traffic and sales, in spite of the stormy start to the day.

"I just can't believe we missed it," Virginia said, shaking her head.

"There's always next year, Ginny," Nathan said. "Or we could do another event for authors sooner. Maybe once a quarter. There are lots of different things we could do."

Nathan was trying to reassure her, but he didn't like the look he noticed pass between the two. It seemed to convey regret and . . . something more?

Hoping to change the subject, because he didn't want to think about what that look might mean, he considered how best to ask about the mystery room he and Grace had stumbled on in the basement. A nurse came in then, checking on Frank and handing him a small paper cup of pills.

Nathan waited, not wanting to mention anything that would worry the Fisks, but too curious to stay quiet. He resolved not to mention hearing anything downstairs late at night.

Once the nurse left, teasing that Nathan should have brought her a treat, too, Virginia gave him a knowing grin.

"How did Grace's visit go? She seems like a delightful young woman."

Nathan shrugged. He felt conflicted where Grace was concerned, like he still had to keep his guard up. "Fun. She was a big help on Saturday, she had fun seeing her dad, and then she headed back early yesterday. She had lots of studying to do and was meeting with a study group at two."

"Good. I'm glad you had some time with a friend. I worry we're working you too hard. A young man like you should be out having some fun. It *is* the last year of your college career."

"Don't worry about me, guys, I'm fine. Working at the bookstore *is* fun. But, hey, I did want to ask you about something . . . I was down in the basement this weekend—Grace insisted I needed some Christmas decorations in my apartment, and I thought I remembered seeing a box for an artificial tree down there. I'm sure it's the one you replaced this year because it was too small. I didn't think you'd mind."

Virginia set her cup of tea down on the floor near her purse. "Of course not, dear. We don't use that old Christmas tree anymore. Did you find it? Did Grace help you decorate it? It's always nice to have a woman's touch in a home."

Frank scoffed. "For God's sake, Ginny, give it a rest. Your subtle hints aren't at all subtle. Let the boy talk."

She shot her husband a look but said nothing more, nodding to Nathan to continue.

"Anyway, when we went down to the basement to find the box, we ran across something I hadn't noticed before."

"What was that?" Frank asked, seemingly more intrigued by this line of conversation than his wife's matchmaking.

"A door."

"A door?" Virginia asked. "Whatever do you mean?"

"In that small corner room, off the main room with all the books."

"The one we always seem to have water trouble in?" she asked, her face still scrunched in confusion.

"No, across the way. The other corner. We moved some boxes around, looking for the tree, and I was surprised to see a small door in the wall. I'd never noticed it before."

Now Frank shifted in his bed, sitting forward and looking spry.

"By God, I'd forgotten all about that door!"

"I'm afraid I'm still not following, boys," Virginia said, looking between the two men.

"Did you open it?" Frank asked Nathan, ignoring his wife.

Nathan considered how best to respond. He didn't want to get into the whole disturbing business about waking up to a weird sound downstairs—nor did he want it to seem like he was snooping where he shouldn't have been—but he wanted some answers.

"It was stuck at first, but we did get it to open," he said, watching closely for Frank's reaction.

"I bet that wasn't easy," Frank said. "No one's had any reason to open that door in decades."

Virginia raised a hand. "*What* door, Frank?"

"Don't you remember, Ginny? There used to be a door between our building and Philip's."

She still looked puzzled. "I don't remember a door between our buildings."

"Sure. It's always been there, although we never really had a use for it. That old room on the other side of the door is still empty, isn't it?"

Nathan frowned. He hadn't seen *that* coming. "No . . . it isn't empty. It's pretty full, actually. Stacks and stacks of old boxes. Some of them are deteriorating, and the contents are spilling onto the floor."

Frank sank back against the raised end of his bed. "That can't be right." Nathan shrugged, watching as Frank stared thoughtfully out his hospital window at the gray winter sky beyond. It wasn't snowing, but there was a heavy cloud cover. Finally he asked, "What was in the boxes?"

Since Frank didn't seem concerned if they'd looked around, Nathan ticked through the items he and Grace had found.

Frank rubbed at his temple.

"Dear, is this too much for you?" Virginia asked. "Is your head starting to hurt again?"

He shifted, patting her hand reassuringly before folding his own across his chest. "No, just trying to remember the details. I specifically remember arranging to have that room cleared out after Philip died and it fell to me to take care of his estate."

"Now, *that* was a time I'd rather forget," Virginia said, shuddering.

"Who, exactly, was this Philip guy?"

Frank looked up, as if he'd forgotten Nathan was there. "My older brother. He owned the building next door to the one that houses the bookstore now. Years ago, he ran a men's clothing store out of there. It was Philip who told us about the building we're in now going up for sale. Virginia wanted to open a bookstore so badly."

"Yes, that's right, dear," Virginia added. "I'd been struggling to find just the right place, and I even had Celia lined up to help us with the purchase, but nothing felt right. Until Philip told us about the building adjacent to his store."

"You guys added the door when you purchased adjoining buildings?" Nathan asked.

"No, it was already there." Frank shrugged. "We never really knew why."

"Did your brother's building pass to you, then, when he died?"

Frank shook his head. "Philip was a widower with a son and a daughter. Everything passed to them, but neither had a head for business. They had no interest in maintaining the store Philip founded and nurtured for twenty years, all the way up until his untimely death. They sold off the inventory and then tried a couple of different enterprises before basically giving up and asking me if I'd help them just rent it out. I agreed . . . but that's when the headaches really kicked in."

Nathan found his comment ironic, given he was in the hospital for brutal headaches now.

Frank continued, not registering the irony in his last words. "One tenant wanted to utilize the basement, but insisted some remodeling be done first. My nephew, clueless as to the cost of such things, agreed. But instead of doing it himself, he gave them permission to make the changes, including adding some interior walls downstairs."

Nathan nodded. "That would explain the wall we saw at the end of the room we found. It was two-by-fours and rough plywood sheets, different from the concrete block walls everywhere else."

"Yes, that's right. I remember telling my nephew to be sure to get all of that old merchandise and junk out of the rooms downstairs before letting the tenant in to do their work. He assured me he'd take care of it. Add *that* to the list of things he said that I shouldn't have believed."

"You think the tenant just sectioned off part of the basement down there, blocking off part of the room and leaving all the junk inside?"

Frank shrugged again. "If there are still boxes down there—and I specifically remember that Santa suit you found—then yes, that *is* what I think. Philip had that suit custom-made. He'd wear it in the city parade every year. Thought it was good advertisement for his men's clothing store, better than some cheap Santa suit bought out of a catalog."

Nathan grinned. "Grace thought maybe the suit belonged to the *real* Santa, it was so nice." He stood and tossed his now-empty coffee cup in the trash. Virginia handed hers to him as well. "I've looked in the windows of that building next door. It's empty. I could see a 'For Sale' sign on the floor. Must have fallen off the window. I take it the tenant didn't work out?"

"No. No surprise there. Got behind on rent, and I eventually had to have them formally evicted. After that, there was no way Philip's kids could pay the taxes. They'd both moved across the country. The property went back to the city. I heard a developer bought it for the cost of the back taxes, but they haven't done anything with it yet."

It was all starting to make sense to Nathan now—especially the Santa suit. But he was still concerned about the partially obscured tracks in the snow, outside the door into the alley. And, of course, why the door was open that second night when they went down to investigate.

"We did see there was a second door out of that storage room," he said. "Into the back alley."

Frank nodded. "Sure—that was where Philip used to receive his deliveries. He didn't have a door on the upper level like we do."

Nathan was careful how he asked his next question. "Would there be any reason for someone to be back there these days? Near the door into the alley?"

"Oh . . . no. I'm sure that door's been sealed up tight for years."

"Interesting. It's just that . . . I walked through the alley this morning on my way to Mabel's to pick up our coffee. I noticed wheel tracks in the snow back there. There's an old cart with a garbage can on it. Someone must have moved it recently."

Virginia sat up straighter. "My heavens, Nathan, whatever made you take the alley? The front sidewalk is much easier."

"I know. I just needed to check to see if I needed to clear snow off the back steps. Tomorrow's garbage day, right? I'll need to take the trash out there today yet."

Nathan's explanation seemed to satisfy Virginia.

"You know," Frank said, thinking, "I wonder if those tracks you saw came from Nick."

Nathan blinked. "Nick?"

"Yeah, you remember—the police officer who came over when I called about the missing money?"

Now Nathan nodded. He'd forgotten the guy's name. Then it dawned on him, at the same time that Frank uttered the words.

"He said he found the empty donation box back in the alley somewhere. I bet *he* moved the cart when he was looking for the missing money."

***

Grace called two days later. Nathan had been tempted to call her after his visit with Frank and Virginia, but then he remembered how awkward he'd felt when she'd left, and he decided to wait to see if she'd reach out to him instead. Part of him was relieved to see her number pop up on his phone. Another part was leery. She wouldn't be done with finals yet—it was only Wednesday.

Why would she call now?

"Hey, Grace. How's your week going?" he asked, slamming the door to his dad's Lexus. He'd just gotten back to the bookstore. The only light inside was from the Christmas tree. It was after 7:00 p.m., and his mom would have closed up two hours ago.

"Hi, Nathan. How are finals going?"

"All right, I think. I haven't *bombed* any of them yet, at least. How about for you? You aren't done, are you?"

"No, not yet. But I just wanted to call and thank you for the fun weekend. And . . ." She hesitated, but Nathan didn't jump in. "And I feel like I owe you an apology."

Nathan let himself into the bookstore. He dropped his backpack on the floor, his keys rattling as he tossed them next to his books. "For what?"

He shifted the phone to his other ear, squatting next to the tree and pulling out one of the pillows he and Grace had used the previous Friday night. He lay down, staring up at their make-believe starry sky, where reflections from the pink and white Christmas lights dotted the tin ceiling.

The last time I got down on this floor, I liked what she had to say. Maybe it'll work again.

"I always wanted to come see Dad at your event on Saturday," she said. "But that honestly wasn't the only reason I drove over early. Of course I wanted to see you, too, don't get me wrong . . . but there was another reason. Remember when I told you about Connor? The guy I went down to Texas to visit, and we parted ways under bad circumstances?"

"You mean the dude whose picture is your phone's backdrop?"

"You saw that, huh? Yeah, that's him. I need to change that."

Nathan sighed. Why was Grace talking to him about this Connor guy? Was he back in her life or something?

"Julie ran into his old roommate. The roommate told Julie that Connor was coming back for the weekend and he wanted to talk to me about what happened between us."

Nathan sat up. *Now* things were starting to make sense. "*But*, instead, you came *here*, earlier than expected. So, let me guess . . . you left so you could avoid seeing him?"

He could picture Grace nodding.

"I did. And I'm embarrassed. I shouldn't have done that. Or, at least, I should have told *you* why I came early. That's why I was feeling so bad on Sunday morning. You're a great guy, and I didn't want you to think I was leading you on."

"Were you?"

"I understand why it might look that way. That's what I wanted to apologize for now. That was never my intent."

Nathan took some time to consider Grace's confession before responding. He lay back down, crossed his ankles, and raised an index finger toward the pinpoints of light on the ceiling, connecting the dots to make imaginary figures. When he realized he'd drawn a heart, he sighed again.

"Did you still end up talking to him on Sunday? Once you got back to school?"

He heard her exhale. "I did. He found me in the library. Once my study group broke up, he was waiting for me in the lobby. I considered walking right past him, but then I decided we probably should talk about what happened."

Nathan rolled over on his side and propped up on an elbow, staring blindly at the Christmas tree. He didn't want to hear about how Grace patched things up with her ex.

"Grace . . . why are you telling me all this? I think I've been pretty clear about my feelings where you're concerned, but I feel like you're sending me mixed messages. I wish you'd have just been straight with me."

A pause. "I wish I would have been, too."

"Guess that's one wish that won't be coming true this Christmas," he said, eyeing the ballerina ornament that would always remind him of Grace.

"But I want to be honest with you *now*, Nathan. Please."

Nathan stayed quiet, waiting for her to continue.

"I think part of me was still hung up on Connor. You see, he was the first guy I dated since I went back to college. When I was so sick, I didn't know if I'd ever get back there. When I did, and I started dating Connor, things finally felt more *normal* again. Do you know what I mean?"

He could maybe understand that, but he still didn't interrupt.

"After talking to him again on Sunday, I realized we have very little in common. There was nothing there, no connection."

Nathan lay flat on his back again, twisting a thread of tinsel around his finger that had drifted to the floor.

Am I supposed to congratulate her for finally getting over a guy she said treated her like dirt? Where is she going with all of this?

"Anyhow, I just wanted to call and try to clear the air. I don't want things to be awkward between us. I think you're a great guy, and I enjoy spending time with you. I was hoping maybe I could come back, maybe the weekend before Christmas, and help you some more in the bookstore. I can't make it this weekend because I'm helping a friend cater a holiday party—I need some cash. But could I come on the twenty-second? That Friday . . . and maybe stay until Saturday night? Sunday will be Christmas Eve."

Nathan shook the tinsel off his finger. He felt torn. It had been great spending time with Grace, but she was all over the board, and he was tired of not knowing where he stood with her. After some thought, he figured sharing his plans for that last shopping weekend would be easier than giving her a direct answer.

"I'm not sure if Frank will be well enough to be back at the store by then or not. That last weekend was when I was hoping to focus on the kids more, give their parents a break so they can do some last-minute shopping. But if Frank isn't better, I don't have a Santa Claus."

"And were you thinking of maybe using that *amazing* Santa suit we found?"

"Oh!" That reminded him that Grace was out of the loop as far as Philip and the building next door. He filled her in on his Monday visit to the hospital and all he'd learned.

"I wonder who all that stuff belongs to, then?"

"*Nobody*, I guess."

"If that's the case, do you think Frank would object to us using the Santa suit?"

"It doesn't matter if we can use the *suit* because we don't have a *Santa*. Unless we find someone else. Maybe I could ask my grandfather. He's usually a good sport about things."

"Or," Grace said, her voice sounding suddenly mischievous, "we could ask my dad to do it. After all, he had that scruff on his face. If he hasn't shaved it off yet, and he lets it grow for another week and a half, he might be able to pull it off."

Nathan laughed; he couldn't picture quiet Grant being up for that. "It would never look like the real Santa."

"But he'd look dang good! If any of the kids ask, he could tell them he'd been to the barber, and they trimmed off a little too much. And maybe the women customers would appreciate a hunky-looking Santa for a change."

"I'm telling him you said that," Nathan teased.

"I don't care. I've been trying to set Dad up for years—obviously with little success. So, what do you think? Would you mind if I came for another visit? I just want to hang out with you, you know, take things slow. I don't want to jump into anything serious again. But don't you think you should have some fun and not work *all* the time during the holidays?"

"Now you're starting to sound like Virginia," Nathan said, again staring up at the ceiling covered in reflected Christmas lights. "Sure, why not? Last weekend was fun, and I could probably use the help around here."

He stayed there, stretched out on his back on the drafty floor, after their phone call ended.

While things with Grace still felt confusing, he was gaining clarity in a different area of his life. Working here at the bookstore felt rewarding, like he was making a difference. Another wish was taking shape in Nathan's mind as he found the brightest spot of white light above. His great-aunt Celia had helped Virginia start this bookstore years ago. When she'd died, she'd arranged for Nathan, along with his other cousins, to inherit a tidy sum of money from her estate if and when they each graduated from college. He wished he could do something with those funds to keep Virginia's bookstore going for years to come.

Maybe that would have been Celia's wish too . . .

CHAPTER 21

Gift of Unfulfilled Wishes

When Frank's diagnosis was finally communicated to them that Thursday, it was a relief to learn the type of headaches he was suffering from were caused by a treatable condition that was more common in older adults. His situation had been complicated by his blood pressure, which they'd had trouble regulating. When Virginia asked why it had taken so long for them to arrive at their conclusion, the doctors assured her it was necessary to rule out other, more serious, conditions. While it was frustrating, they were both relieved at the doctor's assurances that Frank wouldn't have to suffer from the mind-numbing pain he'd been experiencing for the foreseeable future.

They were finally releasing him.

An unexpected side benefit of Frank's illness—at least from Virginia's perspective—was her ability to fully embrace the commitment she'd made to herself during his duck-hunting weekend to get back some independence. She was driving again, handling more of the household tasks she'd let Frank take care of in recent months, like paying bills and buying groceries, and she was nursing her husband back to health. While she never would have wanted Frank to get sick, she herself was feeling stronger. Ever since that morning when she'd sat in the back of the ambulance with Frank, watching their home shrink as they sped toward the hospital, Virginia had felt a surge of something akin to power flow back into her core. If she didn't step up, who would see to Frank?

It felt great to be driving again, despite the less-than-ideal road conditions. Other than the one unfortunate incident with the garage door, she was getting her confidence back when she sat behind the wheel. Slowly slipping into the habit of allowing Frank to chauffeur her around town, insisting she give up her keys when her eye doctor mentioned deteriorating peripheral vision, had been a blow to her confidence. Frank had ignored the part where the doctor said her eyesight was *very slowly* diminishing.

She didn't blame her husband. Letting herself fall into the trap of thinking her best years were behind her was her own fault. Frank had the best of intentions. After all, he'd been taking care of her for over forty years. She'd been allowing the circle that made up her world to shrink a nearly imperceptible bit each day.

While her withdrawal had initially been slow, and then more dramatic when all of Karen's troubles surfaced, the realization of what she was allowing herself to become was a shock, like being doused in ice water. She was missing out on so many of the things that used to bring her joy. She missed the evenings she used to enjoy at their local theater, directing young people and helping with costumes. Her bridge group still met weekly, but her old spot had been filled by someone else when she quit attending regularly.

Once Frank was feeling better, she'd see about getting her spot back at the card table. She also needed to find out which play the local theater group planned to produce and how she might be able to get involved. Summer was always a busy time for shows, but the work at the theater would begin months earlier.

"Where is that blasted doctor?" Frank said, sitting on the edge of his hospital bed, fully dressed in his street clothes for the first time in nearly a week. "He needs to release me."

"He said he'd stop in during his rounds this morning. Be patient, dear. I'm sure it won't be long now."

"Have you called Nathan yet?"

"Yes, yes, I told him you'd be home soon. Or at least I told his *voicemail.* I think he finishes his finals today."

"Good, good."

Virginia again took in her husband's appearance. The past few weeks had been hard on him, both physically and emotionally. She knew he struggled with this sudden reversal of the roles they'd assumed in their marriage. *He* usually fussed over *her*. Now it was her turn to structure her days to see to his needs.

She also knew he hated it.

They needed to talk. To take a hard look at what her and Frank's lives had become and make some changes. She didn't know what that would look like, but she finally realized that if she didn't want to continue on this slow decline she'd been on, they'd have to fight against what had become deeply ingrained habits. She missed the vitality she used to feel.

Frank glanced out the window. "It's starting to snow. I'll drive us home."

No time like the present to get started on those changes, Virginia thought.

"Don't be ridiculous, Frank. I've been doing fine, driving all week. I'll get you home safely."

Voices in the hallway and the swooshing of the curtain into Frank's room curtailed any further argument. His doctor, along with a nurse, had finally arrived.

"What do you say we get you out of here, Frank?" she said.

***

"Watch this intersection," Frank directed, pointing through the windshield to the busy corner ahead. "It's always slick when it snows."

Virginia sighed but bit her lip. His habit of *helpful* commentary any time she drove was the impetus for her allowing him to drive more and more often in the recent past. It had seemed easier to let him drive than to tolerate his advice, which often led to arguments. Now she'd do her best to tamp down her irritation at his words. But she wasn't giving up the keys again.

"I'll park in front, so it's easier for you to get in the house," Virginia said, turning down their street instead of the alley. She still needed to get someone over to fix the garage door and didn't need Frank seeing the damage she'd caused on his first morning home.

"Now, Ginny, I do *not* want you to be coddling me. I'm perfectly capable of walking from the garage to the house."

"Not coddling, dear. The back path still has lots of compacted snow on it, so it's slippery. The last thing I want is for you to fall and crack your head on the ground, now that you finally shook that headache. Nathan did a nice job clearing the front walk, so that's more manageable. There's still some ice, but it's better than behind the house."

Frank continued to grumble as she pulled up in front of the house, careful to match up Frank's door to the walkway shoveled out of the snow. She parked some distance from the curb to give them both room to maneuver. Snow banks on the side of the road were high, and she wanted to hold on to his arm, give them both some stability. She may have committed to acting younger, but she wasn't stupid. She could slip on the ice just as easily as he could.

Once inside, Frank stopped to remove his shoes and hang his jacket in the front hall closet, just as he'd done for decades. "Have I mentioned how sick of this cold weather I am? Imagine not having to battle snow, and ice, and heavy winter coats. I wish we could pack up the car and head to Florida. I've got buddies that go with their wives from the first of January until April."

"I know, dear, you've reminded me of that fact every day this week." Virginia also removed her shoes and outerwear. "Why don't you go get settled in the front room, and I can pull some lunch together? Your show is on."

"Good idea. I need to catch up," Frank said, heading for his recliner.

"It's recording," Virginia said with a shake of her head. As far as she knew, Frank's soap opera was her husband's one guilty pleasure. No one would believe her if she told them he watched it religiously. Not that she was *allowed* to tell anyone.

"Are you going to join me?" Frank asked. "We never get to watch it at lunchtime. We're usually at the bookstore."

While she didn't particularly care to watch the show, she'd do it because he asked her to sit with him. Frank would do it for her. It was the little things, after all these years, that kept the spark alive.

After lunch, Frank nodded off in front of the television. They'd already agreed she'd run down to the bookstore to check on Nathan—or Jess if he was still at a final—and see if there was anything that needed her attention. The poor boy had been holding things down long enough. And maybe she could even convince him to run back to her house to look at her garage door.

The store was surprisingly busy when she arrived. Parking spots in front of the bookstore, normally open, were full. She ended up parking closer to Mabel's bakery. Not that she minded—despite having just eaten lunch, she craved a cup of her favorite tea, made the way only Mabel could prepare it.

"Aren't *you* a sight for sore eyes," her friend greeted her as she pushed through the heavy front door.

The glass in the door sported a new painting of three choir boys in white robes and little cowlicks sticking up from the tops of their heads, surrounded by sprigs of holly. Virginia found it quaint.

"Who's the artist?"

Mabel grimaced, nodding her head toward the kitchen in the back. "Tansy. She *insisted* on hanging this garland across my front display cabinet, too. It looks like Christmas threw up in here."

Virginia laughed loudly. Mabel, despite her big heart and wise words, was a Scrooge at heart.

"She's talented, Mabel. I think the painting on the door is a nice touch."

Mabel snorted, busying herself with Virginia's tea. "I've missed making this for you every afternoon. I take it Frank was able to go home?"

"Finally. He'll be all right, but that was scary. These golden years aren't so golden."

"Guess it all depends on your perspective. To hear Tansy tell it, being twenty-five isn't so golden either."

While she hadn't intended to stay for a visit, something in Mabel's tone held her back. "Here I thought you were going to tell me the golden years are great if you just keep a positive attitude." When her teasing didn't elicit much of a response from Mabel, she shrugged out of her coat and motioned to the table in front of the window where they sometimes took their afternoon tea.

Mabel nodded, bringing Virginia's tea over, along with a cup of coffee for herself.

"Do you want to talk about it?"

Her friend glanced back toward the kitchen. Virginia heard an oven door slam shut.

"Tansy's very gifted, as you can see. But she's troubled, too. I thought, or at least *hoped*, that by the time she was in her mid-twenties she'd have found a bit of stability in her life. She does make progress—once in a while—but then she'll inevitably hook up with the wrong kind of guy, and she starts the downward spiral again."

"Is that what's brought her back this time? It's been, what, three years since she last sought you out?"

"Yeah. I suppose. That brother of mine is fed up with her, so she has nowhere else to turn. I hope she figures it out this time. She seems to want to try."

Virginia searched her friend's face. Time had left a network of wrinkles across her ruddy skin, the lines deepest around her warm brown eyes. Those eyes were always so expressive. Today, they reflected concern.

"And if she doesn't?"

Mabel, usually so decisive, grimaced. "Honestly? I don't know. I'm not sure I'd have the heart to kick her out. She's been through so much. Losing your mom when you're twelve is life-changing. And I know she blames herself for what happened. Ridiculous, obviously, but perception is reality."

The front door opened and a young couple entered hand in hand.

"Be right with you," Mabel said, waving.

"Take your time, we don't know what we want yet," the woman said, clasping her hands behind her back as she checked out Mabel's mouthwatering display of treats, many decorated for the holidays.

Mabel turned back to Virginia. "But hey, at least she gave me a few hundred dollars a couple weeks ago. Said it was for rent. I was surprised since I thought she was flat broke, but I wasn't about to complain."

Nathan's guilt-ridden eyes swam up in Virginia's mind. He'd felt responsible when their money went missing. She hated the thought that popped into her brain. Tansy may have her issues, but that didn't mean she'd steal a donation box.

Would she?

"I better go help them," Mabel said, standing and pushing her chair back in, the feet scraping the floor. "Thanks for stopping in. Tell Frank I'm glad he's home."

Virginia nodded to her friend as she took another sip of her tea. She heard the male customer ask who'd painted the choir boys on the door. He *liked* it, apparently.

Mabel's weathered face softened as she smiled. "Why, my niece painted that. She's quite talented, isn't she?"

Virginia prayed Tansy wasn't behind the missing money. She knew all too well how horrible it felt when someone close turned out to be a thief and a liar. She didn't want Mabel to ever have to experience that type of pain—the kind Virginia felt when Karen's crimes came to light. Or maybe, if Tansy *was* behind the stolen money, perhaps she'd felt desperate, facing an impossible situation. While Karen's wayward ways had been spurred on by greed, Virginia's own past had taught her one can never know the length you'll go to when loved ones are threatened. Years ago, Virginia had also "hooked up with the wrong kind of guy," to quote her friend, and she'd stolen to survive.

Who am I to judge?

***

By the time Virginia made her way to the bookstore, two of the parking spots up front were open. Letting herself in, she welcomed the chiming of her little bell above. The smell of apple cider and cinnamon enveloped her along with soft piano music. She glanced around her store, taking it all in. She'd missed it.

"Hello, Nathan," she said, walking slowly toward the counter where he was on his computer, even enjoying the click-clacking of her heels on the vinyl tile. She didn't see any customers at the moment. "Is your mom still here?"

Nathan shut his laptop and turned his attention to her.

"How did you know my mom was here? Did you talk to her?"

Silly boy. Maybe he would have thought to put on the cider, but she doubted he'd think to play the Christmas music.

"Lucky guess. It looked busy when I pulled in a bit ago. Good to see. I stopped down to see Mabel," she said, holding up her paper cup of tea and then placing it on the counter.

Nathan sat on one of the stools behind the counter. He motioned to the other one next to him.

"How is Frank doing? Feeling better?"

Virginia hung her coat up on the coat rack and joined Nathan. "He *is* feeling better. Still ornery, but on the mend. I cannot believe we are only a little over a week away from Christmas already! What do you have planned for this weekend?"

"This weekend will be pretty simple. Originally, we'd talked about maybe having some kind of event, but after bringing authors in last weekend, and what I hope to pull together for next Saturday, the day before Christmas Eve, I'm just planning to hit social media hard. I have a fun new twist I could add to our marketing, but I wanted to get your input first."

She cradled her paper cup of tea. "You have me intrigued. Go on."

Nathan grinned. "I still want to have Santa and Mrs. Claus available for the kids that last weekend before Christmas. Now, I know that doesn't sound too original, but we'd jazz it up. Here's where the twist comes in. You know how kids ask Santa for whatever they want at Christmas?"

Virginia nodded, smiling. She'd always loved the giving spirit of Christmas that Santa Claus had come to represent.

"Well, I was talking with Grace"—Virginia's smile widened, but Nathan plowed on—"and we decided that sharing our wishes with others at Christmas time shouldn't have to stop when we grow up."

"What do you mean?"

Nathan shrugged. "It's kind of hard to articulate. But it just feels like . . . I don't know . . . some of the magic of Christmas is lost, the older we get. You know . . . wishes . . . belief . . . it all tends to fade away, replaced with long 'to do' lists and overspending."

"That sounds a bit cynical, Nathan," Virginia pointed out.

"Cynical or not, I'm afraid that's the way most people approach the holidays these days," Nathan said, getting off the stool.

She was surprised to hear the disillusionment in the young man's voice. Her eyes traveled to the gorgeous tree in their front window, the ornaments scattered over its surface.

But is he wrong?

Personally, ever since she'd been young, she knew some people thought she was a dreamer, a hopeless romantic. People like her mother, who'd never understood her passion for things like art and words. But even *she* had let some of her desires slip by the wayside. Wasn't her unfinished manuscript a prime example?

And what about Frank? This last health scare had her questioning her stance she'd taken in regards to this very place she loved so much. Frank wished to spend some of their time down south, in warmer climates, to escape the hard Minnesota winters. But because of Book Journeys, she'd never allowed him to pursue that wish.

Finally she said, "Well, I can't argue with that. But do you think there's any way to change that?"

Nathan leaned a hip against the counter, glancing between Virginia and their front window display. "I'm not sure. But even if we can give people a moment or two of fun, of reconnecting with some of their biggest wishes, I think it would be fun to try. Haven't you had fun finally pursuing your wish of giving Frank his book?"

"Of course! I'm just sorry I've had to put the whole book thing on hold since Frank got sick. I'll get back to it when he feels better, maybe have it ready for him for our anniversary this summer. But back to your bigger question as it pertains to our customers: I think it would be wonderful to encourage their wishing and dreaming. Perfect time of year for that. But how are you proposing we do it?"

"Wait right here," Nathan ordered, heading in the direction of the storage room.

Virginia watched him go, even more curious now. She got off her stool and walked to the tree, her old ornaments beckoning to her. She touched a silver sleigh hanging proudly on a high branch. It had been years since she'd thought much of Santa Claus and the magic he represented to children everywhere. It seemed anywhere she turned now, men in cheap Santa suits were ringing bells to collect money for good causes or looking exhausted on mall benches, listening to a streaming line of crabby children, forcing smiles for overpriced photographs exhausted parents could take home.

Nathan wasn't the only one who'd become cynical.

Her outstretched hand traveled over to her prized nutcracker, and she carefully removed him from the tree. It wasn't easy; the hanger crimped hard around the wire branch, plastic needles poking at her fingers. As she brought him down to eye-level, she felt the cold, heavy weight of the old glass in her hand. His surface bore tiny cracks she'd never noticed before.

Kind of like me and Frank, Virginia realized with a smile.

She again thought back to her father, and the way the man had done his best to satisfy her demanding mother. Despite everything, she'd always known her father loved her mother, although she'd never personally understood his devotion to the difficult woman.

My poor Frank isn't so very different. We've lived our life doing the things I wanted to do. He's asked for so little. What have I done to help him enjoy things important to him?

"Is something wrong?" Nathan asked, causing her to jump. She'd been lost in her thoughts and hadn't heard him return. She turned toward him, still holding the nutcracker.

"Wrong?"

He pointed at the ornament in her hand. "Is it broken?"

Why would it be broken?

She turned back around and placed her nutcracker back on the tree. "Of course not, it's fine."

After again securing the nutcracker on the tree, she gave Nathan her full attention and saw what he was holding.

"Oh my, would you look at that," she said, fingering the fine fabric of her now-dead brother-in-law's custom-made Santa suit. "When you mentioned this the other day, I'd forgotten how *spectacular* it was. I can't believe it was tucked away, forgotten, for all these years. What a blessing you found it!"

"It is something, isn't it?" Nathan said, grinning. "I can still hardly believe Grace and I stumbled across it. Wouldn't it be cool to use this next weekend?"

Virginia nodded, thinking of her tired husband resting on their couch at home. "It would be fun . . . but Nathan, I'm afraid Frank won't be up for it. He wasn't thrilled to play the Scarecrow at Halloween, and after his hospital stay I can't imagine he'd want to wear this for a bunch of children next weekend."

Nathan laid down the pile of clothing across the counter, speaking as he arranged them so Virginia could once again appreciate the craftsmanship of each piece. "Oh no, I realize that. I could maybe try to pull it off, but I'd make a pretty young and scrawny Santa Claus."

"Do you have someone else in mind?" Virginia asked, bending over the suit to have a closer look. The details were exquisite. Whomever Philip had found to fashion this years ago had truly created a thing of beauty.

"Grace thought her dad might do it."

Virginia hadn't yet met Grant Johnson. "He isn't very old either, is he?"

"I'd guess he's mid-forties, maybe fifty. He's not quite as tall as I am, but he's more filled in, and when he was here last weekend he was sporting some decent facial hair."

"But he hasn't agreed yet?"

"Not yet," Nathan said, "but I have a feeling Grace can talk him into almost anything."

"And did you want a *Mrs.* Claus?"

Now he turned his full-wattage smile on her. "It wouldn't take much to change up that Glenda the Good Witch costume you wore for Halloween into a brilliant Mrs. Claus getup."

Virginia paused, but quickly realized she wouldn't be able to pass on an excuse to wear that lovely gown again. "You've been doing some thinking on this, I see. I suppose you want to bring that delightful little red couch down here for us to use, too?"

"I did *wish* we could do that when you first showed it to me," he reminded her, still grinning. He seemed particularly excited with this twist on granting wishes.

"I guess you did, didn't you?"

Virginia let her eye travel around her store. She'd spent years here, doing her best to provide books people would enjoy, books they could escape into or use to learn more about things they were interested in.

"Have you ever thought about how *books* help make wishes come true?" she asked, meeting Nathan's eye.

He laughed. "See, here you've been in the wish-granting business all these years and didn't even realize it. And that's what I want to focus on between now and Christmas. Let's help remind people to *wish* and to *dream* . . . and to pursue those dreams again."

Virginia picked up the tufted Santa hat and settled it on top of her snow-white hair, her eyes twinkling. "Let's do just that."

CHAPTER 22

Gift of a Vision

*G*race was somehow able to convince her father that he'd make an excellent Santa Claus. It hadn't been easy, she'd told Nathan over the phone on Sunday, but he'd agreed to do it. Both Grace and Grant would come over early the following Saturday morning and spend the day before heading home to celebrate Christmas.

While Nathan was disappointed that she wouldn't be coming earlier, maybe it was for the best. Fewer temptations and all that.

He'd been hitting social media hard since getting Virginia's approval of their ideas, posting photographs showing snippets of the fancy suit they'd found alongside stacks of beautiful books and the tagline *Book Journeys: Capturing Wishes for the Young and Not-So-Young.* It seemed to be resonating. The posts were getting lots of likes and shares.

Virginia shook her head in amazement when he showed her what he'd done. "I remember when we'd work with someone to design a print ad for the local newspaper. I can't believe how the world of advertising and marketing for businesses has changed. I'm thankful we have you to help us with that, Nathan."

The one thing Nathan *didn't* bring up to Virginia again was her book. He did, however, email Grant, Grace, his mother, and his writing professor, Michelle, about Virginia's comment regarding her manuscript. All agreed to keep going on it, despite Virginia's hesitancy to work on it now that Frank needed her more.

Michelle reported that the editing was going well. (Nathan had emailed her the file after they'd all gone out to dinner.) Grant offered to work with her on any rewrites and corrections that were needed, swearing to do his best to keep it in Virginia's voice. Nathan was relieved to have him as part of the team.

Polishing up the manuscript was a big part of the process, but they would also need to get a cover produced, figure out the logistics behind using what Grant had referred to as "print on demand," and all the other things it would take to convert what had begun as a handwritten story on a stack of old paper into a physical book that Virginia would be proud of.

While Nathan was nervous about proceeding without Virginia's guiding hand, it still felt like the right thing to do. She'd done some self-editing on the file he'd typed up for her before Frank got sick, and because she'd been using the store's laptop, he had access to it. He kept an eye on the date stamp of her file, watching for any changes she might make on her own, but the date didn't change; she seemed preoccupied with other things.

With Grant and Michelle working on the story itself, Nathan and Grace offered to figure out the cover but would be sure to get everyone's input on it as well. Jess would help figure out how they'd pay for the cover and any copies of the eventual physical book they'd want to order.

There was lots of work to be done so Virginia could give Frank the book for his birthday, but Nathan had to set that aside until they got past Christmas.

In the week leading up to their last Saturday event before the holidays, Nathan worked hard to create hype around their theme; but he was stuck on one thing. He'd been racking his brain for some kind of giveaway they could use for the kids visiting Santa. He didn't want to settle for a candy cane, but he worried that something like a cookie might be bad with all the food allergies these days. When he'd mentioned his dilemma to Grace, she reminded him about the ballerina jewelry box she'd found in their mystery room.

"What about it?" Nathan asked. He remembered the small box, and how it had played a tune when Grace wound it up, but he didn't see how they could make use of that now.

She sighed. "Nathan, think *creatively* for once." He started to protest, but she interrupted. "Make them *wishing* boxes."

"Wishing boxes?"

"Sure. Why not? It looked like there were lots of them. Extra stock, I suppose."

Nathan hated to admit he wasn't following. "So . . . they're *not* jewelry boxes, then?"

"Focus, Nathan. They're little musical boxes, but you can call them anything you want."

"I guess little girls might be excited to get a box when they talk to Santa, but I doubt most boys will want a box with a ballerina twirling around inside."

His comment gave Grace pause. "At the risk of stereotyping anyone, you might be right. I hadn't thought about that. But what if you pulled the little ballerina off? Make sure the music still plays, but instead of a twirling dancer . . ." She thought for a moment, then said, "See if you could take two silver star stickers and stick them together on top of the little rod instead. *Boom* . . . a wishing box!"

On Thursday, he headed to the basement while Virginia helped customers. He wrestled the old dresser away from the chair, blocking the aqua door. When he opened it, everything looked the same as it had when he and Grace were down here before.

Now, where are those music boxes?

He rummaged around a bit before spotting a familiar-looking box. Sure enough, lots of smaller white boxes were inside. He pulled one out and opened it, removing a small white music box. He estimated there were forty or so similar white boxes, neatly stacked in the larger one.

Now he just had to see if Grace's suggestion to switch out the ballerina would even work—and if Virginia would be okay with them giving the boxes away.

***

On Saturday morning, Grace helped Nathan move the red loveseat out of his apartment and down the stairs, and get it situated near the Christmas tree.

Virginia was already moving around the room in her pretty, sparkly white dress, now topped with a short red jacket trimmed in silvery fur. She looked to be floating, the wide skirts hiding her feet.

Nathan had laughed when she'd arrived an hour earlier. "Where did you get *that* costume addition?"

Virginia stroked the soft fur lining her neck. "I still have connections at the theater in town. I had to dig deep, but I found this beauty in a trunk left over from their production of *Little Red Riding Hood*. I think it adds just the right touch, don't you?"

While Grace and Nathan set up the visiting area under Virginia's critical eye, Grant headed to the bathroom to don the Santa suit. When he came back a few minutes later, Grace squealed in delight at the sight of him.

"Dad, you make the *perfect* Santa!" she exclaimed.

Grant tugged a sleeve down where the burgundy velvet fabric was bunched up underneath the fur-trimmed cape. He had put on everything, including the hat, leather gloves, and thick-soled black boots. "This all fits surprisingly well, but do I really look *old* enough to pass for Santa? Or *fat* enough? Tell me I don't have the paunch or white hair yet."

Grace circled her father, tugging here and there to get everything lined up correctly. "You look like a hunky, silver-fox Santa instead of the lumpy, jolly, traditional Santa. The ladies will love it."

Nathan stood nearby, surveying Grant in his costume with a critical eye. Grace had been right to suggest her dad for the role. He looked *dang* good.

Virginia heard them and came over to investigate. She'd already met Grant when he'd arrived earlier that morning. She covered her mouth with one gloved hand, her eyes glistening.

"Grant, you look *dashing* in that getup! Philip, my dear brother-in-law, may he rest in peace, never *dreamed* of looking that good."

Nathan noticed Grant's cheeks flush in embarrassment, adding to the Santa look.

"Nathan, you must get a picture of our suave Santa and post it. I guarantee that'll draw our female customers in."

"Hey, wait a minute," Grant protested, his cheeks flushing even more. "I thought I was here for the kids."

"Kids . . . and paying customers," Virginia teased, winking at him.

"Enough already." Grant pulled off the gloves and hat in deference to the heated room. "You guys are rotten."

Virginia and Grace laughed.

Even Frank had insisted on coming over to enjoy the day. He'd been sticking close to his desk, making his way through some of the paperwork that Nathan wasn't sure how to deal with, but now he looked over and laughed at their antics.

Grace stepped away and then quickly joined them again, this time carrying a large cardboard box. Nathan, spying her, took the box and set it in front of the loveseat. She took one of the smaller white boxes out, opened it, and grinned in approval at the star where the dancer used to be. It was perfect.

She handed the box to Nathan. "Better tell Dad about these."

Taking the box, he turned back to Grant while Grace got down on her knees and started piling the small white boxes next to where Grant would be sitting.

"We thought we'd give each family one of these little wishing boxes when they either visit with you or purchase something."

"Everyone?" Grant asked, astonished as he held the box. "These look pretty nice just to give away."

"It's a long story, but suffice it to say we found these in the basement—same place we found that suit you're wearing, actually. They've been down there for decades, and we—actually, *Grace*—came up with the idea to turn them into 'wishing boxes.' "

Nathan took the box back from Grant, turned it over, and gave the little knob on the bottom two twists, then flipped it back over and opened the box. The little star rotated while the song about sugar plum fairies played.

"Kids always ask for things from Santa. You know—toys, bikes, whatever. But *adults* get so caught up in the busyness of the season, they forget about the magic. We want people to start wishing again, and to write their wishes on little slips of paper to slip in their magical boxes. It'll encourage them to make some of those wishes come true. Maybe it's a little corny, but hey, people are eating it up on Facebook."

Grant grinned, holding his hand out to take the wishing box again. "Leave it to my daughter to dream up something like this. I guess *I'm* the one that'll have to explain to the kids what these are for, then?"

"The kids, and any adults that might want to sit and visit with you."

He chuckled. "Like *that'll* happen."

Nathan shrugged. "You never know. That suit is one of a kind. And our finding it in a secret room adds to the mystery. I wrote a short story about it and posted it online twenty minutes ago. I'm hoping it will create more buzz."

"What do we do on the off-chance we run out of boxes?"

Virginia overheard Grant's question from where she'd been tweaking the display of books nearest their Santa visiting area. "No worries. I have Mabel on standby. She has boxes of old canning jars we could use. We may just be giving out wishing *jars* by the end of the day!"

***

It didn't take long for Nathan to question his decision to post his short story about the found Santa suit and wishing boxes—but only because the line to sit and visit with Grant and Virginia, aka Santa and Mrs. Claus, was starting to wrap up and down the aisles. His intent had been to provide an easier shopping experience for parents by creating a distraction for the kids— at least that had been his *original* thought; now he feared he was cutting into the parents' day instead, forcing them to wait in line because so many people, kids *and* adults, had shown up.

Their wishing boxes were gone by noon. Nathan made more than one trip to Mabel's for boxes of turquoise-hued canning jars. Grace was improvising, tying white ribbons with silver paper stars on the end that she'd cut out of aluminum foil around the tops of the jars.

Jess stepped in to help as well when they'd stopped to see how the day was going and arrived to a crowded store. When Nathan explained about the wishing boxes, she smiled at her old friend Grant. "*My* wish is that you'd find a real-life Mrs. Claus, instead of living like a hermit, writing your wonderful books."

Grant smirked at her comment, mouthing *"Cute"* at her as another child climbed up on his knee.

Nathan and Grace overheard their exchange, grinning to each other. Grace had filled Nathan in on her latest matchmaking scheme where her father was concerned. She hoped to spark some interest between her dad and Michelle, Nathan's teacher. They'd called her, suggesting she stop down at the bookstore to say hello to Frank, since he was back. That way she'd also get a chance to talk to Grant; Grace had been sure the teacher-turned-editor would appreciate what a handsome Santa he made. Unfortunately, she had other plans for the day. Despite that, Grace was determined to get them together later.

Lots of people wanted their pictures taken with Santa and Mrs. Claus, and Nathan was mad he hadn't thought of it sooner. He'd mentioned this to Mabel and Tansy when he'd picked up the first box of jars, and Tansy had offered to help take digital photos, most likely with the customers' own phones.

And so the day proceeded, everyone staying busy—even Frank as he sat on a stool at the sales counter, ringing up customers. Nathan checked on him more than once.

"I'm just fine, Nathan. It does my heart good, seeing all of these people stopping in and enjoying themselves. Have you noticed how no one seems frazzled or upset, even with the wait? I bet that isn't the case in *other* stores the day before Christmas Eve. You should be proud of yourself. Today really came together."

"Thank you for letting us use the Santa suit and give away those old music boxes. Those were the key, they really were."

Frank shook his head. "Only a small part of it. Your efforts to remind people to find the magic of the holidays, to *wish* for things again—that's what people are responding to."

Nathan appreciated Frank's words. In the rush of the day, he'd lost sight of the wishing component.

He smiled as a customer, similar in age to the Fisks, brought a stack of four books to the counter and set them in front of Frank.

"I am *so* excited about these," the woman said, tapping the books on the counter. "Uffdah! Those were getting *heavy*. I was at a loss as to what to get for my four girlfriends. I knew if I got them one more candle, they'd smile, say 'Thank you,' and I'd see it out on the table at their next garage sale. But I saw your post, read your story—I think it was called 'Forgotten Wishes'—so when we met for our Saturday coffee this morning, I asked them all what they'd wish for if they could ask Santa for anything."

Frank slid the pile of books closer, looking to see what she'd picked out. "Let me guess. One wants to try her hand at calligraphy, someone else would like to travel to Ireland, one is into photography, and the last one . . ."

He held the fourth book up, confusion on his face.

The woman laughed. "Betsy said *she'd* wish for her husband to get his sex drive back."

Nathan burst out laughing while Frank, cheeks bright red, quickly set the other books on top of the novel. The racy cover included a very attractive, older than average, scantily clad couple poised atop a black motorcycle. Nathan remembered reading the back blurb when he'd noticed it on the shelf weeks ago.

Leave it to Virginia to find a very niche book like that to stock.

"What? They bought one of those three-wheeled trike doohickeys, and they're planning a road trip," the customer replied, winking at Nathan while she held her credit card out for Frank. She turned away, smiling sweetly at Frank after he processed the sale, swinging her holiday bag full of books.

Nathan slapped the counter. "Maybe the wishing thing *is* helping. And it's good to see a little color in your cheeks, Frank."

***

The day was an unparalleled success. They'd given out all of their wishing boxes—then all of their substitute wishing *jars*—their sales would likely be the highest the Fisks had ever experienced, and the next day was Christmas Eve.

Grant had stripped down to a short-sleeved T-shirt and jeans, hot after a long day in the Santa suit and countless kids hanging close. "I can't believe I'm saying this, but I'm looking forward to a cold walk down the street to my car."

Grace and Nathan labored upstairs, putting the red loveseat back where it belonged. Jess had given Frank a ride home, as the day had worn him out. Tansy had gone back to the bakery with a handwritten note to Mabel from Virginia, promising her friend she'd replace all the canning jars they'd given out.

Virginia and Grant had a quiet moment alone.

"Thank you, Grant, for being such a good sport today," Virginia said. "I know it couldn't have been easy, having all those kids crawling all over you."

Grant chuckled. "It wasn't too bad—most of the time. Anytime I get to spend all day at a great bookstore like yours is a good day. By the way, I think you forgot to tell me what you wished for this Christmas. I can slip the coat back on if you want to confess."

The older woman laughed. "That won't be necessary. I don't need the jacket to know you'd help me with my wish if you could. Honestly, my wish would be to do something for Frank to repay him for everything he's done for *me* through the years. These past few weeks, when he's been so ill . . . it's really opened my eyes to the reality that we better start doing all of those things we've both wanted to do. Up until this point, most of what we've done has been for me."

Grant glanced toward the stairs leading to Nathan's apartment, but the kids weren't coming back down yet. "What about your book? You still plan to give that to Frank, don't you?"

"Grace told you about that, did she? Yes, yes. I hope to. I'd thought maybe this Valentine's Day, but that's never going to happen, so I'll aim for our anniversary in August. But I meant we should *do* more things. The poor man has always wanted to head south in the winter. He hates snow and cold. I've never wanted to be away from the store that long. I always thought it had to be either-or, not both."

Grant nodded but said nothing at first. Virginia sighed, settling onto a nearby stool.

"What if you went south for a long visit?" Grant suggested. "Maybe a few weeks, a month? Nathan could watch the store for you."

"Oh no, I couldn't ask Nathan to do all of this by himself," she said, motioning around the store. "He's heading into his last semester of college. The boy will have too much to do to work full-time. Some of his classes are in the middle of the day, during store hours. He *had* to take them to graduate."

Grant stroked his beard. "Nathan loves this place, Virginia. I get the sense he doesn't want to go anywhere else after graduation. He's been asking me all about publishing and writing. Either he's thinking about doing some writing himself, or he'd like to help authors get their work out into the world. Perhaps both."

"Ah, yes, goals I can personally relate to," Virginia said, staring at her twinkling Christmas tree.

"Virginia . . . I'm probably speaking out of turn here—and it isn't my place to share this with you—but were you aware of Nathan's inheritance he received from his great-aunt, Celia?"

She was surprised by his question. While she knew that Celia had passed her own small ownership interest in Book Journeys to Nathan's mom, she hadn't heard anything in regards to *his* inheritance.

"No, I don't know anything about that," she replied.

"All I know is Nathan receives some money from Celia's estate when he graduates from college. All the great-nieces and nephews do if they graduate with any post-secondary degree. I only know this because Jess mentioned it to me awhile back when one of the other kids was considering dropping out of college."

"Oh, dear. Does that mean Nathan won't have to work after graduation? I'd hate to lose him."

Grant laughed. "Oh no, it isn't *that* sizeable. But I wouldn't be surprised if he's been thinking how he might use those funds for the bookstore, maybe to buy in to your business or something."

"Oh, *gracious* . . . I'm not ready to give it up yet." Truth be told, Virginia hated to even entertain such an idea.

Grant held up his hands in reassurance. "That isn't what I'm suggesting, either. Maybe you can work out some kind of transition over time. But hey, I've already stepped way out of bounds here. I've never even discussed any of this with Nathan. I just know he loves this store and seems very intent on seeing it succeed, despite the changing landscape of the book industry."

"You've given me lots to think about, Santa," Virginia said, smiling at Grant.

"I'll give you one more thing to consider. My sister lives in Florida, and she has a rental property down there that they recently finished renovating. She didn't think she'd have it available until February, but when I talked to her last weekend she told me to keep my ears open for any snowbirds who might need a place in January. If you like, I could get you some pictures of the house. Maybe you give Frank his wish by taking him to Florida this January."

Before Virginia could react to this, Nathan and Grace made a racket as they pounded down the wooden stairs.

Grant pulled a set of car keys out his pocket. "We're gonna have to get going. I hope you and Frank have a wonderful Christmas, Virginia. Thank you for such a fun day."

"I think it might just be an extra special Christmas this year," Virginia said, smiling despite the pain in her feet after such a full day. "Very special, indeed."

CHAPTER 23

Gift of a White Christmas

*N*athan hoped he'd done enough.

As he drove over to his grandparents' house to celebrate Christmas Eve with his family, he thought back over the past two months since he'd moved into his new apartment and started working with the Fisks. From the beginning, he knew November and December would have to be good for business, or Frank might make good on his recurring threat to close the bookstore. Now, given Frank's health struggles, Nathan better understood why the older man might feel that way. On top of that, Virginia had told him Frank was turning sixty-five the day after this coming Valentine's.

On the flip side, Virginia loved her bookstore. Nathan had noticed a change in her since he'd discovered her hidden manuscript. Initially, he'd mistaken her for a frail woman, even a little scatterbrained. Frank took care of *her*—or at least that was how Nathan saw it. It just went to show how initial impressions could be misleading. Virginia was smart, creative, resilient, and anything but frail. It couldn't have been easy for her, waiting for an ambulance to arrive to pick up her ailing husband. Nor could it have been easy when Karen screwed up so badly. Add to that the death of her mother within the last year, and Virginia had held up surprisingly well.

Maybe resiliency came with age. Or maybe women were just tougher, stronger. Look at how amazingly his mom handled all the crap his dad put her through over the last few years.

Yes, Nathan felt like he'd given it his best shot—something his grandfather always talked about. "Do the best you can, every single day. Everything else is outside of your control."

But was it enough?

Virginia had pulled him aside earlier that morning, wanting to visit with him about something she was considering. If she could find some additional help for the store, she said, would Nathan mind if Virginia and Frank went south for the month of January?

Her question surprised Nathan. He'd overheard his employers arguing about that very point quite often. Frank was tired of Minnesota winters and wished they could go south for a few months each year. Virginia didn't want to leave because of the bookstore. The winter months, after the holidays, were always quiet. Frank used to think they couldn't afford to hire someone full-time for the first quarter of the year, nor would Virginia entertain closing for a few months.

"Why now, Ginny?"

Virginia had shrugged, a small smile on her lips. "Santa suggested it last night."

"What? *Grant?*" Nathan wasn't following. How would Grant even know this was something Frank wanted to do?

"I think he was still in 'Santa' mode, even though he was out of costume by then. We were visiting while you and Grace wrestled that red couch back up to your apartment. He was curious about what my wish would be if I could ask Santa for anything. It was then that I realized my wish would be to grant *Frank's* wish. Those blasted headaches of his reminded me that he—we—aren't getting any younger. We all like to think we can go on and on as we always have, but we can't. Besides, change can be good. At least that's what I keep telling myself."

She'd gone on to explain that she had an idea regarding who she might be able to bring in during January to help Nathan, as she knew he'd also be busy with his final semester of school, but she didn't want to pursue that until she'd had a chance to talk to Nathan first. After all, this wasn't what he'd signed up to do. He'd assured Virginia that he'd do whatever she needed him to do so she could grant Frank's wish. After all, hadn't he and Grace been the ones to dream up the whole "Capturing Wishes" theme?

As he turned onto his grandparents' street, he felt content. Starting with his fun new Halloween window display, all the way through their successful day at the bookstore yesterday, Nathan *did* feel he'd done his best.

And now he could relax and celebrate.

***

Nathan felt as if he'd stepped back in time as he let himself in through his grandparents' back door. The warm air that surrounded him smelled of ham, with an undercurrent of pine. His Aunt Val was stirring a pot on the stove, while lots of his other family members wrapped gifts, covering both the kitchen island and the floor near the television with paper, ribbons, partially wrapped boxes, and bags.

"Did I take a wrong turn and end up at the North Pole?" he joked, his arrival as yet unnoticed.

Waves and shouts of greetings commenced.

Nathan's youngest cousin, Jake, approached. "Hey there, Nathan! Got more presents for us to wrap?"

Nathan grinned down at the precocious little boy. Jake grinned back, his smile missing two front teeth. He pulled a stack of books out of the box he'd carried in, handing them to Jake.

"Who should they go to?"

"I put a sticky note with a name inside each one. I followed Robbie's directions, so I hope I got everyone."

Jake nodded, the six-year-old arms drooping under the weight of the books. "Sounds good. I'll get them wrapped."

Nathan couldn't help but laugh, nodding to Val before he went to find Robbie. "Just wait until Jake's a teenager. He's going to keep you up at night," he cautioned his aunt.

"Like that's anything new. He's been doing *that* since the day he was born," she said, sliding a cookie sheet covered with rolls into the oven.

"Oh, hey, Val, I've been meaning to thank you."

"For what?" she said, straightening up and setting the oven timer.

"When the Fisks had me over for Thanksgiving, I helped Frank get dinner on the table. I don't think I fully appreciated how much work that takes—and there were only *three* of us. You are a saint, feeding this crew like you do."

Val looked taken aback by the compliment. "That's nice of you to say, Nate. I guess I've just always done it—*and* I enjoy it. Gets me out of dish duty."

He laughed. "I'll gladly help with dishes from here on out if you'll keep feeding us. Holidays wouldn't be the same without you and your cooking."

Val dropped the potholder she'd been holding onto the kitchen island and wrapped her arms around her oldest nephew. Nathan returned the hug, the top of his aunt's head low on his chest.

She's short, but she's mighty, he thought before pulling back.

"Now get away from me before you make me cry," she ordered, pointing toward the gift-wrappers.

***

"Robbie, it's cool that you set all this up," Nathan said as he helped his younger cousin take stacks of wrapped presents out into the other room where his grandparents had a second Christmas tree set up. The gifts were for his uncle's tenants, displaced by the fire around Thanksgiving; they needed to be kept separate from all the family presents they'd exchange after dinner.

"Hey, it's no big deal. I guess I get a kick out of helping people at Christmas," Robbie replied, kneeling to arrange the gifts. "I don't think Uncle Ethan has a clue we're doing this."

"All the better."

"They're here!" Jake yelled from the kitchen.

Robbie shot up at the announcement and ran back to scoop up the mess they'd made with their last-minute wrapping. Nathan followed. Robbie's mom, Renee, was already on clean-up duty.

"Nathan, quick, grab these, and we'll get this cleaned up," Renee ordered, and Nathan took the last pile of gifts from her.

He'd just finished arranging them under the spare Christmas tree in the living room and turned off the lights when he heard Uncle Ethan and Lizzy enter the house to a round of hellos similar to those he'd received an hour earlier. Most everyone was here now. He turned back toward the tree for a minute, staring into the multi-colored lights, the cacophony of voices of his crazy family members behind him all blending together.

I wonder how Dad is spending Christmas Eve this year?

It had been a while since his dad had attended one of these family Christmas celebrations. In recent years he'd always claimed to be working, but Nathan often suspected that wasn't true. How ironic that this year he really *did* know where his father would be spending Christmas.

Behind bars.

***

The family gathered around his grandparents' long dining room table and two smaller card tables, all covered in the same gold tablecloths and set with the same white china they'd used for as long as Nathan could remember. Thanksgiving dinner with the Fisks had been special, but he'd missed this.

Grandpa George tapped his water glass with his fork, the clear ringing successfully capturing everyone's attention. Now his Grandma Lavonne would caution his grandfather to be careful not to break her crystal, and then everyone would surprisingly quiet down for the blessing.

"George, be careful!"

We can always count on Grandma.

"Thank you, everyone, for gathering with us tonight to celebrate the birth of our Lord. I remember, two years ago, when we handed each of you a special envelope from my dear sister, Celia. It seems like yesterday. Where did those two years go? But the passing of time has certainly brought about plenty of changes," George said, slowly scanning around the dining room table. "Welcome, Matt and little Harper, now *official* members of the family, to our Christmas tradition. Family is what the holidays should be all about, and we're blessed to have you as part of ours. When we handed out those envelopes, I doubt any of us could have imagined the chain of events that would follow. You've done so many good things with the legacy Celia left behind. She'd be proud of each and every one of you."

"I'm not doing such a great job in that department, Dad," Ethan chimed in, referring to the aftermath of the fire—he'd inherited the fourplex rental from Celia. This remark caused a few groans around the table.

"Nonsense, son. That fire had nothing to do with you, and now you are doing your best to help your tenants," George countered.

Jake snickered as he squirmed, glancing over his shoulder in the direction of the hidden gifts. Nathan, standing nearest him, poked the boy in his side. "Dude, be quiet," he hissed at Jake. "Don't spoil the surprise." Nathan shook his head at Robbie when he caught him glaring at Jake. He'd pull Jake out of the room if he had to. They couldn't let Jake tip Ethan off, this close to the reveal of the gifts for his tenants. "Keep quiet and be respectful of Grandpa," Nathan warned Jake, then glanced up to see George looking their way. "Sorry, Gramps. Keep going," Nathan said, Jake looking sheepish next to him.

"As I was saying," George began again. "Amid all the change we've faced, we say thank you to God for keeping us safe and providing. Change will continue, and more trials lie ahead, because that is how life works, but as long as we stand together, we can get through most anything. Thank you for this wonderful meal and the gift of your son, Jesus. Amen."

Others echoed the "Amen" before taking their seats.

"Dig in, everyone!" Lavonne ordered, grinning at their family gathered there.

***

Val's dinner of scalloped potatoes and ham—a family tradition—was quickly devoured (also a family tradition). Nathan, as the oldest of the grandkids, surprised everyone when he ordered the adults to relax while the kids cleared the dishes. He hadn't been kidding when he'd thanked Val earlier. The other cousins were *not* impressed, but they complied. The family exchanged gifts after everything was cleaned up. Finally, George ordered everyone to take their gifts to their assigned bedrooms and clean up the wrapping paper.

"Hey, Dad, I need to call Mom and wish her Merry Christmas, but I forgot my phone in your truck," Nathan heard Lizzy tell Ethan.

"Just use mine," Ethan said, pulling his phone out of a pocket after shoving his handful of discarded wrapping paper into a garbage bag.

"I *really* need my phone, Dad. Would you mind grabbing it for me? I need to take Grandma's gifts back to her room. Her knee is sore."

Nathan watched in amusement, knowing it was all a ploy to get Ethan out of the house for a minute so the rest of them could sneak into the other room with the presents. He had to hand it to her: Lizzy was a decent actor.

Ethan sighed, propped the half-full garbage bag against a nearby chair, and dug his truck keys out of his jeans pocket. "You kids can't go ten minutes without your damn phones." He was still muttering as he walked out of the room, and then the back door shut behind him.

Robbie started waving everyone out of the family room and toward the living room. "Hurry up, you guys, he'll be right back!"

Nathan helped Robbie get everyone moving. They'd just gotten people into the front living room when the back door opened and shut again.

Lavonne, who was standing next to Robbie, held a hand up, warning people to be quiet. "Ethan, honey, can you come in here a minute? I need some help."

Footsteps echoed from the kitchen. "What do you need, Mom? I suppose we better start loading everyone into the vehicles and get over to the church so we can all sit together—" Ethan drew up short when he saw his whole family gathered in the living room, everyone staring at him. "Why is there another tree in here? And what the heck are all these presents for? Didn't we just open everything?"

"Robbie, why don't you tell your uncle what you've been up to?" Lavonne suggested.

"Oh, are these for another toy drive?" Ethan asked Robbie. "I remember you working at one of those a couple years ago."

Robbie laughed. "Not exactly. This year I thought we'd help out some much *older* kids."

Ethan just stared at him, confused.

Nathan met Lizzy's eye from where she stood on the stairs. She gave him a thumbs-up, obviously pleased with her successful help in the ruse.

Her gesture brought back a powerful memory of his own father giving him a similar sign, when, as a gangly fourteen-year-old, Nathan had made the winning basket at the tail end of a close ball game. He'd quit the team after that year, having never cared much for sports, and that was the only game his father had bothered to attend; but the flush of excitement he'd felt over the man's rare encouragement stuck with him. Now, as he watched Ethan interact with Lizzy and her brothers, he felt a pang of jealousy. He'd never have that type of relationship with his own dad.

Nathan's aunts, Renee and Val, stepped forward, and Renee said to Robbie, "Come on, son, I think you might have to spell it out for Ethan. Maybe you should have borrowed that Santa suit again this year. He's not catching on."

I have an amazing Santa suit I could have lent him, Nathan thought, but he stayed silent, letting Robbie enjoy his well-earned spotlight. His cousin had worked hard to pull this together.

"Why would Robbie need one of Santa's suits?" Jake piped in.

Nathan laughed when he saw Renee mouth *"Sorry!"* to Val. While he felt short-changed in the dad department, he knew he was lucky to be a part of this family.

Robbie went on to explain what was going on to Ethan. Ethan seemed incredibly touched by everyone's generosity.

"We thought maybe it would be fun if a few of us delivered them tonight," Robbie said, motioning to the stacks of gifts. "We can all go to church tomorrow morning instead of tonight."

After a round of hugs, everyone helped Ethan load the gifts into the back of his pickup. The truck could hold five. Robbie would, of course, go along to help deliver the presents to Ethan's three tenants, and one of Ethan's sons wanted to go, too. Grandpa George and Matt, Renee's husband, took the two other spots.

Nathan was happy to stay back. His conflicted emotions, shifting back and forth between hating and missing his dad, were exhausting. Plus, it had been a crazy two days, and the plan was for everyone to spend Christmas Day out at Whispering Pines. He needed some sleep.

***

Nathan fumbled with the fishing line, his fingers numb from the bite of icy lake water. Seth's daughter, Kaylee, kneeled next to him, watching his every move. The teen had flown in from Texas to spend the holiday with Seth, and he'd brought her out to Whispering Pines again to celebrate Christmas with Jess and the whole family. Kaylee had never tried ice fishing before, so Nathan offered to teach her the basics.

It was a bright day, the temperature near twenty degrees—nice for Minnesota in December. Sunshine glinted off the ice and snow around them, and the sky glowed a brilliant blue. Much of his family was out on the ice, halfway through an extremely competitive fishing tournament. With an hour to go, Nathan suspected it would come down to two of his cousins, Julie and Robbie. While Nathan had done some ice fishing through the years, Julie reminded them all that she'd gone often with her dad when she was much younger.

She hadn't forgotten what her dad, Jim, had taught her.

At least Jim took *her fishing,* Nathan thought. Any fishing he'd done growing up had been thanks to his grandpa or his uncle. Jim had been a fun guy, unlike his own dad.

Once Nathan had Kaylee set up again after she'd brought in a small perch, he sat back in his folding chair, not bothering to put his line down his assigned hole again. With so many of them fishing, and his two measly fish he'd tallied up so far, he didn't stand a chance. He'd help the younger kids instead.

Watching Julie and Robbie now, he wondered if they thought of Jim at all during the holidays. Jim had died more than ten years earlier. Maybe Robbie didn't remember much about him, but Julie certainly did. She'd mention him occasionally, her pain still evident over her loss.

Jim—and the disease that killed him—was what had brought Grant and Grace into their lives in the first place. Two years ago, they'd all been shocked to learn his parents had adopted Jim as an infant . . . *and* that he had a twin brother. Grant was that twin, and he'd reached out to Jim's adoptive parents because his only daughter, Grace, was also very ill. She needed a transplant, and sometimes families proved to be a match. Both Jim and Grace had suffered from aplastic anemia. While the disease eventually took Jim, Grace had recovered. Nathan hated to even think about how sick she'd been when they'd first met.

A commotion on the ice pulled Nathan's attention back. Julie was screaming something about a big fish, and George was rushing toward her as she struggled with her rod, bent nearly in half. Then time slowed and Nathan watched in horror, barely daring to breathe, as his grandfather slipped, arms flailing. Nathan feared George would hit the ice hard, maybe really hurting himself. Nathan sprang to his feet, wanting to help, but the ice provided no traction. One foot slipped out from under him, and he went down on one knee, pain radiating up his thigh, stealing his breath. So much for helping.

He thanked God when his grandpa was able to grab hold of Julie's chair, saving himself from a fall. No one noticed Nathan's clumsiness, and he was just pushing himself back up to his feet when there was more yelling. Now Julie was launching herself across the ice toward Jake while the boy tried desperately to grab the stubby fishing pole she'd dropped. Jake was sliding toward the hole, and while Nathan doubted Jake's body could fit through the opening in the ice, he was going to get wet. Nathan cringed, too far away to do anything to stop the events unfolding before him. As he watched, he noticed Julie's grasping fingers slow Jake's momentum, and just as the kid's arm disappeared down the hole, Ethan reached Jake's side and grabbed the back of his parka, plucking him up off the ice.

Luke, Jake's father, was even farther back from the action than Nathan. Now that it was obvious that everyone would be all right, Luke sank back down onto his folding chair, shaking his head. "That kid is going to be the death of me," Nathan heard him mutter.

Thinking the show was over, Nathan turned back to check on Kaylee.

More hollering ensued. Now Jake and his brother, Dave, were yelling at each other, and then Nathan heard Jake yell at George.

You're taking it too far, kid.

"You guys, knock it off!" Luke yelled, but his command was lost in the racket of their bickering.

A squeaky screen door slammed onshore, and Val's voice cut through the noise.

"*Jake Patrick Davis*, what are you doing out here?! You better not be yelling at your grandfather! Get over here right now!"

Nathan checked Luke's reaction. The man was sitting back, arms crossed over his chest, looking between his son on the ice and his wife on the shore. He must have sensed Nathan looking at him, and he glanced his way.

"I think I'll let Val take this one," he said, his face breaking into a confident grin.

Nathan had to agree. It sounded like Val was up to the task for this round of discipline. Jake had pushed too far this time.

***

Nathan was starving. By the time they got the ice fishing gear stowed away, he'd hoped the turkey dinner scheduled to cap off the day would be ready. But there was one last contest planned: snowman building. They'd finish that before it got too dark, and dinner would come after. Knowing he'd either have to build a snowman or set the table, he opted for the outside task.

Having seen little of either of his sisters, he sought Lauren out. He found her in one of the lodge bedrooms, studying chemistry, while Harper napped on a pile of blankets on the floor nearby. Lauren held a finger over her lips, then pointed to Harper. Nathan motioned for her to step outside of the room. She followed him after making sure the baby monitor was on. Their mom had the other one out in the kitchen.

"What's up?" she asked Nathan, hugging her textbook to her chest.

"Why are you studying on Christmas?" he asked, torn between disgust and admiration over his sister's dedication.

"I have cramps, so I didn't feel like doing much," she said, as if this were a perfectly logical explanation. Nathan cringed at the oversharing of information. Lauren, a college freshman, was probably still learning how to balance her homework load. Nathan knew she was much more concerned with maintaining a spotless GPA than he'd ever been. She'd wanted to be a doctor ever since she was a little girl. "Besides, I won't get into med school with mediocre grades."

Nathan rolled his eyes. "For crying out loud, it's *Christmas*. Do you want to build a snowman?"

Now she laughed. "Listen to my big brother, spouting lines from a Disney movie."

"I might have sat through *Frozen* a time or two with Harper," he admitted, smirking back. "But seriously, it's a contest. Are you in?"

"Ah . . . no . . . someone has to watch Harper, and it's too cold outside," she whined, sounding thirteen instead of eighteen.

He hated it when she made up excuses just because she didn't want to do something. *Reminds me of Dad.* He almost voiced his little comparison out loud, but held back. As he'd just reminded her, it was Christmas. He needed to play nice.

"Forget it," Nathan said, turning his back on her. He didn't care about the snowman contest either. He was so hungry he was starting to get a headache.

Besides, Lauren might be on to something, hiding out in this part of the lodge. He'd become accustomed to peace and quiet, living alone and working in bookstores. The calm in this part of the lodge was a nice break from the chaos.

He wandered, enjoying the quiet and avoiding setting the tables. The lodge looked different now compared to when Renee first took it over two years ago. She'd added bedrooms so the retreat business she now ran with Jess's help could include overnight accommodations. Near the front door of the lodge, to the right, was a new sitting area, conducive to small group meetings. To the left was a wall that had remained untouched during the remodel.

The paneled wall was covered from top to bottom with framed pictures. Nathan had never bothered to pay them much attention before. Now he stopped and studied them, light from a window across the hall playing across the glass-covered photographs. A few were colored prints, fading with time, but most were black-and-white.

One picture in particular caught his eye. Something about it made him think of Virginia's book. Her story included a close group of friends, set in the 1960s. This black-and-white snapshot was older than that, but the women in the picture seemed familiar for some reason.

"What are you doing, honey?"

Nathan jumped, clutching at his heart.

"*Shit*, Mom, don't sneak up on a guy like that!"

"Not sneaking," she said, squinting at him. "Why aren't you outside, building a snowman?"

"I needed a partner, and Lauren wasn't up for it, so I decided to pass, too." He didn't go on to admit he was avoiding kitchen work.

"Those are neat, aren't they?" Jess said, nodding toward the wall of pictures.

"Yeah, they are. Lots of memories captured up here," Nathan agreed. "Hey, Mom, have you gotten very far on Virginia's book?"

Although he'd emailed her the draft of the manuscript at the same time he'd emailed it to his professor so she could start her edits, Jess hadn't mentioned it.

She groaned. "Oh, honey, I haven't had a chance yet. Tonight. That's my plan. I figured today would wear Harper out, so maybe I could get some time to myself tonight, once all the craziness of Christmas is behind us. I didn't want to pick it up and start until I knew I had a decent chunk of time to dedicate to it."

"No worries. I just ask because there's something about this picture that reminds me of Virginia's book."

Jess stepped around him so she could get a better look at the picture. "That's your great-aunt, Celia, and a bunch of her friends," she said, glancing back at Nathan.

He looked again. "It is? Huh. Maybe that's why it caught my eye."

"Or maybe Virginia's story includes bits of Celia in it. Remember, they knew each other. Celia was good friends with Virginia's mother, and Virginia lived with Celia when she was younger. Maybe Celia influenced the story."

Nathan shrugged. "Could be, I guess."

"Now I can't *wait* to get started on her manuscript," Jess said, glancing at the watch on her wrist. "But we better get dinner on the table. They'll be done with the snowman contest soon. Why don't you help? You can start by going and getting that pack of napkins out of my trunk."

Based on the look she shot him, Nathan could tell his mother knew exactly why he'd been hanging out in the deserted part of the lodge.

Do mothers have some type of internal homing device, ever on the lookout for slacking children? Nathan wondered as he headed out to his mom's Land Rover. He still couldn't get away with *anything* where she was concerned.

CHAPTER 24

Gift of Extra Holiday Compassion

*V*irginia could not *wait* to talk to Mabel. Her dear friend would probably flip when she heard Virginia had lined up a month-long trip to Florida. Frank's reaction had been priceless when he discovered the printout of their flight itinerary in his stocking on Christmas morning.

"Honey, I know how long you've wanted to do this, and I'm sorry I've been such a wet blanket," she'd said after he'd hugged and kissed her in delight. Frank, seldom outwardly demonstrative, couldn't contain his excitement.

She hadn't dared tell him the flights were refundable. They still needed to be sure his headaches were gone for good. Plus, they'd need coverage for the store. Nathan couldn't be expected to do it alone.

That was the other reason she needed to talk to Mabel . . . and to Tansy.

Virginia still suspected Tansy might have been somehow involved with the missing donation box, stolen from the bookstore under Nathan's watch. Was she utterly mad to consider asking Tansy to come work for them when they went south?

Probably, if my suspicions are accurate.

But Virginia also believed in second chances. She knew how desperate a person could sometimes feel, causing them to make terrible choices they wouldn't normally consider. She'd done it herself. While no one would ever know she'd stolen that innocent woman's pocketbook so many years ago, she'd also made plenty of other mistakes that Celia *had* known about . . . but the woman still took her and Karen in, asking for little in return.

Now it might be Virginia's turn to pay it forward and do the same.

But only if Tansy is honest with me.

Nathan would be back in the afternoon, after spending Christmas with his family. Virginia needed to open the store at ten, but it was only nine. She had time to visit Mabel and her niece.

The sidewalks and streets were quiet at this hour; hopefully shoppers would be out later, searching for after-Christmas specials. Virginia admired the holiday decorations as she strolled to the bakery, hung high overhead on light poles and strung across Main. She'd always marveled over the special beauty of Christmas decorations—at least up until the calendar flipped over. Once New Year's Day had come and gone, thin coatings of dust became apparent and surfaces began to look cluttered. It was time to stash the decorations away and start with a clean slate. This sentiment extended beyond holiday décor. One often felt the need for new beginnings in early January.

That would certainly be the case for her and Frank this year. What might Nathan do with the front window when he took their holiday display down at the bookstore? She and Frank were flying to Florida on the second of January, and Virginia hated to take the tree down before New Year's, so it would be up to Nathan what to do next.

It's just a window, Virginia scolded herself. *You'll be back in time to make it pretty for Valentine's Day.*

She couldn't help but feel apprehension. It would be hard to leave, even if it was only for a month.

Virginia pushed through the cheery door into the bakery, taking another look at the choir boys. *Anyone who can paint sweet faces like that cannot be a bad person.*

"Hello, Mabel. I hope you had a nice Christmas."

"Hi, Ginny! Be with you in a minute," Mabel said in a rush as she carried a miniature wedding cake into a small side room Virginia knew her friend used for cake-tasting.

Virginia was glad to see their usual table by the front was free. Customers sat at the other round iron tables. She took her coat off, folded it over the back of the ice-cream-fountain-style chair, and sat.

"Tea?" Mabel asked as she came out of the side room. She looked frazzled. If Mabel was busy, she didn't want to add to her burdens.

"No, dear, black coffee would be fine."

Mabel brought over two cups of coffee. "You have good timing, friend. I have ten minutes until an appointment with a potential bride."

"That's exciting . . . though a little odd, the day after Christmas," Virginia said, wrapping her hands around her paper cup to warm her fingers.

"It is, but the bride is from out of town. She's home for the holidays. The actual wedding isn't until June. I tell you, the first few months of the new year are looking to be pretty quiet. I'm afraid I won't be able to keep Tansy on much longer."

Virginia nearly took the opening Mabel had unknowingly provided, but she was too excited to tell Mabel about their upcoming trip to wait any longer.

"Guess what I gave Frank for Christmas?"

Mabel looked surprised. "Did you get your book done early for him?"

"Oh no, dear, that will take more time. With him getting sick on me, I've barely scratched the surface. I may be able to finish it up by summer . . ."

Waving to a couple as they left the bakery, Mabel shrugged. "What then?"

"We're going . . . to *Florida*."

"Really?" Mabel said, turning her full attention to Virginia. "When?"

"Next week."

"Next *week*? Is Frank well enough to do that?"

Now it was Virginia's turn to shrug. "I think so. I *hope* so. He's excited about it. He has a check-up this week, so we'll be sure to clear it with his doctor. If she gives Frank the green light, I have to find someone to help Nathan cover the store for a month."

A bell similar to the one Virginia used at the bookstore jingled as the bakery door swung open and two women entered. The younger of the two looked like a near clone of the older one, other than the obvious age gap. The older one was immaculately dressed with smooth blond hair and tanned skin.

Mabel glanced at the clock on the wall behind the cash register. "They're early. I'm sorry, but I need to go. But, Virginia, would you ever consider hiring Tansy to help out over at your store? That might solve both of our problems. She's proven herself to be a hard worker over the past month."

Virginia searched Mabel's familiar face for any hint that her friend had reservations about Tansy. All she saw was an eagerness to help both her niece and her friend.

Maybe I'm wrong . . . I shouldn't judge Tansy.

"If she's here now, I'd love to visit with her about it."

Mabel smiled, some of the tiredness around her eyes seeming to dissipate. "She's here."

Virginia watched as Mabel greeted her potential customers and then excused herself to go in the back. While Virginia waited, the two got settled in the side room, and the other group of three teenagers occupying the table against the wall got up and noisily left the bakery. "Oh, to be eighteen and have our whole lives ahead of us again," she said to no one in particular as the giggling group of girls yanked open the door and strolled down the sidewalk. Life had looked quite different for her at eighteen. She'd never want to go back to those days.

"Mabel said you wanted to see me?" Tansy said, pulling Virginia's attention back to the bakery. Tansy took Mabel's vacant seat.

Virginia grinned at the smudge of flour on the younger woman's nose. *How many times have I seen something similar on Mabel?*

"Yes, hello, Tansy. How was your Christmas?"

Tansy seemed to relax at the question. "It was nice. Quiet, but nice. I think Mabel enjoyed it, too. I know she often spends Christmas alone, but we had each other this year."

Virginia met and held Tansy's gaze, doing her best to read her. Was there a touch of guilt in her expression?

"Thank you again for your help at the bookstore on Saturday. I know our customers appreciated the photos you took."

Tansy smiled. "It was fun. Seeing those kids so excited to talk to Santa was refreshing, you know? They're still so innocent at that age. We forget how thrilling it used to be to believe in something." As she spoke, a look of melancholy stole over her features.

"My dear, you're never too old to believe in something," Virginia said.

Tansy leaned back against the cold wrought iron of her chair, expelling a sigh as she did so, her lips pursing in resignation. "It isn't necessarily *age* that wakes you up to the realities of life."

Virginia hated to hear the cynicism in Tansy's voice, but she recognized it. She'd felt the same way when, as a young mother, the rose-colored glasses had been ripped off her face by the realities of drug abuse and addiction. This girl certainly reminded Virginia of herself at Tansy's age—minus the daughter she'd struggled to protect.

"What are your plans, Tansy? Do you plan to stay around here?"

Tansy sat up straighter in her chair. "I'd like to, but honestly, I don't think Mabel can afford to keep paying me. We stayed busy over the past month, delivering cookies and holiday treats to businesses and for parties, but that will fall off now. She hasn't said anything, but I know she's worried."

"Where would you go?"

Tansy stared out the window, seeming to consider how best to respond. Virginia gave her time.

"I may have to go home. Dad has room, but he kicked me out, so I'd have to convince him to let me come back."

"Do you mind me asking why he asked you to leave?"

Tansy's eyes swung back to Virginia, her face taking on a hard edge Virginia hadn't noticed before. "Look, I screwed up, okay? There was this guy . . ."

There is always a guy, Virginia thought as Tansy's voice trailed off. She waited for Tansy to go on.

"This guy, I liked him. But he was bad news. He was into something he shouldn't have been, and I was too naïve to see it at first. When I finally realized what he was doing, I knew I had to get away before he pulled me into that world with him."

Virginia laid her hand over Tansy's where it rested on the tabletop. "Tansy, what was he doing?"

Tansy pulled her hand back, her eyes traveling around her aunt's bakery, seemingly unable to meet Virginia's gaze.

"Tansy?"

"He was dealing drugs, okay? And he was using *kids* to help him get it into the middle school. I had no idea."

"Did he try to involve you?"

"Hell *yes*, he tried to involve me," Tansy spat out, bitterness dripping from her tone. "And I nearly did it, too. He could be *so* convincing, you know? The plan was to introduce me to a guy he called his *main man*. Stupid me thought his contact was maybe a teacher or something. I was shocked when this kid strolled up to us in the parking lot. He couldn't have been more than ten."

Tansy visibly shuddered at her memories. Virginia flashed back to the hovel she'd lived in for a short time with Bryce. People, stoned out of their minds, lounging all over the house in various stages of dress, most as young or even younger than her back then. Maybe things hadn't changed that much. At least there wasn't a child involved in Tansy's situation. Virginia still had nightmares about the discussion she'd overheard that fateful night . . . someone encouraging Bryce to *sell* his own baby daughter . . .

"After that, I knew I had to get out. But I owed Kip money. Earlier, when Dad kicked me out, I'd moved in with him. He said I could, but I had to pay half the rent. Sleeping with him didn't count toward payment."

Maybe this was worse than Virginia had imagined.

Then Tansy shook her head as if trying to shake off the terrible memories and remembering her audience. "I'm sorry, Virginia, you don't want to hear all the sordid details. I saw a chance to get out, and I took it. I hopped on a bus and came here, never dreaming he'd follow me."

"But he did?"

Tansy hung her head. "He did. And I'm ashamed to admit it. Aunt Mabel has never been anything but kind to me—and because of me, he came here."

Virginia doubted Mabel was aware of this. She'd said nothing about it.

"Has he threatened you, Tansy?"

"Sure," Tansy replied, shrugging one shoulder as if playing it off. "He said he was looking for the money I owed him. I'm still not sure how he found me. Probably a friend of mine. She likely told him where I'd gone. I think they got together after I took off."

Nice group of friends, Virginia thought—although who was she to judge?

"So he followed you here?" she prodded.

"Yeah, he did. He showed up out of the blue one day when Mabel was making a delivery. Thank *God* she didn't see him."

"Is he still around? Still bothering you? Because we could get you some help, you know."

Tansy finally met Virginia's eye. "Nah. I took care of it. Paid him the four hundred bucks he said I owed him and he took off. But I worried he'd come back."

"Did he?"

With a shake of her head and a resigned glint in her eye, she sighed. "No. I think he would have kept coming, but there was a big drug bust back home. He got picked up in a sting. Last I heard he was going away for a long time."

Now it was Virginia's turn to sigh. It was a relief hearing that part of Tansy's life was likely in the past now. But she still had to know the truth.

"Tansy . . . Mabel mentioned you were flat broke when you came here. Where did you get the money to pay Kip?"

Tansy offered no response. Virginia let the question hang in the air between them, giving the younger woman time. The murmur of voices could be heard coming from the tasting room, but they were low. The only other sound was the soft strains of "Baby, It's Cold Outside" playing in the background.

Mabel's niece stood up, her chair scraping against the tile floor. She wandered over to the painting she'd done on the door, and with one fingernail she scraped a curl of black paint off the tallest choir boy's hair. "I was picturing that boy, you know, the one in the parking lot at the school, when I painted this. I bet this was how he looked before Kip got his grubby hands on him . . ."

"Where did you get the money, Tansy?" Virginia asked again, more softly this time.

"I had to make him leave, Virginia. I couldn't have him here, maybe threatening Mabel. She doesn't deserve that. She took me in, no questions asked. She's always been here for me, ever since my mom died."

Although Virginia figured she already had her answer now, she needed Tansy to admit it. She waited.

Finally, Tansy came back and plopped back down onto the chair across from Virginia. "You already know, don't you?"

Virginia just stared. She wasn't letting her off that easy.

"How did you know I was the one who stole the donation box?"

"I didn't. Not for sure. But Mabel mentioned you'd paid her some money, too, back around that same time, and she had no idea how you came up with it. I remembered you'd brought over some cups for our cocoa bar when we ran out. You'd have known where the box was, and that Nathan might not be able to watch things as closely, being there alone part of the time."

Tansy bent over, resting her forehead on her arms on their table. "I'm so ashamed." Virginia could barely make out the girl's muffled words. She waited some more. Finally, the girl straightened. "I'm sorry, Virginia. I stole the box. I'll find some way to pay you back. It was so wrong, and I've felt terrible ever since. I'll *pay* you *back*," she repeated, a desperate edge to her voice. "But . . . can you not tell Mabel about this? It would crush her."

At Tansy's words, a vision of Celia sprang into Virginia's mind. Celia, her mother's friend, coming up to her at her estranged husband's funeral, offering to take her and Karen in, after her parents had walked away, leaving her alone by Bryce's fresh grave. Virginia had never known exactly why Celia had been so kind, so giving. But she did know, without a doubt, that she had turned Virginia's life around that day.

"Are you going to tell my aunt?" Tansy asked again, her eyes pleading.

"Tansy, many years ago, when I was a little younger than you, a friend of my own mother's did something for me that literally saved my life, and that of my baby daughter. To this day I've never really understood why. In the end, I guess the reason doesn't matter. But I know that when someone is truly sorry for something they've done, they can turn things around. Are you willing to do that? To stay out of trouble and make something of your life?"

A glimmer of hope seemed to enter Tansy's eyes. "I *am*, Virginia, I *really* am. Being here with Mabel, coming in early with her every morning and seeing what it takes to run this bakery . . . I can see how rewarding hard work can be. Dad always just laid around after he got home from the factory, drinking beer and complaining about having to get up and do it all again tomorrow. I didn't have much hope for the future. But here, working with Mabel, I can see now that it can be different. I don't ever want to go back there."

Virginia took her hands, and this time the girl didn't pull away. "Will you promise me you'll never do something stupid like that again? Steal from someone to cover your own mistakes?"

"I promise."

"Can I trust you?"

"Yes. I screwed up. But I want to make it up to you. How can I make it up to you?"

Virginia thought the woman looked sincere. Did she dare?

Celia hadn't been afraid to dare.

Now Virginia knew it was her turn.

"I have an idea how you can pay me back," she said to Tansy. "But any more screw-ups and you're on your own."

With that warning, she stood, slipped her coat back on, and picked up her purse. The background music shifted to "It's the Most Wonderful Time of the Year." Virginia grinned—that song had been Celia's favorite.

"But something tells me your mistakes are in the past," she continued, winking down at Tansy. "Welcome to a brighter future."

She turned and left the bakery, and as she pushed through the door onto the sidewalk, she felt confident she'd made the right choice.

It was what Celia would have done.

CHAPTER 25

Gift of Yuletide Fun

"Guess what's sitting in our living room, right next to the TV?"

"Hello to you, too," Nathan said, grinning when Grace jumped right into conversation the second he answered her call. He popped the top on the beer he'd just grabbed out of the fridge when his phone rang.

"Guess!"

"Grace," he said, laughing, "I have no idea. Did you get a new gaming system for Christmas?"

She snorted. "Yeah, *right*. No, it's a big old ice fishing trophy dated 1965!"

Nathan wasn't surprised, but he still laughed. "Julie was pretty proud of that thing, you know. The good news is you might only have to look at it for a year. It's meant to be a traveling trophy, and I could give her a run for her money next year."

"The way I heard it, you weren't even in the running," Grace teased.

He could have denied it or blamed it on helping out the younger kids instead of focusing on catching fish himself, but he was still glad Julie won. "You know, she said she used to go with her dad when she was young, so I thought it was pretty cool when she won. Her dad died over ten years ago now, and he's hardly ever mentioned anymore. Do you think that bothers her?"

But then he remembered that Jim was Grace's uncle, and she'd lost her mom, too, when she was still a kid. He could have kicked himself for his question, feeling insensitive. "I'm sorry, Grace. I guess you face the same thing."

"Don't apologize. Heck, *your* dad isn't around either, even though he's still alive."

"Yeah, but that's different. My dad screwed up royally. He doesn't *deserve* to be talked about fondly."

Grace was quiet, as if considering what he'd said.

Nathan regretted his words—despite the truthfulness behind them. "I'm sorry. It's been a weird holiday . . . I keep thinking about Dad, even though I don't *want* to."

"I'm sorry you're so bitter about all that."

"Wouldn't you be if you were in my shoes?"

"I don't honestly know how I'd feel. It would be hard not to love my dad still, even if he did something terrible."

Nathan sat back on his bed, propping pillows behind his back so he could lean against the headboard. He'd gotten back from Whispering Pines that afternoon, put in a few hours of work, and was ready to do some mindless Netflix binging when Grace had called. "Wait, how did this conversation turn so deep and dark? And why are we discussing *my* feelings? Just because I can't catch a fish doesn't mean I deserve to be psychoanalyzed. Let's talk about something else. What did you do for Christmas?"

Grace laughed. Nathan could hear voices in the background.

"Are you at your apartment?" he asked, thinking he could hear Julie's laugh.

"Yeah, I just got home a little bit ago. Julie and Zoey are yacking about something out in the kitchen. Well, let's see . . . after we left the bookstore on Saturday, we drove over to Dad's. In the morning, we got up and drove to my aunt and uncle's house in Brainerd. Spent Christmas Eve and Christmas Day with them. It was fun. Their kids are a little younger, middle school and high school. Some other relatives came over, too. It was noisy, there was lots of food, and it was exactly what a Christmas should be."

"What kind of stuff did you do?" Nathan enjoyed listening to Grace talk. He realized she ran hot or cold: sometimes she was talkative, other times quiet, almost aloof. Maybe that was just her personality. She'd certainly had to live through some tough times.

"I don't know, the usual, I guess. Oh, we did go ice skating. That was fun. It'd been a long time since I'd strapped a pair of figure skates on."

Nathan could picture her, gliding gracefully over the ice, her long, nearly white hair streaming out behind her. "Maybe we could go skating some time. I've got an old pair of hockey skates stashed away at Mom's somewhere."

"It was epic. I hip-checked my obnoxious, hockey-playing little cousin. I sent him right into the boards. Apparently I popped him in the nose, too, because there was blood. *Lots* of blood."

"Jeez, Grace, what an animal!" Nathan laughed, mentally scratching the graceful image he'd conjured up of her.

"Consider yourself warned."

Their conversation continued, Nathan keeping her talking. She asked some about his holiday, too, although she already knew some of what he'd done through talking with Julie.

"What are you doing this week?" she asked. "Are you working?"

"Probably mornings, yeah. Virginia isn't letting Frank come in much. She wants him to get back to a hundred percent. Because get this—they're taking the entire month of January off and flying to Florida!"

"No way!"

"Yeah, way. I guess it was your dad that suggested it in the first place. Frank claims he's wanted to go south in the winter for years, but Virginia never wanted to leave the bookstore."

"And now they have you! But wait . . . you'll be back in school for the last half of the month. How are you going to manage that?"

Nathan took a sip of his beer. "Virginia talked to Tansy. Do you remember her? She took pictures when your dad was playing Santa."

"Sure. From the bakery."

"Right. I guess her and Virginia and Mabel worked things out."

"Cool," Grace said. "Guess that means you won't be the low man on the totem pole anymore."

"Guess not."

Nathan could hear Julie yelling for Grace.

"Do you need to go?"

"Probably. Julie and Zoey want to walk down to the pizza place a few blocks over. I just wanted to call and say hey."

"I'm glad you did. Have fun, I'll talk to you later."

Nathan dropped his now-silent phone onto his bedside table. Suddenly his night alone watching Netflix didn't sound so fun. He'd have liked to go hang out with friends, too, but it was late, and none of his old buddies lived close. He'd barely even talked to any of them much since he'd moved over to the bookstore.

He finished his beer. He'd have to find something fun to do for New Year's.

***

"Here's the box for my ornaments. Please be sure to wrap each one individually and only put one in each of the separate slots inside this special container."

Nathan rested a reassuring hand on Virginia's shoulder. She'd insisted he follow her back to the storage room so she could show him where all the decorations would go when he took down the front window display. "I'll be very careful with them, Ginny. Don't worry. I've got this."

She shook her head, muttering, as she left the room and headed for the coffee pot in the reading nook. She'd seemed out of sorts to Nathan for the last few days. Probably nervous about leaving for Florida.

"Are you and Frank doing anything fun tonight, for New Year's Eve?" Nathan asked as he followed her out, hoping to distract her.

"Oh yes—I plan to rush home, put on my gold-sequined party pants, help Frank into his black leather suit, and the two of us will go out clubbing."

He had to bite back a snort. The woman was waving her hands as sarcasm dripped from her words.

"Make fun now, Ginny, but I bet you used to own a pair of gold-sequined pants back in the day."

She spun on her heel to face him, hands on her hips. "Of *course* I did, child. I remember when we'd go down to the Elks and spend hours dancing and drinking Tom and Jerrys . . . *in the middle of the day!* We'd wear silky party pants, halter tops, and big dangly earrings. That was back when people knew how to have fun. People don't know how to have fun anymore."

He held his hands up in self-defense. While their earlier New Year's celebrations sounded fun, her tone had an angry bite to it as she described what she obviously thought of as better times. "Jeez, what's gotten into you? I was teasing."

Virginia visibly deflated as Nathan's words sunk in. "Oh my goodness . . . I've been on a tear all day, haven't I?"

There was no use denying it. "Pretty much," Nathan agreed.

"I'm sorry."

"Forget it," Nathan said. "I know it's hard for you to leave your baby, even if it *is* in my capable hands, and only for a month."

Virginia sat down in one of the wingback chairs, motioning for Nathan to take the one across from her. The store was open, but no customers had stopped in yet. Nathan sensed she had something important to say.

"I wasn't going to bring this up until we all saw how things went in January, but it's been bugging me, ever since Grant said something right before Christmas," she said, fiddling with the chain that kept her glasses around her neck.

"Was this during the same conversation when he suggested you visit Florida for a month?"

His question surprised her. "Why, yes, I suppose it was."

"What is it?" Nathan prodded. He hoped Grant hadn't let anything slip about Virginia's book. They'd had lots of back and forth through email during this somewhat quieter week between Christmas and New Year's. Michelle and Grant were making good progress with the edits, and Grace had found a possible cover designer. They just needed to decide on a style of cover, and then they could get going on that, too. Now that they'd made plans to surprise both Frank *and* Virginia with the book at Valentine's Day, Nathan didn't want Virginia to find out about it.

"Grant mentioned your inheritance from your great-aunt, Celia."

Now it was Nathan's turn to be surprised. While he'd been secretly contemplating how he might be able to use the money his great aunt had so generously left him, he'd said nothing about it to anyone else. His dream was to invest it in this place, but he had no idea how realistic that was, straight out of college and with no other access to funds. He'd hoped the Fisks might consider letting him buy in as a partner.

"He did?" Nathan asked, hedging to see where she was going with this.

"Please don't be upset with him. He was afraid he might be speaking out of turn. But I'm glad he said something. What are your plans after graduation, dear?"

Now that she'd opened the door, he figured he didn't have anything to lose by being completely candid with her.

"I'd hoped to stay on here after graduation, Ginny. But I wouldn't be able to continue just to work part-time. If I stayed, I'd hoped to invest in the store somehow, someday. I'll have to start paying back student loans, and while the apartment upstairs is awesome, someday I'll want a bigger place. Honestly, I think I'd either have to work toward partial ownership of this place, or I'll have to go get a 'real job.' " He made air quotes with both hands as he said this last part.

"What makes you think this isn't a real job?" Virginia asked. He hoped he hadn't offended her, but she looked more curious than upset.

"That didn't come out right. Of course it's all *real*, but . . . look, we all have concerns about keeping the store open, right? I worry that we need different things to offer in the future, things to keep drawing people in so customers don't just default to ordering all their books online."

"That's valid. But what could you do?"

"What if we tried some new things? Offered a meeting space for book clubs? Or writer groups? Maybe some courses, even?"

Virginia listened intently. "I like that. But we don't have much for space."

"But you *do*," he said, watching her closely.

"Where? Unless you want to give up your apartment . . . but that isn't a very large area up there."

"What about the basement?"

"The basement? Why, Nathan, that is jam-packed with old books. Besides, it's musty down there."

Nathan got up, took two bottles of water out of the small fridge in the corner of the reading nook, and handed one to Virginia.

"True. But I've been dying to get down there and take a closer look at those books. Would you mind if I spent some time down there when you're gone? See what you have for back stock? Maybe come up with a game plan to sell or even donate some of it?"

He'd been dreaming of finding some "diamonds in the rough" down there—maybe early books of authors who went on to find success, or even who went no further than their first book but had real talent. Frank had said Virginia had been very generous with new authors through the years, stocking their books here when larger bookstores wouldn't give them a chance. He'd grumbled that they got stuck with lots of them, but Nathan had different ideas.

"Of course, I wouldn't mind. Have at it," Virginia said. "But I still don't think the basement is usable space."

Nathan considered this. She might be right. The steps going down were narrow, rickety. Fixing them would take funds, and even then, it wouldn't be accessible to everyone. The only other way into the basement was through the doors he and Grace had discovered, but those passed through the building next door. The building that was sitting empty and an eyesore compared to some of the other revitalizations that were happening around them.

"Could we do anything with the building next door?" he asked, his brain firing off a new volley of possibilities, none of which he'd even considered before now.

"We?" Virginia asked. "The *city* took the building back. The rumor was they'd sold it to a developer for the back taxes. Didn't Frank tell you that?"

Nathan sat forward in his chair, energized by their brainstorming. "I know, but they haven't done anything with it. Are you sure the sale went through?"

"Well . . . no, not really. It's sat vacant for so long, I never even give it a thought anymore. It's just there, you know? At least I hadn't thought about it until you and Grace ended up finding that back room full of stuff. Saving Philip's Santa suit made my heart happy."

Nathan nodded. He'd wanted to get back down there, too—find other hidden treasures in the boxes. When he'd mentioned doing so to Frank, the man had told him to feel free. "Would there be room next door to set something up, maybe for meetings or classes?"

Virginia's gaze went to the front window. "Heavens, it's been *years* since I've been in there. But, yes, I suspect there would be. But all these ideas of yours are exhausting me, Nathan."

Laughing, Nathan apologized for his enthusiasm.

"Oh, no—don't ever apologize for that. It's that youth and excitement that keep the world fresh. Why don't you do some research while we're gone? Brainstorm all you like. I tend to agree with you, Nathan. If we want to keep this place open much longer, we need to breathe some life into things. But, just so we're clear, I'm not ready to walk away yet. I want—no . . . I *need* . . . to still be involved."

He smiled. "I wouldn't want it any other way, Virginia."

***

Nathan closed the bookstore midafternoon to give Virginia a ride home. Her car was in the shop, but she needed to get home to finish packing and make some final arrangements. They were leaving in two days.

When he got back, he was surprised to see the customer who had flirted with him, Amanda, hanging around outside the store.

"Don't you know there's a law against loitering downtown?" he teased. He felt a twinge of guilt, again, for never having called her.

But the smile she gave him seemed to indicate she wasn't upset. Instead, she pointed to the sign he'd stuck to the door. "Says you'd be back in fifteen minutes. I believe the law allows for up to thirty minutes of loitering before they haul you away."

"You might be right," Nathan laughed, digging out his keys. "What are you shopping for today?"

She shrugged as he held the door open for her. "I was hoping you'd have a new recommendation for me. My TBR pile is getting low."

"TBR?"

"Sure—you know, my 'To Be Read' pile," she said with a laugh. "You know, as a bookseller you should really keep up with the lingo."

"Ah, yes. It's a shame when one's TBR pile gets too low." He shrugged out of his jacket and tossed it onto the stool behind the counter. "Did you have a nice Christmas? Hey, did your brother like the book you picked out for him?"

"He seemed to, although he's moved on from dating the girl who liked to read to some chick with two kids, so it might never actually get read. Let's say he isn't known for sticking with one thing for very long."

Nathan laughed. "At least you tried."

He was glad she'd stopped in. Amanda was easy to talk to. If his feelings weren't all wrapped up in knots over Grace, who he *still* couldn't read, he'd have worked up the nerve to ask Amanda out.

She beat him to it.

"Say, do you have plans tonight?"

He almost stuttered. "Tonight?"

"Yeah. You know . . . New Year's Eve?"

"Yes, I remembered it's New Year's. Do you think all I do is work?" He'd made tentative plans to join a group of his old buddies at a house party on the edge of campus, but he hadn't been able to muster much excitement at the prospect.

Amanda wandered over to the table displaying current bestselling titles, running her fingers over some of the covers. "The thought crossed my mind. You've been here almost every time I've stopped in."

He couldn't argue with that. "I was maybe going to hang out with some buddies. Why?"

"There's a group of us heading out to the Barn. I thought maybe you might like to join us."

"What barn?"

"*The* Barn," she repeated, laughing. "It's this neat place that has a big annual New Year's Eve celebration. They offer a smorgasbord, and then hayrides complete with spiked hot cocoa, followed by a live band up in the hayloft. It's twenty-one and older, so there aren't a bunch of drunk teenagers around. We went last year and had a lot of fun. We thought we'd go again. There are about ten of us."

Her offer sounded much more appealing than the house party that *would* be full of drunk teenagers. He was tempted, remembering how he'd wished he had a better group of friends to hang out with these days.

"I wouldn't be the only guy, would I?"

She laughed again. "Of course not. About half and half. But don't worry, it isn't a *date* thing. Not couples."

The Barn was sounding better all the time.

"Where can I meet you all?"

***

They were meeting at six in the mall parking lot and taking three Ubers out to the New Year's Eve party. No one wanted to worry about having to drive home afterward.

When he'd texted his old roommate that something had come up and they should go on to the house party without him, he got a quick text back.

Dude, you're pathatic

He may be *pathetic,* but at least he'd learned to spell during his school career. He was suddenly even more glad he'd decided to take Amanda up on her offer.

As he dug through a tote of winter clothes he'd stashed in his closet, looking for his boots, his cell rang.

It was Grace. He hadn't heard from her since they'd talked the day after getting back from Whispering Pines. He'd taken her silence to mean she was enjoying "taking it slow," just as she'd requested. But that didn't mean he had to sit home alone on New Year's.

So why do I feel guilty? he thought as he answered his phone.

"Hi, Nathan! What are you up to tonight? Want to drive over and go out with me and Julie and Zoey? Ben is coming, too, and bringing the guy Zoey kind of liked."

Julie and Ben, Zoey and that guy, me and Grace . . . this is definitely a date *thing. Couples.*

He glanced at the time. He was supposed to be at the mall parking lot in fifteen minutes. He'd already bailed on his buddies. He couldn't do the same to Amanda. She deserved better. Besides, if Grace had wanted to spend New Year's Eve with him, she should have called sooner.

"I'm sorry, Grace, but I have plans."

"Plans? Really?"

Why is that so hard to believe?

"Yes, plans. I would have called you, but I wasn't sure you wanted me to. You know, 'taking it slow' and all."

While he hated that his comment might come across as whining or passive-aggressive, he'd had about enough of her back and forth where they were concerned. He'd wanted to date her for months, but she'd been reluctant to commit to anything. Maybe he should see where things might be able to go with Amanda. *She* seemed more than willing to spend time with him, and she was straightforward about it.

He heard Grace's sigh through the phone. "I guess I deserve that. Can I ask what you're doing?"

"Sure," he replied, trying to keep his tone light. "I'm going to some party at this place called the Barn. Ever hear of it?"

"No. Who are you going with?"

"Remember that girl, Amanda? From the bookstore? She stopped in a little bit ago and invited me."

"Ah. Okay," Grace said, a hint of irritation in her voice now. "Go have fun on your date. Sorry to bother you."

Click.

The satisfaction he'd felt when mentioning Amanda's invite was fleeting. Now he just felt . . . lonely again.

***

Amanda's friends were fun. Dinner included a baked potato bar, hot dogs, salad, and a variety of homemade desserts. Nothing fancy, but it was a festive atmosphere, and the food was good. They served keg beer, and for a $40 cover charge, the hayride and dance were included with the meal.

One of the other girls in the group had been in the bookstore before with Amanda. Two of the guys, brothers, were old college friends of Amanda's. Nathan missed the other connections she had quickly rattled off when she'd first introduced everyone in the mall parking lot.

Nathan was having fun, trying to put his conversation with Grace out of his mind. Had he missed a chance for them to finally start acting like a couple? She hadn't sounded happy when she thought he was going out on a date. But then the picture on her screensaver flashed through his mind—the one with her and Connor. Grace had things to figure out. He deserved a night of fun with friends.

"Come on, grab some hot chocolate over here and follow me," Amanda said after they'd bussed their trays following the meal.

Nathan groaned. "I don't know. I'm pretty stuffed."

"Trust me, you are going to want to try this," she assured him, offering him a friendly smile.

One of the guys in their group bumped into him from behind as they made their way over to the line forming near the door. "Sorry, bud."

Nathan nodded. "Did you come to this last year, too?"

"Yeah. It was fun," the guy replied. "It left me with a hell of a hangover to start the New Year off, but it was worth it. Thought I better pace myself a little better this year."

They continued to talk while the line moved slowly. It turned out the guy was working in the city offices now.

"Hey, you wouldn't happen to know anything about who owns an old building downtown, would you? Does your office work with that kind of thing?"

"I'm sure I could find out. Those are public records. Want me to check on something for you?"

Nathan filled him in as to which building he was curious about and why.

"Call me next week. I'll see what I can find out for ya."

"Cool, I appreciate that, man," Nathan said, surprised to have made the connection with one of Amanda's friends.

Later, with everyone crammed onto benches in an old farm trailer piled high with straw, Nathan found himself pressed up tightly against Amanda's side. Across from them were a guy and girl from their group, arms around each other, looking very much like a couple in the moonlight.

He leaned over to whisper in Amanda's ear. "I thought you said this wasn't a *couple* thing."

She shrugged, her eyes on the moon and not him. "Those two? They're on again, off again all the time. We never know what to expect. She's afraid of commitment but gets all lovey-dovey with him whenever she feels like it. We're all used to it by now. I used to feel sorry for him. Now I find it all . . . pitiful," she said, finally meeting his eye.

She isn't talking about you and Grace, he thought to himself, trying to make out the color of Amanda's eyes in the moonlight. It was too dark, and he couldn't remember noticing their color before. But Amanda leaned ever so slightly toward him, and his eyes fell to her lips. Did he dare?

The wagon wheel banged through a hole, jostling everyone on the benches, laughter ringing out. "Hey, buddy, are you trying to kill us back here?" someone shouted to the man leading the team of horses.

Maybe he should have taken Amanda's friend's advice and not drank quite so much.

The moment was lost, but not forgotten.

CHAPTER 26

Gift of Zebra Prints and White Linen

*N*athan groaned, rolling over onto his back and covering his face with a pillow.

His head was killing him.

He lay there, his mind going over how the evening had unfolded. After the near-kiss in the hay, Nathan had avoided being alone with Amanda the rest of the night. She hadn't let on that anything was off, still as pleasant and talkative as ever. While he wasn't usually much of a dancer, he couldn't remember sitting out a single song once the band started playing. They'd danced as a group, the temperature upstairs in the barn rising with the bodies and exertion, despite the frigid temperature outside.

When the clock struck midnight, there'd been friendly hugs and quick pecks all around, all in good fun—except for the one couple he'd asked Amanda about earlier. They snuck off, only to return later, the guy's shirt half-untucked and the girl's hair snarled.

Nathan suspected that poor guy felt worse than he did this morning.

Or better.

Then he remembered the Uber ride back to town. He'd checked his phone, noticing pictures Julie had texted to him. She'd added *Wish you were here!* to one of them, and Nathan could see they were out on a different dance floor. Grace was in the background of one of the shots, some guy hanging on her.

Grace should have been hanging on me, *but no, I had to be stubborn. Try to make her jealous.*

He groaned again when he remembered he hadn't kept that particular comment to himself. Amanda had overheard him, leading to a discussion about his relationship, or whatever it was, with Grace. He was afraid he'd said too much, but she was nice about it. When she invited him out to breakfast with the group, he declined. He stayed with the Uber, after dropping everyone else at an all-night restaurant. Nathan went back to the bookstore. He'd have to figure out a way to pick up his car from the mall.

"If you ever get over her, call me sometime," Amanda had said just before she'd slammed the door as she got out.

Something occurred to Nathan then, despite the brain-fog he was suffering. He pulled up the texts his cousin had sent him.

He bit his tongue to keep from cursing. It probably wasn't even worth getting upset over again. A guy *was* hanging on Grace in one of the shots, and now, when Nathan looked closer, he recognized him. It was the same guy, Connor, from her phone before—the one she'd supposedly broken things off with.

Enough was enough—no more of Grace's games.

He owed Amanda an apology.

***

Nathan had no food in his apartment. He showered, pulled on sweats, and headed downstairs, each step causing his head to throb.

They wouldn't be open on New Year's Day, and Virginia had made him promise not to work—although he was tempted to get started on the front window if he could get over this hangover. He was about to head out to find food, maybe drive to the grocery store, when he remembered his car was still in the mall parking lot.

His phone rang.

"Hey, Mom, Happy New Year."

"Happy New Year, son!" she replied, her voice sounding much too chipper to his ear. "Did you do anything fun last night?"

"Yeah, went out." His voice sounded terrible, even to his own ears.

If Jess noticed, she didn't comment. "What are you doing today, then?"

"I was going to go get some groceries, but my car's not here. We used an Uber last night."

"Why don't you sit tight? I'll swing by and get you."

Before he could even respond, she'd hung up.

"Sure, Mom, why don't you do that," he said aloud to the empty store.

He looked around, trying to think of something to occupy himself, since it would take Jess nearly an hour to "swing by" if she was coming from Whispering Pines. He'd promised Virginia to take the day off. He didn't have any homework, since classes hadn't started back up again, and his head hurt too much to read.

The door to the basement caught his eye. He'd been dying to dig around down there again. Maybe this was the perfect time. He grabbed the flashlight, even though it wouldn't be dark down there this time of day, took a minute to down some aspirin along with half a bottle of water, found a pocket-knife to help open boxes, and unlocked the basement door.

All was quiet as he climbed down the stairs. He flipped the lights on, despite the muted sunlight finding its way into the basement through the small windows. The stacks of books on tables in the large front room beckoned to him, but he ignored them.

Another day. Promise.

He went straight back to the corner room, unblocked the aqua door, and pulled it toward him. The room beyond looked just as he'd left it when he'd come down to get the music boxes.

Where should I start?

Grace had already poked through most of the boxes nearest the aqua door. Neither of them had done much digging in the area on the other side of the windows stacked against the outer wall, just past the door to the outside. Nathan made his way back there, using his flashlight to brighten up his path. He didn't want to fall over anything, as Grace had done.

To the right of the door, he found a tall stack of boxes, piled higher than his head and two deep. He pulled one off the top and used the pocket-knife to slice the brittle masking tape open, encountering very little resistance against the blade. The first box was full of paper bags. No markings, not exciting. The next box contained the same thing. Maybe they'd already found the only treasures down here.

He went to pull off another box, revealing an area previously hidden by the boxes.

In the glare of the flashlight beam, blank eyes stared back at him.

"Holy shit!" he cried, jumping back.

It only took him a second to realize it was a mannequin.

He laughed—then moaned in pain. The aspirin hadn't taken care of his headache yet.

Curious what else might be behind the boxes, as digging through them wasn't revealing anything interesting, he slid them out of the way as best he could. His flashlight beam had just come to rest on a pile of blankets in the corner when he heard a voice behind him.

"Nathan! Are you down here?"

"Back here, Mom!" he yelled back, surprised she was already here.

"*What* are you doing?" she asked, then she stopped and looked around. "What *is* this place?"

"This is that room where we found the Santa suit. Remember, I told you about it."

She nodded, continuing to peer around the messy, dim room.

Another voice: "Jess, where'd you go?"

"Seth's here, too?" Nathan asked.

"Yeah, we were going out for lunch, since we stayed home last night. Lauren insisted we go for a New Year's date. She's watching Harper," she explained to her son before turning back to the colored door she'd just come through. "Back here, hon!"

"I'm glad he's here. He digs around in old buildings all the time. Did you tell Seth about this place?" Nathan asked Jess as he watched for Seth to come in.

"Just briefly."

Seth's big body filled the narrow door frame. "What are you doing, Nathan?" he asked, echoing Jess.

"Seeing what else is down here."

Seth looked up, back over his shoulder, and took a few steps into the room. "This isn't part of the Fisks' basement, is it? It seems like we're under the building next door."

"We are. I'll explain later. But, guys, come here. I just found something a minute before Mom came in here."

Nathan turned back around to face the pile of blankets, curious about them but also very glad he wasn't down here alone anymore. Jess reached his side, and Seth looked over his shoulder. He was afraid he was looking at some kind of bed . . . like someone had been staying down here.

"What is *that*?" Jess asked as Nathan slowly approached the pile, ready to jump back if something nasty was under those blankets.

"Nathan, wait," Seth said, grabbing his arm. "Give me that flashlight." Nathan did as he was told.

Seth took two steps forward and then used the heavy, long flashlight to prod into the center of the pile. When nothing happened, he used the flashlight to lift one corner carefully and look underneath.

"Be *careful*," Jess hissed, holding on to Nathan's arm with both hands.

Seth crouched down, pinched the edge of the blanket, and slowly lifted it.

Something metal rattled out and fell to the floor with a *clank*. It was a flask.

"Looks like somebody might have been sleeping down here, once upon a time," Seth said, now more aggressively rummaging through the blankets.

Nathan's mind flew back to the night when he and Grace thought they heard something in the bookstore—and then the door into this room had been mysteriously open.

"Like . . . recently?" Nathan asked, not wanting to believe it could be true. The door at the top of his apartment stairs didn't lock. What if someone *had* been in the bookstore? They could have snuck upstairs while he and Grace were sleeping . . .

"I can't tell. These blankets are old, but if someone was squatting in here, they'd probably make use of what was here. Do you have any reason to believe someone has been in here recently?"

Nathan sighed. "Maybe it's just my imagination going crazy . . . but there have been a couple things that seemed odd lately." He went on to tell them about the noises, the tipped boxes, and how the door had been locked one night then ajar the next time they checked.

Seth must have noticed Nathan glance toward the outer door. "Huh, would you look at that—someone probably came in through that way, maybe looking for a place to warm up."

Nathan walked over to the door, and Seth followed. The older man tested the lock, then took a closer look at it.

"So do you think someone could open that?"

"Yeah, I think they could . . . and without too much trouble."

Jess had stayed in the background, but Seth's comment brought her charging forward. "Nathan, we need to call the police. This isn't safe."

Seth spun to face her, placing his hands on her shoulders. "Jess, breathe. This is all speculation. We don't know that anyone has been in here. Maybe the things Nathan noticed can all be explained away."

"Yeah, no. I'm not buying it," Jess said, her eyes taking on that stubborn glint both Nathan and Seth recognized.

"Mom, I don't want to deal with the police. Heck, I don't even know if we should be in here. I don't want to upset the Fisks. Seth's right. It was probably just our imagination."

She paused. Nathan thought maybe Jess was coming around. His own initial fear over his discovery was being replaced with a twinge of sympathy. He struggled to understand how anyone would be desperate enough to sleep in this forgotten, filthy room, among the mice and who knows what else.

Virginia's sense of empathy for people in hopeless situations must be rubbing off on me.

"Look, I have some tools in my truck. I know a thing or two about locks. I think I could tighten this one up, maybe even install a bar across that smaller door over there that leads into the Fisks' basement," Seth said, motioning toward the aqua door. "Then we could be certain no one can access the bookstore through here. What do you say?"

Jess chewed on her bottom lip, considering. "You could do that right now?"

Seth nodded. "Won't take me long. Thirty minutes and we're out of here."

"Oh, fine," Jess said. She gave Nathan a look. "I don't want to upset the Fisks either, you know."

True to his word, Seth made quick work of securing both doors. As they were leaving, the pile of old windows stacked against the wall caught his eye. He whistled. "These are *nice*. It's a shame these windows are down here, just taking up space. I could sell them in a heartbeat."

As an owner of a business that specialized in buying and selling architectural salvage, Seth would know quality when he saw it. Nathan didn't doubt he could sell the cool old windows. Maybe other stuff down here, too.

Jess sneezed. Then sneezed again. "Anybody else hungry? I could use some lunch," she said, dabbing at her nose with the back of her hand.

"You wouldn't last long on the job with me, Jess, if a little dust bothers you," Seth said, glancing her way with a smile.

"And that's why I help you out with your business on the *bookkeeping* side," she reminded him, grinning back.

"Come on, Nathan, let's go feed your mother. Maybe you and I can come back down here again soon. I'd like to see what else is here."

***

They all climbed into Seth's truck, agreeing to get Nathan's car after lunch. He let out a low whistle when Seth pulled into one of the nicer restaurants in the area. Definitely not one Nathan had ever been able to patronize before—not on a college student's budget.

"I've heard this place is great, but I didn't think they were open for lunch."

"They aren't usually, but they're running a New Year's Day special. Besides, I helped the owner with some of his design elements inside. Thought I'd give him some business in return."

As they all climbed out of the pickup, their breath puffed out on the frigid air.

"It's gotta be twenty degrees colder than it was last night—and it wasn't exactly balmy then, either," Nathan said, hunching up against the cold, trying to keep his neck protected with his jacket.

The snow and ice covering the parking lot crunched underfoot.

Inside, it took a minute for his eyes to adjust to the dimness: dark, rich wall coverings, heavy carpet on the floor, and white tablecloths; one wall was even covered in a zebra-print wallpaper yet somehow managed not to look gaudy.

Nope, definitely not in my league.

It occurred to him then that his headache had slipped away. Lunch at a nice place with family was a pleasant surprise, and the perfect way to usher in the new year with class.

"Maybe I should send Lauren a picture of this place, rub it in a little that we're here and she's home changing diapers."

"How about you *don't* do that," Jess replied, looking at him sideways while they waited for the hostess to show them to their table. The place was hopping. Seth must have called ahead. Once they were seated, a waiter offered them wine. The thought of alcohol in his still-empty stomach threatened to reignite his headache. He settled for water. They ordered, and while they waited for their food their discussion turned to Nathan's activities the night before.

"What did 'going out' consist of last night, if you don't mind my asking?" Jess began.

Here comes the inquisition.

He told them about the food, hayride, and dancing at the Barn.

"I know that place," Seth said. "Lots of fun."

"Was this a group of friends I know?"

"No, Mom, you haven't met this group. One of them has stopped in the store a few times, and we've gotten to be friends, so when she swung by the bookstore yesterday before I closed, she invited me along."

"Oh, so this wasn't a *date* thing, then?" Jess sounded disappointed.

"No. It was not. Just a bunch of guys and girls, hanging out. It was fun, though."

"Is she cute?"

Nathan shrugged. "Yeah, she's cute, but I don't know her very well. She was actually at the store one day when you stopped in."

Jess pulled a bread roll out of a linen-lined basket in the middle of the table, tore it apart, and buttered it. "I guess I don't remember."

Looking to change the subject, Nathan asked what Lauren did, if anything, the night before.

"She stayed home. Julie called, invited her along, but it sounded like they might be going to some bars and Lauren didn't want to cramp their style. That reminds me—I thought they were going to call you, too?"

"Grace did call, but I'd already made plans with Amanda and her friends, so I had to pass. Julie sent me drunken dancing texts throughout the night, though, so I didn't *completely* miss out."

"Hmm."

"What? I know that *hmm*, Mom."

"Oh, nothing. I was starting to wonder if maybe Grace might not have a little bit of a crush on you."

Nathan grunted. "I think Grace is struggling to get over an old flame." It ticked him off when he saw a look pass between Seth and his mom, almost like a non-verbal *I told you so,* but he let it go. "Maybe I'll ask Amanda out. She's fun, and I liked her friends."

He was saved from any further talk about his lackluster love life by the arrival of their food. The plate of baked chicken, mashed potatoes, and asparagus was a delicious distraction. Jess dug into her pasta, and Seth flaked off a large bite from his salmon.

"This should be enough food for the whole *day,*" Seth said between bites.

"Oh, say, Nathan, guess what? I finally had a chance to finish Virginia's book last night! I *loved* it! You were right to encourage her to do something with it."

Nathan was relieved to hear high praises from his mom. She was an avid reader and a straight shooter. If she hadn't liked it, she'd have said so.

"It *is* good, isn't it?"

"What's the next step then?" Seth asked. "Don't you want to have that thing done in, like, a month?"

Jess nodded. "Six weeks, but even that isn't much time. I called Grant this morning. He and Michelle are still passing it back and forth. They hope to be done with it in a week or two."

"And then?" Seth prodded.

"I honestly don't know too much about all the steps we'll need to take."

Jess looked at Nathan. "Nathan?"

"I've been researching when I can. Talking to Grant about the process, too. Once the book is fully edited, he's got his formatter lined up to make it look pretty, for lack of a better term. As far as the exterior, we'll need to find a cover designer. Grace found us someone, but she's looking for input on the image and title and stuff."

"I can't wait to see Virginia's name in big bold letters on the front of this book," Jess said, her eyes lighting up. "And we have to come up with an amazing dedication for the front."

Nathan hadn't given a thought to the dedication. "I'll maybe leave that touchy-feely stuff up to you, Mom. But you bring up a good point about her name. Earlier, before Virginia had even had a chance to read her manuscript again, I joked with her about maybe putting her book out under a pen name."

Surprise registered on Jess's face. "Really? Is that what she wanted to do?"

Nathan tried to remember their exact exchange, but the details were fuzzy. "I'm not sure . . . I think *I* brought it up first."

"If she didn't come right out and say she didn't want to publish under her own name, then I say *no way* to a pen name. For God's sake, Virginia has been carrying this wish to be a published author around in her heart for decades!"

Nathan looked to Seth for any possible guidance. He shrugged and raised a hand in Jess's direction. "I wouldn't go against that, man" was all he offered.

She's right, of course, Nathan conceded. Virginia should be proud to have her name associated with her amazing story.

Jess twirled a forkful of noodles and shoved them into her mouth, nodding for Nathan to go on, as if her edict settled the matter.

"Got it. We'll go with Virginia's actual name as the author. Once the inside and the outside of the book are ready to go, I plan to load it up to an online distributor. I hear their platform isn't too difficult to figure out, and they'll do print-on-demand for us."

Based on the blank look on Seth's face, the term was foreign to him.

"All that means is we won't have to order a huge stack of the books. They'll print as many books as we want to order. They serve wholesalers. You can order one, or a hundred, or a thousand."

"I had no idea," Seth said. "I was envisioning a print run costing thousands of dollars, and I was getting hung up on that. If you're surprising Virginia and Frank with this book, who's paying for things on the front end?"

Jess, pushed her half-eaten bowl of pasta out of the way and laid her napkin on the table. "I'll take that home for later. I can't eat another bite," she said, folding her hands on the tabletop. "That's a fair question, Seth. We can get a cover done, have the book formatted for an estimate Grant gave me, and order a small supply of Virginia's books for her bookstore for around a thousand dollars. Remember, Michelle isn't charging us for editing. She's doing it to gain the experience, with the hope Grant and the Fisks can send work her way in the future."

Nathan was glad Jess had thought through the finances. He hadn't given much thought to the upfront cost in the excitement and rush to get the book done as a surprise—although he did have one idea, based on something Seth had said earlier.

"I might have an idea where we can get the thousand dollars," Nathan offered.

Jess looked at him, interested. "Okay, let's hear it."

"What if we sold some of the stuff in that back storage room?"

Jess sat back in her chair, clearly surprised by the idea. "Can we even *do* that?"

"I think we can. Frank said to feel free to get rid of the stuff if I had time. He doesn't seem to think it has any value. But there's a big box of old *Life* magazines down there. I was kind of curious, so I looked online, and some might be worth about five bucks apiece. I bet there are at least a hundred of them in there."

Nathan scooped up the last of his potatoes, shoving them into his mouth.

"And those windows we saw leaning up against the wall down there are worth something, too. I could sell those for you," Seth offered.

Jess glanced between the two men. "What I mean is, do you think you have permission to *sell* the stuff? The room isn't part of the Fisks' building. Someone else owns it. And it's not like we can call Frank or Virginia up and ask *them* for advice. Not if we want the book to be a surprise."

"Mother. No one has paid any attention to that stuff in something like thirty years. The city sold the building to an investor—at least we think, I'm checking on that—and that room we were in was completely walled off. They don't even know the room is there. But when I find out who actually owns the building, I'll ask, all right?"

"Yes, please. I'm not a hundred percent comfortable removing anything more from that hidden room until you get the proper permission. It feels a little unethical."

"Mom, the stuff all belonged to Frank's brother when he died. The brother's kids didn't want it. They told Frank they cleaned it all out, but they must have been too lazy to actually do it. What more do you want? Unless you have an extra grand lying around that's burning a hole in your pocket."

Jess laughed, holding up her palms in surrender. "Just make sure first. Then, if you get the green light, see what you can get for all that old junk. Maybe we could get an even bigger print run of Virginia's book and offer them for sale in the store."

"Jess, remember, one man's junk is another man's treasure. Don't wound me with your 'junk' comments. It's how I make a living," Seth reminded her. The smirk on his face told Nathan he was teasing.

"Who knows—maybe we can sell some of those old books in the Fisks' basement too," Nathan went on. "We could earn some extra cash and rent the whole building next door. Offer some kind of courses or something. You know, diversify the income streams for the bookstore."

Jess grinned at her son. "I like the way you think, kid. You must be almost a college graduate or something."

"Haha," Nathan shot back, shoving a big forkful of chicken into his mouth with the manners of a five-year-old.

***

Once the idea to sell things out of the back storage room to fund Virginia's book took hold, Nathan got busy. His contact at the city, the one he'd met on New Year's Eve at the Barn, reached out to the investment company that now owned the building. They had assumed the building was empty and didn't want to bother with the logistics to have the old merchandise cleared out. They sent their written permission through the city offices, authorizing Nathan to proceed with disposal of the items. Seth helped.

Grant and Michelle held up their end of the bargain, completing their work by the end of the first week and passing it on to a professional formatter.

Nathan split his time between the store, his new classes, and learning what he could about the mechanics of independent or indie publishing. It was as if a whole new world was opening up to him. He secretly hoped this wouldn't be the last book he helped put out into the world.

Tansy turned out to be a big help at the bookstore. She did great with customers and had a flair for displays. She helped Nathan change out the front window, and together they came up with a simple, aesthetically pleasing design, welcome after the intricate holiday display. The only part of the business she shied away from was the business end. She let Nathan handle customer checks, credit cards, and the cash as much as possible. When Nathan asked her about it one day, she'd replied that Virginia had assured her Nathan would handle all of that. He didn't mind. With Frank gone, it gave him a chance to see the business from all angles.

He had yet to talk to Grace again. He was still mad at her for apparently hooking up with her ex after she'd told him she was done with the guy. He'd even gone so far as to call Amanda to ask her to a movie, but she was on a month-long work trip out of town.

The group working on Virginia's book shared cover input with Grace through email. They settled on a cover that Nathan hoped would make Virginia proud. Everything was coming together. Valentine's Day was going to work great for the big surprise. The books were ordered and should arrive a week before February 14th.

Three days before the Fisks were expected back, Nathan's phone rang. It was Virginia. He'd talked to her once a week since they'd left, so he knew they were enjoying themselves, but he was excited to get them home before Frank's birthday.

"Hi, Virginia! I'm glad you called. Listen, I've been thinking. We should probably do some type of event for Valentine's Day, don't you think?"

He actually had a large party planned already. The invites were out, and the food ordered. He just needed to convince Virginia it was a good idea without letting on that her book was at the heart of the celebration.

"Hello, Nathan. Things must be going well, you sound excited. Yes, I agree, we should do something fun for Valentine's Day, now that I'm sure we will be back in time."

Her comment gave him pause. "What do you mean, 'back in time'? Is everything all right?"

"Oh my, yes. We are having so much fun! In fact, we even looked into staying a bit longer. Of course, I would have checked with you on that before we finalized anything, but unfortunately the place we're staying in is only available until the end of January. So we'll be back as scheduled."

"You have no idea how glad I am to hear you say that, Ginny," Nathan said, his shoulders sagging with relief. He'd had a momentary panic when she'd mentioned staying longer, picturing the bookstore full of people, refreshments, and copies of Virginia's new book on February 14th. Everything would have been in place—except for the guests of honor.

After a beat of silence, Virginia's voice came over the line again. "I'm surprised to hear you say that, Nathan. Is there some problem back home? Are things not going as well as you've been saying?"

Get a grip, or you're going to ruin the surprise!

"Oh no, nothing like that, Ginny. And I'm glad you two are having so much fun. I was just worried that maybe Frank's headaches were back or something and you were concerned about the flight home, since it's only three days away."

"Bless you, Nathan. I appreciate your concern, but we are both feeling fit as a pair of fiddles. Looking forward to seeing you soon!"

He hung up, smiling.

Me too, Ginny.

CHAPTER 27
Gift of Captured Wishes

"*I* just *love* Valentine's Day, don't you?" Virginia asked Nathan as she arranged some of her all-time favorite romance novels on the front table in the bookstore.

Nathan looked down at her from his perch high on a ladder in the front window. One of the long strands of paper hearts he'd strung a week ago had fallen overnight. "Never been a big fan, to be honest, Ginny, but today should be fun."

He may not put much stock in a holiday dedicated to love these days, but he supposed he *had* enjoyed it as a kid. Trying to build the best Valentine's box to win the inevitable contest in school, chocolates or candied hearts taped to silly little cards classmates exchanged, and even a middle school Valentine's Day dance where he'd first slow-danced with a girl—those had been fun times.

Today promised to be fun as well . . . but Nathan hoped Virginia still hadn't caught on to what they'd been up to with her manuscript.

"I don't understand why you have things looking so sparse up here, though, Nathan," Virginia said, hands on her hips as she surveyed the section of the store nearest the door. "You did a beautiful job in the front window, *again*, but explain why we're making our customers roam the aisles to find a book instead of using the tables up here? I've never only had two tables in the front . . ."

"I told you, Ginny. I'm paying close attention to buyer's habits, and one thing buyers don't appreciate is feeling overwhelmed. They prefer wide open spaces and room to browse."

Even as he said it, he knew his excuse was a stretch, but the lie couldn't be helped. The real reason was because Nathan needed room to put a third table back up, dedicated strictly to Virginia's book, but of course he couldn't tell her that.

"I *am* sorry you and Frank couldn't stay in Florida for a few extra weeks," he said, hoping for a distraction. Of course, he wasn't sorry at all, but it sounded good.

"I was, too, Nathan. But it was a silly notion. The place we were staying at was beautiful. I should have expected it to be booked for the next few months."

"Will you go back next year?"

Virginia nodded, her normally snow-white hair gleaming with a touch of pink in the morning sunlight. She'd added a special rinse during her last trip to the beauty shop—something she told Nathan she did every February to celebrate Valentine's Day. "We're already booked for January *and* February next year. I can't believe I was so stubborn about going. We should have started an annual trip, right after Christmas, *years* ago."

"Good thing you finally granted Frank his wish to visit Florida, huh?"

Making her way from the table of bestselling romance books to the one other table currently set up in the front of the store, Virginia ran her fingers over several different book spines. "Thank you for taking the time to start going through all those books downstairs. I *love* that you picked out some of the old romances and brought them up here for your Valentine's party."

Nathan climbed down off the ladder and carefully maneuvered the bulky thing away from the window display. He loved the way the window had come together. They'd found two vintage signs in the now-thoroughly-vetted basement storage room, one a mock-up of a kissing booth sign like at a county fair back in the 1960s. The other was of a small, dark-haired child in a pair of heart-covered pajamas, sporting the words BE MY HONEY BUNNY across the bottom. Where they'd come from, and how, or even *if,* they'd ever actually been used before, they'd never know. But the rigid cardboard signs gave special flair to their window display for February, the pinks and reds a nice contrast to the bleak winter days outside.

"Finding books specific to romance down there was Tansy's idea, actually. But aren't some of these old covers great? They've been a big hit in my posts advertising our little get-together today."

The front door jangled and in came Jess, carrying a large white box from Mabel's bakery.

"Cupcakes are here! Where do you want them?"

Nathan hurried over and took the box out of his mother's hands. "Over here," he said, taking them back to where he planned to set them out midafternoon for the party.

"I hope Frank doesn't mind us using the party today to celebrate his birthday, too. He doesn't like a fuss," Virginia said.

"I know, but it might help bring more people into the store. And you know Frank. He's usually up for things that stand to increase foot traffic."

Virginia laughed. "He *is* a practical man, isn't he?"

Jess looked around the store. "It looks great in here, guys. I like the way you've opened things up a bit—more room to walk."

The front door opened to squeals. Harper burst into the store, running as best she could on wobbly legs, launching herself toward her big brother. Seth wasn't far behind.

Nathan scooped her up, getting a better look at her face, a red rim of some sort ringing her mouth. He wiped at it, but it wasn't coming off.

"Mabel heard she had her first birthday a few weeks ago and she gave her a tiny little cake to celebrate. Of course, the frosting was bright red for Valentine's Day," Seth explained.

"Hello, Seth. It's good to see all of you," Virginia said, patting Harper on the head. The one-year-old tried to squirm away, not having any of it.

"Great, sugar-induced attitude," Nathan said with a groan, setting Harper down.

"I'm surprised you're here already," Virginia said to Jess. "Frank's birthday party doesn't start until three."

There was more activity at the front door. Grant, Michelle, and Grace all walked in, bringing a rush of cold air and pink cheeks.

"Man, it's *cold* out there!" Grant said, clapping his hands together for warmth.

"Well, hello," Virginia said, looking around at everyone. "Was there some miscommunication about the time for the party? I'll have to call

Frank, have him come over. He was waiting at home for the repairman to fix the garage door. By the way, thanks for trying to fix it, Nathan, but the door keeps getting stuck on the tracks."

Nathan laughed, thinking back to the mess Virginia had made of the garage door earlier in the winter on a particularly icy day. Despite their best efforts, they weren't able to hide her little accident from Frank after all.

"No, don't call him. The party is still on for this afternoon. But there's a little something we wanted to talk to you about first, Ginny. Why don't you come sit down back here?" Nathan suggested, walking back toward their reading nook.

He waved to the chair he knew to be Virginia's favorite, and let some of the other adults fill the remaining three. Jess corralled Harper onto her lap. Everyone else stood.

Virginia complied, but glanced with suspicion between them. "Is this an *intervention* or something? Because I promise you, I don't have any addictions. Well, other than maybe this place. And books. I *love* books, and I will not apologize for it."

Everyone laughed, and Virginia seemed to relax, although her face still wore a curious expression.

"Nathan, why don't you start?" Jess suggested.

He took a deep breath, excited to finally share with Virginia what they'd all been working so hard on for the past couple of months. But he was nervous, too. Would she appreciate their efforts, or be upset they took her book in secret and ran with it? He stepped forward, standing next to Grace, who exchanged a tentative smile with him. Then he turned his full attention to Virginia.

"Virginia Fisk . . . we have a surprise for you."

"That much is obvious, child. Out with it! While I love surprises, the suspense is killing me," Virginia prodded, a big grin on her face.

Nathan knew Virginia enjoyed the drama.

"All right. I've been debating about how best to tell you this, but I couldn't come up with anything clever, so . . . here it goes. We finished your book for you so that you could give it to Frank today, as you originally planned."

Virginia showed no visible reaction to Nathan's announcement other than her smile fading away.

Is she upset? Did I overstep?

Nathan waited, although the suspense was now killing *him*. Was she mad?

The only sound was from Harper as she tried to squirm out of Jess's arms.

Virginia raised a shaky hand and adjusted her blush-tinted hair—something Nathan had noticed her do before when she was nervous. "My . . . *my* book?"

Jess stood, passed Harper to Seth, and knelt in front of Virginia, capturing both her hands with her own.

"Ginny, Nathan told us about the story you wrote for Frank. The manuscript he found in the desk upstairs. He was so excited to help you turn your story into a physical book for Frank's birthday. He couldn't keep his excitement to himself. But when Frank got sick, and you had to put it aside again, he worried you might change your mind. Both he and Grace had already read it and insisted it needed to be turned into an actual book for Frank to enjoy. For the *world* to enjoy."

Virginia listened intently, still looking confused. "But I don't understand. How could you turn that pile of paper into a real book without me?"

Jess looked around at her friends and kids. "We all took a piece of the process. All except Harper, of course. It came together very nicely, if I do say so myself." She released Virginia's hands and stood back up, kicking her leg where it must have ached from kneeling. "Nathan, why don't you show Virginia?"

"Oh—sure!"

He spun on his heel to grab a copy from under the sales counter. He'd hidden it there earlier in the day. It felt solid, *real* in his hand when he walked it back to Virginia and passed it to her with a flourish.

"Ta-da!"

With still-shaking hands, she took it, staring at the inch-thick book in awe. Her pale fingers traced the title, the image, and her own name in bold white letters across the bottom. Turning the book over, she giggled when she saw a picture of herself staring back from a corner of the back cover.

"My . . . *heavens* . . . I guess I'm a real author now. And I love the title: *Friends First*. However did you come up with that?" Virginia asked.

"Your story explores the essence of friendship," Nathan said, motioning toward the book she clutched in her hand. He'd loved the image Grace found of a vintage Volkswagen minivan, driving down a dusty road, passengers' arms extended out the windows. The vibrant image exuded freedom and fun. "But you also said something at Thanksgiving that really stuck with me."

"Thanksgiving?"

"Sure. Remember how you told me about the early days of your relationship with Frank?"

Nathan watched Virginia closely, bursting into a grin the moment he could see she'd put it all together.

She nodded her head slowly. "Frank and I . . . we were friends first, before things blossomed into so much more."

Her eyes misted over as she looked gratefully up at Nathan.

***

Nathan had never seen Virginia so excited. So happy.

She might still be in a bit of shock.

He was glad they'd decided to give her the book early, before the party started, instead of in front of Frank. After all, it was *her* book, and she had the right to be the one to present it to her husband. They'd just helped get it across the finish line.

Shortly after giving Virginia her copy of the book, Jess, Seth, and Harper had headed home. "She'll be a bear at the party if she doesn't get a nap in," Jess explained, promising to be back at three.

"Do you want to lay her down upstairs, Mom? That's a lot of driving."

But Jess had insisted. Grant and Michelle left as well, heading out for lunch, also promising to return. Their exit left just Grace, Nathan, and Virginia in the store. The party wouldn't start for a few hours yet. There were few customers around yet.

"Can we go pick you up some lunch, Ginny?" Nathan offered.

Virginia had been paging through her book, her face still glowing. She glanced his way but went right back to the hardback volume she held in her hands. "Sure, sure . . . that would be fine, Nathan. Perhaps a sandwich from the deli two blocks over? You kids go. I want to sit with my book for a while. Then I suppose I will need to figure out how I'm going to present it to Frank at his party."

Nathan looked to Grace, and she gave him a slight nod.

"We'll be back in a bit then."

As he walked past his boss to grab his jacket out of the back, Virginia snagged his hand, squeezing tightly.

"Nathan, this is probably the nicest thing anyone has ever done for me. And you were right. I was starting to have doubts again as to whether or not I could turn this into a real, *actual* book. Becoming a published author has been one of my deepest desires since I was a little girl. You made my wish come true."

***

"Well, I'd say that went better than we could have hoped," Grace said as Nathan closed the door to the bookstore behind them. They turned in the direction of the deli, taking them past the front window of the bookstore. Grace stopped, facing the display of tissue hearts, an old kissing booth cardboard sign, and a table of romance books. A clear plastic riser stood in the middle of the table. Nathan would set Virginia's book onto that pedestal for the world to see, once Virginia handed the first copy to Frank. "You should be proud, Nathan."

As Nathan gazed at his Valentine's window display, he *was* proud. And he was relieved. He'd worried about Virginia's reaction to them running ahead with her book. But he could breathe easy now.

The only thing that would make the day even better would be if this tension between him and Grace could somehow go away. As they stood on the sidewalk, facing Book Journeys, a cold wind snaking over the top of the buildings around them and down the collars of their winter jackets, he racked his brain for something to say that wouldn't make him sound like a moron. But it was Grace who spoke first.

"You know, Nathan, I was *really* mad at you that night."

He nearly asked "Which night?" but he knew the answer. He waited instead, giving her time to start the conversation.

A beeping sound penetrated the cold air, catching both of their attentions. Turning away from the window, they saw two city workers across the street, putting up an electric lift next to a streetlight pole. Both wore bright-yellow caution vests, the guy on the ground running the lift, the one in the bucket holding a banner of some sort in his hand. The banner snapped in the wind.

"Man, it's gotta be cold up there," Nathan said, wondering what they were putting up in place of the deep-blue flag sporting a snowflake.

Grace shivered. "It's cold down *here*. Can we walk?"

"Sorry. Sure," Nathan agreed, bumping her shoulder with his own when he turned again toward the deli. "It's cold, and I'm starving. What were you saying?"

Grace let out a loud sigh. "That night . . . awhile back. You know, when I called and invited you out for New Year's but you had other plans? I'd misread the situation with us. It hurt to find out you were going out on a date with someone else."

Nathan sighed right back. "I admit it—I let you think it was a date. But it wasn't. Not really. I was sick of not knowing where I stood with you, so I guess I thought maybe if *you* thought someone else was interested, you might see me differently. It made more sense at the time. When I admit it out loud now, it just sounds juvenile. For that, I apologize."

Grace kicked at a chunk of ice on the sidewalk, her feet protected from the cold with gray boots that reached her knees. She looked great, as usual, her long legs keeping pace with his. He didn't know how to interpret her silence.

Nothing unusual there either.

"I saw the picture, you know," he said when she remained quiet.

The bright winter sun caused her to squint when she looked his way.

"What picture? My phone wallpaper?"

"No—Julie sent me a few texts on New Year's Eve. You were all out on a dance floor. *Wish you were here* type of thing. You were in the background, and that guy had his arms around you."

"That guy?"

They'd crossed the street against the red DO NOT WALK sign, reaching the other side safely with little traffic. Nathan stopped on the corner. Grace pulled up short, turning to face him.

"Yeah, Grace, *that guy.* Connor. The one we talked about weeks ago. The one you said you broke up with and you were working on getting over. It looks like you have more work to do. That is, unless, the two of you kissed and made up."

Nathan searched her face, wondering if he'd find the truth there that he so desperately needed. He was done with the games. They weren't kids anymore, not really, and he was ready to move on. Either they could have a *real* relationship, or he'd chalk it up to one of life's tough lessons. The holiday season was over. Virginia's book was done. They no longer had something they needed to work on together. He could handle whatever they'd decide today, on this sidewalk, on what was supposed to be the most romantic day of the year. But they *would* decide.

At least Virginia would experience the heady thrill of romance today. There was that.

Grace nodded, as if she realized this was it. Maybe she was tired of the dance, too.

"It was hard to get over Connor. He was the first real relationship I've ever been in. But I can see now, with the benefit of hindsight, that I wouldn't be happy with him."

"You looked pretty happy on that dance floor."

"I *was* happy—because we'd just had another deep discussion about the fact that I was no longer interested in being with him. I told him that before Christmas, but he didn't believe me. He's one of those types of people who think they can charm their way through anything. But I wasn't buying it anymore. Instead, I was pointing out girls to him that I thought he should ask to dance. He was just drunk enough that he was playing along."

Unbidden, an image of Nathan's father popped into his head. Will, that charming smile of his plastered onto his face, the one Nathan had come to recognize as a mask. That smile seldom reached his father's eyes. If that was the kind of guy Grace had dated, and if she was done with him, she was lucky.

"Why are you even telling me this, Grace?"

Hands buried in her white winter jacket, her pale hair dancing on the icy breeze, Grace stepped close, directly meeting his gaze. "Because. I've been stupid. Afraid. I didn't want to get hurt again. But now, seeing how excited Virginia is to finally give the book she wrote *forty years ago* to a man she says saved her as a young woman, and she still loves today, I realized something. I want something real, too, with someone who could be my best friend. Someone I like to laugh with . . . explore creepy basements with. I wish he'd give me a second chance."

Nathan searched her eyes, wanting to believe her, but tired of the games.

She pulled one hand out of her jacket pocket, and Nathan saw something flutter to the sidewalk. A small rectangle of paper, landing face down on the frosty concrete.

He bent down to pick it up, intending to hand it back to her. But he paused. His name was on the card, printed in bold black letters. *Book Journeys* was printed under his name, with the third row reading MANAGER. His phone number and email were listed across the bottom.

"What's this?" he asked, not understanding why Grace would have what looked to be a business card with his name on it in her pocket.

She shrugged, smiling up at him. "I talked to Virginia one day when they got back from Florida. I called her to see if they'd had fun. We talked for quite a while. She was appreciative that my dad encouraged her to take Frank on that trip. It got us talking about wishes, and when she asked me what I thought *your* wish might be, I told her I suspected you hoped to run Book Journeys for them someday."

"You did? You talked to Virginia about me?" he asked, unsure how he felt about that.

"Sure. Virginia assured me you're pretty much already running the bookstore, the day-to-day at least. She made the comment that she wished they'd hired a manager five years ago, that it was working out so well with you now."

"She called me the *manager*?"

Grace laughed. "She did. I thought it might be fun to have some business cards made up for you. You know, kind of a *grown-up* Valentine's Day card. Like the little cards we used to give our friends in grade school, but a bit more adult."

Still holding the card Grace made up for him in one hand, he touched her cheek with his other. He thought back to his discussion with the Fisks over the Thanksgiving table, about how long Virginia had to work to get Frank even to notice her. While their start might have been rocky, they'd managed to weather the many storms they'd inevitability faced through the decades. It gave him faith that relationships can work if you find the right person. Maybe things could work out with Grace.

Especially since we were friends first, too.

He ran his thumb over her bottom lip and then bent to kiss her, standing right there on the corner, half a block away from the deli.

A passer-by honked. An older man, roughly Frank's age, walked by, smiling. "Happy Valentine's Day, kids," he said with a tip of his hat before crossing the street.

***

Frank was irritated. He'd noticed the small sheet cake, on a table by the coffee pot, surrounded by dozens of cupcakes. The cake bore the words *Happy Birthday, Frank* in thick red letters, and pink and red roses of frosting rimmed the dessert.

"You couldn't just let us celebrate a nice, quiet birthday at home tomorrow, could you, Virginia? You had to go and make a big deal about it. You know I've never liked parties thrown on my behalf."

"I know, dear, but it's not every day the love of your life turns sixty-five. It's a special occasion, worthy of a party."

Nathan watched Frank glance at his Timex and tried not to laugh. "What time did you say this shindig was supposed to start? Three? And what's with the table over there, draped in a white cloth? I should have known you were up to something, Ginny. You and Nathan have been acting suspicious lately."

Nathan held up his hands, doing his best to keep his expression innocent. "I'm not the romantic one here."

Virginia smiled. Nathan wondered if she was nervous. She'd be handing Frank the book soon.

People were starting to show up. Nathan had been making posts all week about a Valentine's party at Book Journeys, tempting people with the promise of special discounts and romances from the past. He'd played with different slogans, trying to put the fun back into Valentine's Day. Similar to Christmas, the holiday had been one of his favorites as a kid, but now he suspected lots of people had come to regard the day as another obligation. A day to order overpriced flowers or boxes of chocolate, all in the supposed name of love. He'd hinted that people should come down to the store and witness a true moment of romance. He'd kept it vague enough to pique people's interest.

The front door opened, and Grant and Michelle walked back in. Frank glanced their way, stopped fussing at Virginia, and looked more closely at the woman. Michelle smiled at Frank, making her way toward him with her arms extended.

"Hello, Mr. Fisk. Remember me?"

"Of *course* I remember you, Michelle! But it's been a long time. What brings you in today?"

Michelle gestured toward Nathan. "I taught a few of Nathan's literature classes. We were visiting after class one evening, and he mentioned working here, for you. I thought it would be fun to swing in and say hello, wish you a happy birthday."

"I'm so glad you did. Tell me, what have you been up to?"

Nathan wandered away to let Michelle and Frank talk. Now seemed a perfect time, with Frank busy visiting with his former student, to help Virginia with final preparations. When he and Grace had returned with sandwiches from the deli, Virginia had handed him a beautifully wrapped package, saying, "Can you put this upstairs, maybe? I inscribed it for Frank.

I don't want him to see it yet. We should set the other copies out on the table, too, as you suggested, and get it covered before he gets here."

They'd done as she'd asked. Frank had indeed arrived just as Nathan was flicking the white linen tablecloth open and draping it over a table, more copies of Virginia's book stacked underneath. With any luck, customers would be interested in her book, too.

Now, it was nearly time. Nathan was about to run upstairs when Jess caught up with him.

"Honey, I need to talk to you for a minute," she said, turning and walking over to a quieter area in the store. Nathan followed, but was anxious to go grab Frank's gift.

"What is it, Mom? I have to run upstairs."

Jess turned back to him, glancing around as if to make sure no one else was in earshot. "I wanted to let you know how proud I am of what you did here for Virginia. And for Frank."

Nathan nodded, appreciating Jess's words but nervous about holding Virginia up. "Well, thanks, Mom. But everybody helped."

Jess laid a hand on Nathan's forearm, giving a slight shake of her head. "None of this would have happened without you. I also wanted to let you know your *dad* is proud of you, too."

Nathan snorted. "Yeah, right. I can't remember the last time Dad was proud of anything I've done."

This time Jess's headshake was more pronounced. "That's not true, Nathan. For all his faults and failures, the love he has for you and your sisters is real."

"Mom, in case you forgot, Dad's a little out of the loop these days. Even if I thought he had the emotional depth to feel anything but disappointment where I'm concerned, he'd have no way of knowing about Virginia's book."

Jess broke eye contact with him then, scanning the room. "Actually, he does know about it. I told him."

"You talked to Dad?"

"I actually went to see him."

"Why would you do that?" Nathan asked, shocked to hear his mom had gone to the prison to see his father. She'd sworn she'd never go back there after her adoption of Harper was final.

"Seth convinced me I should. He said Will might benefit from getting updates about you kids once in a while. I took Will a few pictures from Harper's first birthday party, and some of you and Lauren at Christmas."

Nathan nearly asked how Will was doing but stopped himself. He didn't care.

"Look, Nathan, I know you're still furious with your father. And that's okay. It's totally up to you when, or even if, you ever want to forgive him. But I also know how hard it is on you, this rift between you and your dad, and I wanted you to know that he *is* proud of you, and for figuring out how to help Virginia publish her book. He asked me to give you this."

Nathan stared at the plain white envelope his mother held out to him, his feelings all stirred up. With a sigh, he took the letter. "All right, Mom. But I have to go, okay? I'll read it later."

"Yes, go. Enjoy this moment," Jess said, giving him a reassuring smile.

Nathan stuffed the envelope into his back pocket and ran up to his apartment to retrieve Virginia's wrapped book off his miniature kitchen table. He remembered sitting there, reading the manuscript he'd stumbled across, months ago. Back then, in the early days of living upstairs, he wondered what secrets the walls of this old building held.

Turns out, quite a few.

They'd discovered some of those secrets, and done what they could with them, to culminate in Virginia's book.

Nathan could hear Virginia downstairs, clapping to get people's attention. He tried to put his mother's comments about his father out of his mind, but it was no use. He needed to read the letter. It would take a minute for Virginia to get everyone organized downstairs. Besides, she couldn't start without him.

Pulling the envelope out of his pocket, he slid his finger under the seal. As he unfolded the single sheet of paper, he immediately recognized his father's messy handwriting.

Dear Nathan,

Your mother shared with me how hard you've worked these past few months, balancing school, work, and helping your employer publish her book. I just wanted to take a minute to let you know how proud I am of all you are doing.

I should have told you that more often.

I know I've disappointed you. My mistakes were unconscionable and I don't deserve your forgiveness.

We've never really understood each other. I accept the blame for that. Through the years, I tried to mold you into a better version of me. But you stayed strong in your own convictions. Perhaps if I'd possessed a fraction of your integrity, I wouldn't be writing to you today from a jail cell.

Thank you for being the man of the family, for taking care of your mother and sisters. It's a job I should be doing, but I failed.

Never again will I question your choices in life. You've grown into an amazing young man, despite having me for a father.

This may surprise you, but I am doing more reading these days. If you feel so inclined, I would love to read this book you've helped bring into the world. I suspect it is the first of many great things in your future.

I love you, son.

Dad

Nathan slowly folded the letter and slid it back into its envelope.

Is he really proud of me . . . ?

He set the envelope down on the table, picked up Virginia's book, and headed for the stairs. The top board squeaked as he hurried down, his feet feeling lighter after reading his dad's words. Maybe it was too little, too late. Maybe not. Time would tell.

But now it's Frank and Virginia's time.

He hurried down the steps. When he reached the bottom, a few people glanced his way, likely curious about the noise he was making. Grace was one of those people. He caught her eye and she gave him a thumbs-up when she saw the package in his hand, much as Lizzy had done at Christmas—and his father had done at the basketball game, so long ago. Nathan winked back. Grace had helped him pull this together for Virginia. He weaved his way through the throng of people as they turned their attention to Virginia, their gracious hostess. He stopped next to Grace.

"I want to thank all of you for coming today. Those of you who know me know I'm a sucker for Valentine's Day. In my humble opinion, the world suffers from a lack of true romantic gestures these days. Readers know that, even if we aren't fortunate enough to have romance in our own lives, we can find it in a book. We can experience great loves through our imaginations, aided by the words captured on paper by others, without the risk of real pain that love can bring."

Nathan grinned, watching his boss in action. She *was* dramatic. Only Virginia would be able to stand up there, in front of a crowd, wearing a pretty flowing red dress and a pink tint to her white hair, and say things like that. He glanced around at the crowd. People were listening intently, not scoffing at her as she waxed poetic.

"If you are fortunate to find love, as I have been, protect it. Tell the one you love how you feel, be the best person you can be for them, and know how lucky you are to have them. Many *many* years ago now, I found that kind of love with a serious, studious man. I had a devil of a time getting him to notice me at first, but once he did there was no stopping us."

Frank, standing to the left of Virginia, muttered something, his face flush with embarrassment. If he hadn't liked the idea of a party in his honor, Nathan knew he hated this. A ripple of nervous laughter flowed through the crowd. Frank might not be the only one embarrassed by Virginia's words.

If Virginia sensed it, she didn't care.

"Frank was the best thing that has ever happened to me. To us. He encouraged me to live the life I'd dreamed of, surrounded with books, and authors, and friends who love literature and weaving stories as much as I do. Thank you, Frank."

Frank angled his body ever so slightly into a bow in her direction. He probably wished she'd wrap this up.

"But there was one pesky dream that I'd ignored. One thing I always wanted to do, but I never found the courage to pursue it. I know for a fact that I'm not alone in this," Virginia said, scanning the faces looking back at her as if searching for others who felt the same way. "I always wanted to write a book. I've loved supporting other authors throughout my career, but I told very few people that one of *my* biggest dreams was to write my own book. Nearly forty years ago, I took my dream so far as to write a story. A story pulled from the depths of my heart, meant to be a tribute to this man who'd saved me. To my Frank."

Now Frank was staring at his wife as if she'd lost her mind. Maybe he was worried she was suffering some type of episode, a break from reality.

"I wrote a story, but then when I encountered the *tiniest* of resistance in the process, I got scared. I took my words, the ones I'd worked so hard to get down on paper, and hid them away. I hid them away both physically and mentally, telling myself I was content to help other authors. I didn't need to *be* one."

The front door opened, the tiny bell above it jingling with the arrival of another customer. The distraction seemed to pull Virginia back to the crowded room.

With a shake of her head, she stepped over to Nathan and took the gift she'd so carefully wrapped from him. She squeezed Nathan's hand, offered him a grateful smile, then turned and walked over to stand in front of her husband. She ignored the roomful of people now.

"Frank, honey, you have given me a life full of love and laughter. You helped me to do so many of the things I'd dreamed of doing when I was a small child, living in a household that didn't appreciate the value of the arts. Today, for your birthday, I wanted to finally give you the present I started for you so long ago. A wise young man convinced me that it's never too late to chase your dreams. I hope you enjoy it."

Frank took the present she offered him, searching her face for answers. Finding none, he looked down at the package his wife had handed to him. With a shrug, he pulled the paper away, letting it fall to the ground, forgotten, as he ran his hand over the front cover of a book, flipping it over to look at the back. There, staring back at him, was his beloved wife, her headshot prominent in the bottom left-hand corner of the book.

"What is this, Virginia?"

Virginia smiled at him, gesturing with her graceful hands at the book he now held in his less-graceful ones. "Why, it's our story, dear. At least, our story as it stood forty years ago, woven into a fictitious world, much like the bedtime story you told our daughter almost every night."

"You wrote this?"

"Yes, honey," Virginia said, gently taking the book out of her husband's hands and flipping back a few pages from the front. "My name is on the front because I'm the author."

Chuckles of laughter rippled through the crowd.

"Please read this," Virginia suggested, pointing at the page she'd turned to as she handed the book back to Frank.

Frank took the book, adjusted his glasses, and peered at the words. He read them out loud. " 'To Frank, my beloved friend. Now is the time to make all of our wishes come true.' "

Frank closed the book, held out one hand to his wife, and pulled her close. He kissed her softly, and the crowd cheered.

A thrill raced through Nathan as he saw the pure delight on Virginia's face, the sense of achievement she must be feeling now that she could finally call herself a published author.

The book her husband now held in his hands was her one elusive life goal she'd never thought she'd hit. Nathan had played a part in it all.

And it felt good.

It felt really good.

THANK YOU!

Dear Reader,

I would like to thank you for reading **Capturing Wishes**. I'm honored that you took time out of your busy days to read this holiday novel. Creating the stories of Virginia and Frank, as well as Nathan and Grace, was a delightful process, and I hope you found yourself cheering them on.

If you don't mind taking a few more minutes with this book, I would really appreciate your leaving a comment on Amazon. Reviews are extremely helpful and greatly appreciated.

Wishing you the very best,
Kimberly

CURIOUS ABOUT THE CELIA'S GIFTS SERIES?

Celia's Gifts series

In the summer of 1942, a young woman's visit to the lake cottage of a friend would commence a series of events destined to weave her family's future to a very special place for generations to come. The young woman was Celia, and that place was Whispering Pines.

Celia would go on to live a long, extraordinary life. She'd excel in the world of business, resulting in financial success she generously shared with others throughout her life. She always supported the underdog. Now Celia's spirit and good work continue—even after her death at 92—through others.

Each book in the series highlights the impact Celia had on people while she lived and on the legacy she leaves to family members. Celia's nieces and nephews will face the inevitable struggles of mid-life while watching their own children deal with those age-old struggles of young adulthood.

Will they survive broken hearts, broken homes, and abandoned dreams?

Their encouraging stories of family, love, and growth will inspire you.

Whispering Pines (Book 1)
When one woman's dull yet comfortable life is upended, can she find the courage to change everything?

Summers at Whispering Pines defined Renee's childhood. Days meant swimming and sun, nights meant ghost stories and campfires. Best of all, summer meant time with Celia, her favorite aunt. Through the years, trips to Whispering Pines would fade to memories. Raising kids alone and a demanding career consumed Renee's life.

Now Celia is gone and Renee's career is in shambles. She'll make the most of her time off, and a spontaneous trip could mean unexpected romance, but when mysterious events begin to swirl around her kids, her worries compound.

How can Renee keep her family safe while she rebuilds their lives? Celia's final gift may provide answers, but there are risks. Why can't things be simple, the way they were when she spent summers at Whispering Pines?

Tangled Beginnings (Book 2)

Often the most difficult of choices can lead to the greatest of joys, but what if the stakes feel too high?

Jess is ready for a fresh start. Her twenty-five-year marriage is over, her youngest is heading to college, and all she wants to do is retreat to Whispering Pines. She's watched her sister Renee make the most of second chances, and now it's her turn.

But when her ex asks her to do the unimaginable, will his mistakes threaten to undermine her new chance at happiness? Long-buried secrets and new accusations tangle together, threatening to ruin reputations and lives. Jess may be the only one who can find out the truth.

Threaded with romance and mystery and ghosts from the past, this novel is bound to make you fall in love once more with the prospect of life and love and forgiveness.

Rebuilding Home (Book 3)

A story of one man's struggle to rethink his vision of the perfect family, true friendship, and what home really means.

When Ethan's wife walks out in search of something more, his **first** priority is to protect his three teenagers from further heartache. He should have been a better husband. Now it's time to be a better dad.

Ethan thinks he's doing a decent job juggling the responsibilities of a business owner, landlord, and recommitted father. But a devastating fire changes everything. Suspicions and doubts threaten all he holds dear. When trust is shattered, can old friendships guide him home again?

Follow Ethan on an emotional journey from fractured illusions, through tangled paths of hope and despair, to the renewed possibility of happiness and love.

Where does Capturing Wishes *fit in?*

We are first introduced to Virginia and Frank Fisk and their bookstore in book 2, *Tangled Beginnings*, where you'll find out more about how the Fisks came to be an important part of Jess's and her son Nathan's lives. *Capturing Wishes* takes place at the same time as book 3, *Rebuilding Home*, but from others' points of view.

What's next?

There will be additional books in the series. This tight-knit family has more stories to tell and other ways to keep Celia's legacy alive. Stay tuned for little sister Val's story, a novel dedicated to Celia, and more.

For all of Kimberly Diede's books, please visit:

www.amazon.com/author/kimberlydiede

AN INVITATION

If you have enjoyed any of the Celia's Gifts books, please join my Reader's Club for periodic updates on future books in this series and my other writing projects.

Go to my website at www.kimberlydiedeauthor.com to sign up.
Then watch your email for your free novella!

To thank you for joining, I will send you this free novella: *First Summers at Whispering Pines 1980*. I hope you'll enjoy this trip back to a time of innocence when Renee, Jess, Ethan, and Val first visit Whispering Pines as children.

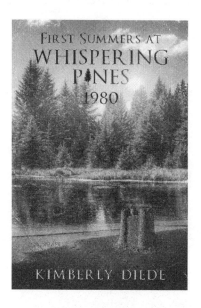

Find out why this family falls in love
with this welcoming Minnesota lake resort
and what pulls them back
time and time again.

ACKNOWLEDGMENTS

Christmas has always held a special place in my heart. Growing up, we celebrated the holiday through decorations, food, and family. And, of course, presents. No one could decorate a home for the holidays like my mom. She'd spend *days* making everything perfect, each room overflowing with holiday cheer. If you were blessed to know my mom, and you ever visited our home in December, you're smiling right now!

These traditions continue at our house. I fill each room with special holiday decorations, and while it amounts to a lot of work, it wouldn't feel like Christmas without the extra effort. And true confessions: I *am* one of those annoying people that put my holiday decorations up before Thanksgiving. It is simply too much work and I enjoy them too much to limit it to only the month of December! Please don't judge me.

Given my love of the holiday season, I knew I wanted to write a Whispering Pines book centered on this magical time of the year. My other books include plenty of holiday scenes, but this was different. I wanted to find a way to have my characters spread holiday cheer beyond their closest family and friends.

Capturing Wishes focuses on two main couples. Virginia and Frank are older and nearing a point in their lives where they are considering leaving their careers. They have so much wisdom to share. Thank you to my readers out there who asked me to include exciting stories revolving around mature individuals. It was so fun to write from Virginia's point of view—I love that woman. Maybe I want to *be* that woman down the road!

And then there is young Nathan—getting ready to graduate from college and feeling the pressures to make career decisions and figure out the complex world of love and relationships. As the mother of three young adults, I had plenty of material to draw upon.

As is the case with every book I write, I owe a big thank-you to my husband, Rick, and our kids, Josh, Alecia, and Amber, for their patience with me. My amazing dad also continues to ask me nearly every time we visit "how the book is coming." And I would be remiss if I didn't thank my extended family for sharing every Christmas with me, through these many years. I love you all.

It was difficult to get two books out this year, but having many of my top-notch readers continue to tell me they can't wait for this holiday book gave me the encouragement I needed to keep my focus! Thank you to everyone who gives of their precious time to read my stories.

Thank you, again, to my editor, Spencer Hamilton of Nerdy Wordsmith, for jumping on the phone with me to brainstorm on ways to make each book, and this series, better. Thank you also to Cakamura DSGN for your patience and creativity, leading to yet another stunning cover. I believe we stayed true to the theme of Whispering Pines, but also incorporated some of the magic that is the season.

Many of you will help me launch this special book, and you have my deepest gratitude, as do all of you who are helping me realize my dream of writing books. I may have started later than some authors, but I've found a way to make many of my own wishes come true.

I wish the same for you!

ABOUT THE AUTHOR

Aunt mary Nierling trying to "hang on"

Pictured here is Kimberly, age 2,
celebrating Christmas with her Aunt Mary.

Kimberly Diede's first novel, *Whispering Pines*, was inspired by her real-life "Aunt Celia," Mary K. Nierling. Mary was a generous, extraordinary, slightly formidable woman who excelled in a "man's world" in the mid-1900s. The Celia's Gifts series is Kimberly's way of honoring her great-aunt and the legacy she left behind. She is currently at work on future novels in the series.

Kimberly lives in North Dakota with her family, spending as much time as she can at their lake cabin in the summer months. When the temperatures dip and the snow flies, she'll be cozied up at home, spinning inspiring tales of family, second chances, and the beauty of everyday people living extraordinary lives. She's obsessed with the Christmas holiday, celebrating every year by trying to convince anyone with a spare three hours to sit down and watch *It's a Wonderful Life* with her. Because life *can* be wonderful, despite our many struggles.

Be sure to follow Kimberly on social media, where she'll share some of the magic she creates around the holidays with you:

Website and inspiring blog: www.kimberlydiedeauthor.com
Email: kim@kimberlydiedeauthor.com
FB: www.facebook.com/KimberlyDiedeAuthor/
Instagram: www.instagram.com/kimberlydiedeauthor/
Pinterest: www.pinterest.com/kdiedeauthor/
Amazon Author Page: www.amazon.com/author/kimberlydiede/

Made in the USA
Las Vegas, NV
08 December 2020